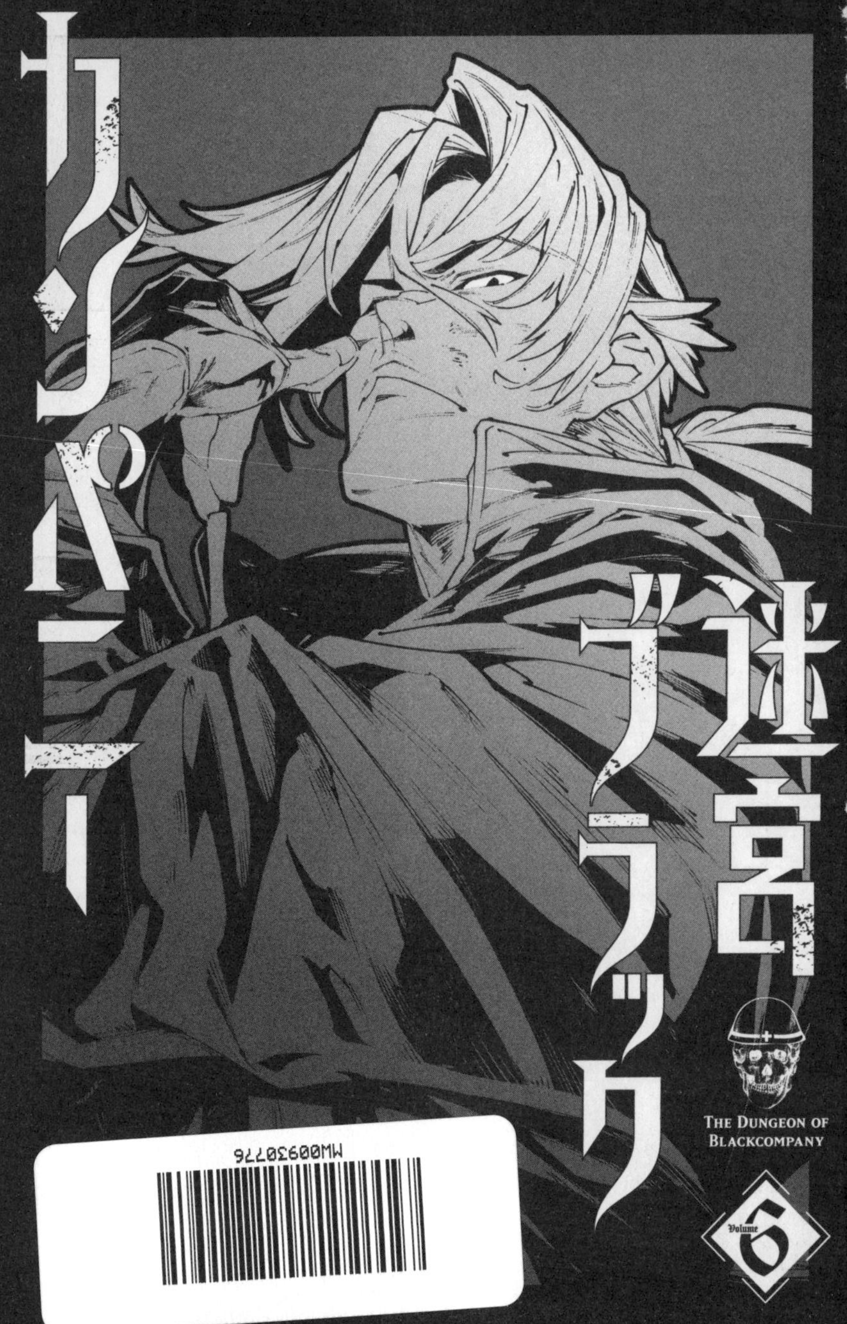
迷宮ブラック
カンパニー
THE DUNGEON OF BLACKCOMPANY
Volume 6

THE DUNGEON OF BLACK COMPANY

CHARACTER

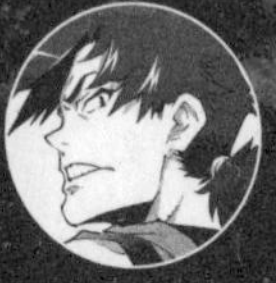

NINOMIYA KINJI

A man with a more conceited and uninhibited way of thinking than anyone else. Summoned to another world by some unknown force and now serves as a dungeon explorer under corporate slavery.

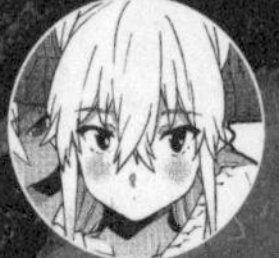

RIM

Lured into being Ninomiya's ally by the promise of a good meal. The strongest monster girl you'll ever see, but quickly became something more like a mascot.

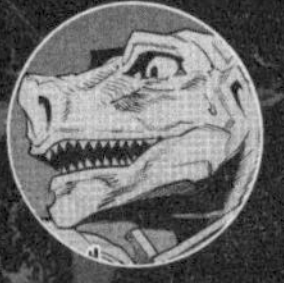

WANIBE

A lizardman who's heavily predisposed to being an underling. Always being used by Ninomiya in his underhanded schemes, but seems to happily take part.

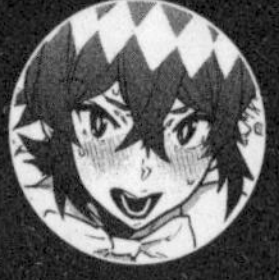

SHIA

A corporate drone with the title of "Hero." Helpful and serious, she always pulls her weight when she comes along.

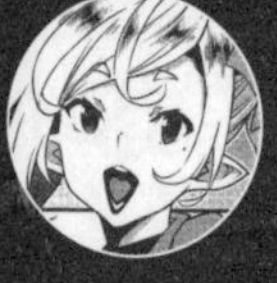

RANGA

A cute, impish and rather feminine magical boy. Accompanied Ninomiya from the future. Belza's descendant.

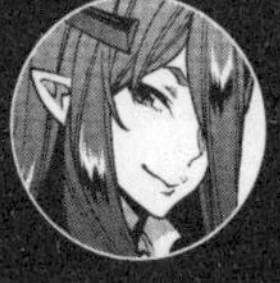

BELZA

Director of the Raiza'ha Demonite Mining Corporation, Detmolt branch. A manager who's willing to sacrifice her employees if it gets results.

STORY

Due to being ripped from his home and thrown into an alternate world, Ninomiya Kinji now has to work for a crooked, exploitative company. Currently, he is trying to clear the dungeon in order to obtain a power hidden in its deepest ruins, with which he plans to overthrow his corporate masters. After helping a shop owner who had her store usurped from her, he got equipment and headed to floor B-4, where he had to manage the chaos taking place there. Having reunited with his subordinates, the ants, he takes Rim's little sister Sky in tow and finally manages to reach floor B-5. He had planned on challenging the ridiculously powerful boss there, but we'll see...

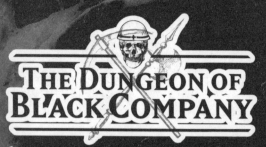

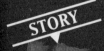

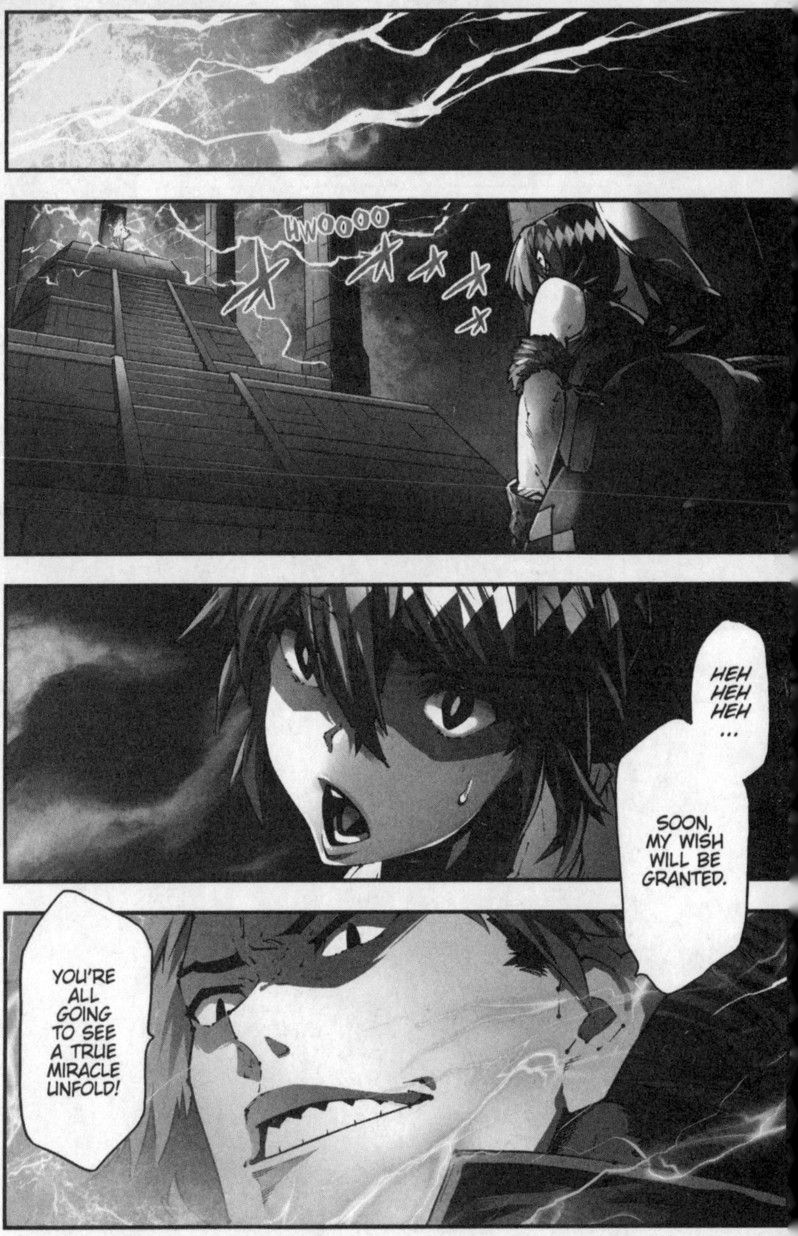
HWOOOO
HEH HEH HEH...
SOON, MY WISH WILL BE GRANTED.
YOU'RE ALL GOING TO SEE A TRUE MIRACLE UNFOLD!

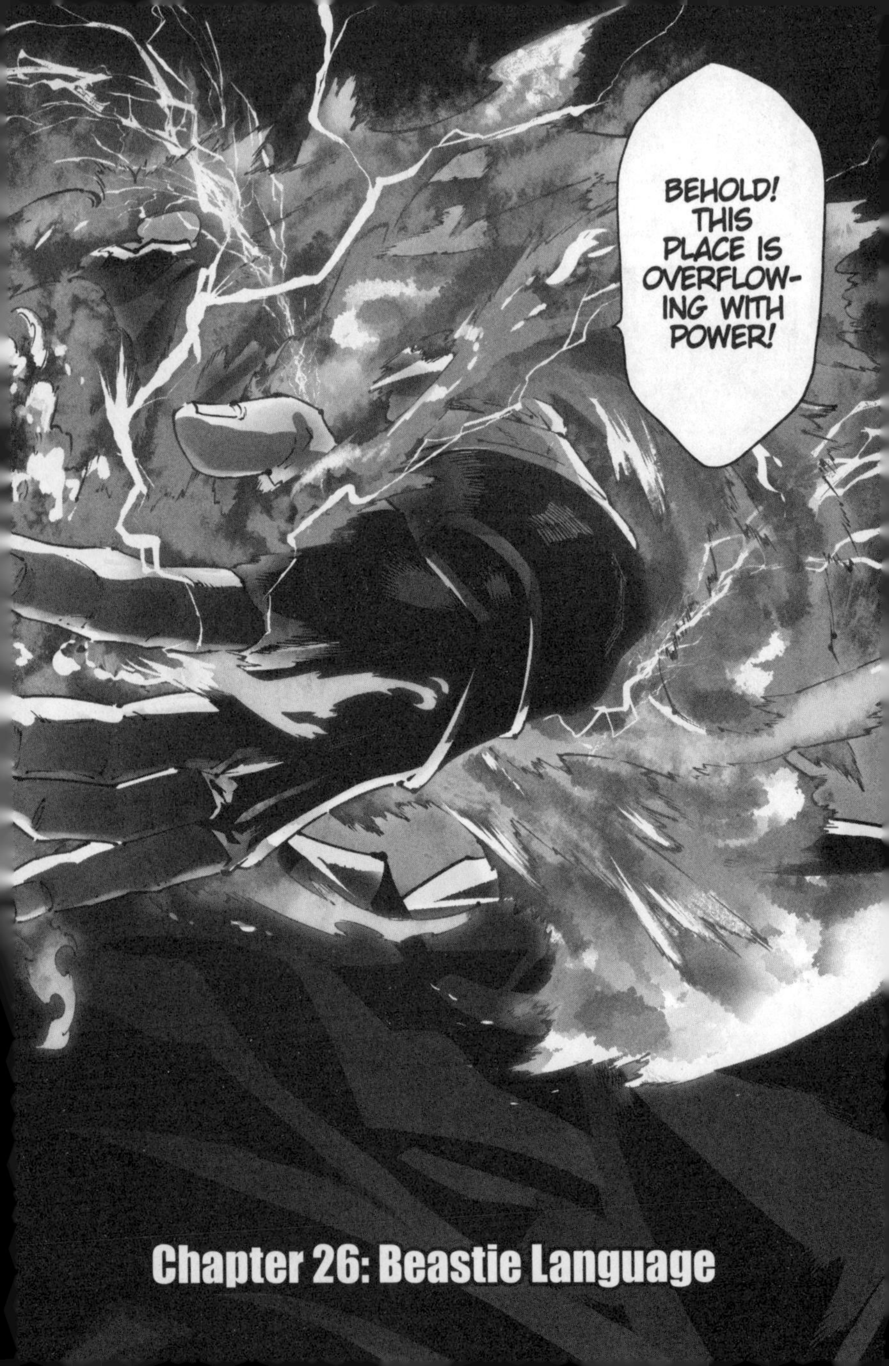
BEHOLD! THIS PLACE IS OVERFLOWING WITH POWER!

Chapter 26: Beastie Language

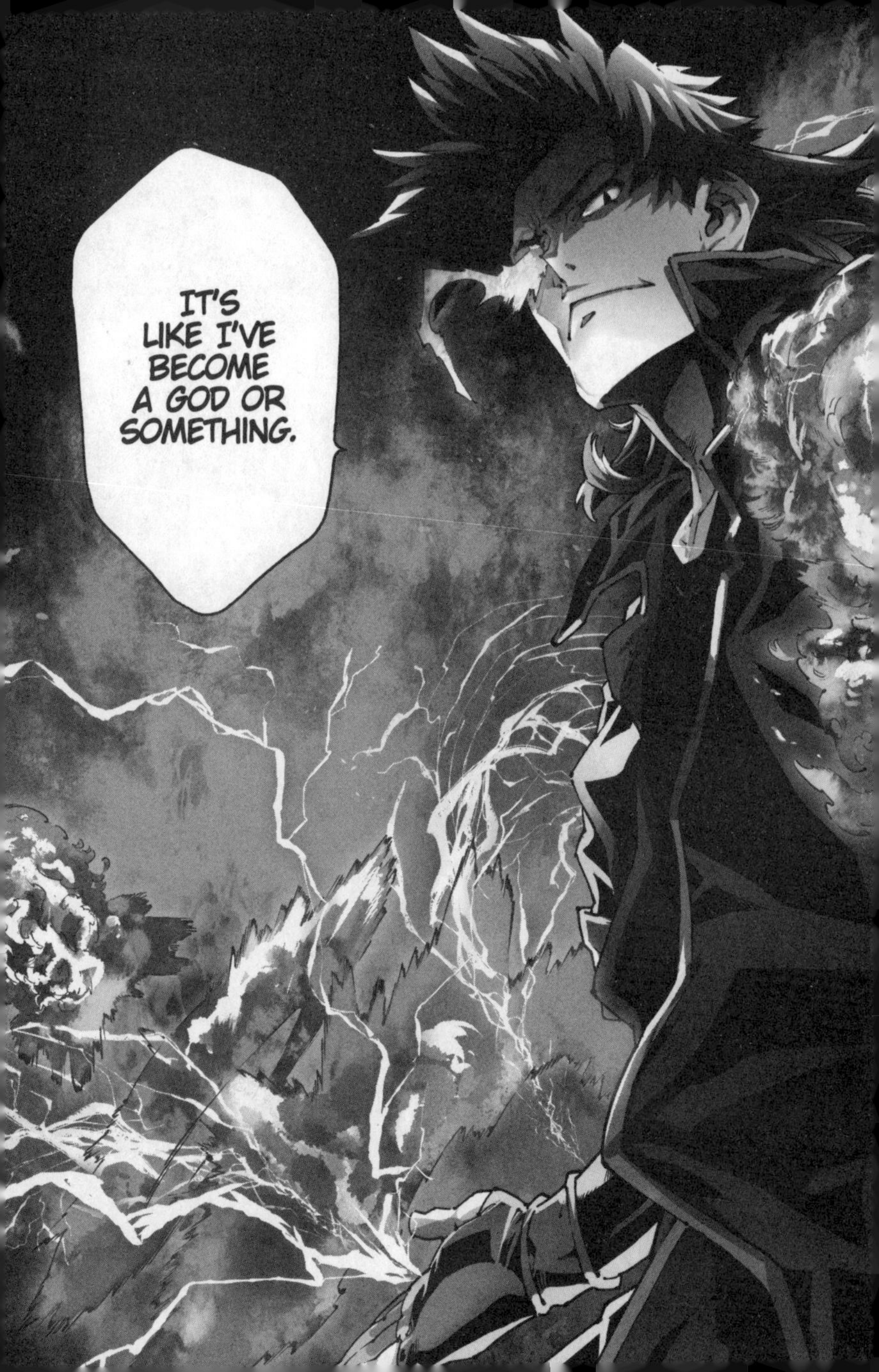
IT'S LIKE I'VE BECOME A GOD OR SOMETHING.

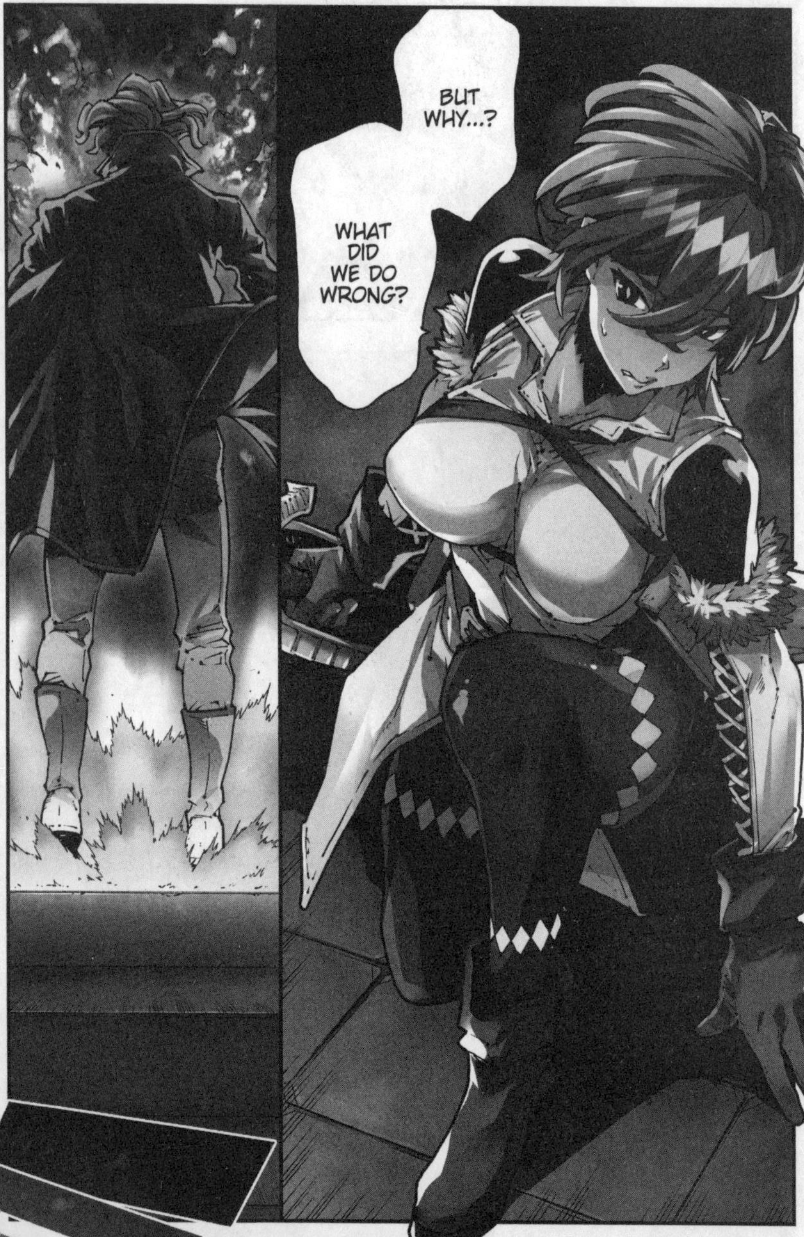
BUT WHY...?
WHAT DID WE DO WRONG?

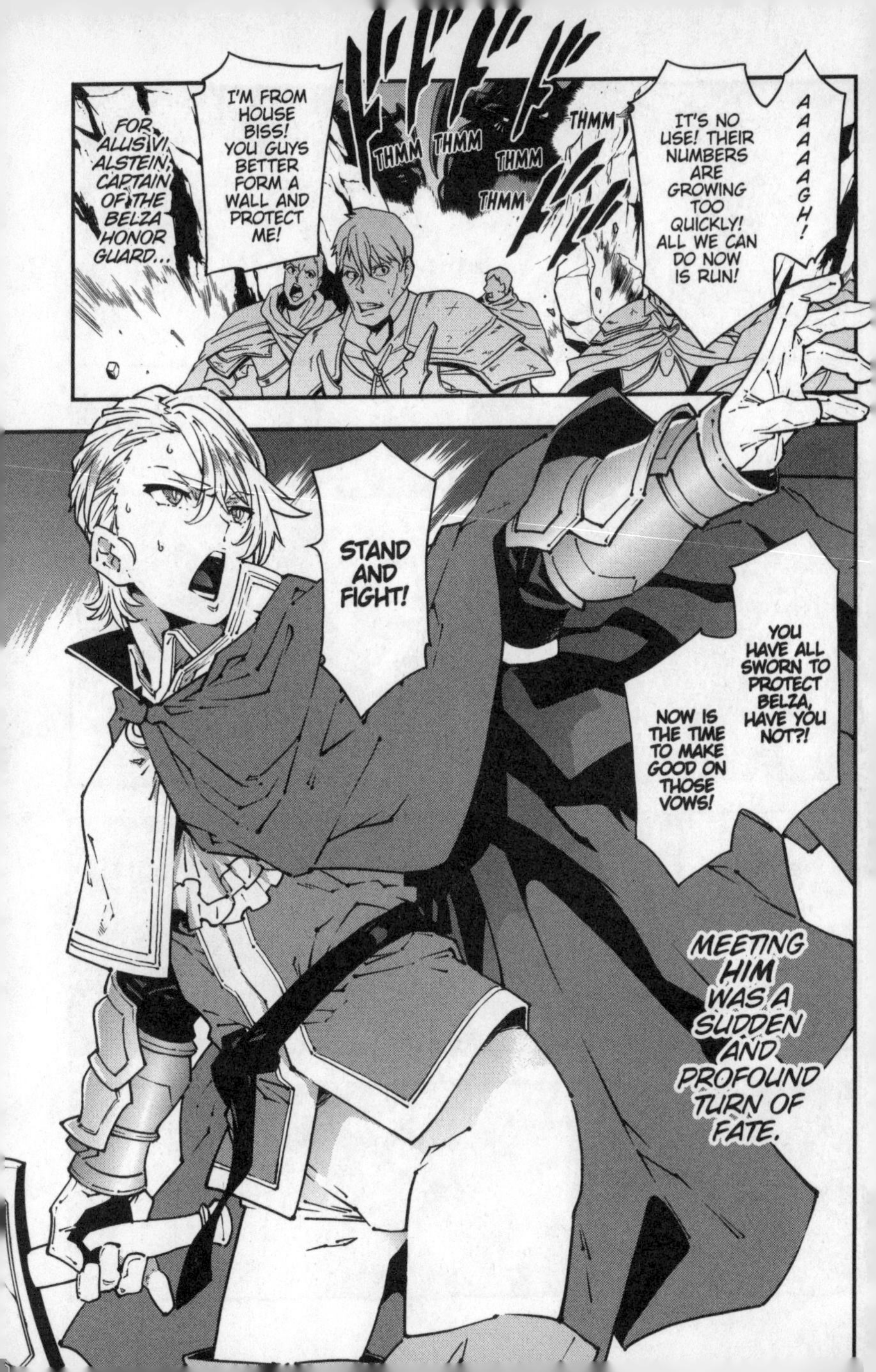
AAAAAAGH!
IT'S NO USE! THEIR NUMBERS ARE GROWING TOO QUICKLY! ALL WE CAN DO NOW IS RUN!
THMM THMM THMM THMM THMM
I'M FROM HOUSE BISS! YOU GUYS BETTER FORM A WALL AND PROTECT ME!
FOR ALUS VI ALSTEIN, CAPTAIN OF THE BELZA HONOR GUARD...
STAND AND FIGHT!
YOU HAVE ALL SWORN TO PROTECT BELZA, HAVE YOU NOT?!
NOW IS THE TIME TO MAKE GOOD ON THOSE VOWS!
MEETING HIM WAS A SUDDEN AND PROFOUND TURN OF FATE.

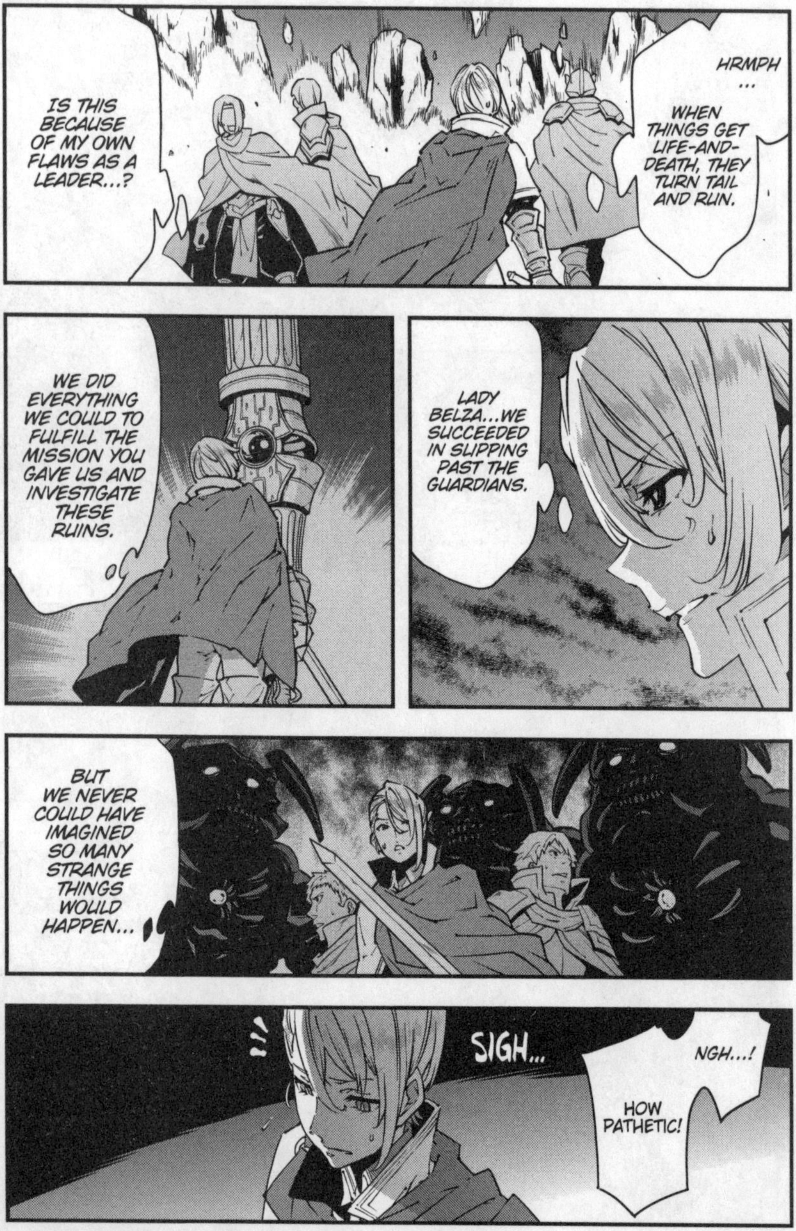
HRMPH... WHEN THINGS GET LIFE-AND-DEATH, THEY TURN TAIL AND RUN.
IS THIS BECAUSE OF MY OWN FLAWS AS A LEADER...?
LADY BELZA...WE SUCCEEDED IN SLIPPING PAST THE GUARDIANS.
WE DID EVERYTHING WE COULD TO FULFILL THE MISSION YOU GAVE US AND INVESTIGATE THESE RUINS.
BUT WE NEVER COULD HAVE IMAGINED SO MANY STRANGE THINGS WOULD HAPPEN...
NGH...! HOW PATHETIC!
SIGH...
!!

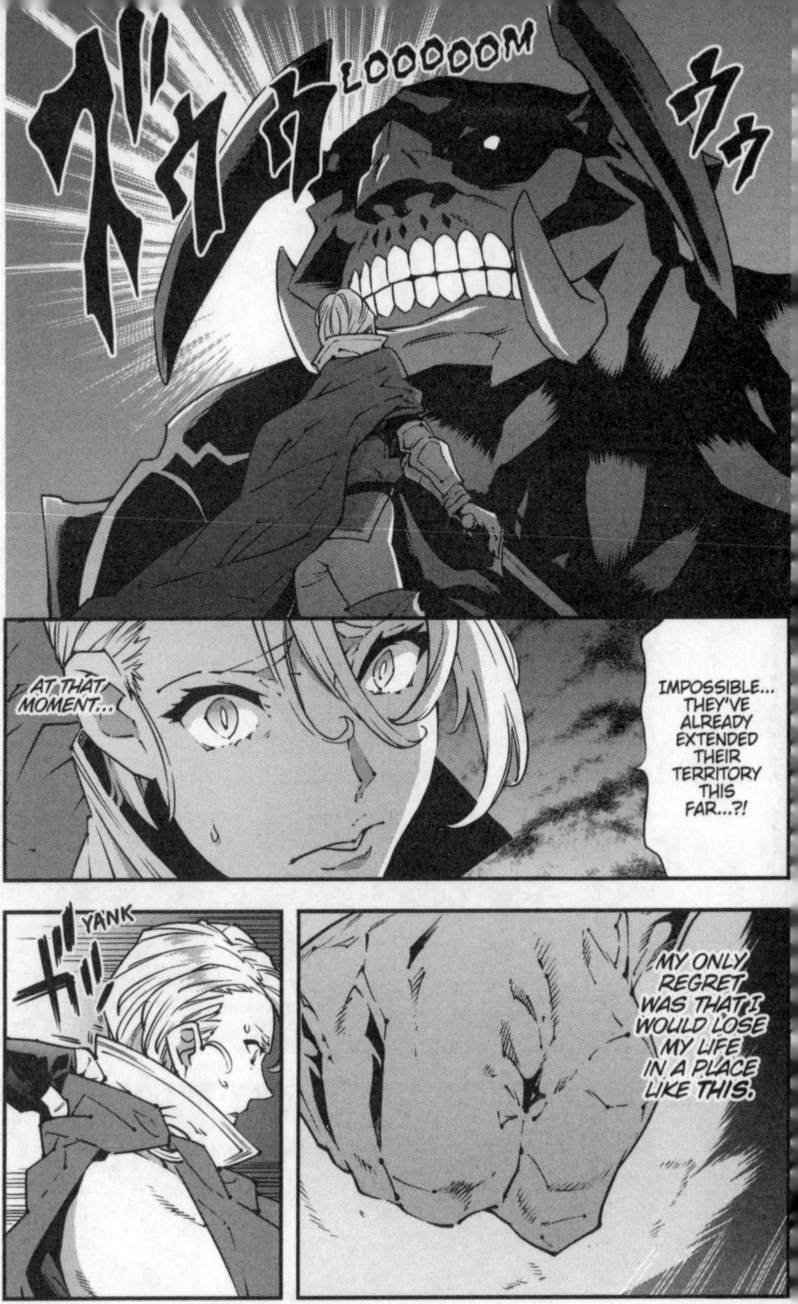
LOOOOOM
IMPOSSIBLE... THEY'VE ALREADY EXTENDED THEIR TERRITORY THIS FAR...?!
AT THAT MOMENT...
MY ONLY REGRET WAS THAT I WOULD LOSE MY LIFE IN A PLACE LIKE THIS.
YANK

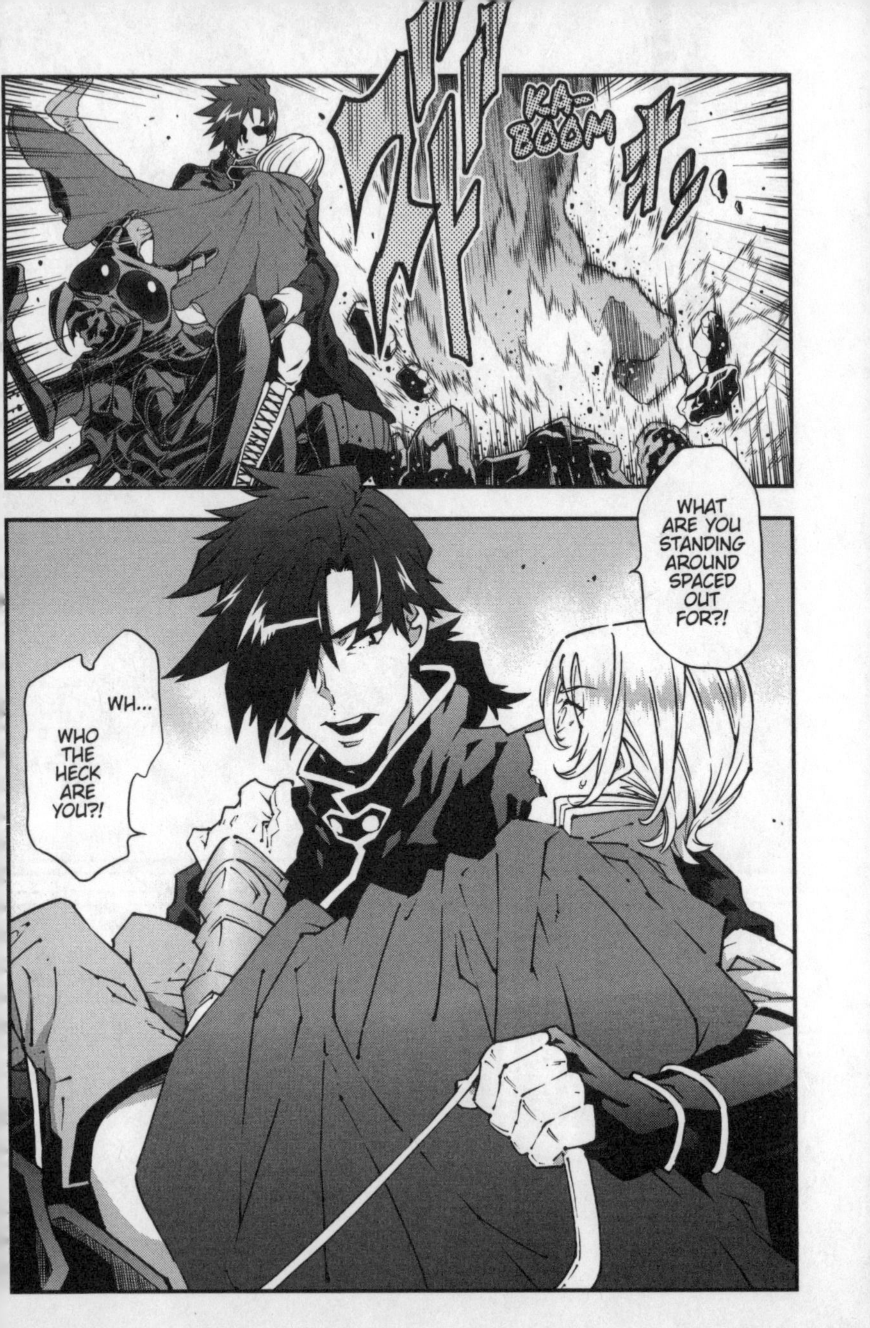
KA-BOOM
WHAT ARE YOU STANDING AROUND SPACED OUT FOR?!
WH...
WHO THE HECK ARE YOU?!

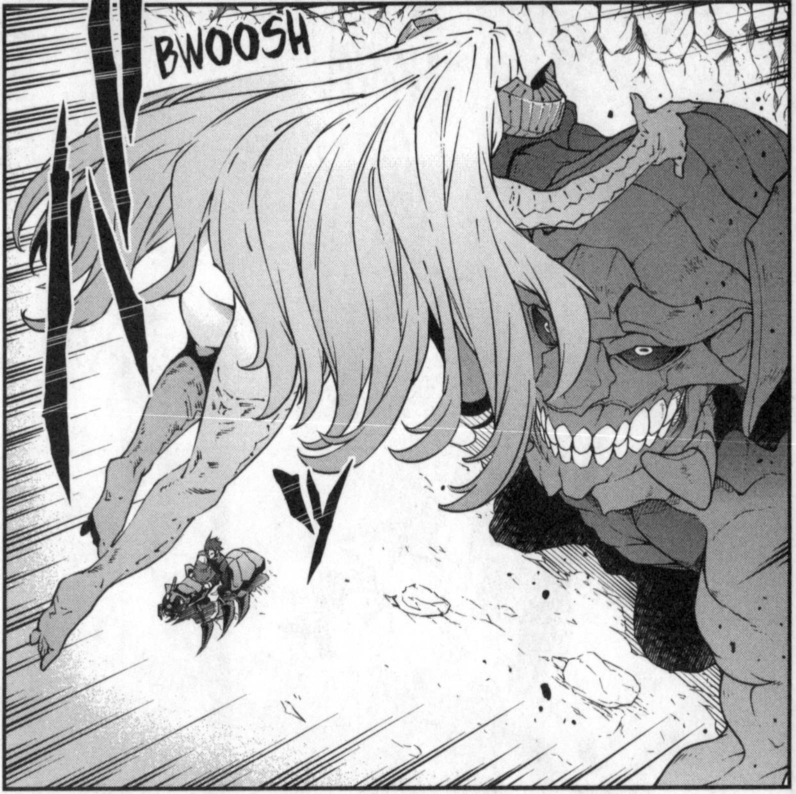
BWOOSH
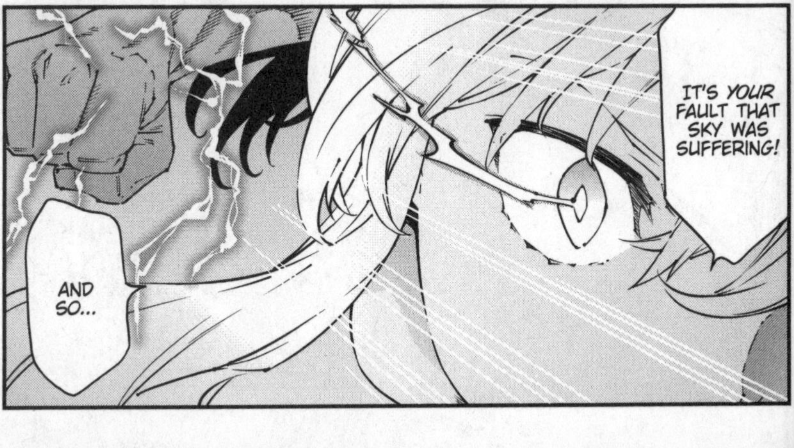
IT'S *YOUR* FAULT THAT SKY WAS SUFFERING!
AND SO...

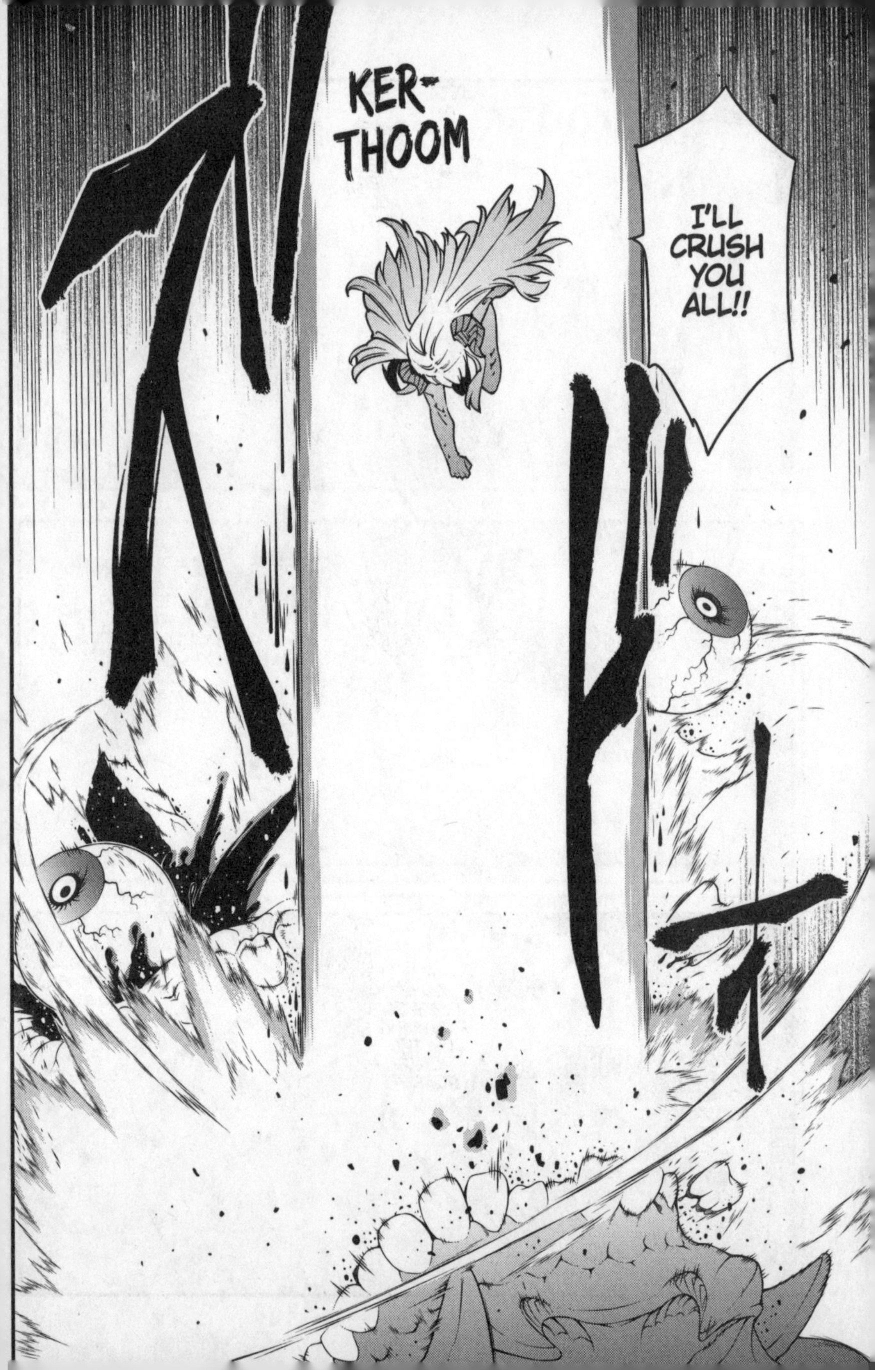
I'LL CRUSH YOU ALL!!
KER-THOOM

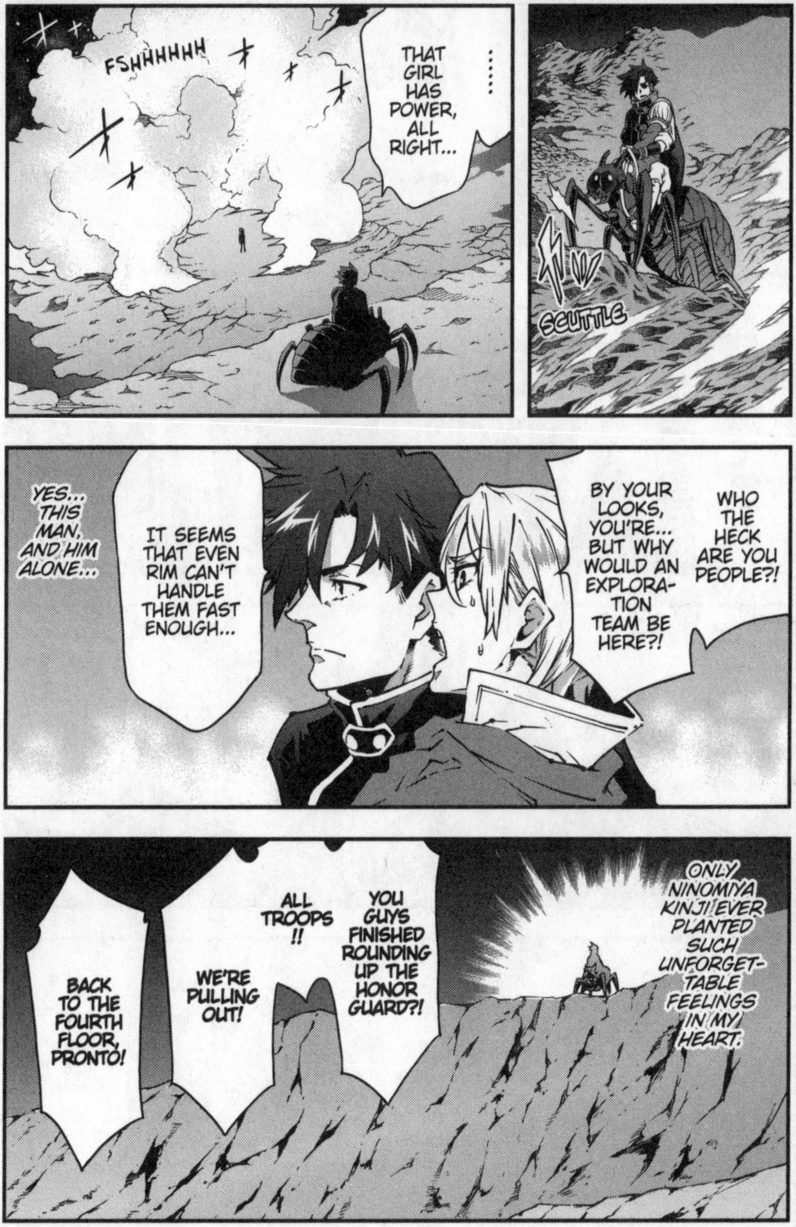
SCUTTLE
......
THAT GIRL HAS POWER, ALL RIGHT...
FSHHHHHH
WHO THE HECK ARE YOU PEOPLE?!
BY YOUR LOOKS, YOU'RE... BUT WHY WOULD AN EXPLORATION TEAM BE HERE?!
IT SEEMS THAT EVEN RIM CAN'T HANDLE THEM FAST ENOUGH...
YES... THIS MAN, AND HIM ALONE...
ONLY NINOMIYA KINJI EVER PLANTED SUCH UNFORGET-TABLE FEELINGS IN MY HEART.
YOU GUYS FINISHED ROUNDING UP THE HONOR GUARD?!
ALL TROOPS !!
WE'RE PULLING OUT!
BACK TO THE FOURTH FLOOR, PRONTO!

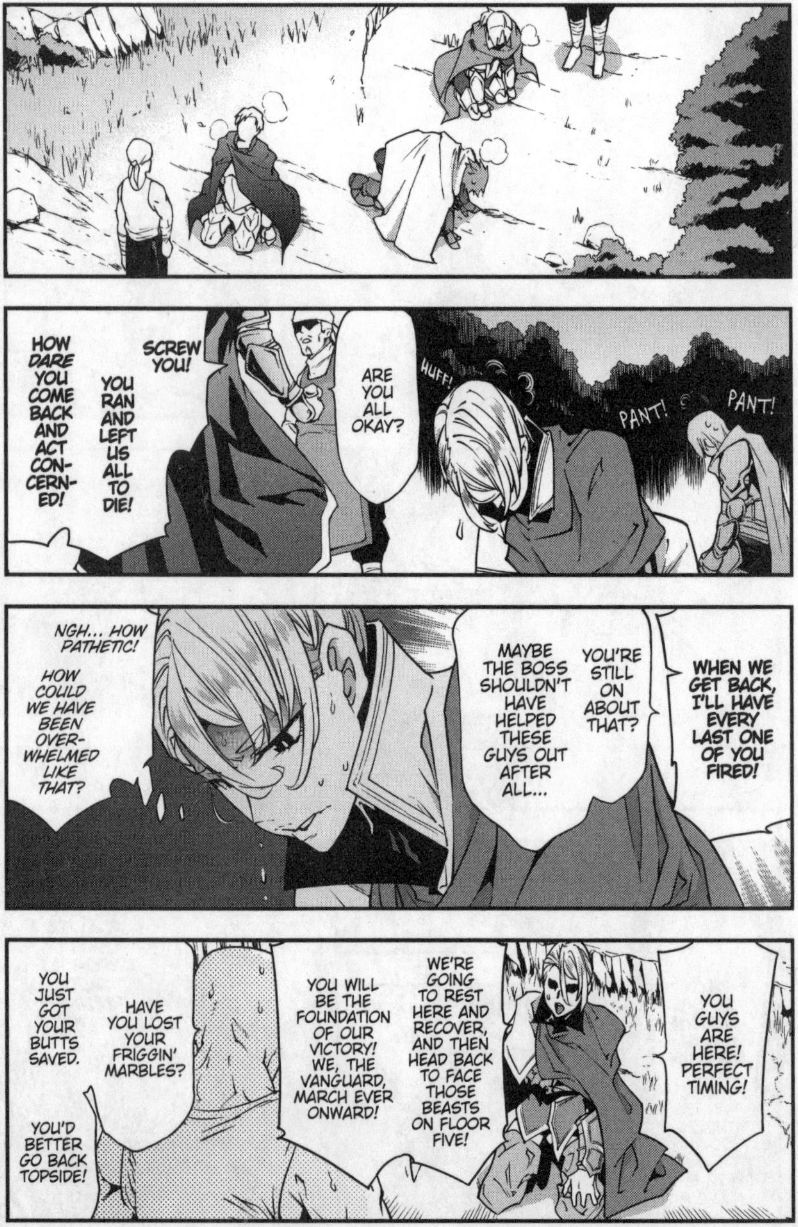
PANT!
PANT!
HUFF!
ARE YOU ALL OKAY?
SCREW YOU!
YOU RAN AND LEFT US ALL TO DIE!
HOW DARE YOU COME BACK AND ACT CONCERNED!
WHEN WE GET BACK, I'LL HAVE EVERY LAST ONE OF YOU FIRED!
YOU'RE STILL ON ABOUT THAT?
MAYBE THE BOSS SHOULDN'T HAVE HELPED THESE GUYS OUT AFTER ALL...
NGH... HOW PATHETIC!
HOW COULD WE HAVE BEEN OVER-WHELMED LIKE THAT?
YOU GUYS ARE HERE! PERFECT TIMING!
WE'RE GOING TO REST HERE AND RECOVER, AND THEN HEAD BACK TO FACE THOSE BEASTS ON FLOOR FIVE!
YOU WILL BE THE FOUNDATION OF OUR VICTORY! WE, THE VANGUARD, MARCH EVER ONWARD!
HAVE YOU LOST YOUR FRIGGIN' MARBLES?
YOU JUST GOT YOUR BUTTS SAVED.
YOU'D BETTER GO BACK TOPSIDE!

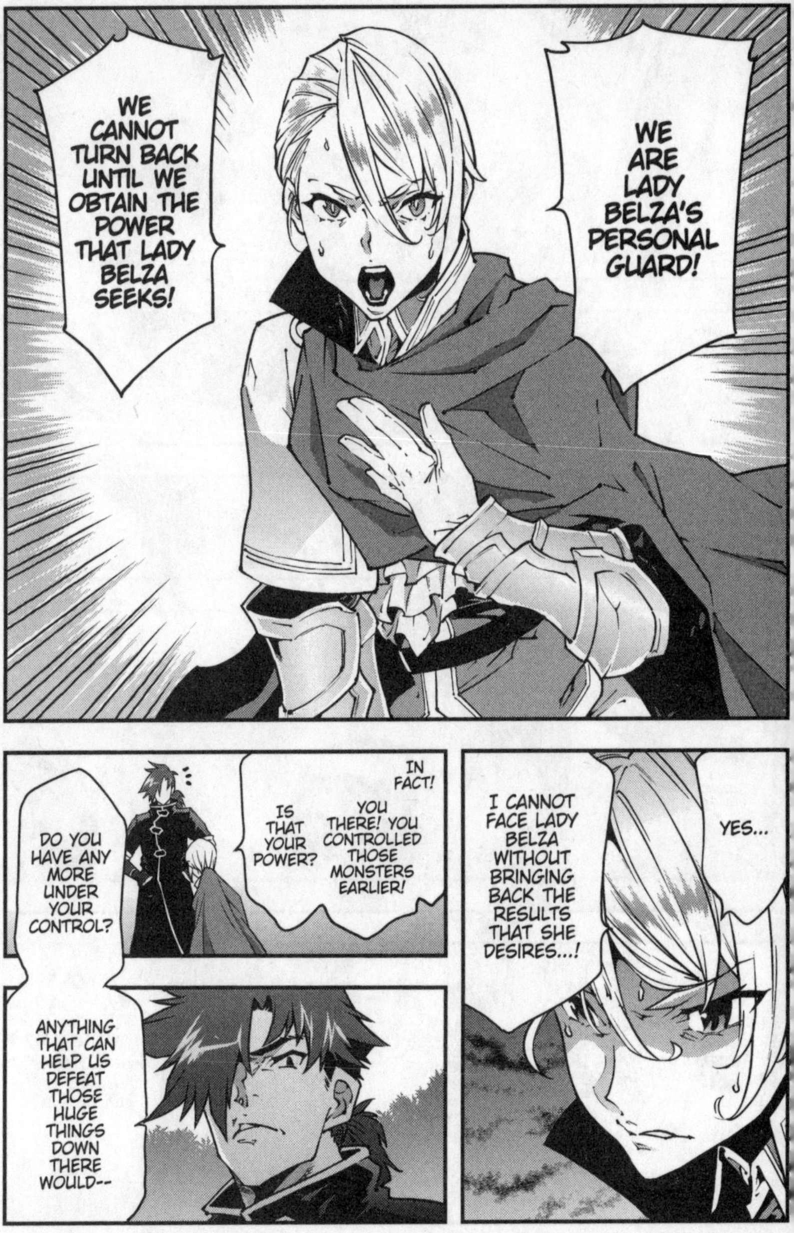
WE ARE LADY BELZA'S PERSONAL GUARD!
WE CANNOT TURN BACK UNTIL WE OBTAIN THE POWER THAT LADY BELZA SEEKS!
YES...
I CANNOT FACE LADY BELZA WITHOUT BRINGING BACK THE RESULTS THAT SHE DESIRES...!
IN FACT!
YOU THERE! YOU CONTROLLED THOSE MONSTERS EARLIER!
IS THAT YOUR POWER?
DO YOU HAVE ANY MORE UNDER YOUR CONTROL?
ANYTHING THAT CAN HELP US DEFEAT THOSE HUGE THINGS DOWN THERE WOULD--

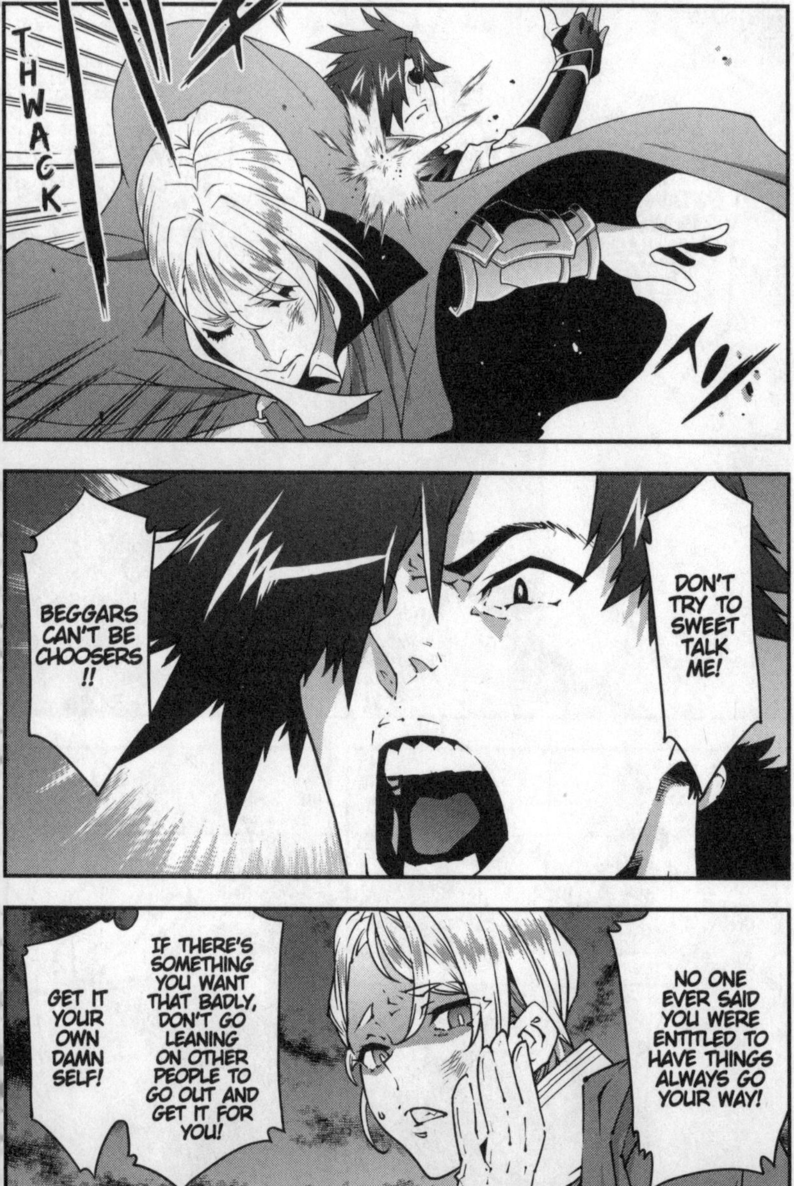
THWACK
DON'T TRY TO SWEET TALK ME!
BEGGARS CAN'T BE CHOOSERS!!
NO ONE EVER SAID YOU WERE ENTITLED TO HAVE THINGS ALWAYS GO YOUR WAY!
IF THERE'S SOMETHING YOU WANT THAT BADLY, DON'T GO LEANING ON OTHER PEOPLE TO GO OUT AND GET IT FOR YOU!
GET IT YOUR OWN DAMN SELF!

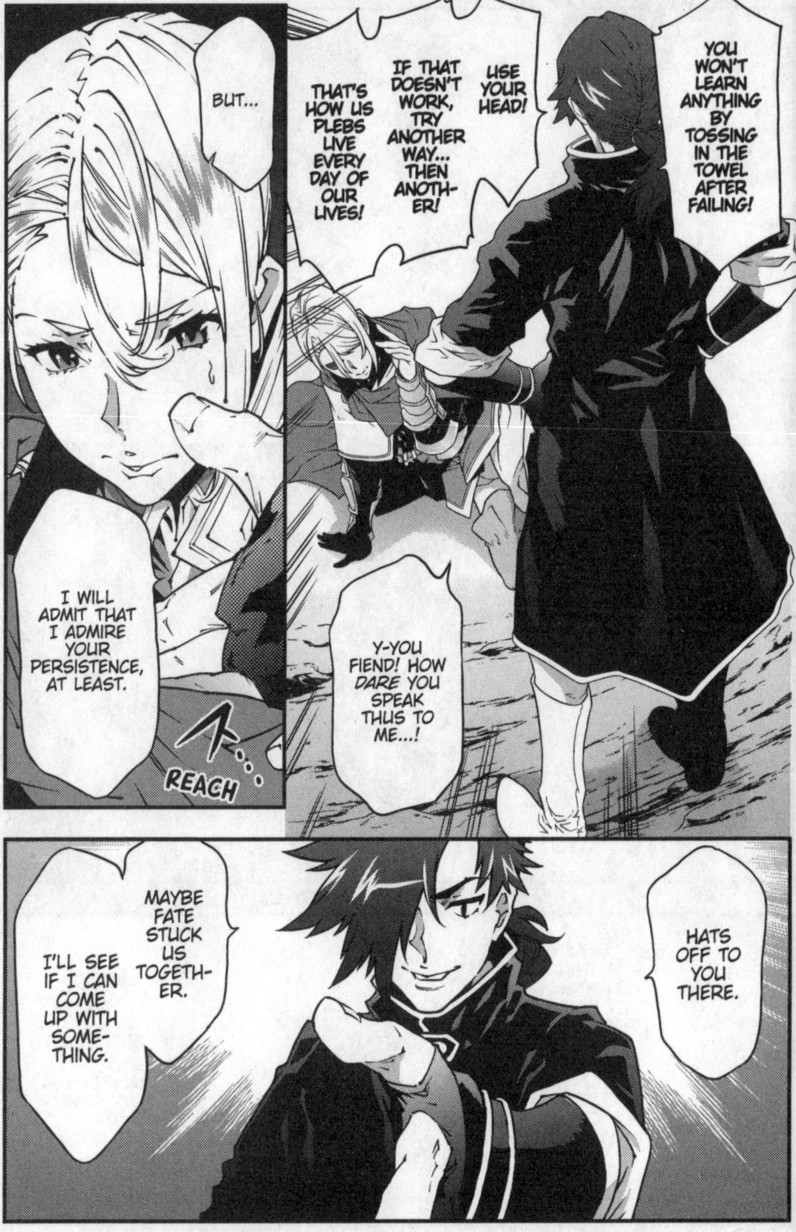
YOU WON'T LEARN ANYTHING BY TOSSING IN THE TOWEL AFTER FAILING!
USE YOUR HEAD!
IF THAT DOESN'T WORK, TRY ANOTHER WAY... THEN ANOTH-ER!
THAT'S HOW US PLEBS LIVE EVERY DAY OF OUR LIVES!
Y-YOU FIEND! HOW *DARE* YOU SPEAK THUS TO ME...!
BUT...
I WILL ADMIT THAT I ADMIRE YOUR PERSISTENCE, AT LEAST.
REACH
HATS OFF TO YOU THERE.
MAYBE FATE STUCK US TOGETH-ER.
I'LL SEE IF I CAN COME UP WITH SOME-THING.

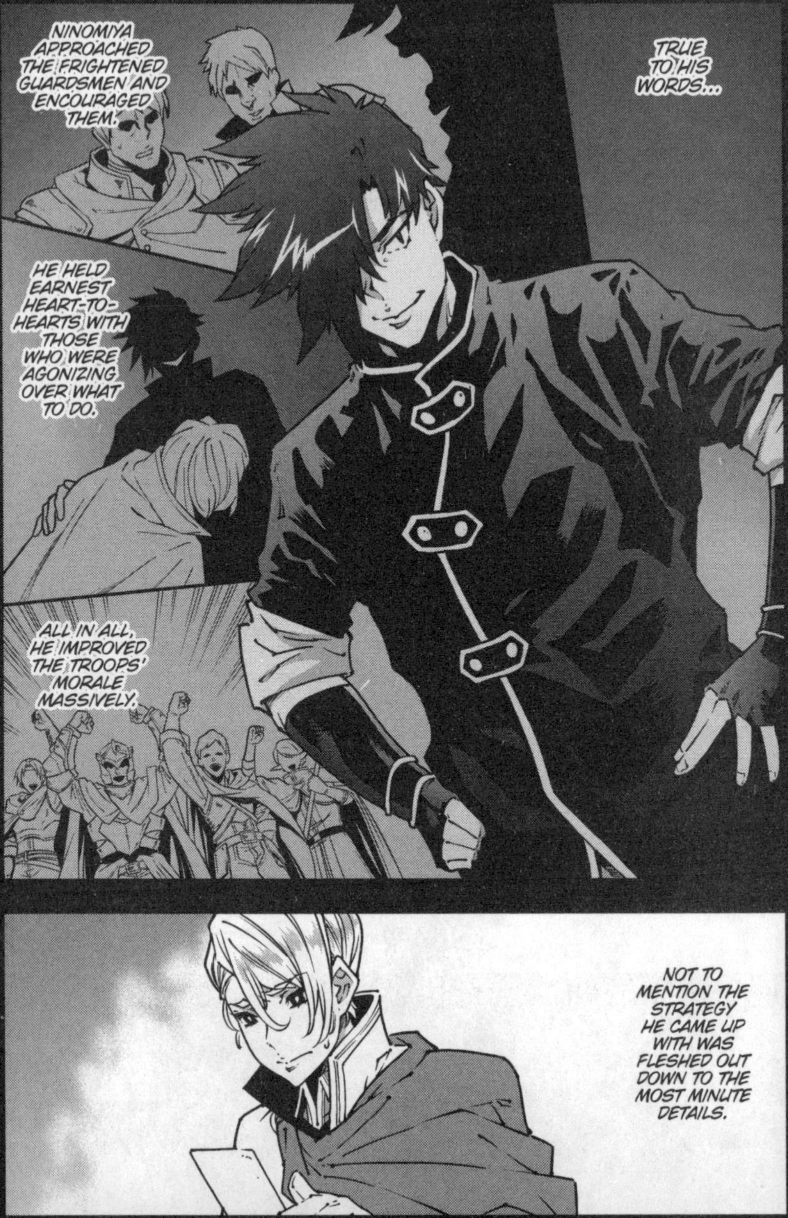
TRUE TO HIS WORDS...
NINOMIYA APPROACHED THE FRIGHTENED GUARDSMEN AND ENCOURAGED THEM.
HE HELD EARNEST HEART-TO-HEARTS WITH THOSE WHO WERE AGONIZING OVER WHAT TO DO.
ALL IN ALL, HE IMPROVED THE TROOPS' MORALE MASSIVELY.
NOT TO MENTION THE STRATEGY HE CAME UP WITH WAS FLESHED OUT DOWN TO THE MOST MINUTE DETAILS.

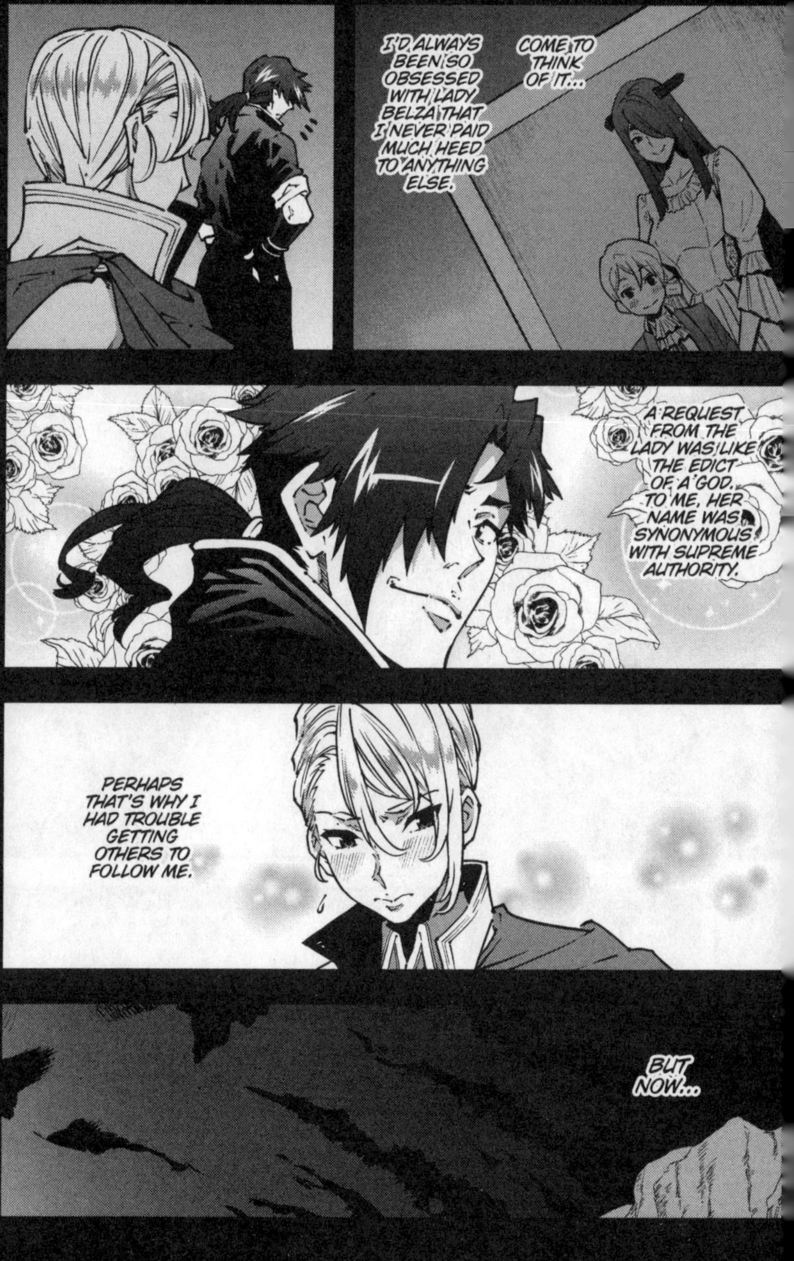
COME TO THINK OF IT...
I'D ALWAYS BEEN SO OBSESSED WITH LADY BELZA THAT I NEVER PAID MUCH HEED TO ANYTHING ELSE.
A REQUEST FROM THE LADY WAS LIKE THE EDICT OF A GOD. TO ME, HER NAME WAS SYNONYMOUS WITH SUPREME AUTHORITY.
PERHAPS THAT'S WHY I HAD TROUBLE GETTING OTHERS TO FOLLOW ME.
BUT NOW...

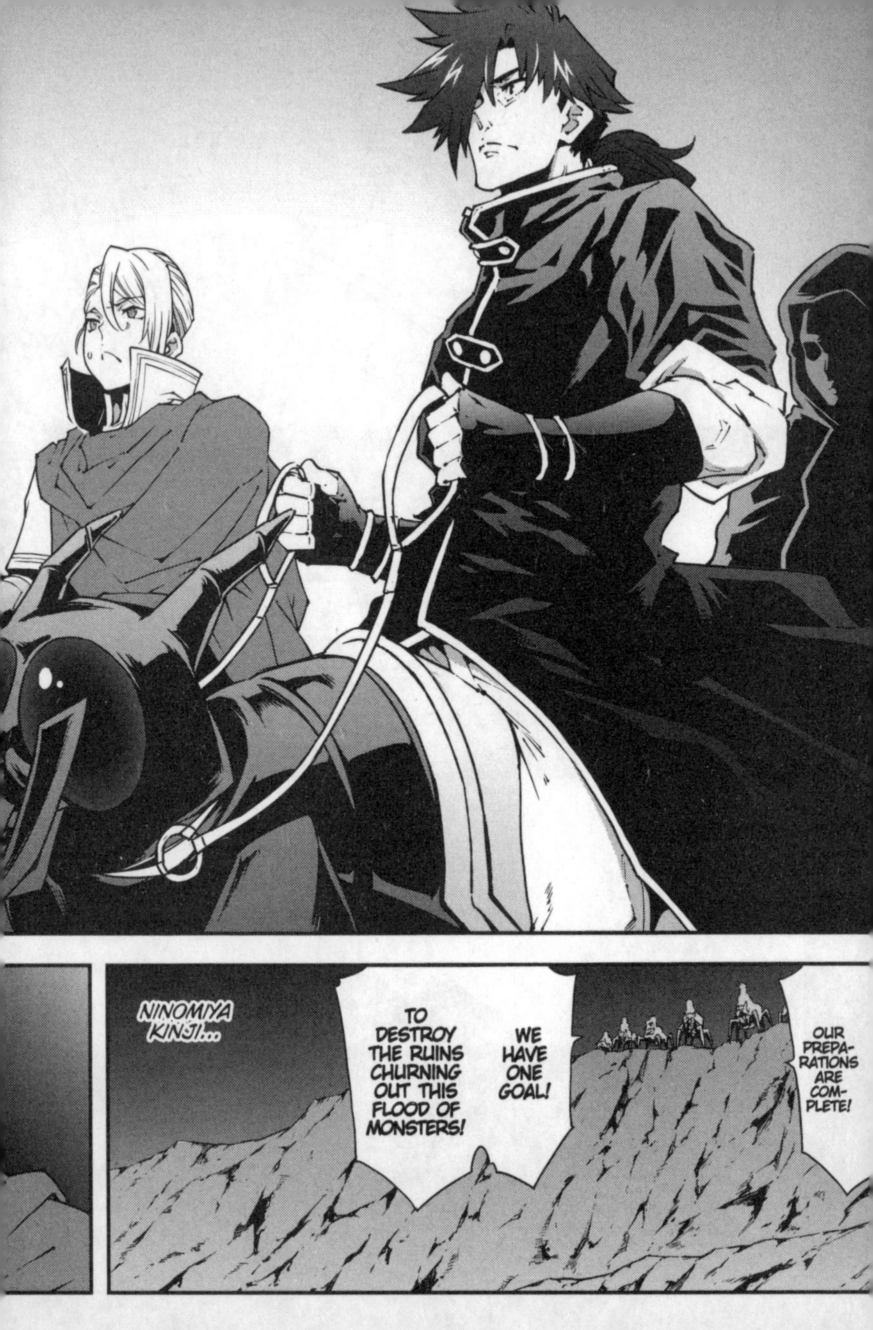
OUR PREPARATIONS ARE COMPLETE!
WE HAVE ONE GOAL!
TO DESTROY THE RUINS CHURNING OUT THIS FLOOD OF MONSTERS!
NINOMIYA KINJI...

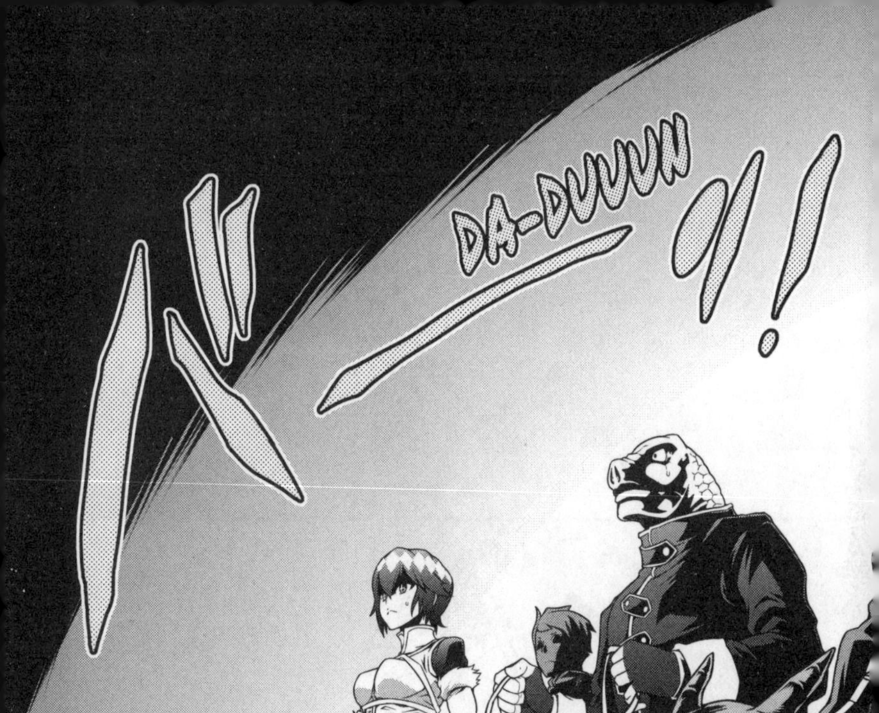
DA-DUUUN!!

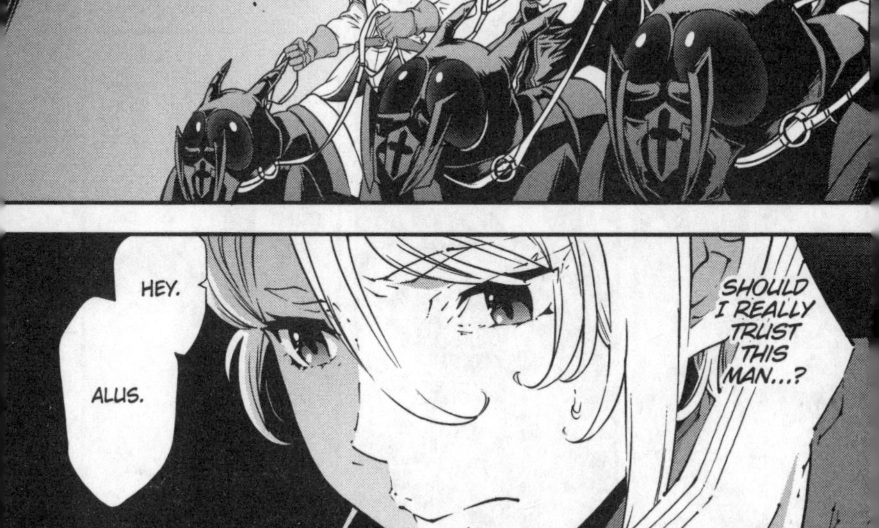
SHOULD I REALLY TRUST THIS MAN...?
HEY. ALUS.

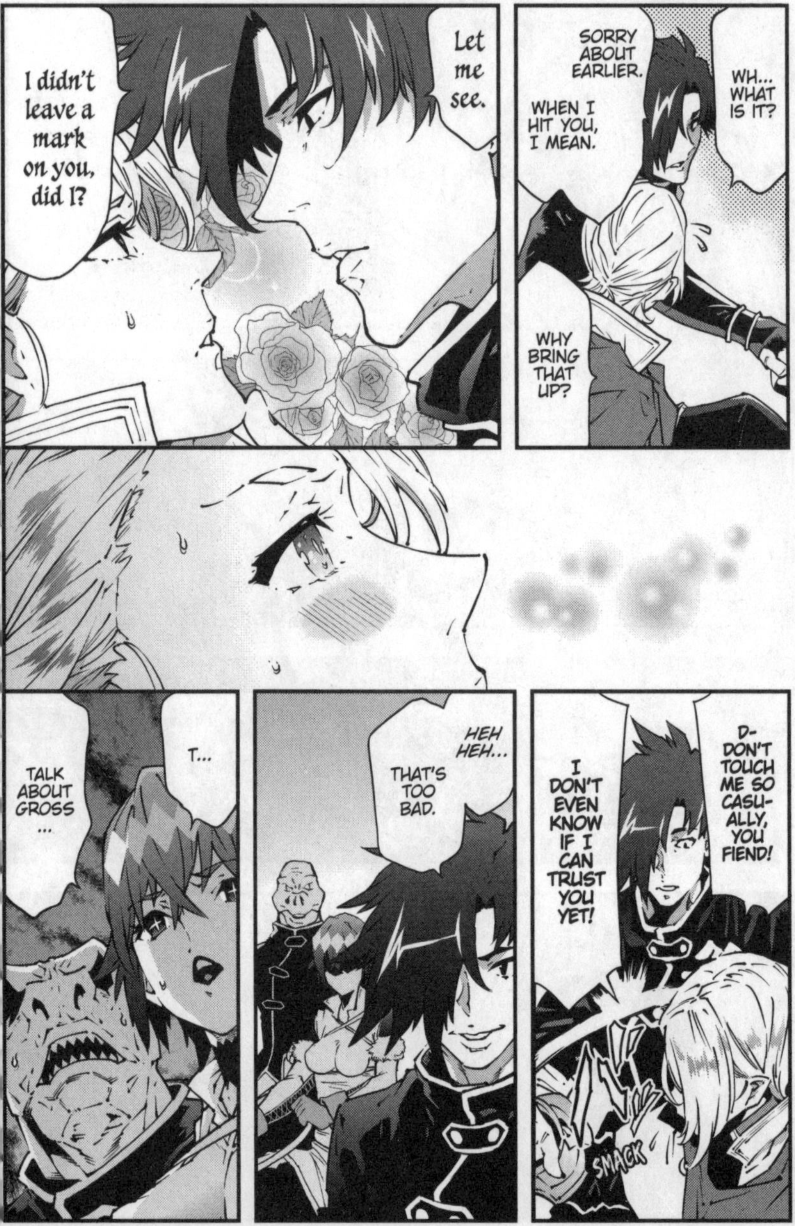
WH... WHAT IS IT?
SORRY ABOUT EARLIER.
WHEN I HIT YOU, I MEAN.
WHY BRING THAT UP?
Let me see.
I didn't leave a mark on you, did I?
D-DON'T TOUCH ME SO CASU-ALLY, YOU FIEND!
I DON'T EVEN KNOW IF I CAN TRUST YOU YET!
SMACK
HEH HEH...
THAT'S TOO BAD.
T...
TALK ABOUT GROSS ...

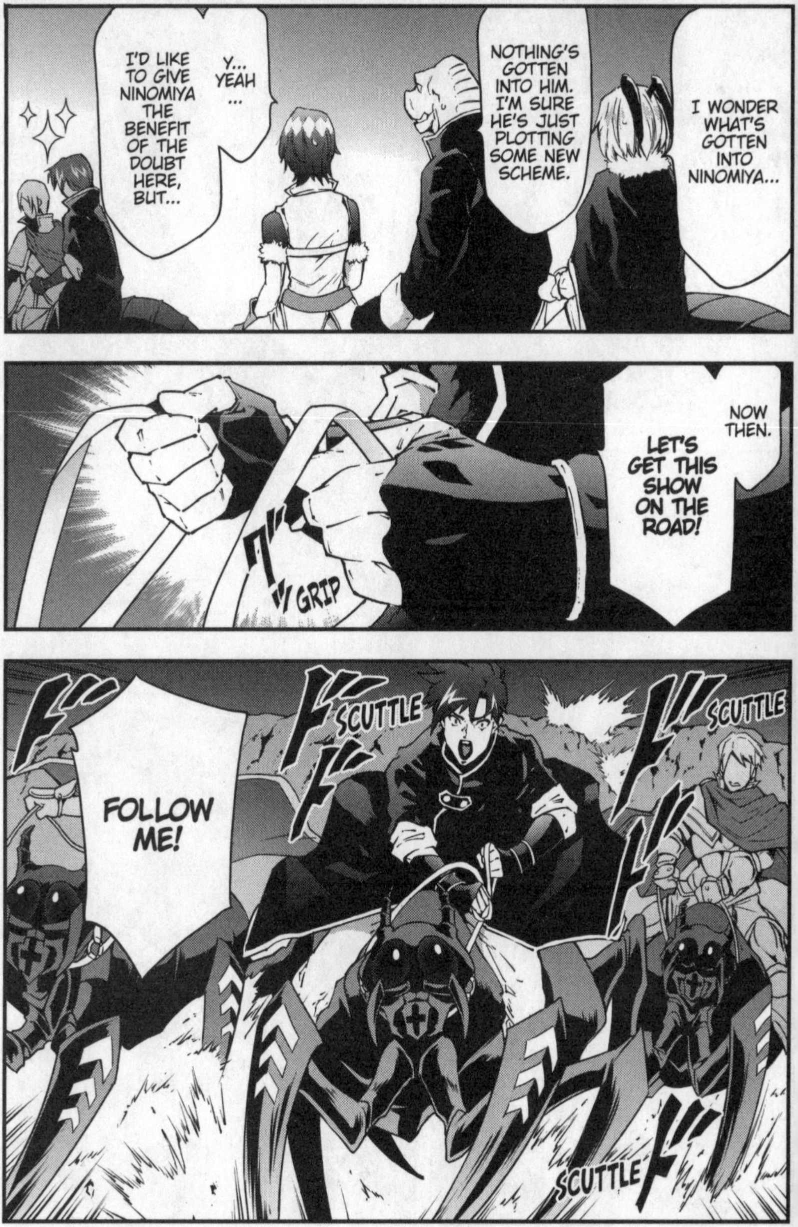
I WONDER WHAT'S GOTTEN INTO NINOMIYA...
NOTHING'S GOTTEN INTO HIM. I'M SURE HE'S JUST PLOTTING SOME NEW SCHEME.
Y... YEAH ...
I'D LIKE TO GIVE NINOMIYA THE BENEFIT OF THE DOUBT HERE, BUT...
NOW THEN.
LET'S GET THIS SHOW ON THE ROAD!
GRIP
SCUTTLE
SCUTTLE
FOLLOW ME!
SCUTTLE

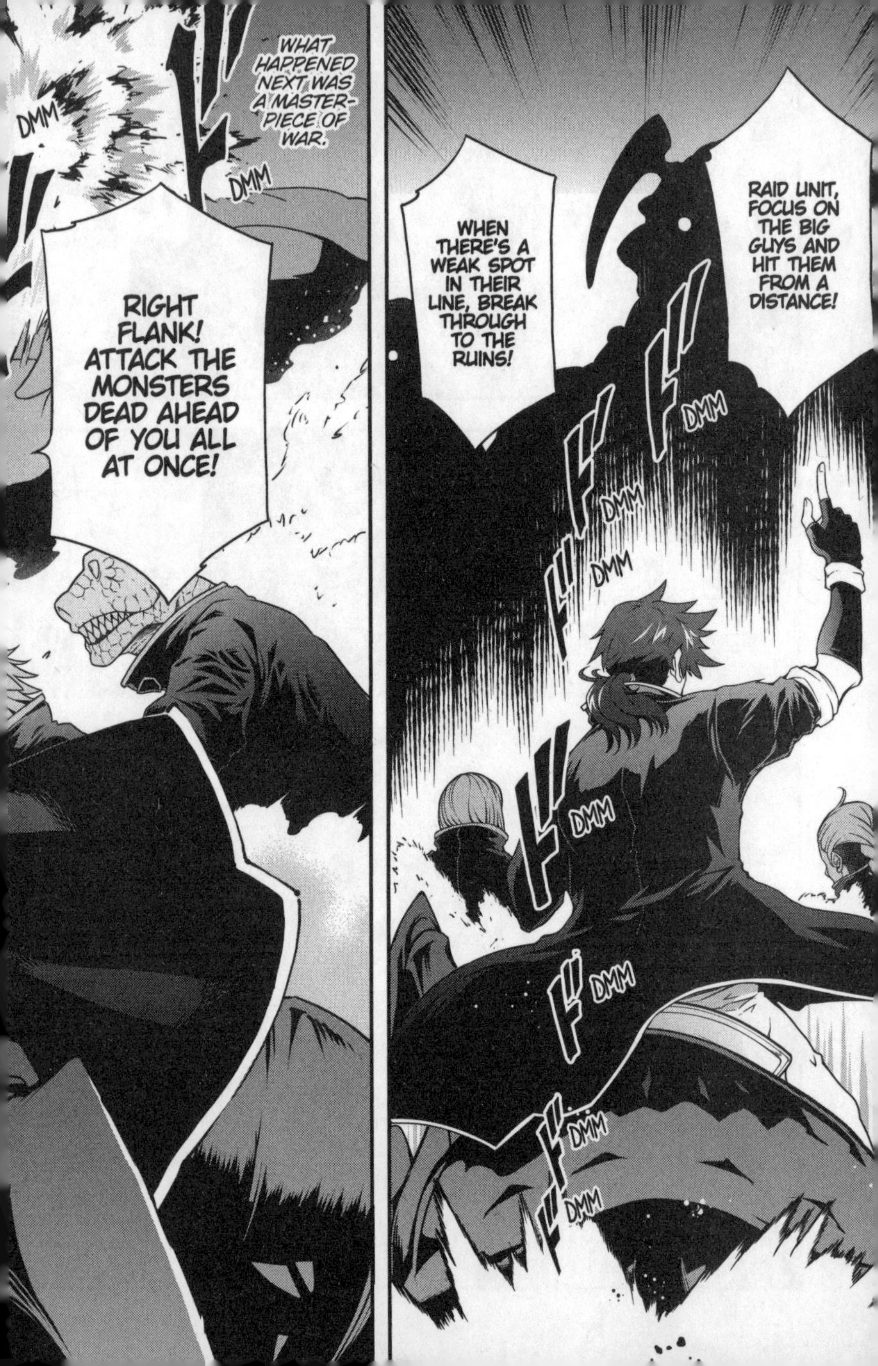

RAID UNIT, FOCUS ON THE BIG GUYS AND HIT THEM FROM A DISTANCE!
WHEN THERE'S A WEAK SPOT IN THEIR LINE, BREAK THROUGH TO THE RUINS!
DMM
DMM
DMM
DMM
DMM
DMM
DMM
WHAT HAPPENED NEXT WAS A MASTER-PIECE OF WAR.
DMM
DMM
RIGHT FLANK! ATTACK THE MONSTERS DEAD AHEAD OF YOU ALL AT ONCE!

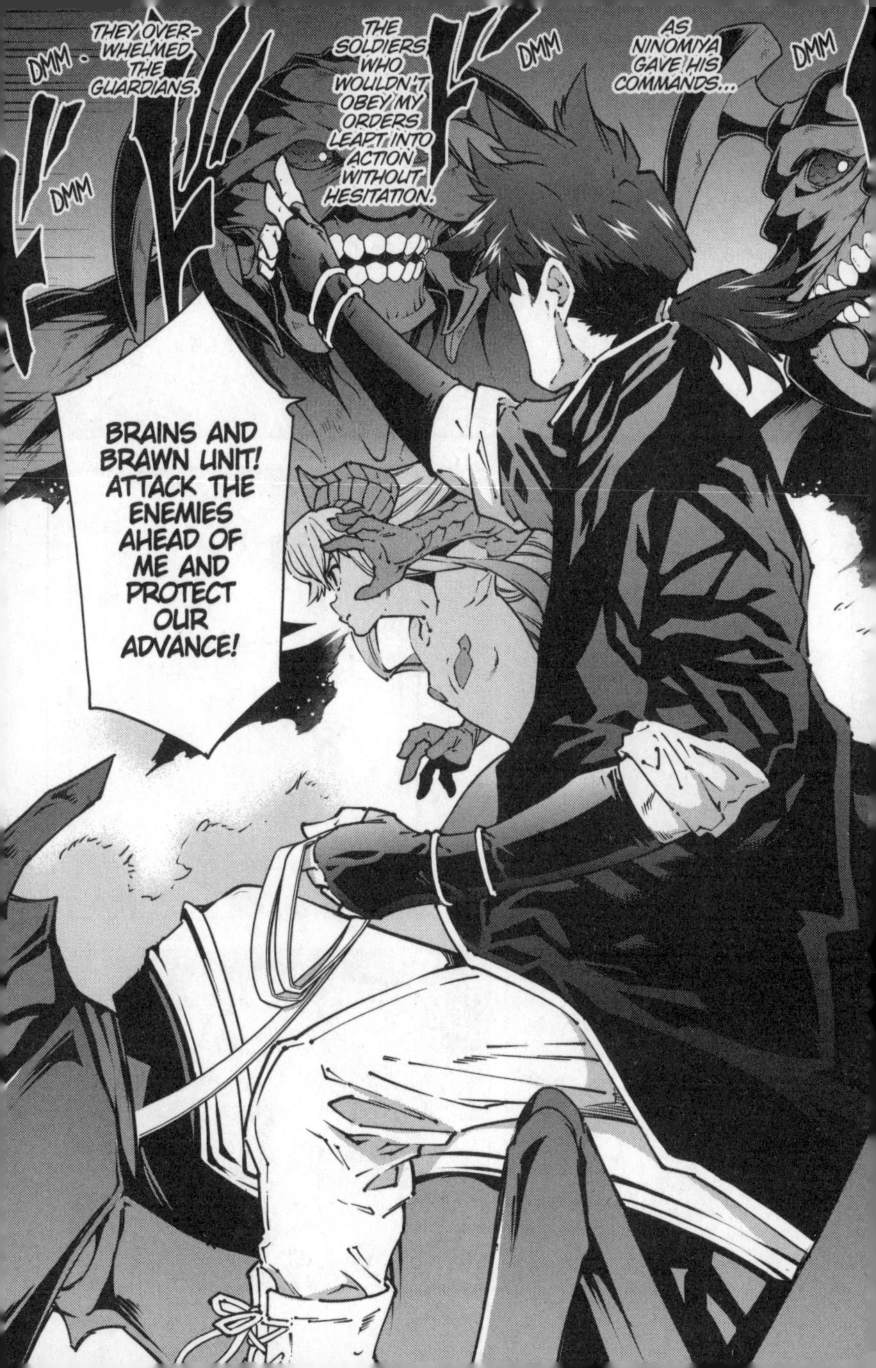
DMM
AS NINOMIYA GAVE HIS COMMANDS...
DMM
THE SOLDIERS WHO WOULDN'T OBEY MY ORDERS LEAPT INTO ACTION WITHOUT HESITATION.
THEY OVER-WHELMED THE GUARDIANS.
DMM
DMM
BRAINS AND BRAWN UNIT! ATTACK THE ENEMIES AHEAD OF ME AND PROTECT OUR ADVANCE!

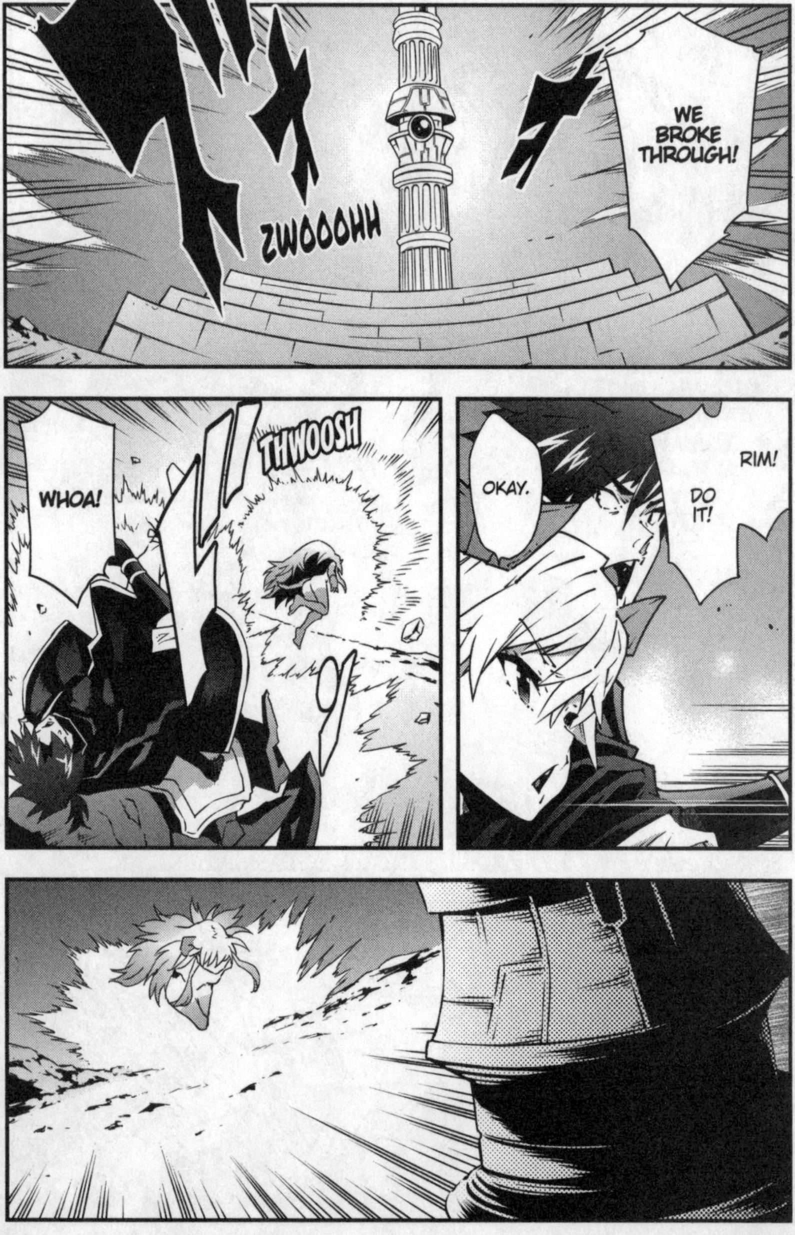
WE BROKE THROUGH!
ZWOOOHH
RIM!
DO IT!
OKAY.
THWOOSH
WHOA!

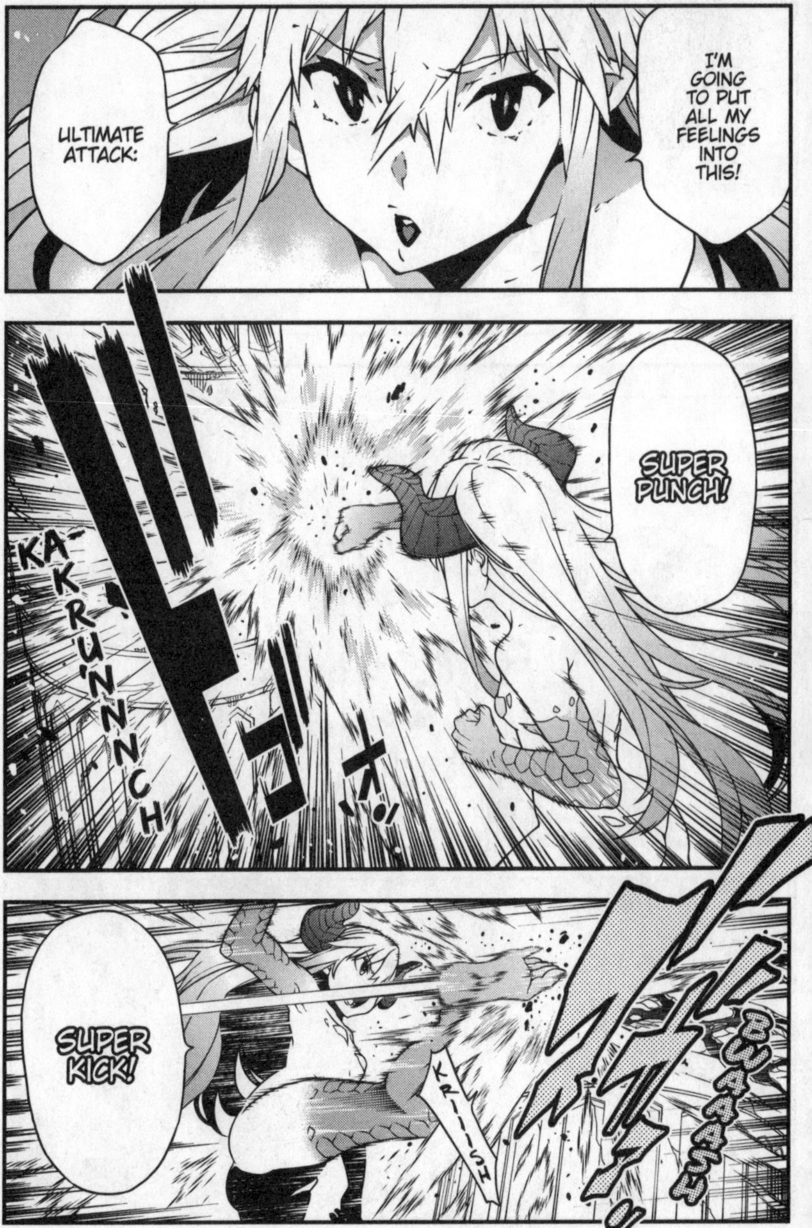
I'M GOING TO PUT ALL MY FEELINGS INTO THIS!
ULTIMATE ATTACK:
SUPER PUNCH!
KAKRUNNNCH
BWAAASH!!
KRIIISH
SUPER KICK!

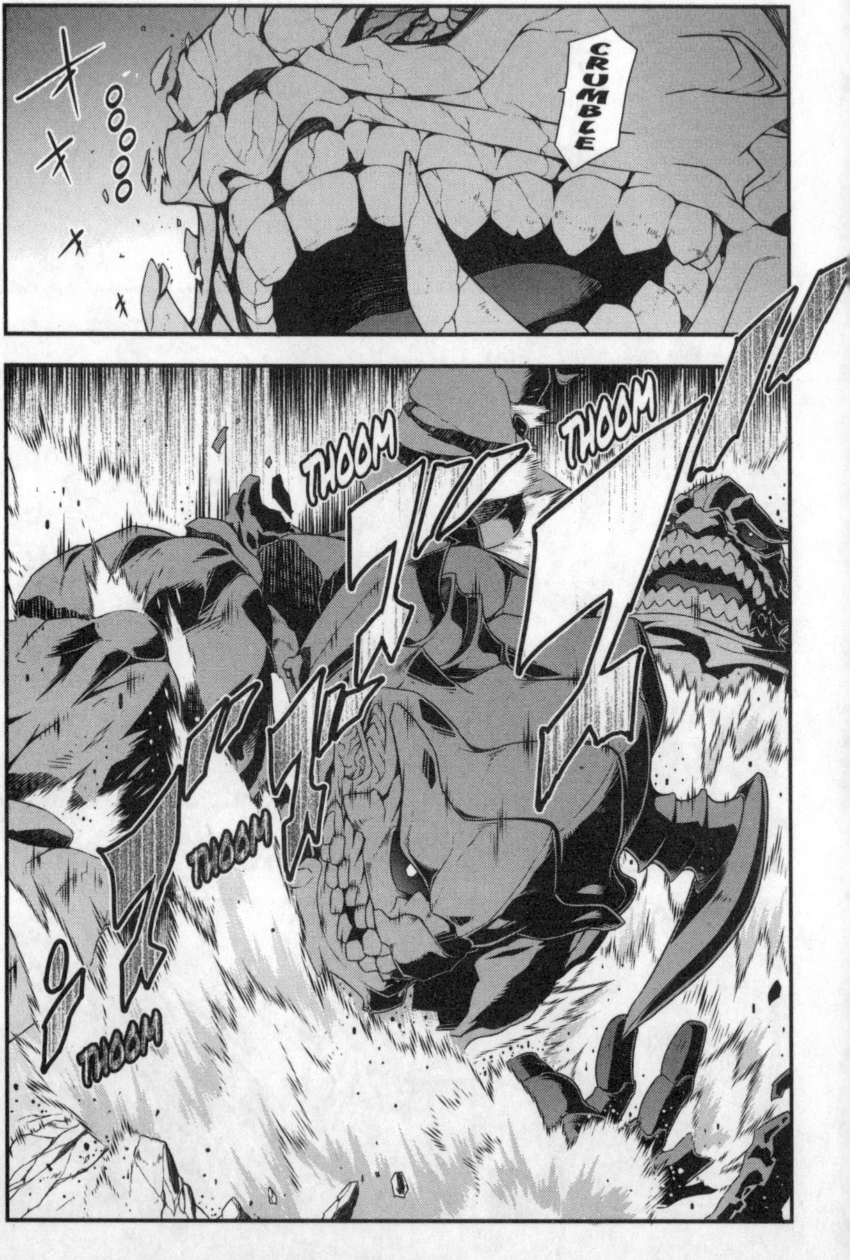
CRUMBLE
...OOOOO
THOOM
THOOM
THOOM
THOOM

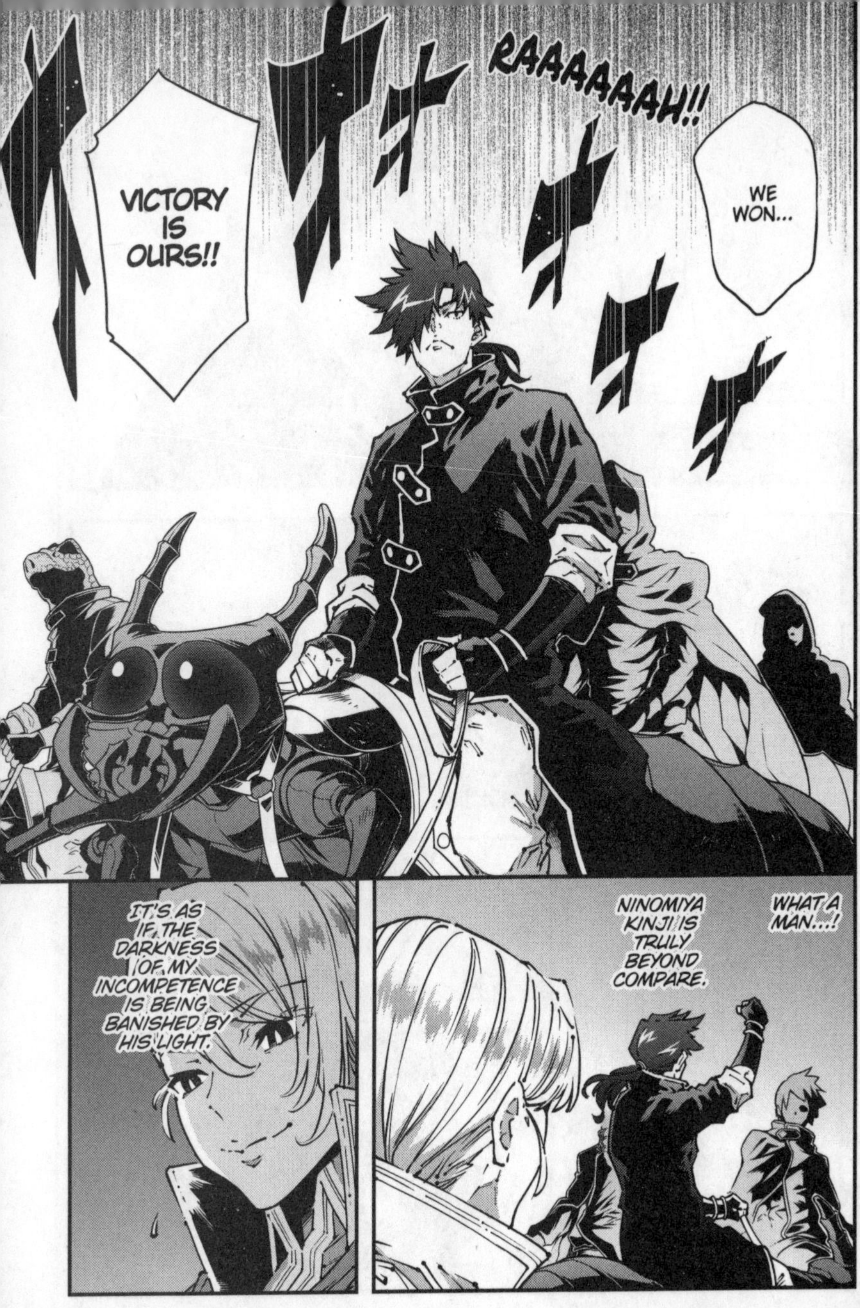
WE WON...
RAAAAAAAH!!
VICTORY IS OURS!!
WHAT A MAN...!
NINOMIYA KINJI IS TRULY BEYOND COMPARE.
IT'S AS IF THE DARKNESS OF MY INCOMPETENCE IS BEING BANISHED BY HIS LIGHT.

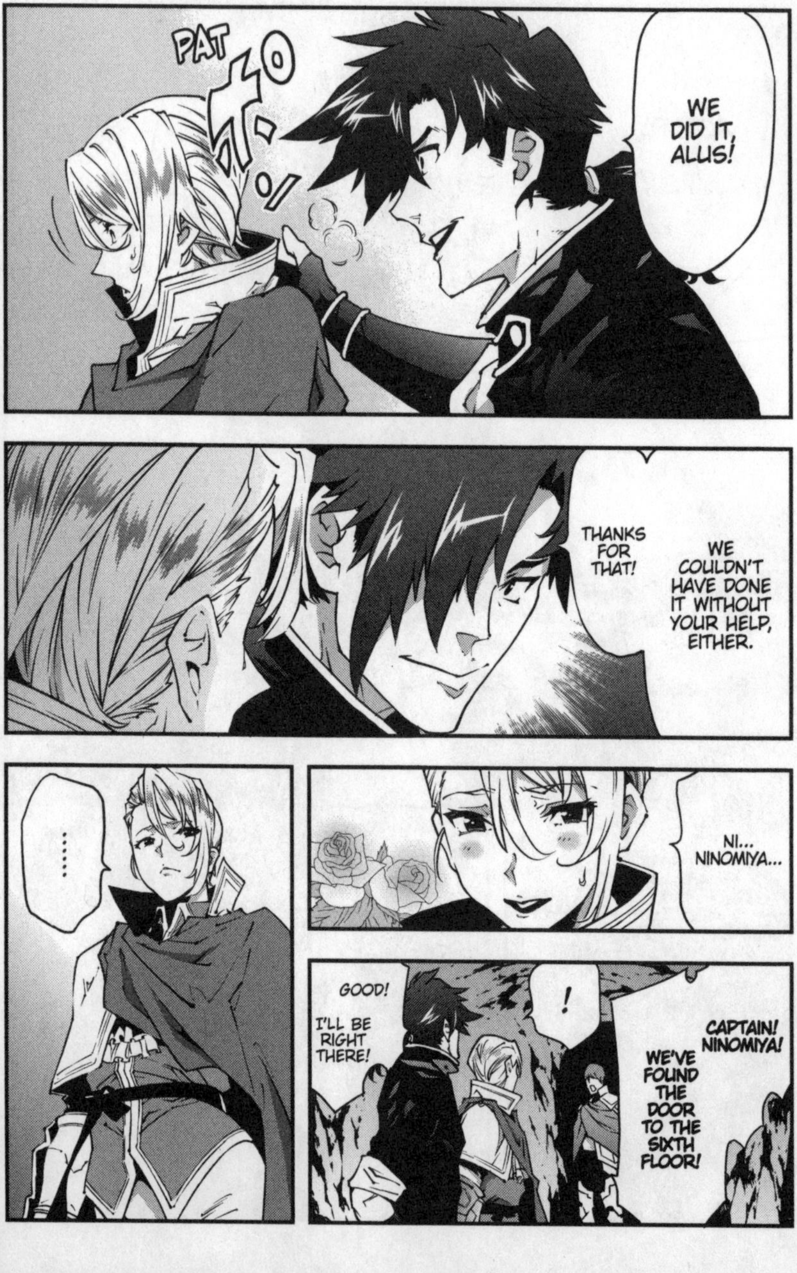
WE DID IT, ALUS!
PAT
WE COULDN'T HAVE DONE IT WITHOUT YOUR HELP, EITHER.
THANKS FOR THAT!
NI... NINOMIYA...
CAPTAIN! NINOMIYA!
WE'VE FOUND THE DOOR TO THE SIXTH FLOOR!
!
GOOD!
I'LL BE RIGHT THERE!
......

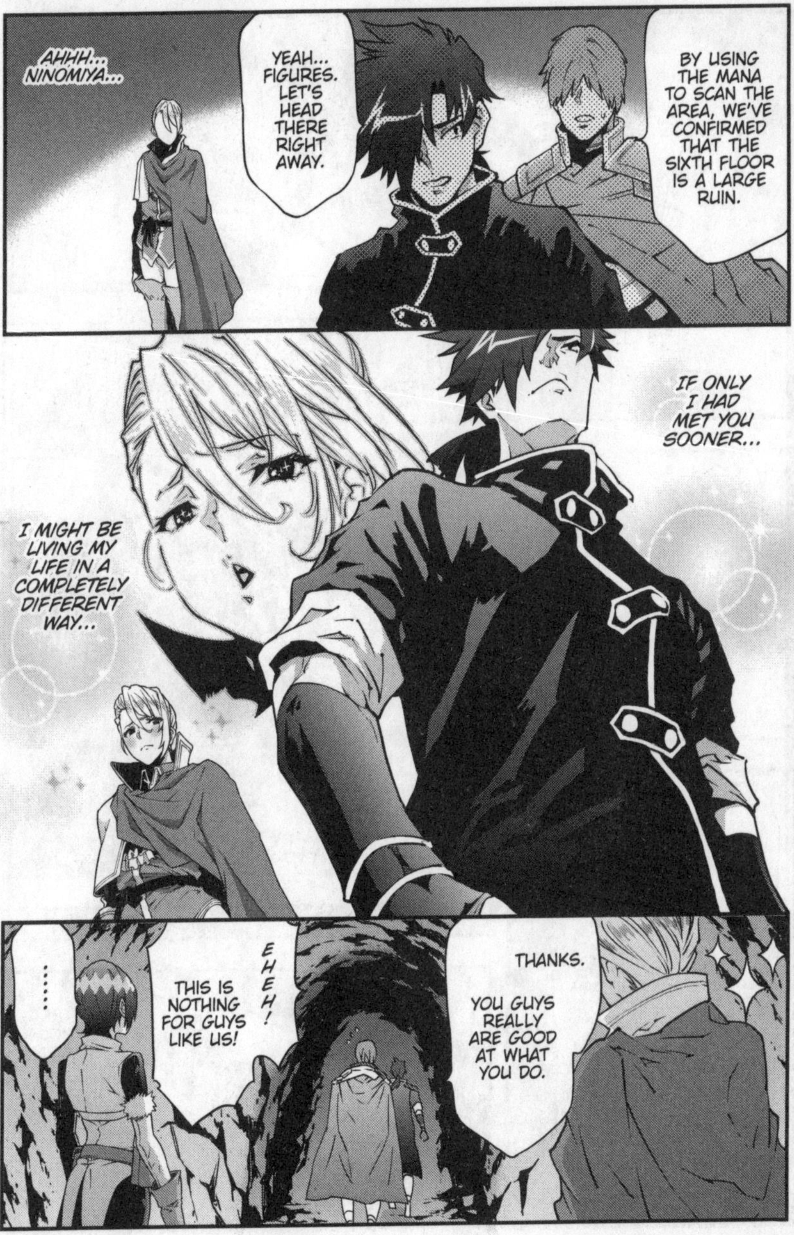
BY USING THE MANA TO SCAN THE AREA, WE'VE CONFIRMED THAT THE SIXTH FLOOR IS A LARGE RUIN.
YEAH... FIGURES. LET'S HEAD THERE RIGHT AWAY.
AHHH... NINOMIYA...
IF ONLY I HAD MET YOU SOONER...
I MIGHT BE LIVING MY LIFE IN A COMPLETELY DIFFERENT WAY...
THANKS.
YOU GUYS REALLY ARE GOOD AT WHAT YOU DO.
EHEH!
THIS IS NOTHING FOR GUYS LIKE US!
......

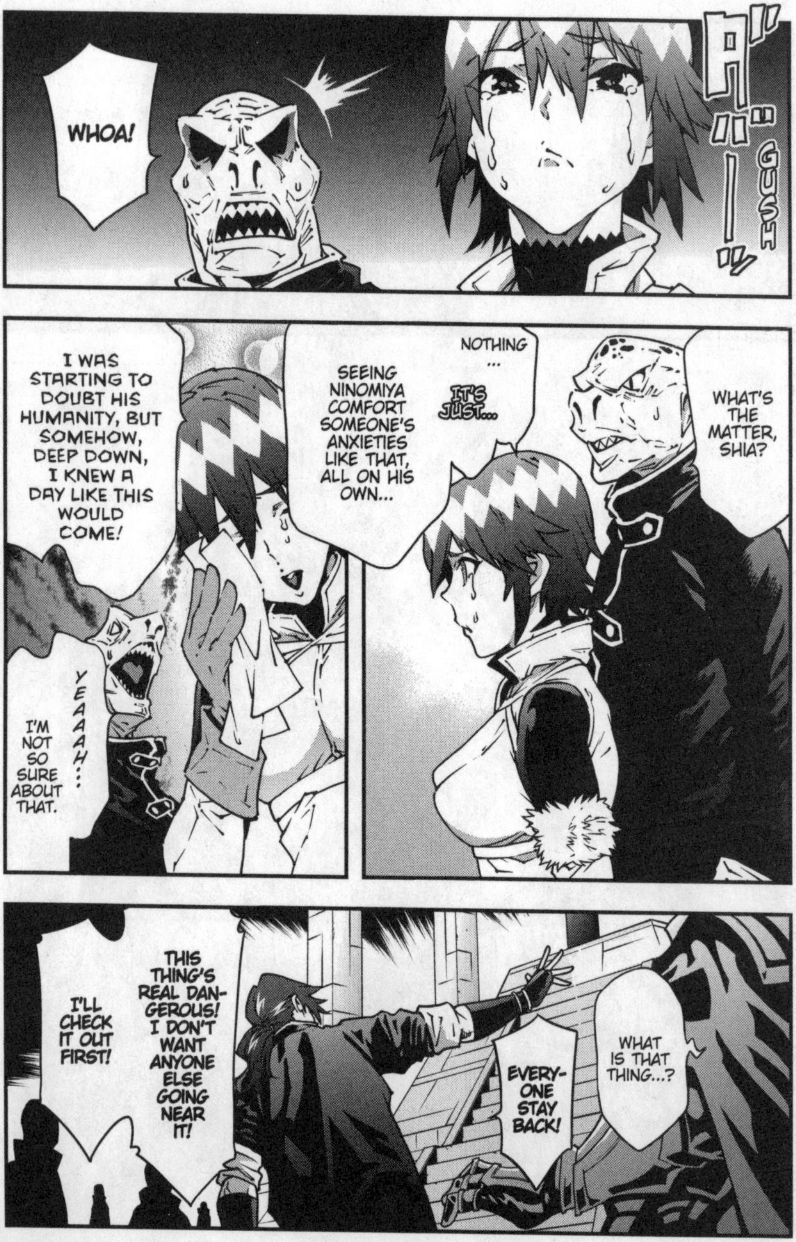
GUSH
WHOA!
WHAT'S THE MATTER, SHIA?
NOTHING...
IT'S JUST...
SEEING NINOMIYA COMFORT SOMEONE'S ANXIETIES LIKE THAT, ALL ON HIS OWN...
I WAS STARTING TO DOUBT HIS HUMANITY, BUT SOMEHOW, DEEP DOWN, I KNEW A DAY LIKE THIS WOULD COME!
YEAAAAH...
I'M NOT SO SURE ABOUT THAT.
WHAT IS THAT THING...?
EVERY-ONE STAY BACK!
THIS THING'S REAL DAN-GEROUS! I DON'T WANT ANYONE ELSE GOING NEAR IT!
I'LL CHECK IT OUT FIRST!

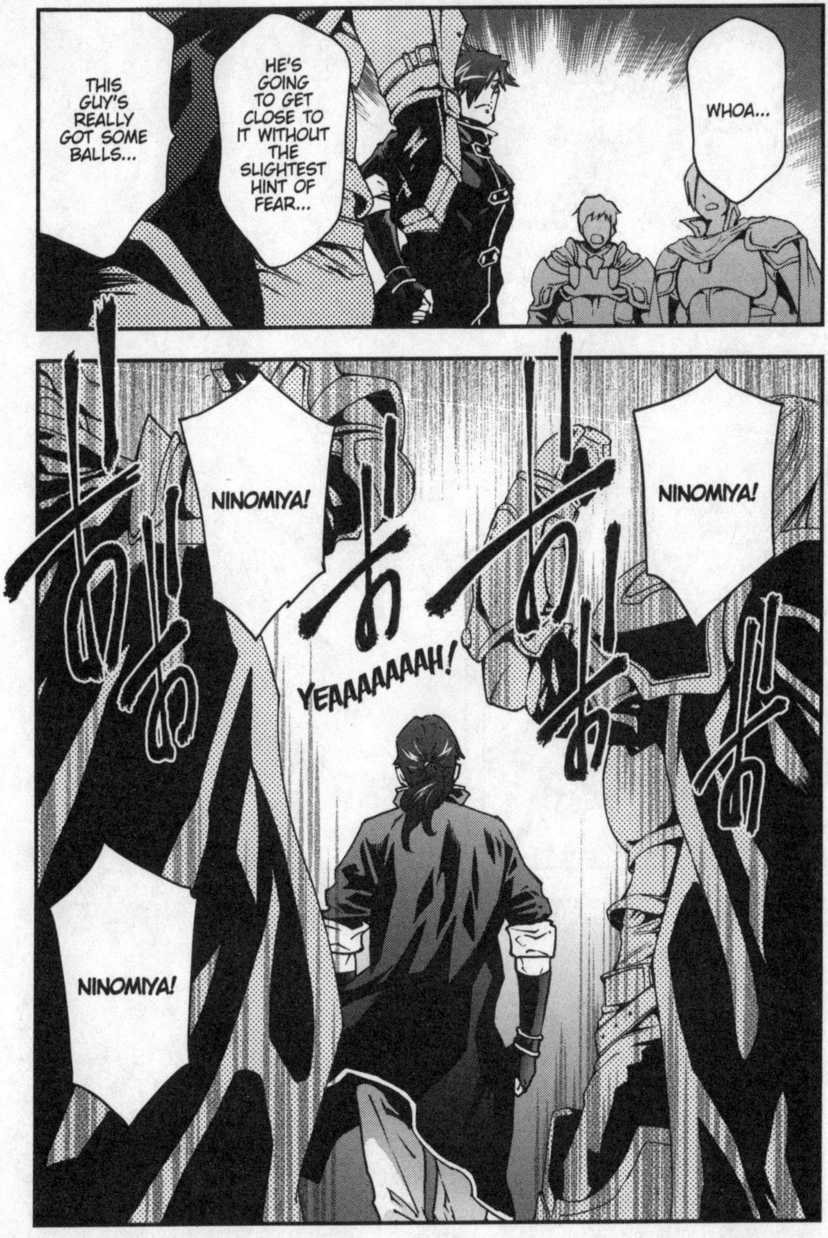
WHOA...
HE'S GOING TO GET CLOSE TO IT WITHOUT THE SLIGHTEST HINT OF FEAR...
THIS GUY'S REALLY GOT SOME BALLS...
NINOMIYA!
NINOMIYA!
YEAAAAAAAH!
NINOMIYA!

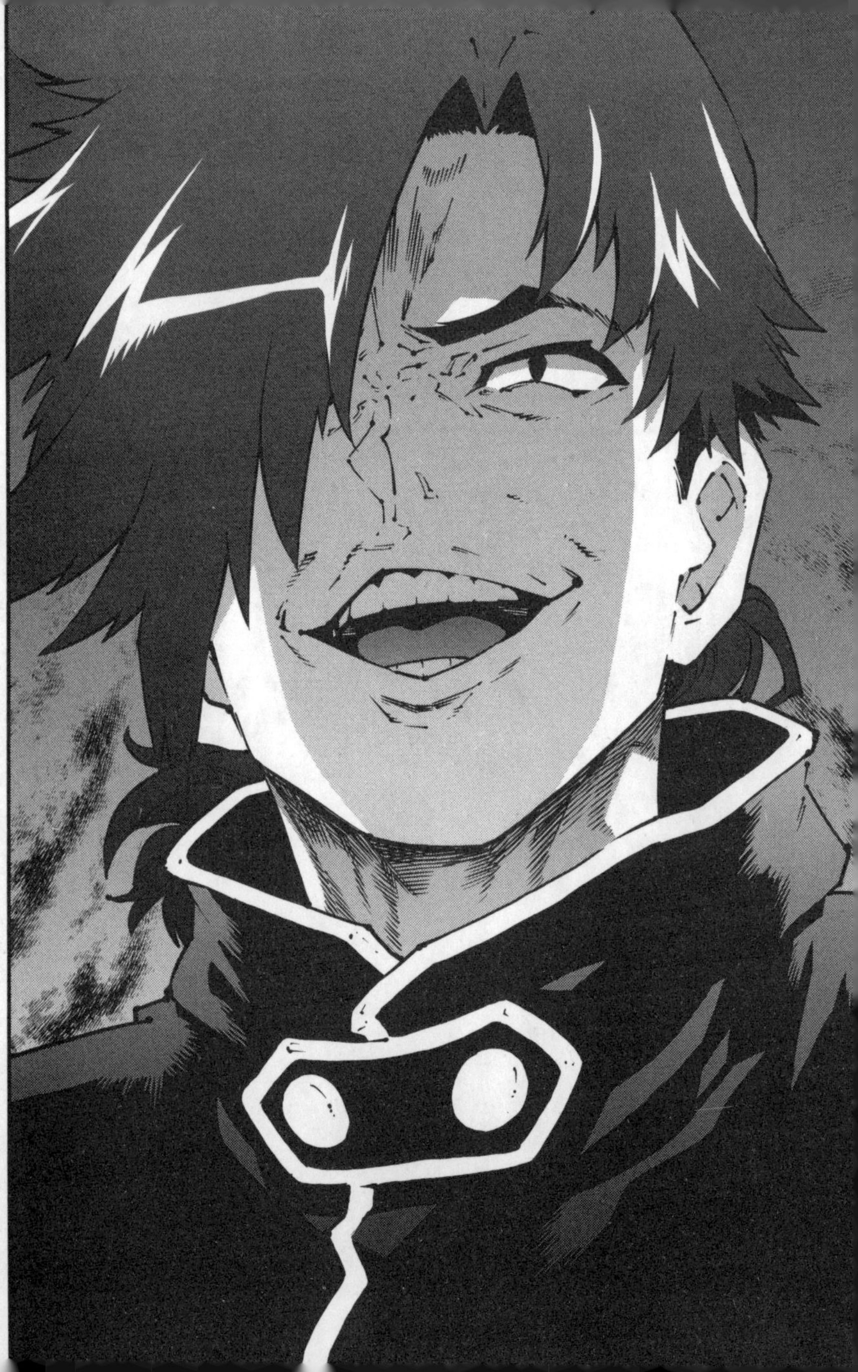

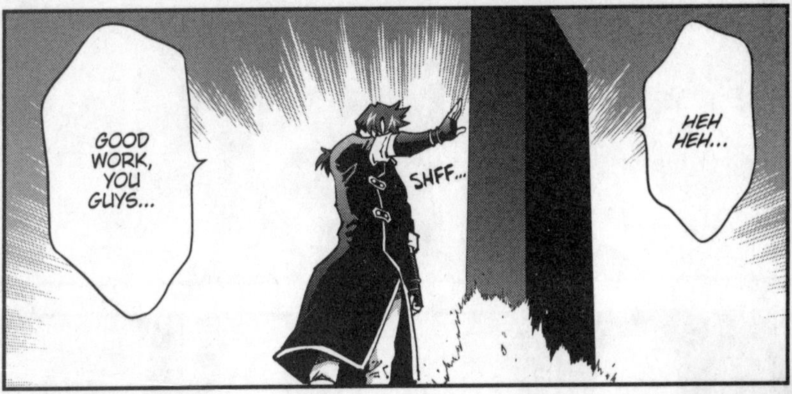
HEH HEH...
SHFF...
GOOD WORK, YOU GUYS...
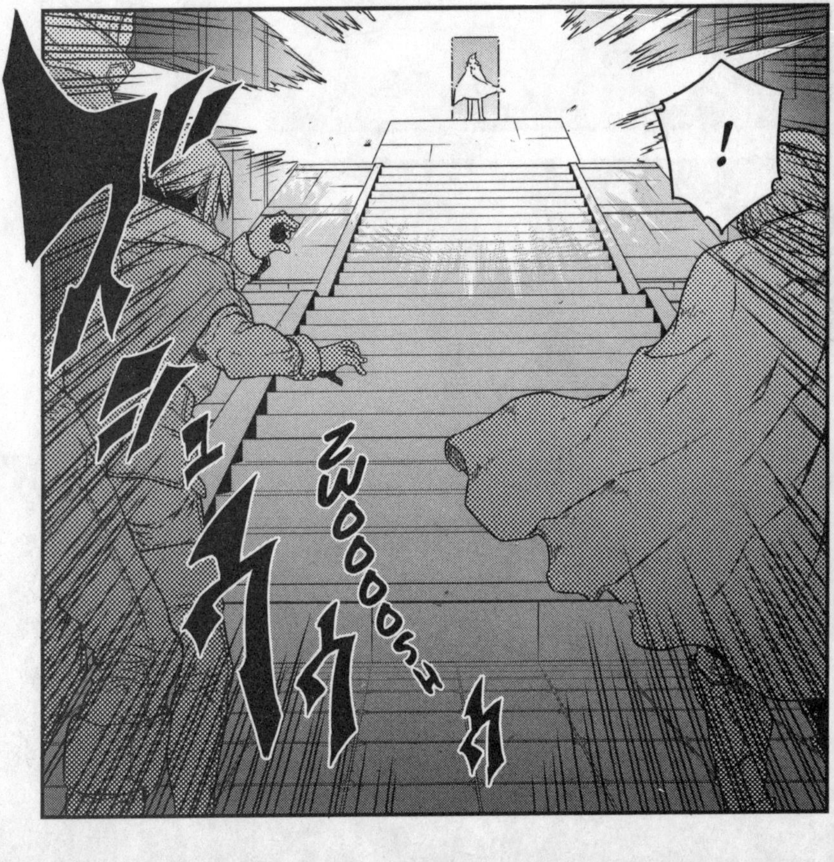
!
ZWOOOOSH

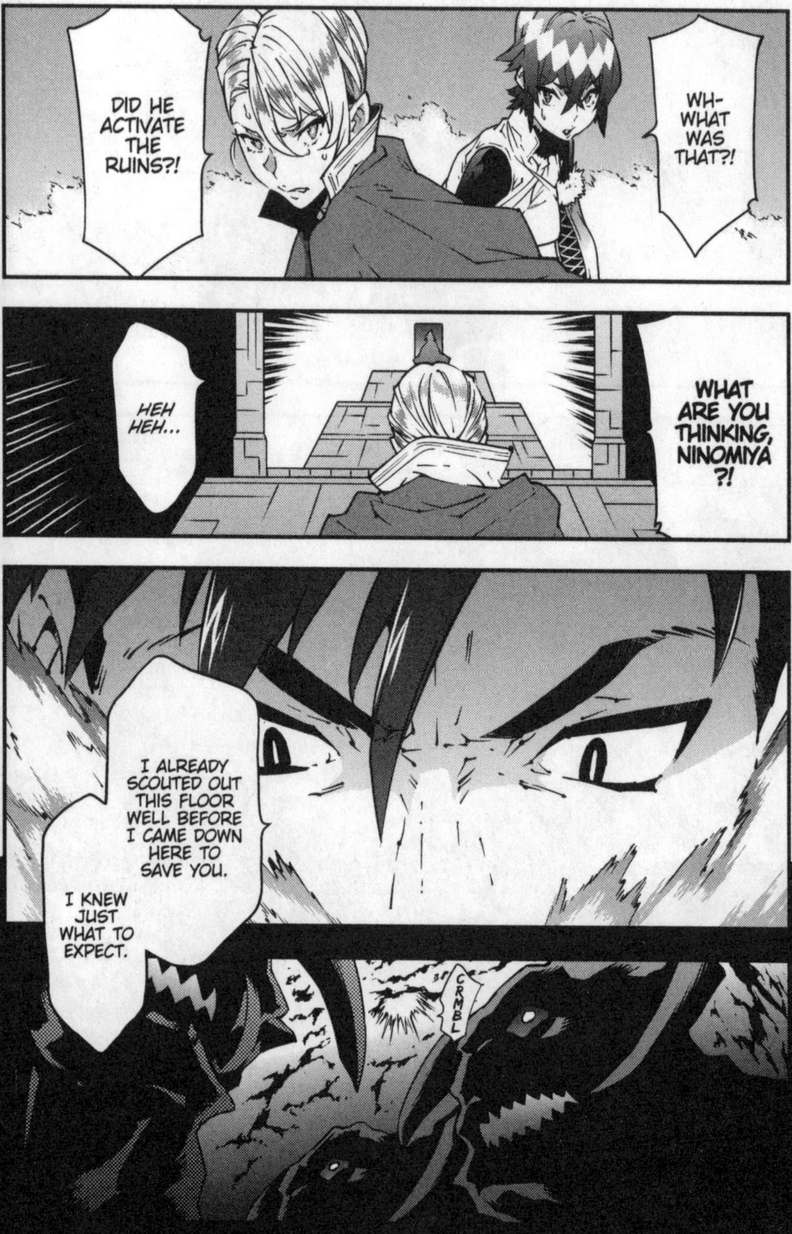
WH- WHAT WAS THAT?!
DID HE ACTIVATE THE RUINS?!
WHAT ARE YOU THINKING, NINOMIYA?!
HEH HEH...
I ALREADY SCOUTED OUT THIS FLOOR WELL BEFORE I CAME DOWN HERE TO SAVE YOU.
I KNEW JUST WHAT TO EXPECT.
CRMBL

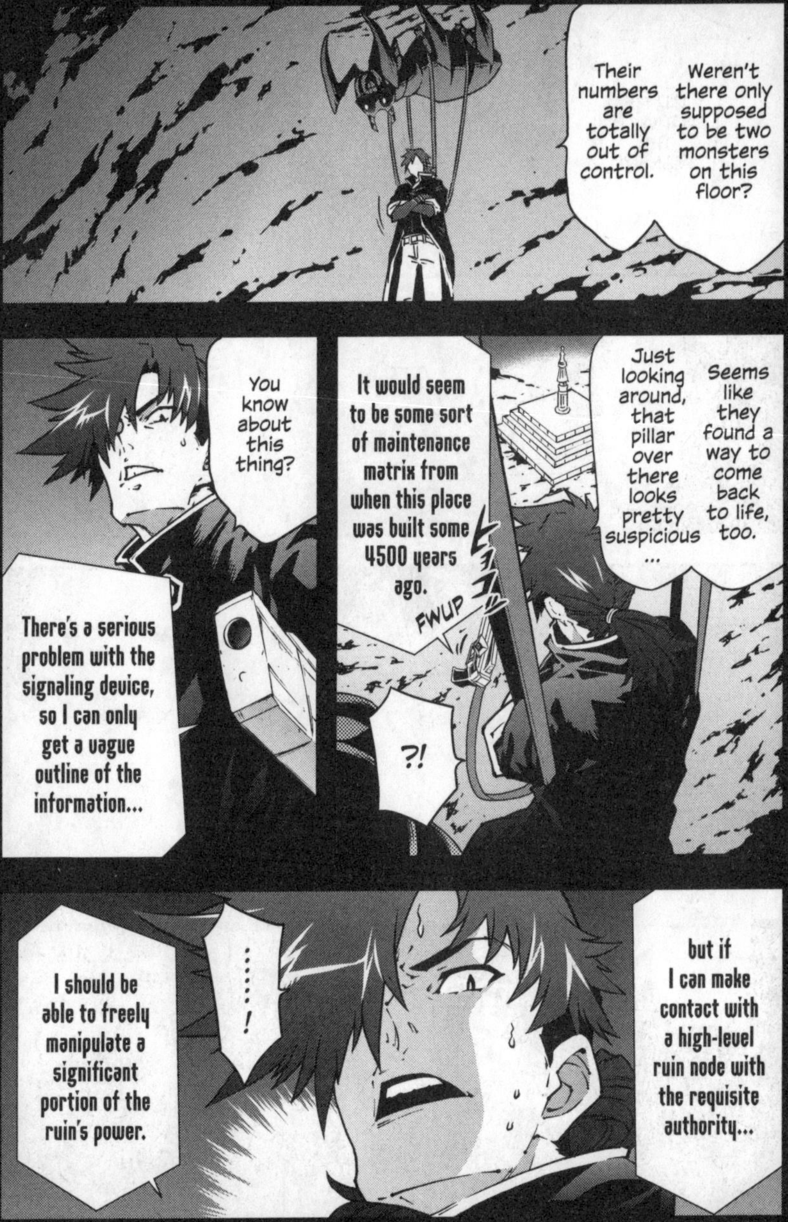
Weren't there only supposed to be two monsters on this floor?
Their numbers are totally out of control.
Seems like they found a way to come back to life, too.
Just looking around, that pillar over there looks pretty suspicious...
It would seem to be some sort of maintenance matrix from when this place was built some 4500 years ago.
FWUP
?!
You know about this thing?
There's a serious problem with the signaling device, so I can only get a vague outline of the information...
but if I can make contact with a high-level ruin node with the requisite authority...
......!
I should be able to freely manipulate a significant portion of the ruin's power.

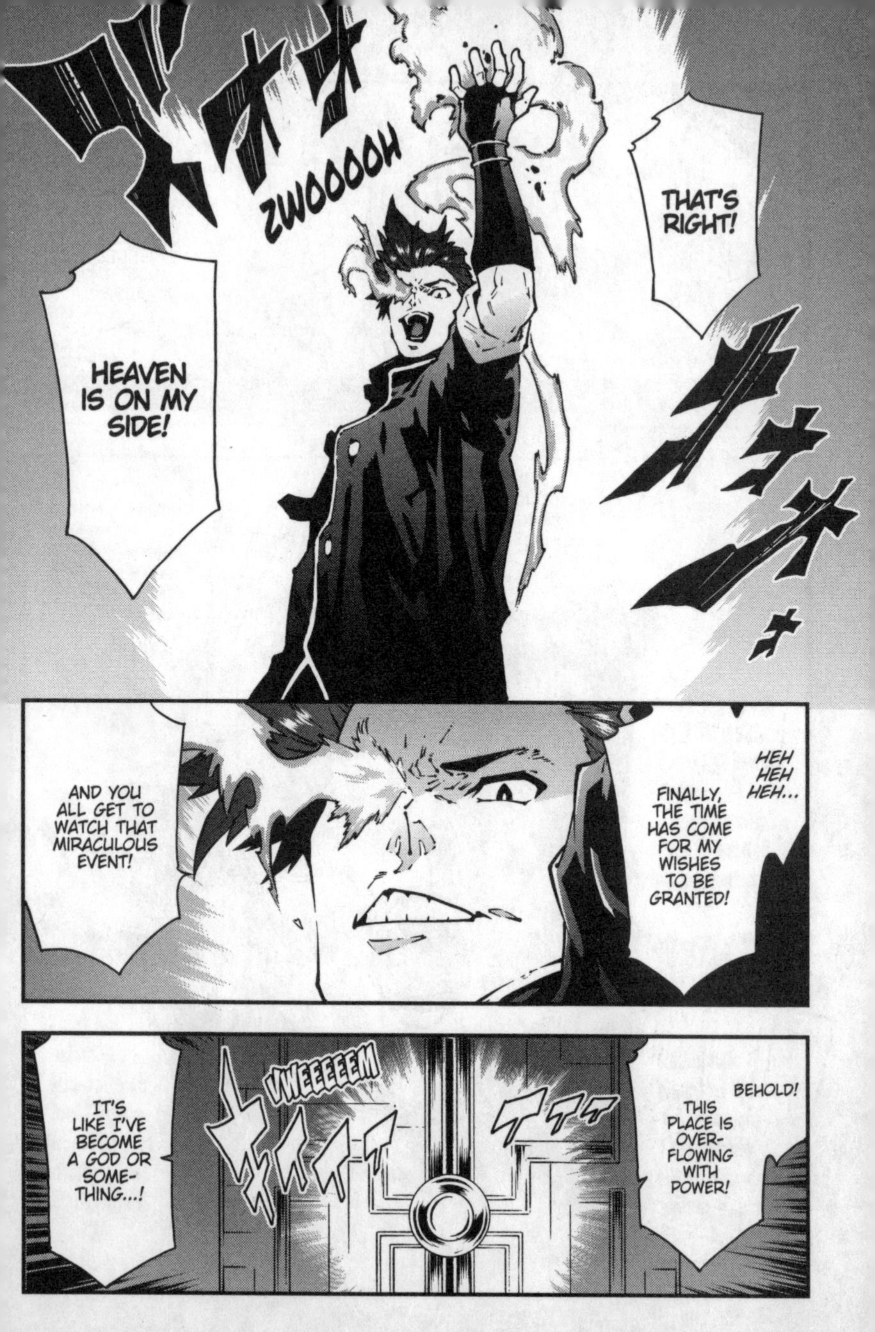
THAT'S RIGHT!
ZWOOOOH
HEAVEN IS ON MY SIDE!
HEH HEH HEH...
FINALLY, THE TIME HAS COME FOR MY WISHES TO BE GRANTED!
AND YOU ALL GET TO WATCH THAT MIRACULOUS EVENT!
BEHOLD!
THIS PLACE IS OVER-FLOWING WITH POWER!
VWEEEEEM
IT'S LIKE I'VE BECOME A GOD OR SOME-THING...!

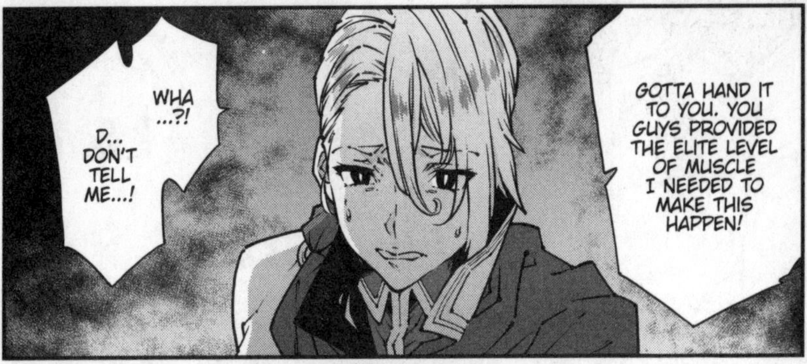
GOTTA HAND IT TO YOU. YOU GUYS PROVIDED THE ELITE LEVEL OF MUSCLE I NEEDED TO MAKE THIS HAPPEN!
WHA ...?!
D... DON'T TELL ME...!

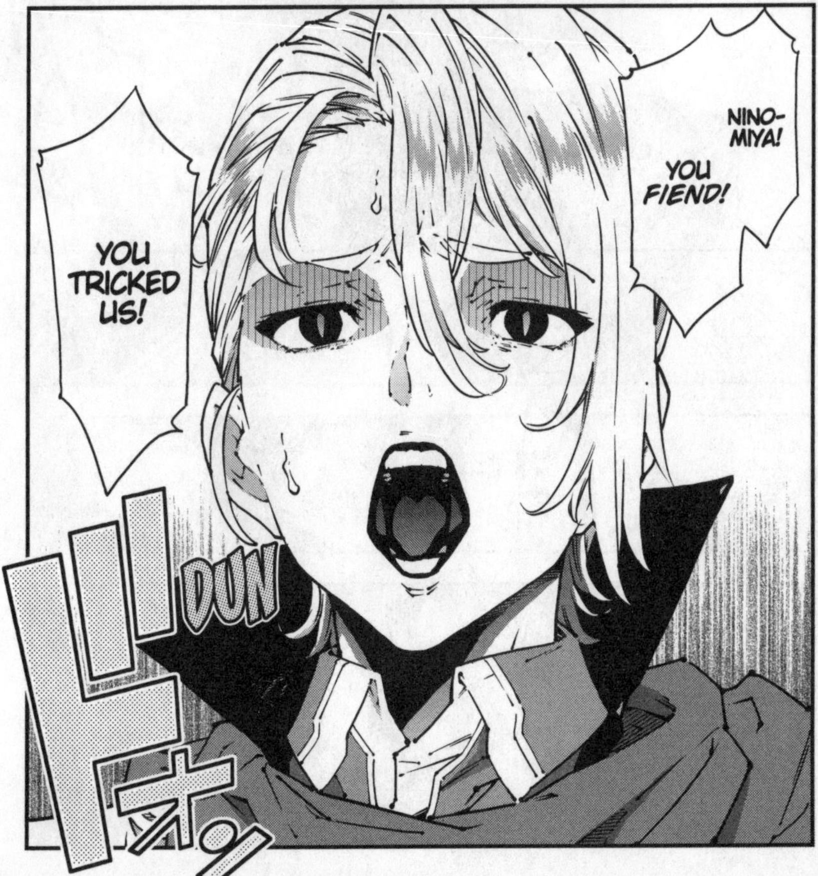
NINO-MIYA!
YOU FIEND!
YOU TRICKED US!
DUN

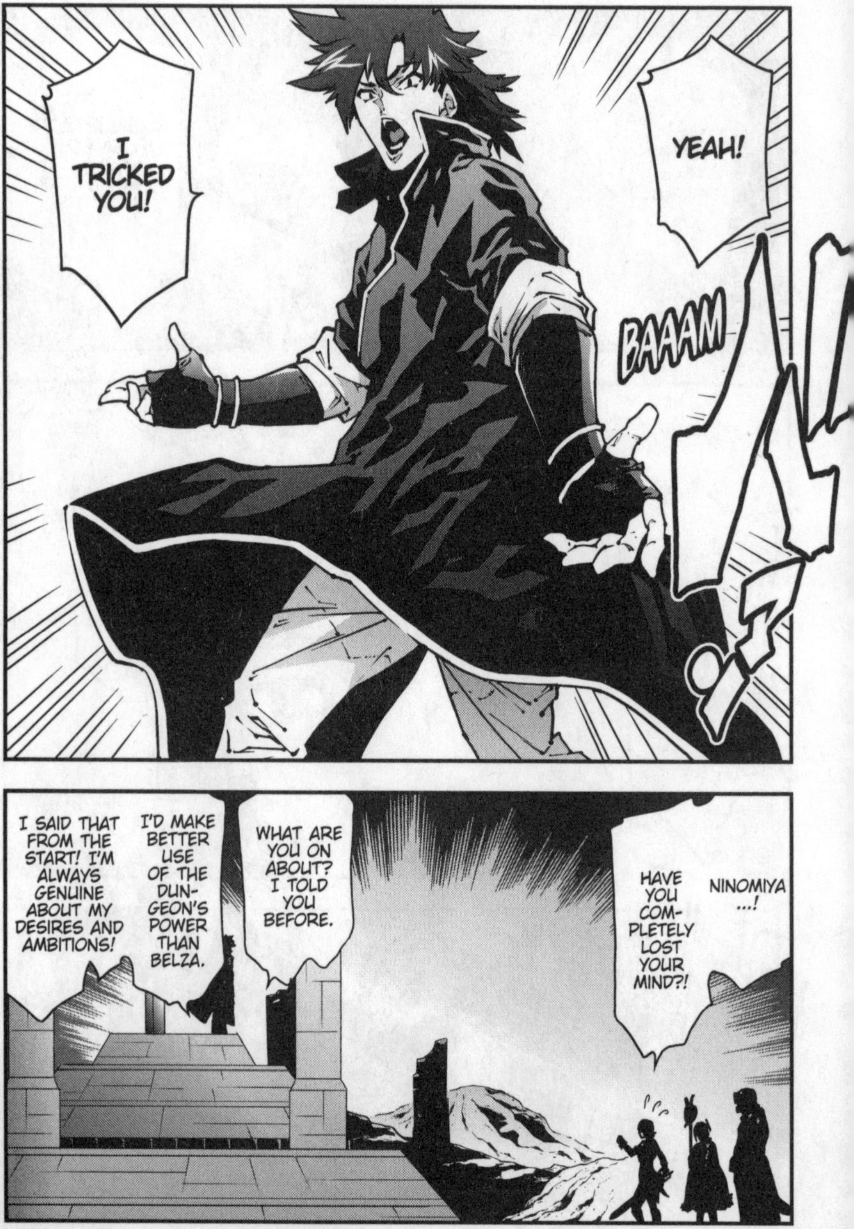
YEAH!
I TRICKED YOU!
BAAAM
NINOMIYA...!
HAVE YOU COMPLETELY LOST YOUR MIND?!
WHAT ARE YOU ON ABOUT? I TOLD YOU BEFORE.
I'D MAKE BETTER USE OF THE DUNGEON'S POWER THAN BELZA.
I SAID THAT FROM THE START! I'M ALWAYS GENUINE ABOUT MY DESIRES AND AMBITIONS!

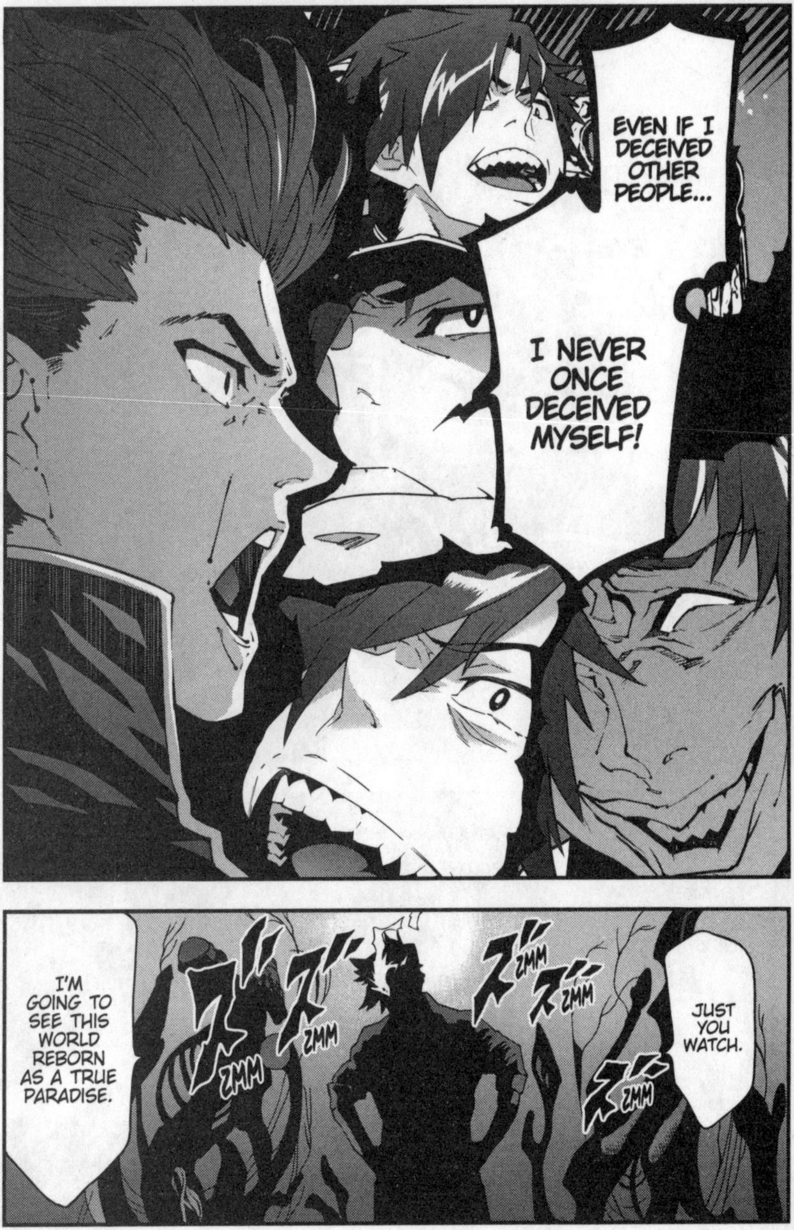
EVEN IF I DECEIVED OTHER PEOPLE...
I NEVER ONCE DECEIVED MYSELF!
JUST YOU WATCH.
ZMM
ZMM
ZMM
ZMM
ZMM
I'M GOING TO SEE THIS WORLD REBORN AS A TRUE PARADISE.

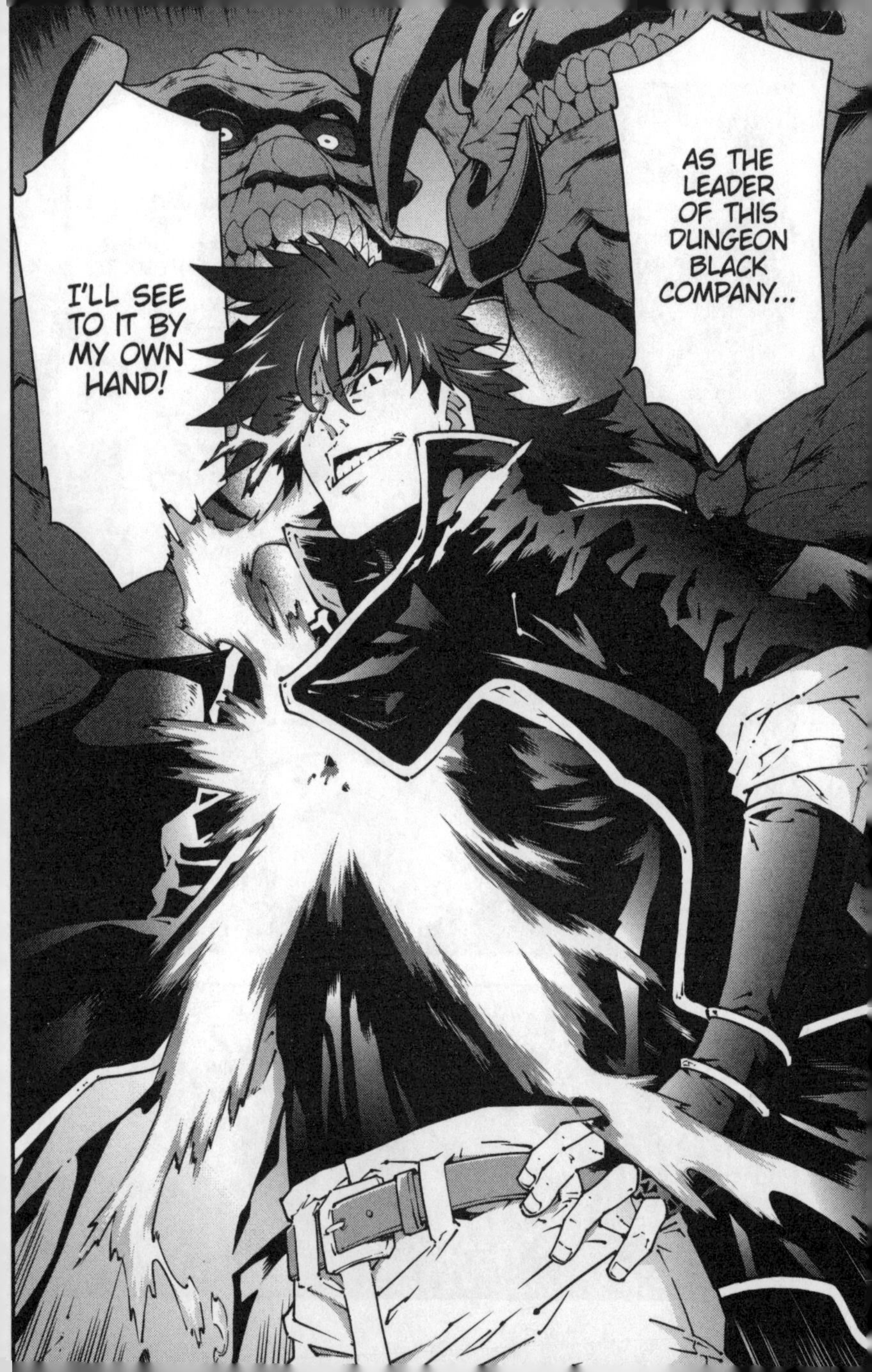
AS THE LEADER OF THIS DUNGEON BLACK COMPANY...
I'LL SEE TO IT BY MY OWN HAND!

BELZA
RANGA'S COSTUME VERSION

THE DUNGEON OF
BLACK COMPANY

Chapter 27: Crash Evolution

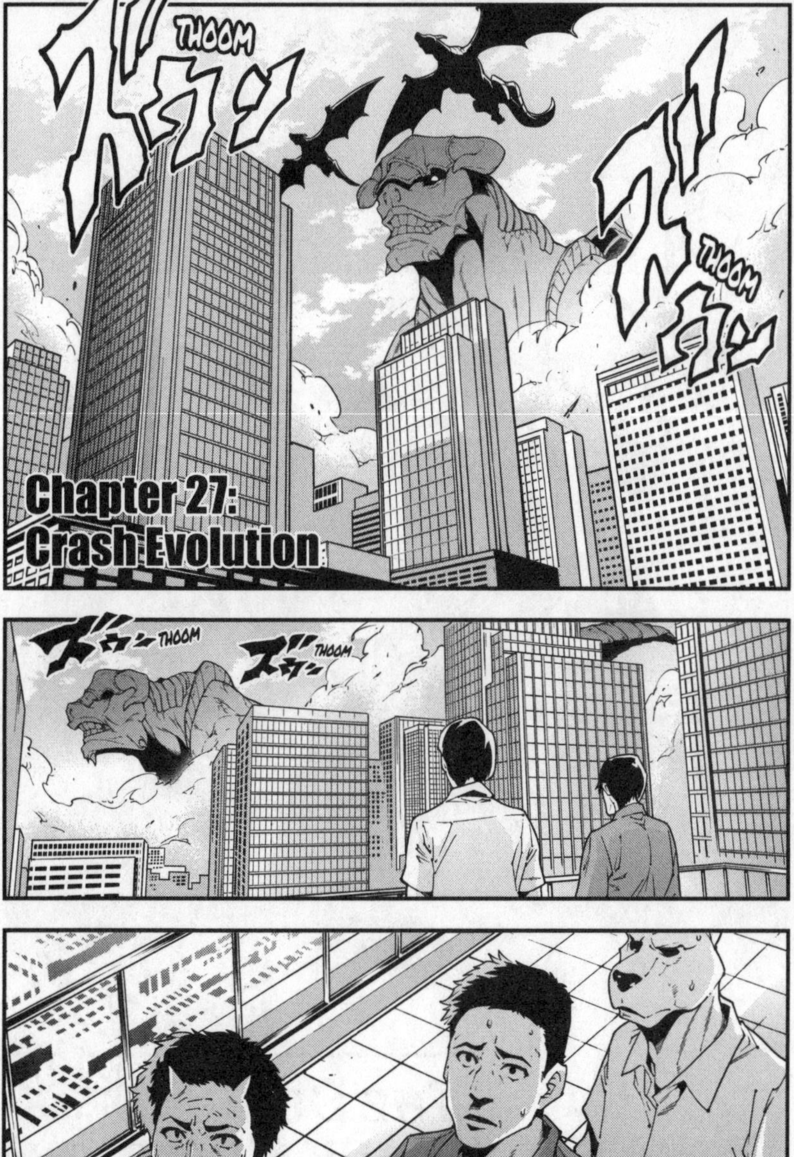
THOOM
THOOM
THOOM
THOOM

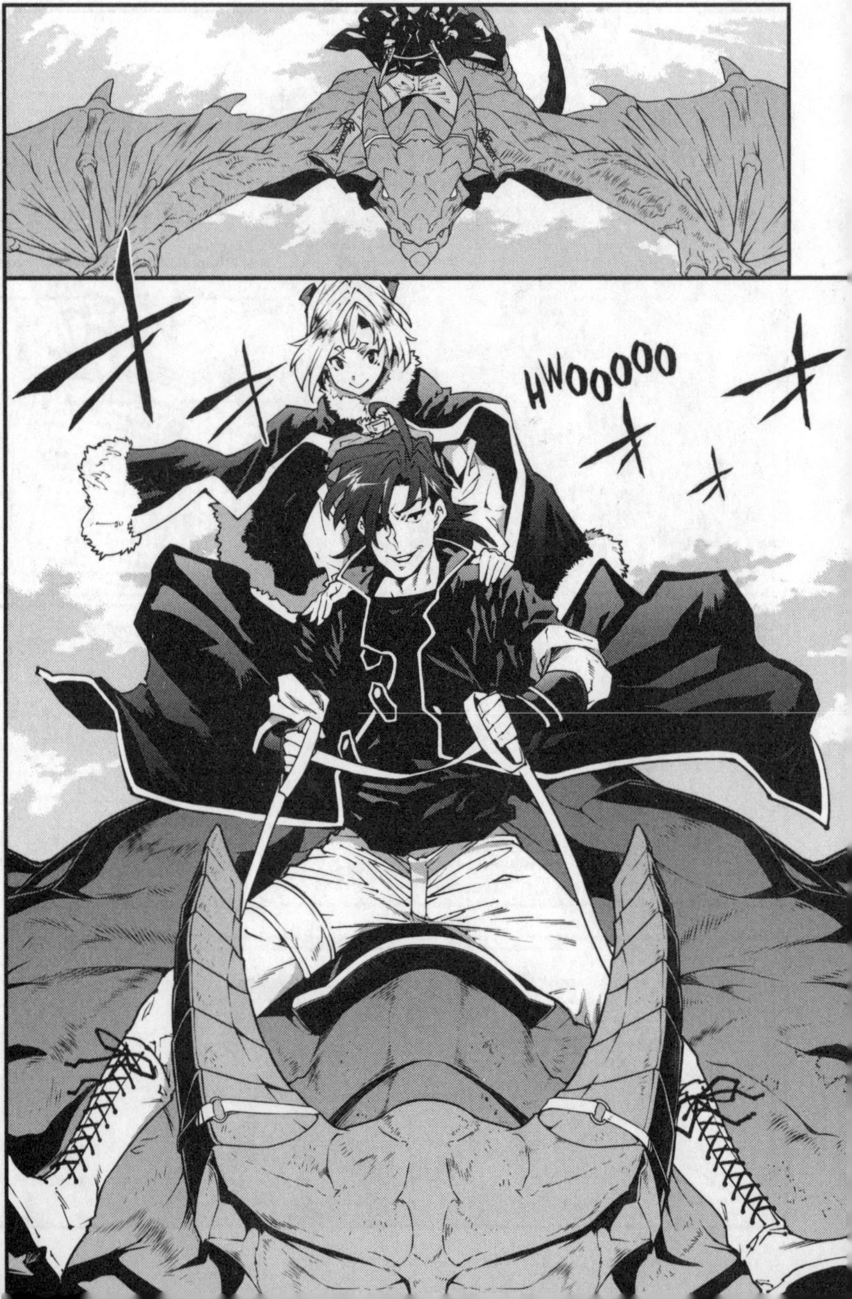
HWOOOOO

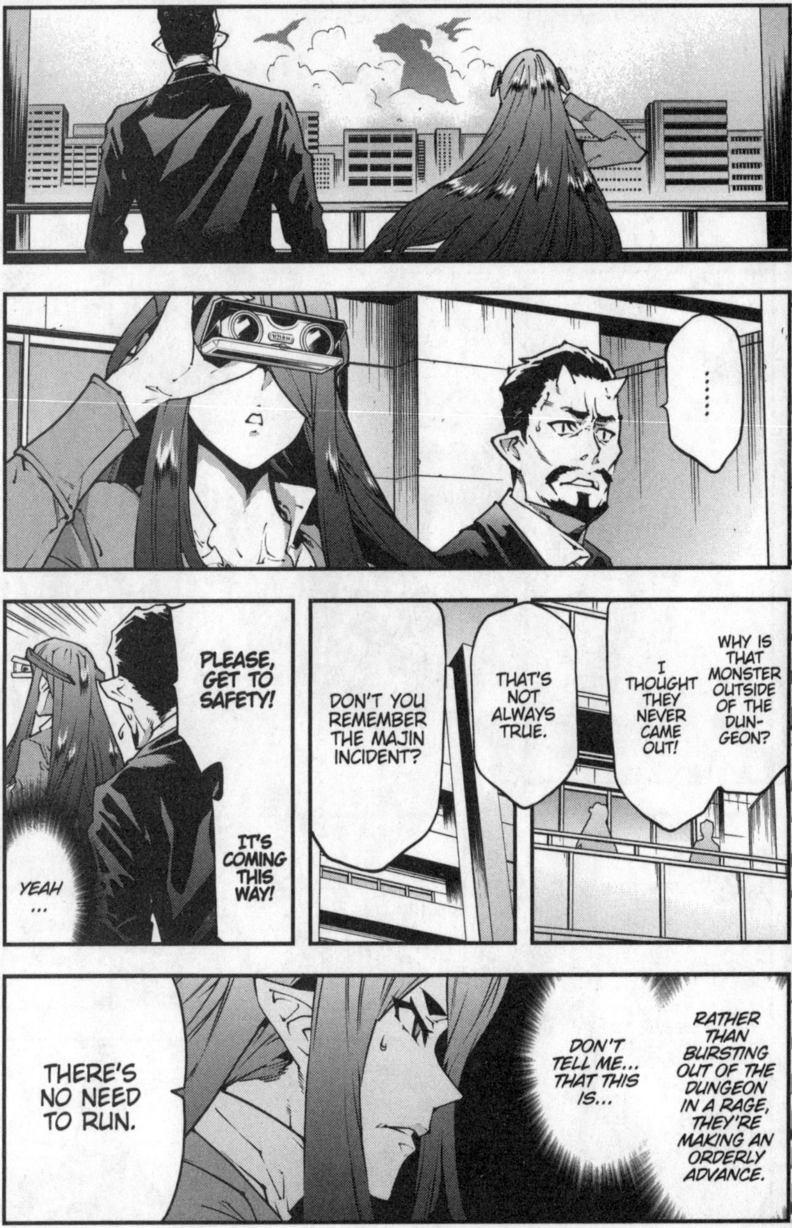
......
WHY IS THAT MONSTER OUTSIDE OF THE DUN-GEON?
I THOUGHT THEY NEVER CAME OUT!
THAT'S NOT ALWAYS TRUE.
DON'T YOU REMEMBER THE MAJIN INCIDENT?
PLEASE, GET TO SAFETY!
IT'S COMING THIS WAY!
YEAH...
RATHER THAN BURSTING OUT OF THE DUNGEON IN A RAGE, THEY'RE MAKING AN ORDERLY ADVANCE.
DON'T TELL ME... THAT THIS IS...
THERE'S NO NEED TO RUN.

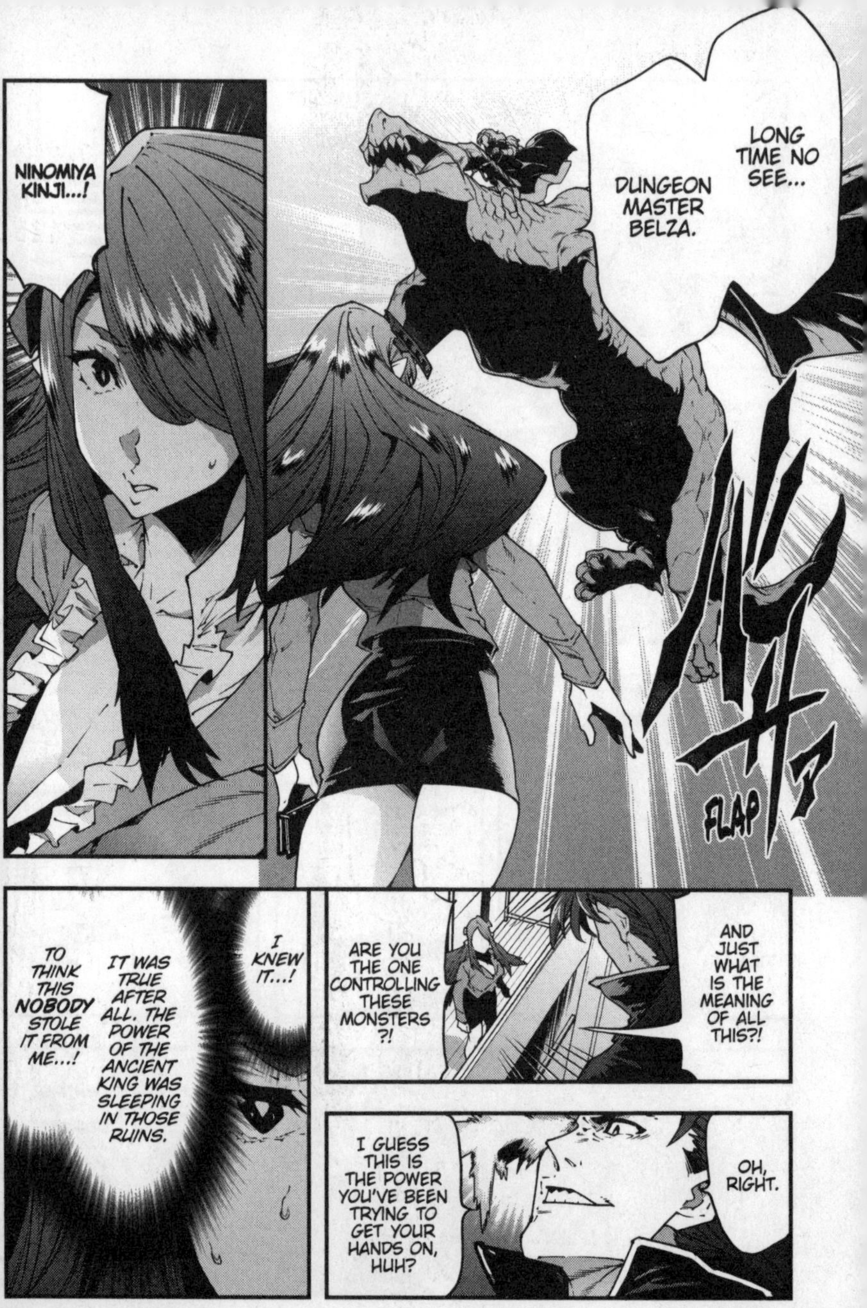
LONG TIME NO SEE...
DUNGEON MASTER BELZA.
FLAP
NINOMIYA KINJI...!
AND JUST WHAT IS THE MEANING OF ALL THIS?!
ARE YOU THE ONE CONTROLLING THESE MONSTERS?!
OH, RIGHT.
I GUESS THIS IS THE POWER YOU'VE BEEN TRYING TO GET YOUR HANDS ON, HUH?
I KNEW IT...!
IT WAS TRUE AFTER ALL. THE POWER OF THE ANCIENT KING WAS SLEEPING IN THOSE RUINS.
TO THINK THIS NOBODY STOLE IT FROM ME...!

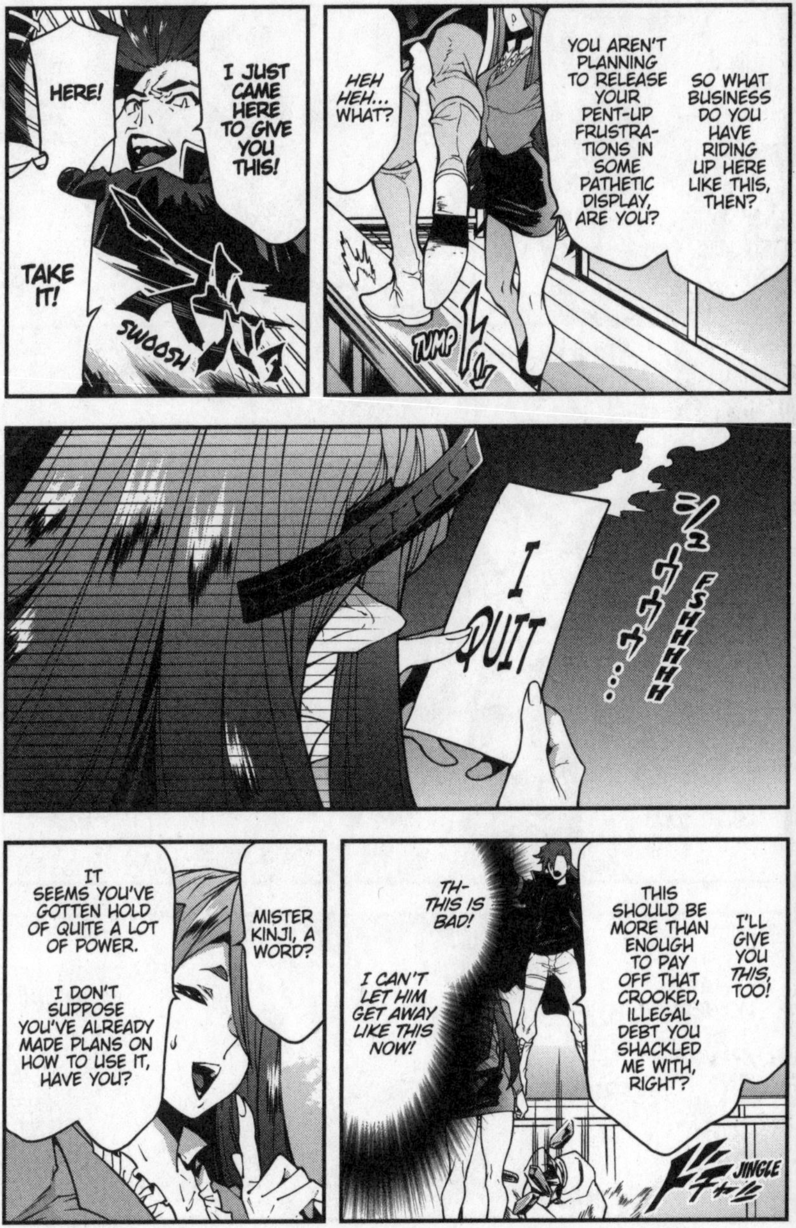
SO WHAT BUSINESS DO YOU HAVE RIDING UP HERE LIKE THIS, THEN?
YOU AREN'T PLANNING TO RELEASE YOUR PENT-UP FRUSTRATIONS IN SOME PATHETIC DISPLAY, ARE YOU?
HEH HEH... WHAT?
TUMP
I JUST CAME HERE TO GIVE YOU THIS!
HERE!
TAKE IT!
SWOOSH
シュウウウ…
FSHHHHHH
I QUIT
I'LL GIVE YOU THIS, TOO!
THIS SHOULD BE MORE THAN ENOUGH TO PAY OFF THAT CROOKED, ILLEGAL DEBT YOU SHACKLED ME WITH, RIGHT?
TH- THIS IS BAD!
I CAN'T LET HIM GET AWAY LIKE THIS NOW!
JINGLE
MISTER KINJI, A WORD?
IT SEEMS YOU'VE GOTTEN HOLD OF QUITE A LOT OF POWER.
I DON'T SUPPOSE YOU'VE ALREADY MADE PLANS ON HOW TO USE IT, HAVE YOU?

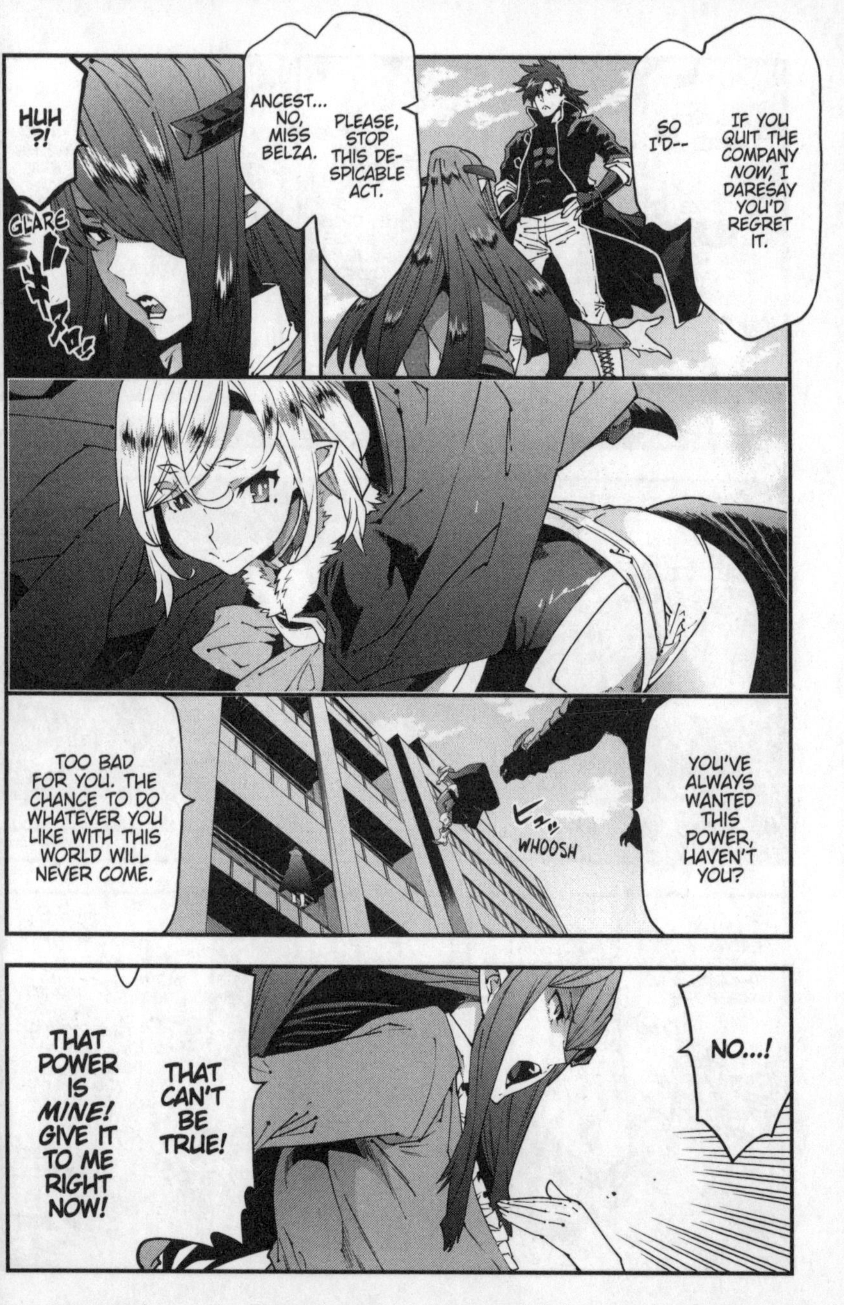

IF YOU QUIT THE COMPANY *NOW*, I DARESAY YOU'D REGRET IT.
SO I'D--
ANCEST... NO, MISS BELZA.
PLEASE, STOP THIS DESPICABLE ACT.
HUH?!
GLARE
YOU'VE ALWAYS WANTED THIS POWER, HAVEN'T YOU?
ヒュッ
WHOOSH
TOO BAD FOR YOU. THE CHANCE TO DO WHATEVER YOU LIKE WITH THIS WORLD WILL NEVER COME.
NO...!
THAT CAN'T BE TRUE!
THAT POWER IS *MINE!* GIVE IT TO ME RIGHT NOW!

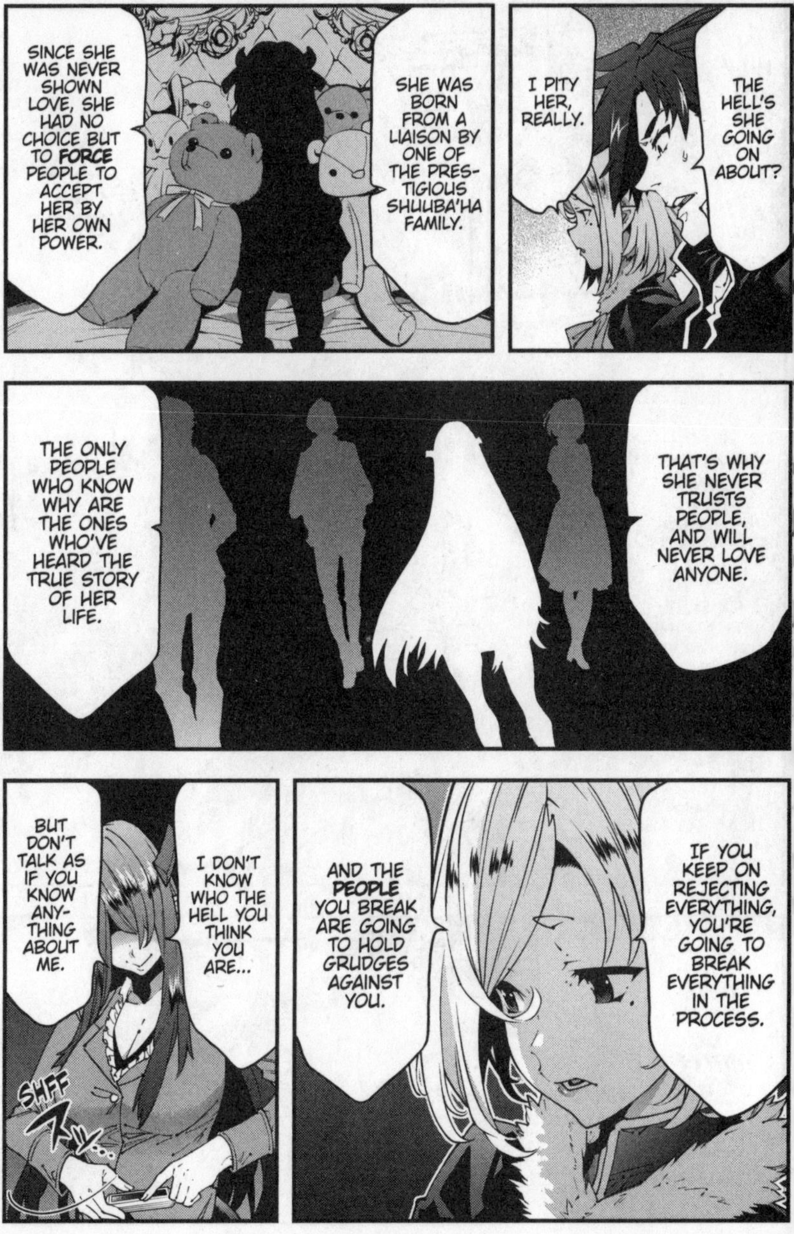
THE HELL'S SHE GOING ON ABOUT?
I PITY HER, REALLY.
SHE WAS BORN FROM A LIAISON BY ONE OF THE PRESTIGIOUS SHUUBA'HA FAMILY.
SINCE SHE WAS NEVER SHOWN LOVE, SHE HAD NO CHOICE BUT TO **FORCE** PEOPLE TO ACCEPT HER BY HER OWN POWER.
THAT'S WHY SHE NEVER TRUSTS PEOPLE, AND WILL NEVER LOVE ANYONE.
THE ONLY PEOPLE WHO KNOW WHY ARE THE ONES WHO'VE HEARD THE TRUE STORY OF HER LIFE.
IF YOU KEEP ON REJECTING EVERYTHING, YOU'RE GOING TO BREAK EVERYTHING IN THE PROCESS.
AND THE **PEOPLE** YOU BREAK ARE GOING TO HOLD GRUDGES AGAINST YOU.
I DON'T KNOW WHO THE HELL YOU THINK YOU ARE...
BUT DON'T TALK AS IF YOU KNOW ANYTHING ABOUT ME.
SHFF

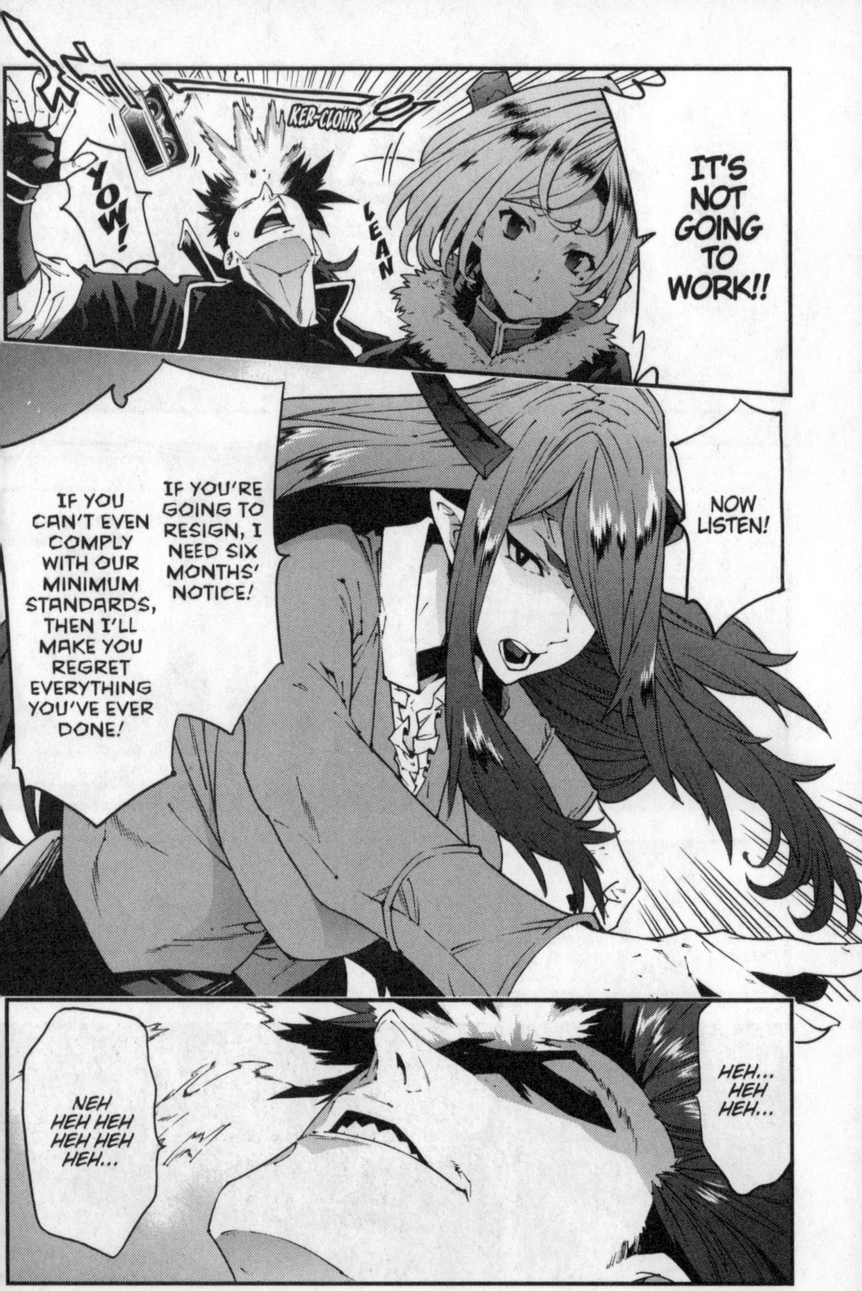
IT'S NOT GOING TO WORK!!
KER-CLONK
LEAN
YOW!
NOW LISTEN!
IF YOU'RE GOING TO RESIGN, I NEED SIX MONTHS' NOTICE!
IF YOU CAN'T EVEN COMPLY WITH OUR MINIMUM STANDARDS, THEN I'LL MAKE YOU REGRET EVERYTHING YOU'VE EVER DONE!
HEH... HEH HEH...
NEH HEH HEH HEH HEH HEH...

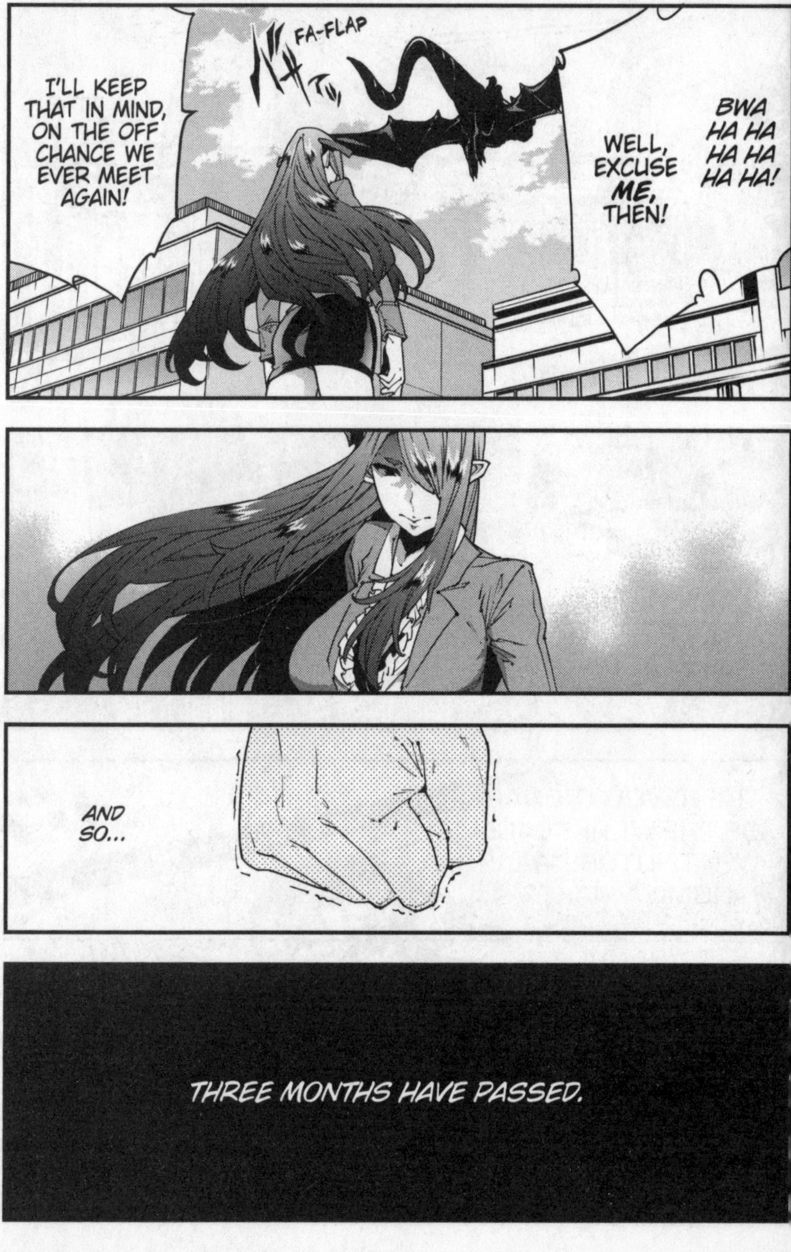
BWA HA HA HA HA HA HA!
WELL, EXCUSE ME, THEN!
FA-FLAP
I'LL KEEP THAT IN MIND, ON THE OFF CHANCE WE EVER MEET AGAIN!
AND SO...
THREE MONTHS HAVE PASSED.

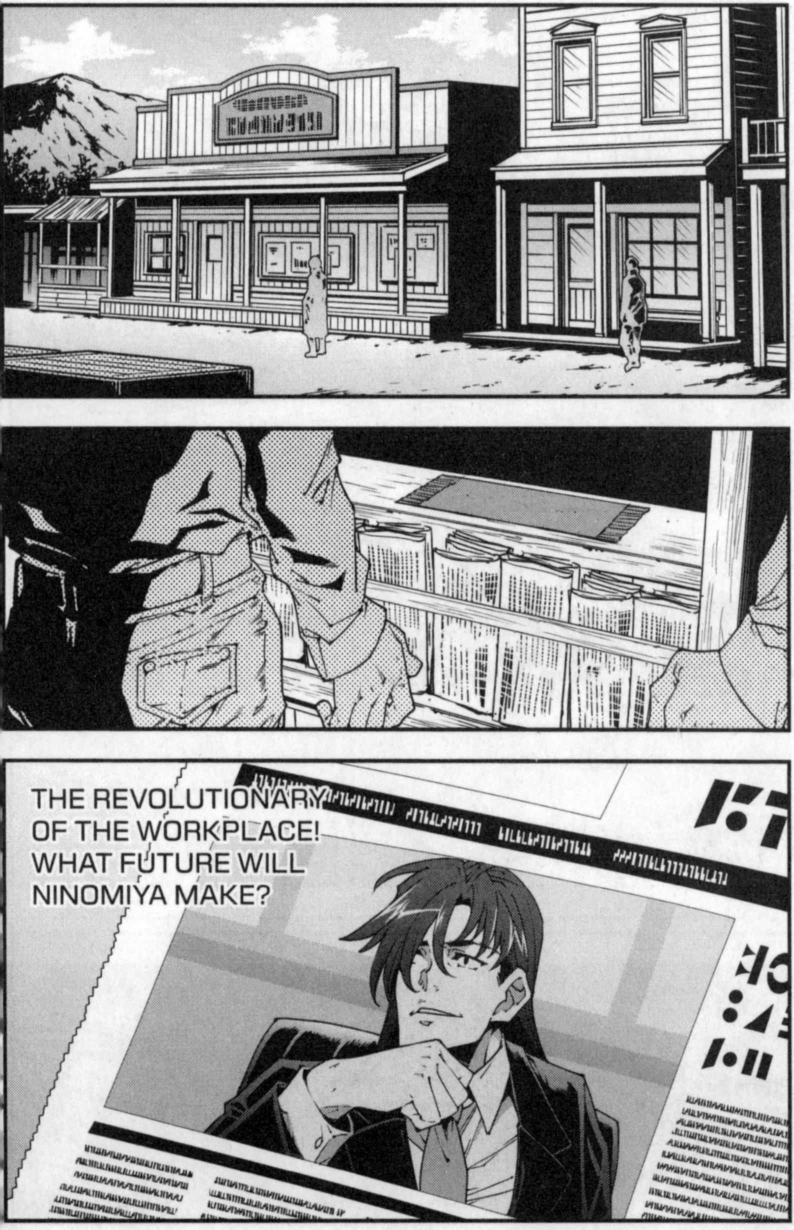
THE REVOLUTIONARY
OF THE WORKPLACE!
WHAT FUTURE WILL
NINOMIYA MAKE?

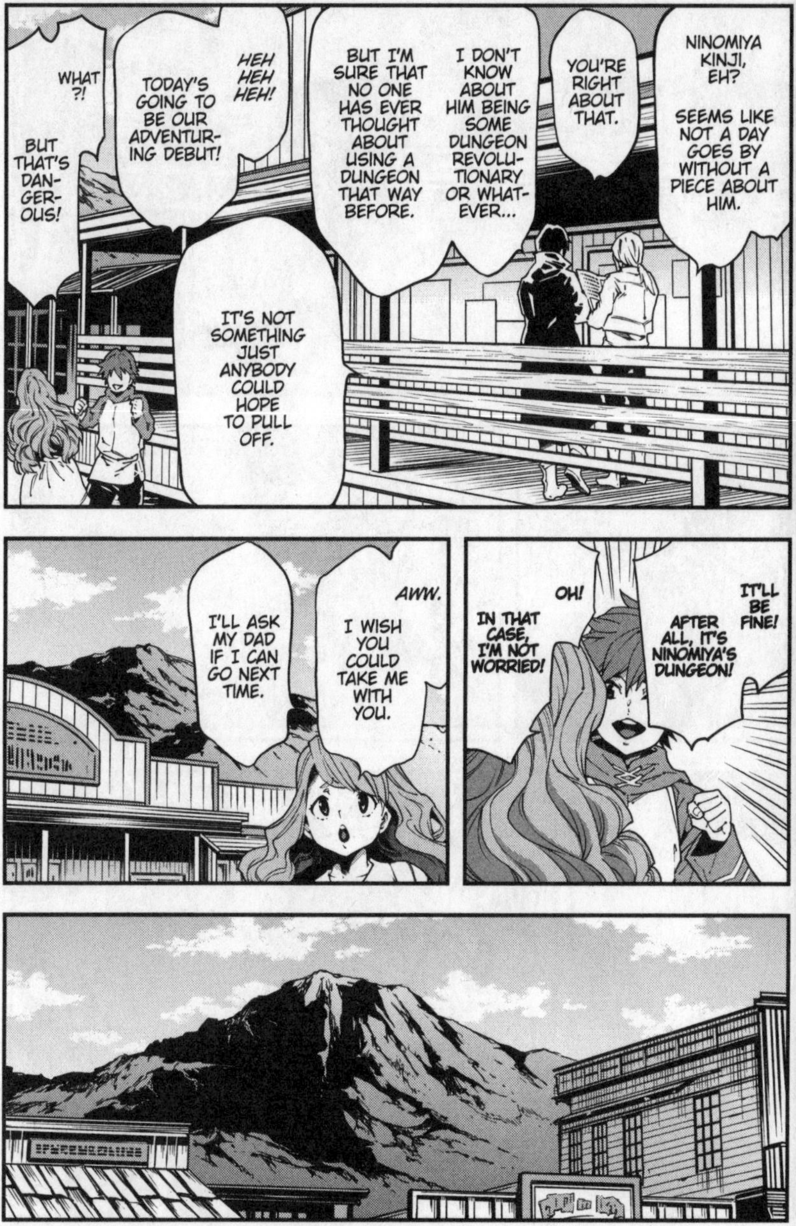
NINOMIYA KINJI, EH?
SEEMS LIKE NOT A DAY GOES BY WITHOUT A PIECE ABOUT HIM.
YOU'RE RIGHT ABOUT THAT.
I DON'T KNOW ABOUT HIM BEING SOME DUNGEON REVOLUTIONARY OR WHATEVER...
BUT I'M SURE THAT NO ONE HAS EVER THOUGHT ABOUT USING A DUNGEON THAT WAY BEFORE.
IT'S NOT SOMETHING JUST ANYBODY COULD HOPE TO PULL OFF.
HEH HEH HEH!
TODAY'S GOING TO BE OUR ADVENTURING DEBUT!
WHAT ?!
BUT THAT'S DANGEROUS!
IT'LL BE FINE!
AFTER ALL, IT'S NINOMIYA'S DUNGEON!
OH!
IN THAT CASE, I'M NOT WORRIED!
AWW.
I WISH YOU COULD TAKE ME WITH YOU.
I'LL ASK MY DAD IF I CAN GO NEXT TIME.

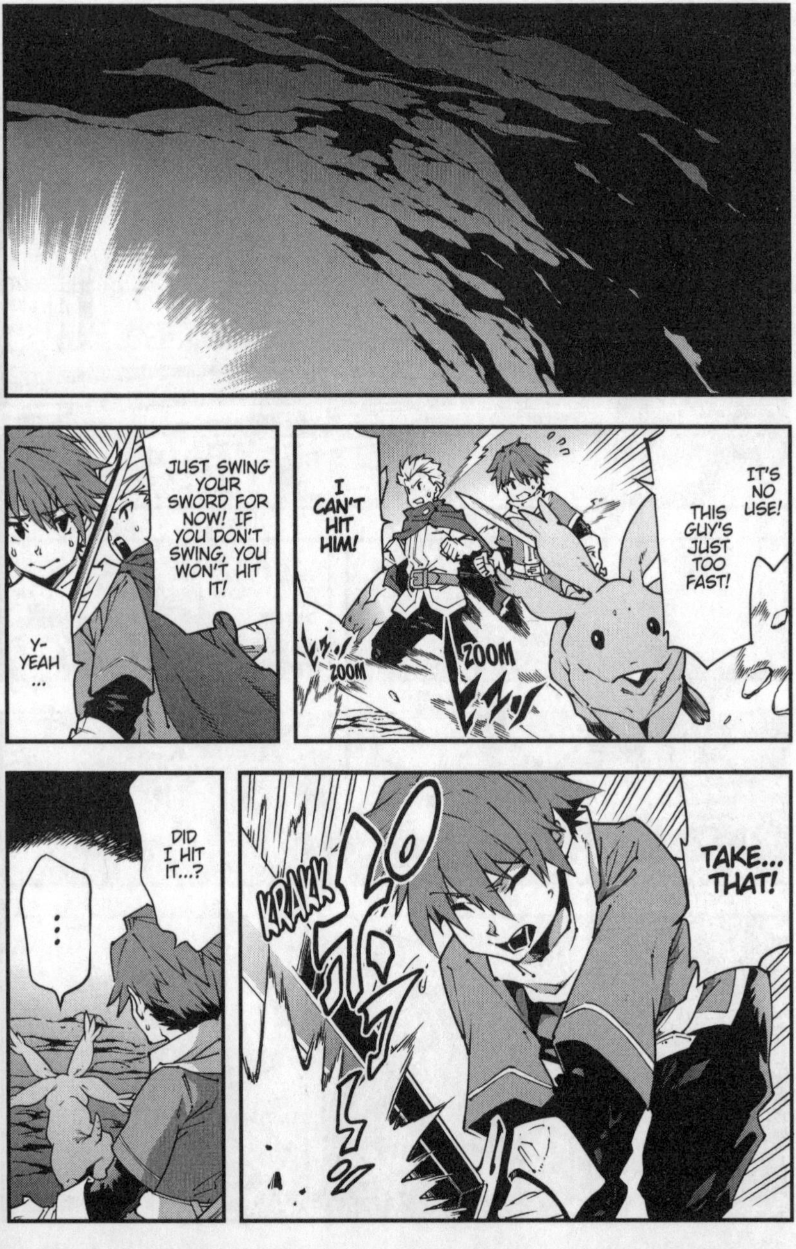
IT'S NO USE!
THIS GUY'S JUST TOO FAST!
I CAN'T HIT HIM!
ZOOM
ZOOM
JUST SWING YOUR SWORD FOR NOW! IF YOU DON'T SWING, YOU WON'T HIT IT!
Y-YEAH ...
TAKE... THAT!
KRAKK
DID I HIT IT...?
...

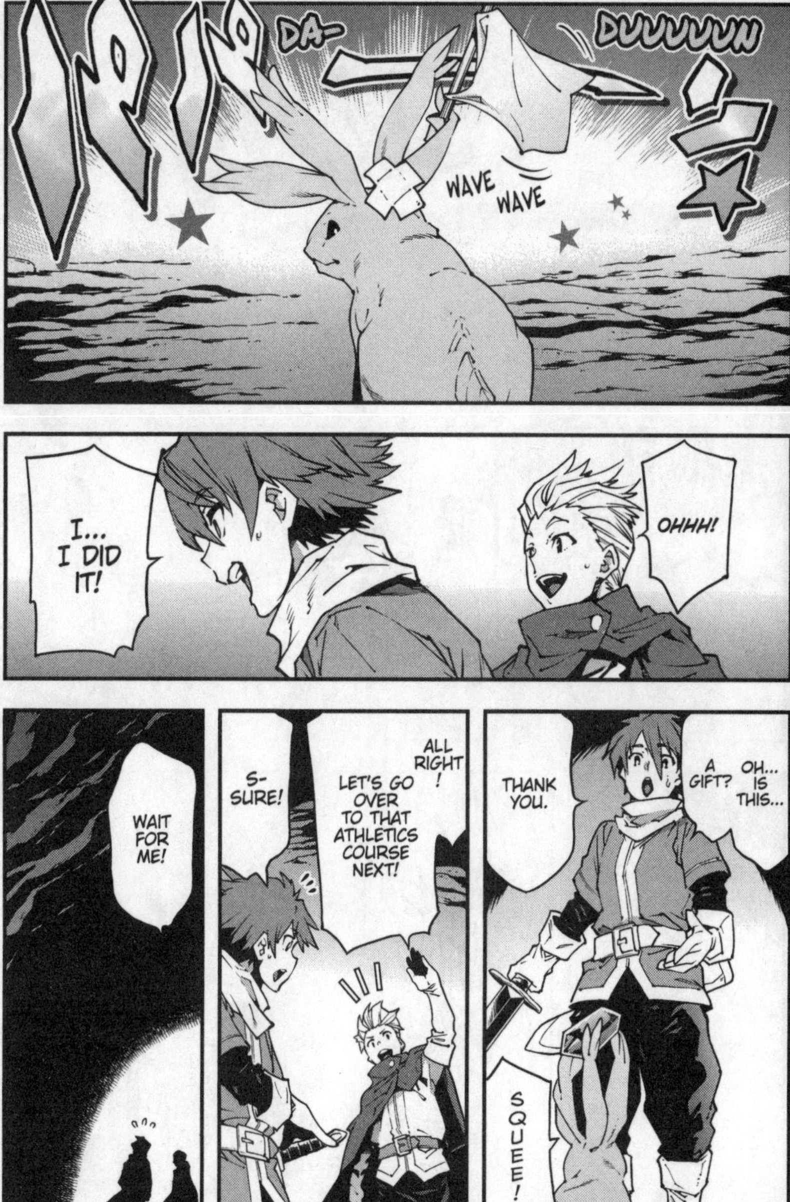
DA-
DUVUVUUN
WAVE WAVE
OHHH!
I... I DID IT!
OH... IS THIS...
A GIFT?
THANK YOU.
SQUEE!
ALL RIGHT!
LET'S GO OVER TO THAT ATHLETICS COURSE NEXT!
S-SURE!
WAIT FOR ME!

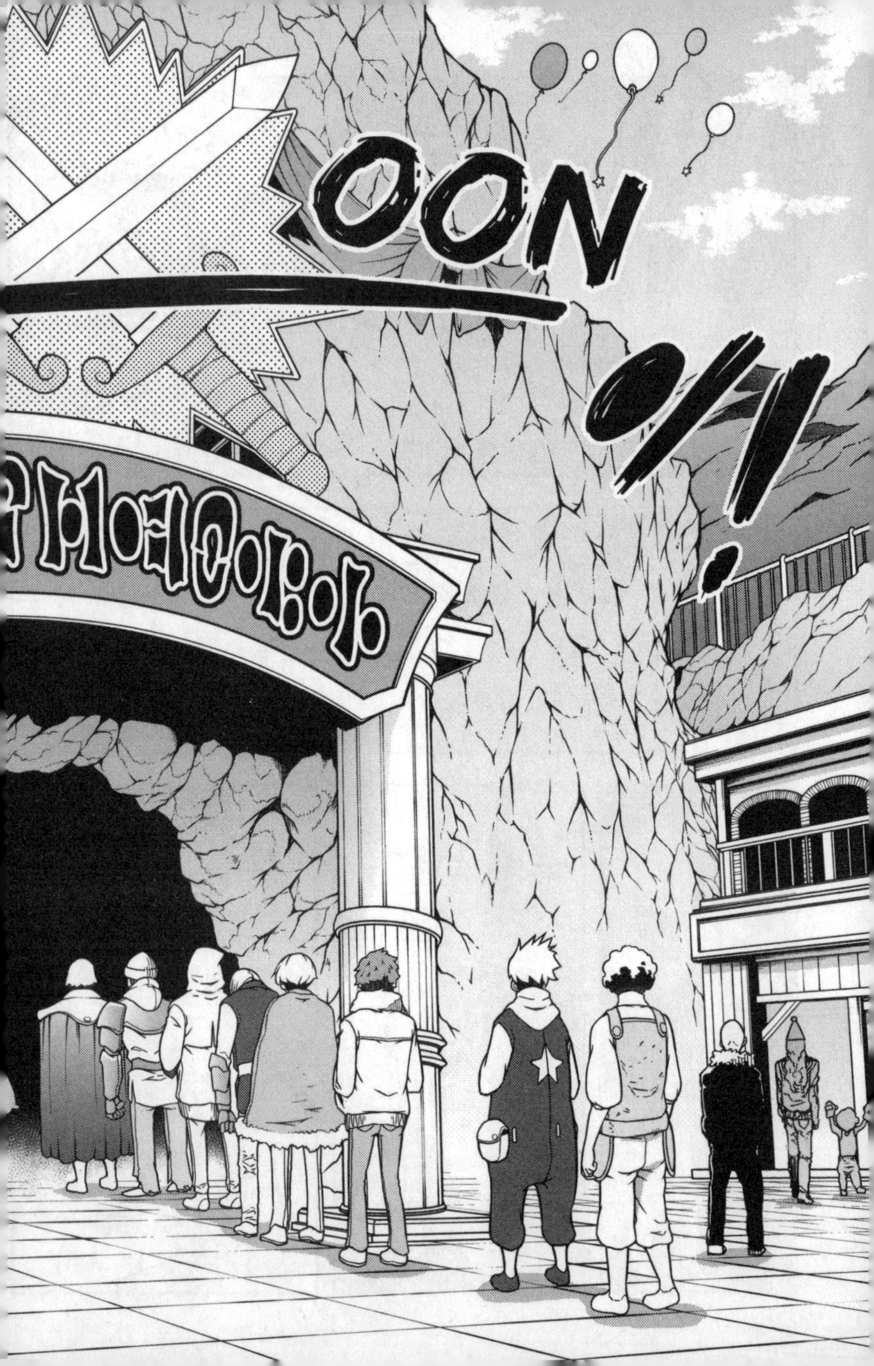
OON!!

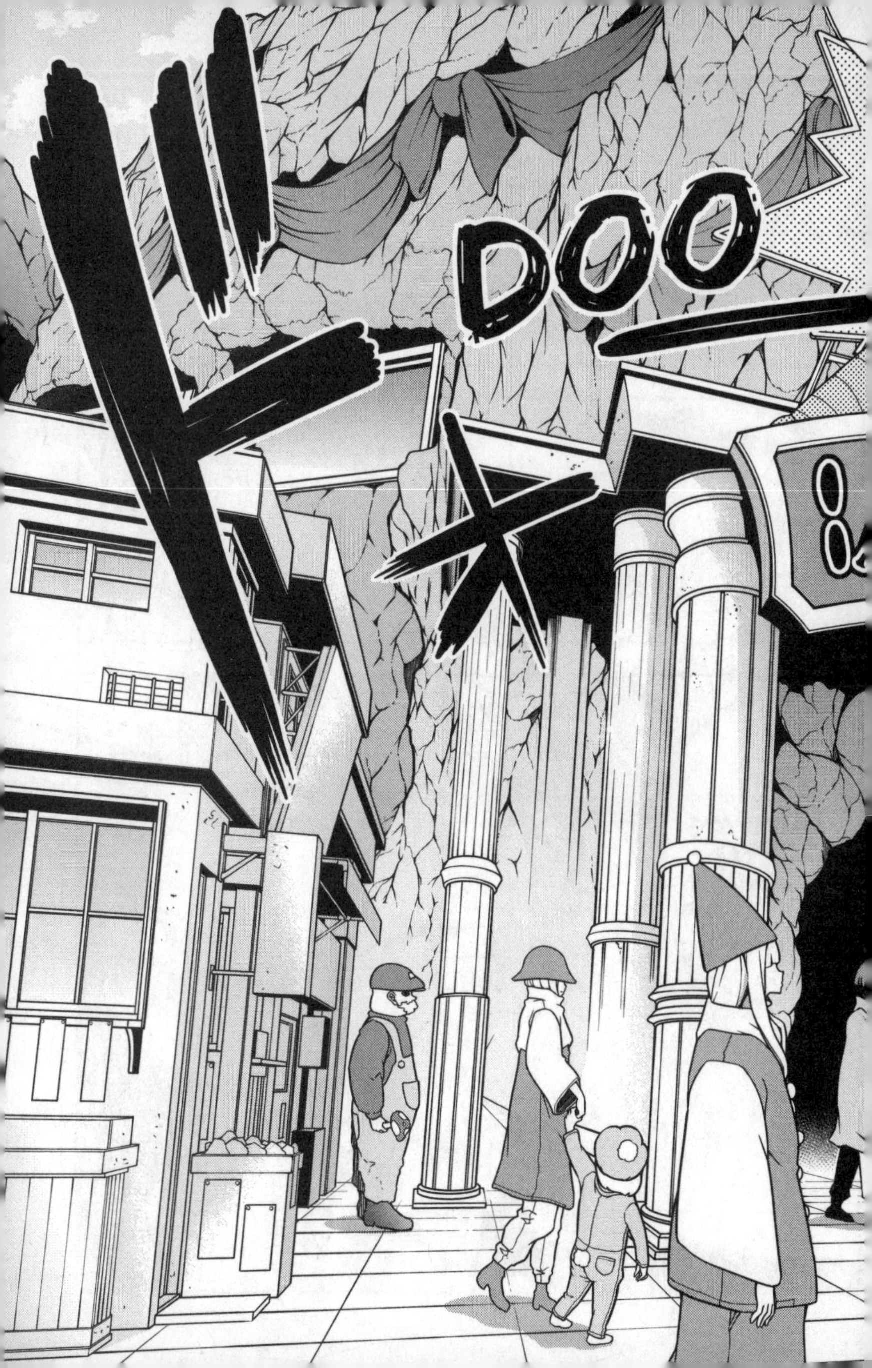
DOO

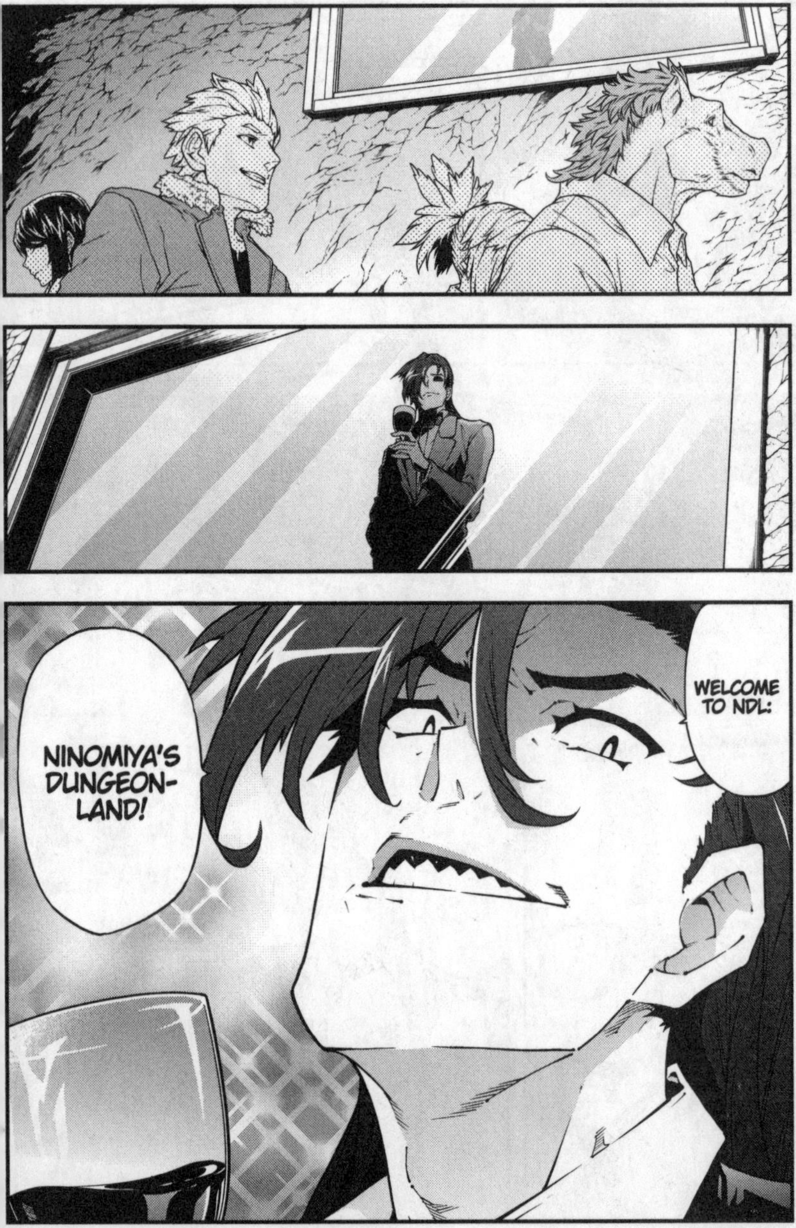
WELCOME TO NDL:
NINOMIYA'S DUNGEON-LAND!

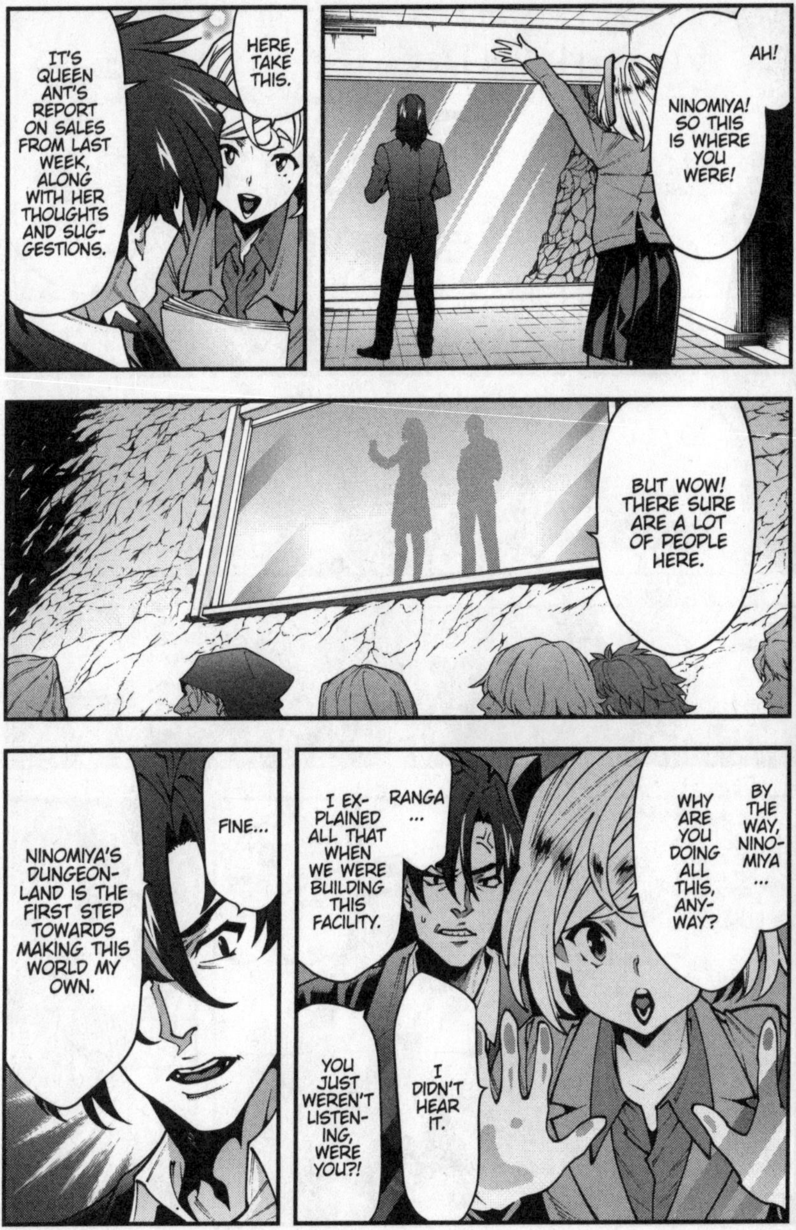
AH!
NINOMIYA! SO THIS IS WHERE YOU WERE!
HERE, TAKE THIS.
IT'S QUEEN ANT'S REPORT ON SALES FROM LAST WEEK, ALONG WITH HER THOUGHTS AND SUGGESTIONS.
BUT WOW! THERE SURE ARE A LOT OF PEOPLE HERE.
BY THE WAY, NINOMIYA ...
WHY ARE YOU DOING ALL THIS, ANYWAY?
RANGA ...
I EXPLAINED ALL THAT WHEN WE WERE BUILDING THIS FACILITY.
I DIDN'T HEAR IT.
YOU JUST WEREN'T LISTENING, WERE YOU?!
FINE...
NINOMIYA'S DUNGEON-LAND IS THE FIRST STEP TOWARDS MAKING THIS WORLD MY OWN.

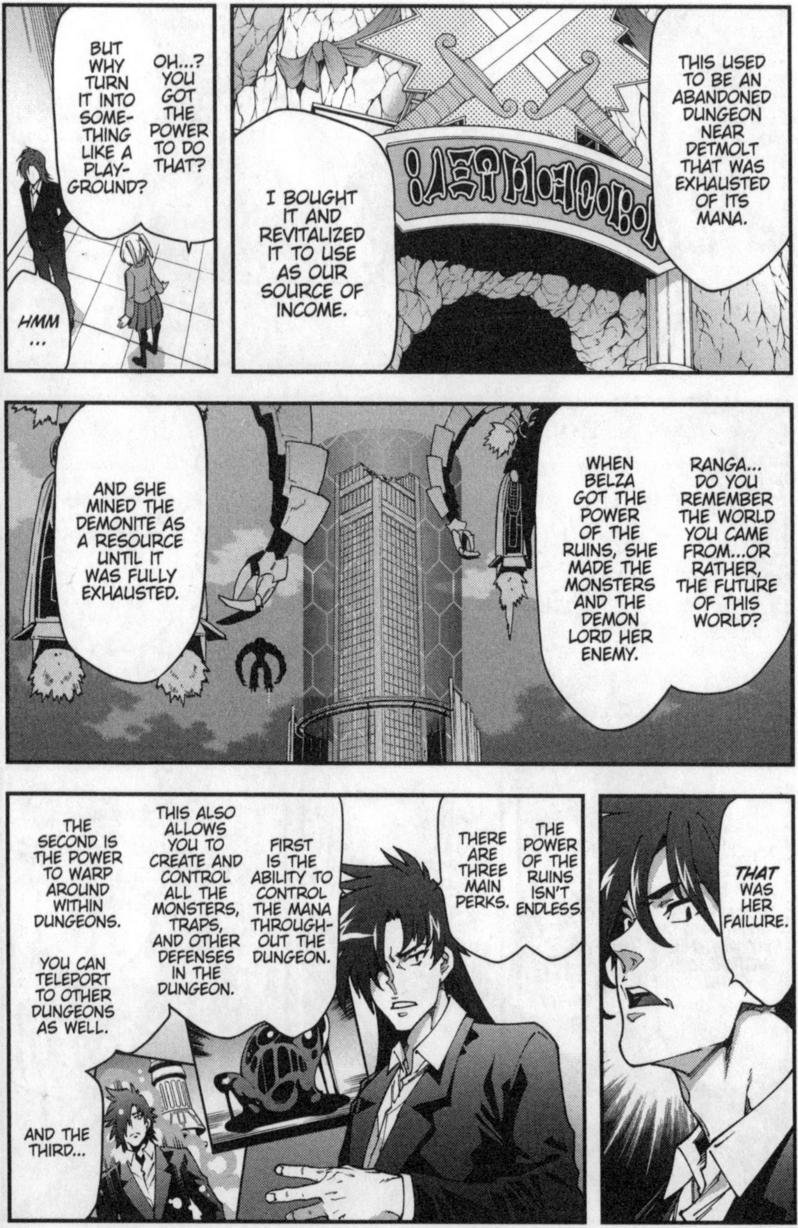
THIS USED TO BE AN ABANDONED DUNGEON NEAR DETMOLT THAT WAS EXHAUSTED OF ITS MANA.
I BOUGHT IT AND REVITALIZED IT TO USE AS OUR SOURCE OF INCOME.
OH...? YOU GOT THE POWER TO DO THAT?
BUT WHY TURN IT INTO SOME-THING LIKE A PLAY-GROUND?
HMM...
RANGA... DO YOU REMEMBER THE WORLD YOU CAME FROM...OR RATHER, THE FUTURE OF THIS WORLD?
WHEN BELZA GOT THE POWER OF THE RUINS, SHE MADE THE MONSTERS AND THE DEMON LORD HER ENEMY.
AND SHE MINED THE DEMONITE AS A RESOURCE UNTIL IT WAS FULLY EXHAUSTED.
THAT WAS HER FAILURE.
THE POWER OF THE RUINS ISN'T ENDLESS.
THERE ARE THREE MAIN PERKS.
FIRST IS THE ABILITY TO CONTROL THE MANA THROUGH-OUT THE DUNGEON.
THIS ALSO ALLOWS YOU TO CREATE AND CONTROL ALL THE MONSTERS, TRAPS, AND OTHER DEFENSES IN THE DUNGEON.
THE SECOND IS THE POWER TO WARP AROUND WITHIN DUNGEONS.
YOU CAN TELEPORT TO OTHER DUNGEONS AS WELL.
AND THE THIRD...

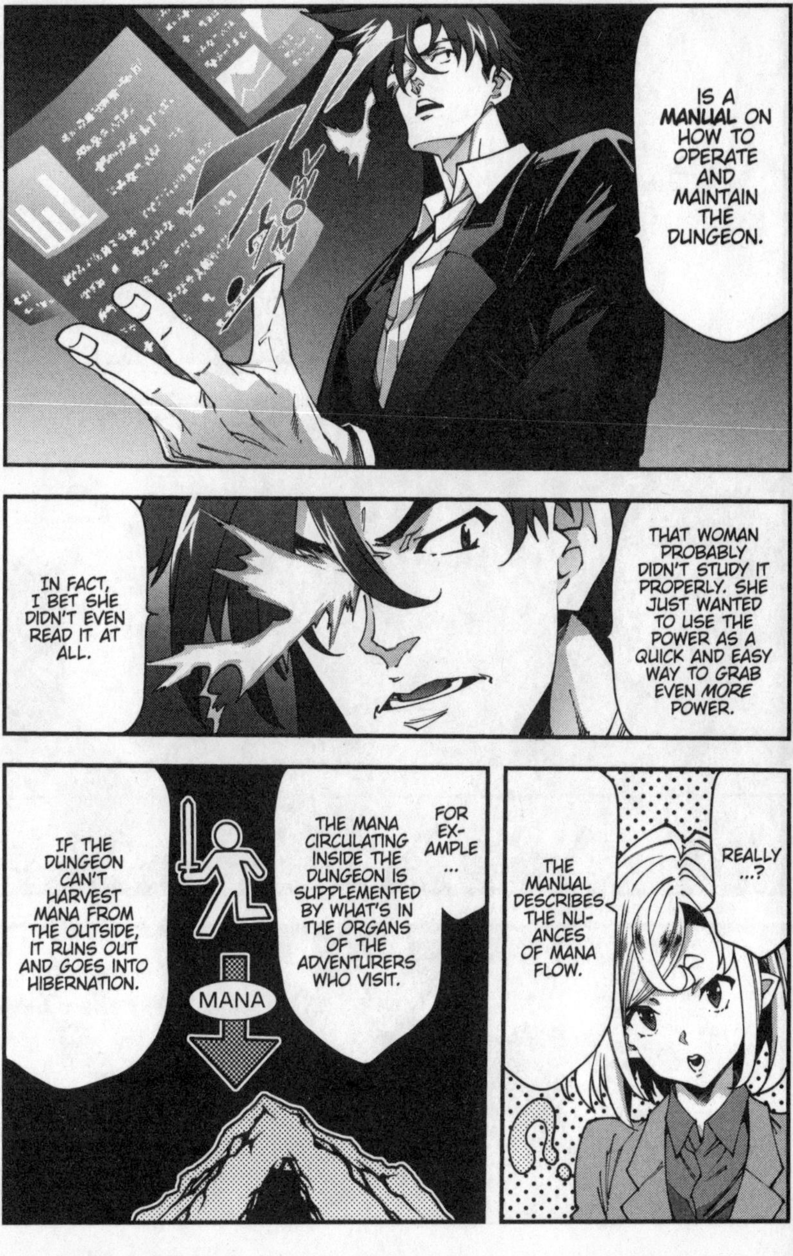
IS A MANUAL ON HOW TO OPERATE AND MAINTAIN THE DUNGEON.
VWOOM
THAT WOMAN PROBABLY DIDN'T STUDY IT PROPERLY. SHE JUST WANTED TO USE THE POWER AS A QUICK AND EASY WAY TO GRAB EVEN MORE POWER.
IN FACT, I BET SHE DIDN'T EVEN READ IT AT ALL.
REALLY ...?
THE MANUAL DESCRIBES THE NUANCES OF MANA FLOW.
FOR EXAMPLE ...
THE MANA CIRCULATING INSIDE THE DUNGEON IS SUPPLEMENTED BY WHAT'S IN THE ORGANS OF THE ADVENTURERS WHO VISIT.
MANA
IF THE DUNGEON CAN'T HARVEST MANA FROM THE OUTSIDE, IT RUNS OUT AND GOES INTO HIBERNATION.

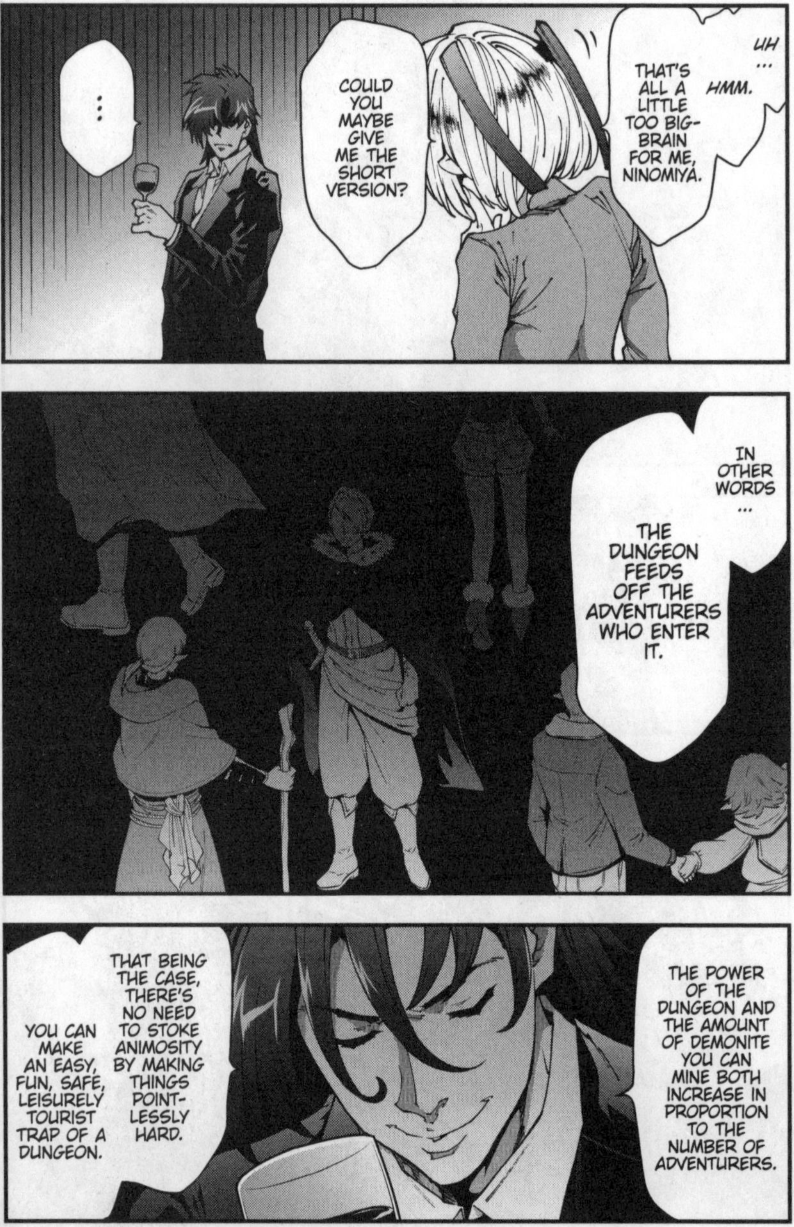
UH... HMM.
THAT'S ALL A LITTLE TOO BIG-BRAIN FOR ME, NINOMIYA.
COULD YOU MAYBE GIVE ME THE SHORT VERSION?
...
IN OTHER WORDS...
THE DUNGEON FEEDS OFF THE ADVENTURERS WHO ENTER IT.
THE POWER OF THE DUNGEON AND THE AMOUNT OF DEMONITE YOU CAN MINE BOTH INCREASE IN PROPORTION TO THE NUMBER OF ADVENTURERS.
THAT BEING THE CASE, THERE'S NO NEED TO STOKE ANIMOSITY BY MAKING THINGS POINTLESSLY HARD.
YOU CAN MAKE AN EASY, FUN, SAFE, LEISURELY TOURIST TRAP OF A DUNGEON.

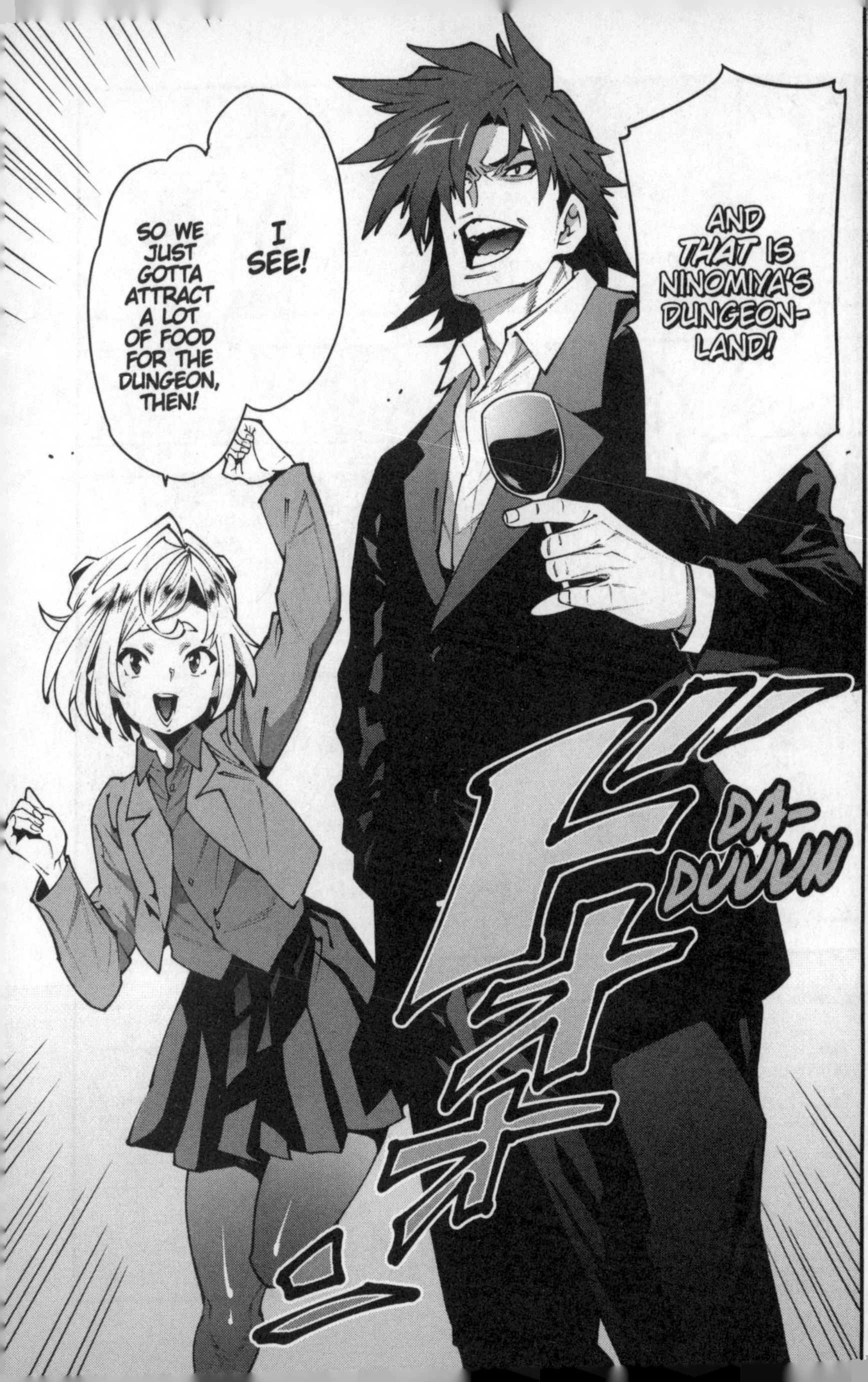
AND *THAT* IS NINOMIYA'S DUNGEON-LAND!
I SEE!
SO WE JUST GOTTA ATTRACT A LOT OF FOOD FOR THE DUNGEON, THEN!
DA-DUUUN

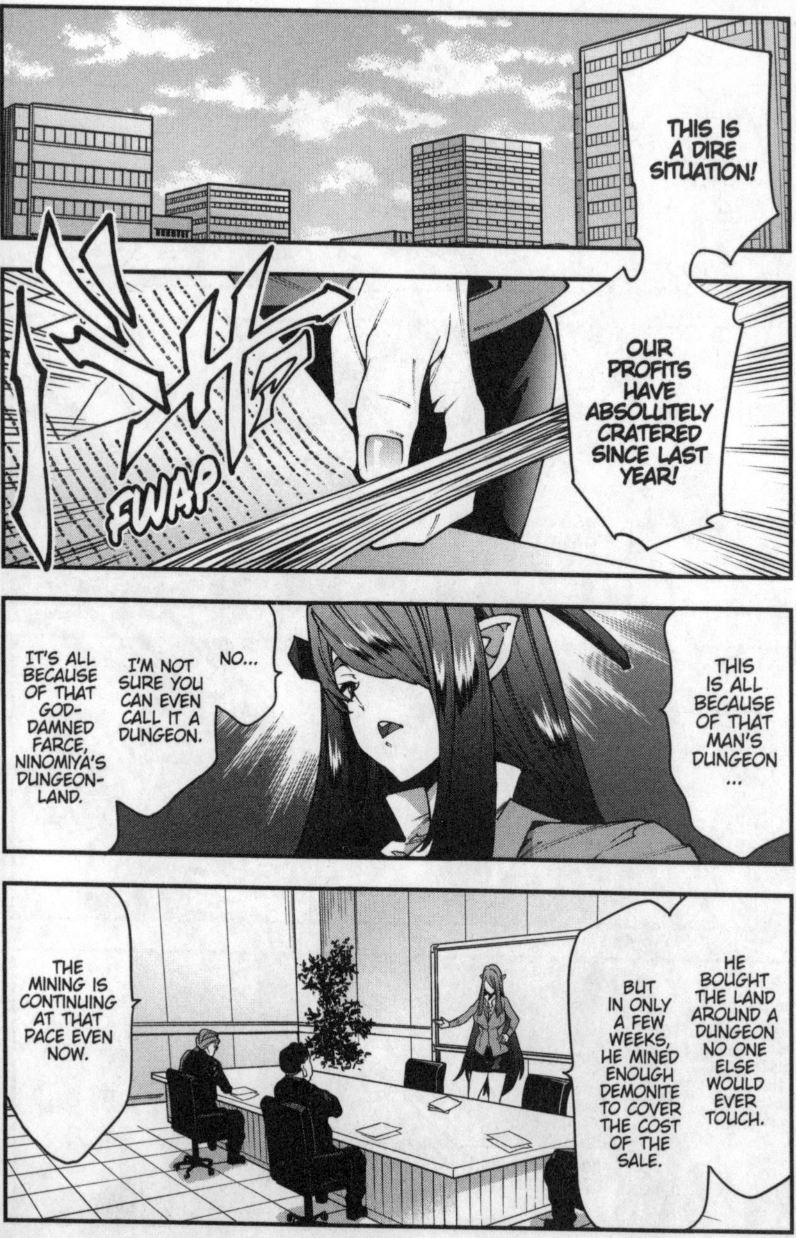
THIS IS A DIRE SITUATION!
OUR PROFITS HAVE ABSOLUTELY CRATERED SINCE LAST YEAR!
FWAP
THIS IS ALL BECAUSE OF THAT MAN'S DUNGEON...
NO...
I'M NOT SURE YOU CAN EVEN CALL IT A DUNGEON.
IT'S ALL BECAUSE OF THAT GOD-DAMNED FARCE, NINOMIYA'S DUNGEON-LAND.
HE BOUGHT THE LAND AROUND A DUNGEON NO ONE ELSE WOULD EVER TOUCH.
BUT IN ONLY A FEW WEEKS, HE MINED ENOUGH DEMONITE TO COVER THE COST OF THE SALE.
THE MINING IS CONTINUING AT THAT PACE EVEN NOW.

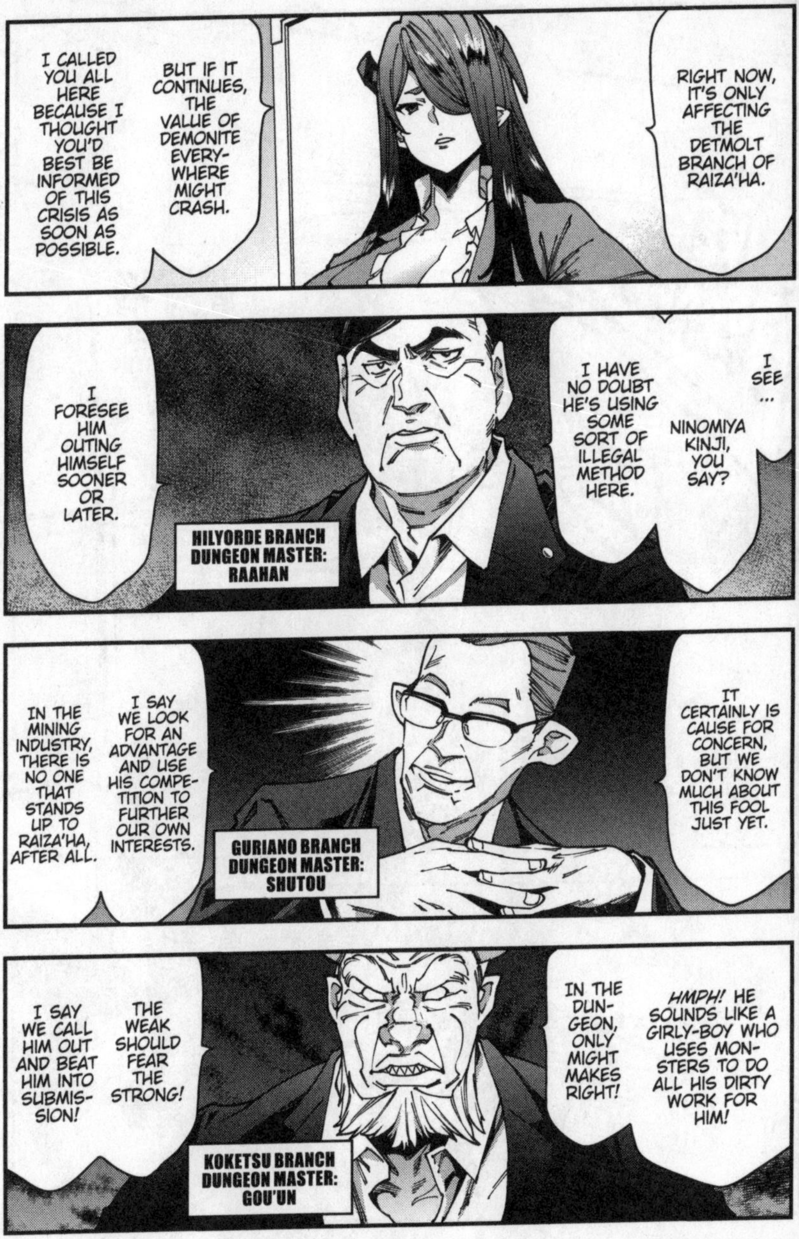
RIGHT NOW, IT'S ONLY AFFECTING THE DETMOLT BRANCH OF RAIZA'HA.
BUT IF IT CONTINUES, THE VALUE OF DEMONITE EVERY-WHERE MIGHT CRASH.
I CALLED YOU ALL HERE BECAUSE I THOUGHT YOU'D BEST BE INFORMED OF THIS CRISIS AS SOON AS POSSIBLE.
I SEE...
NINOMIYA KINJI, YOU SAY?
I HAVE NO DOUBT HE'S USING SOME SORT OF ILLEGAL METHOD HERE.
HILYORDE BRANCH DUNGEON MASTER: RAAHAN
I FORESEE HIM OUTING HIMSELF SOONER OR LATER.
IT CERTAINLY IS CAUSE FOR CONCERN, BUT WE DON'T KNOW MUCH ABOUT THIS FOOL JUST YET.
I SAY WE LOOK FOR AN ADVANTAGE AND USE HIS COMPE-TITION TO FURTHER OUR OWN INTERESTS.
GURIANO BRANCH DUNGEON MASTER: SHUTOU
IN THE MINING INDUSTRY, THERE IS NO ONE THAT STANDS UP TO RAIZA'HA, AFTER ALL.
HMPH! HE SOUNDS LIKE A GIRLY-BOY WHO USES MON-STERS TO DO ALL HIS DIRTY WORK FOR HIM!
IN THE DUN-GEON, ONLY MIGHT MAKES RIGHT!
THE WEAK SHOULD FEAR THE STRONG!
I SAY WE CALL HIM OUT AND BEAT HIM INTO SUBMIS-SION!
KOKETSU BRANCH DUNGEON MASTER: GOU'UN

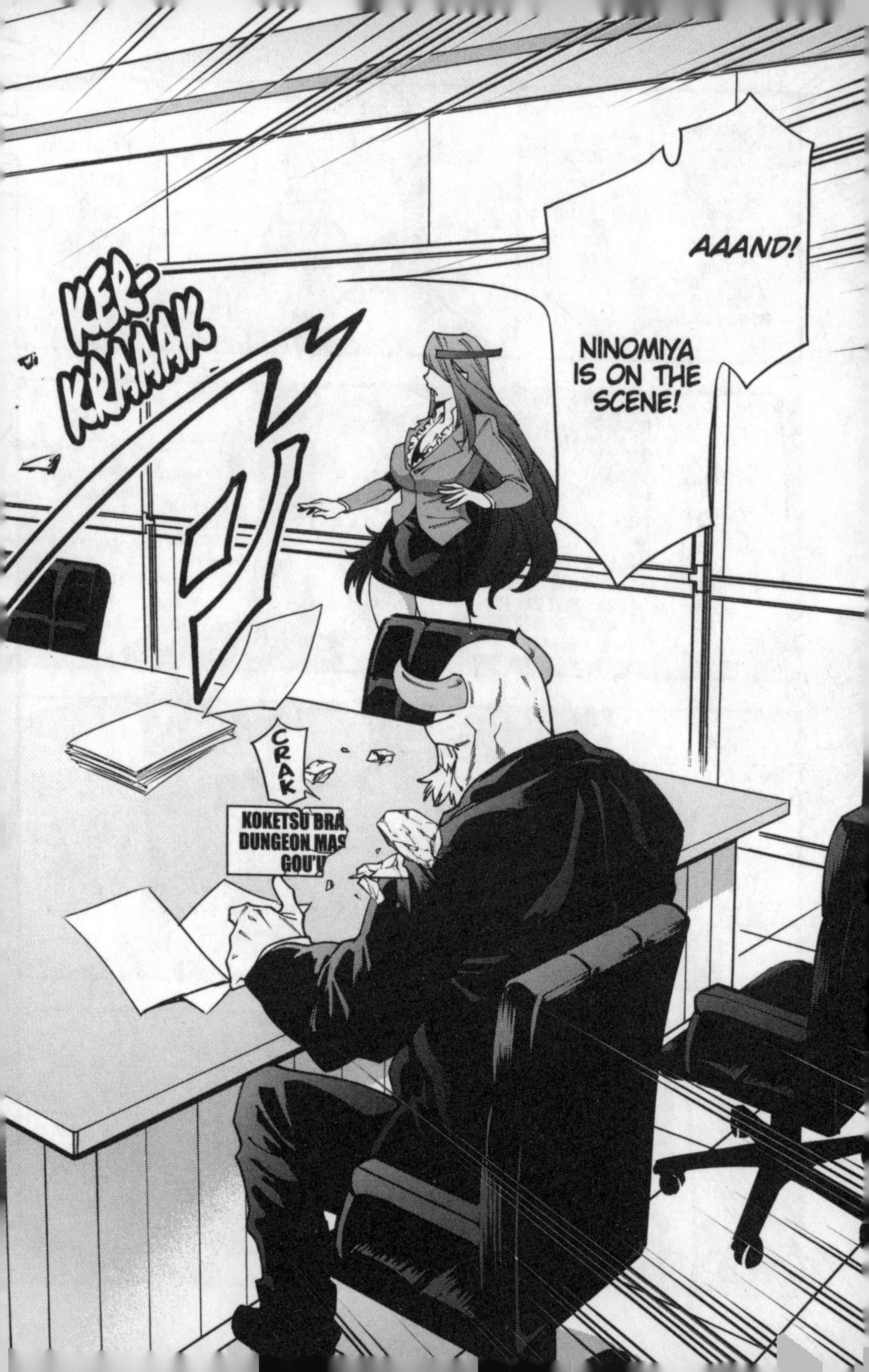
AAAND!
NINOMIYA IS ON THE SCENE!
KER-KRAAAK
CRAK
KOKETSU BRA
DUNGEON MAS
GOU'

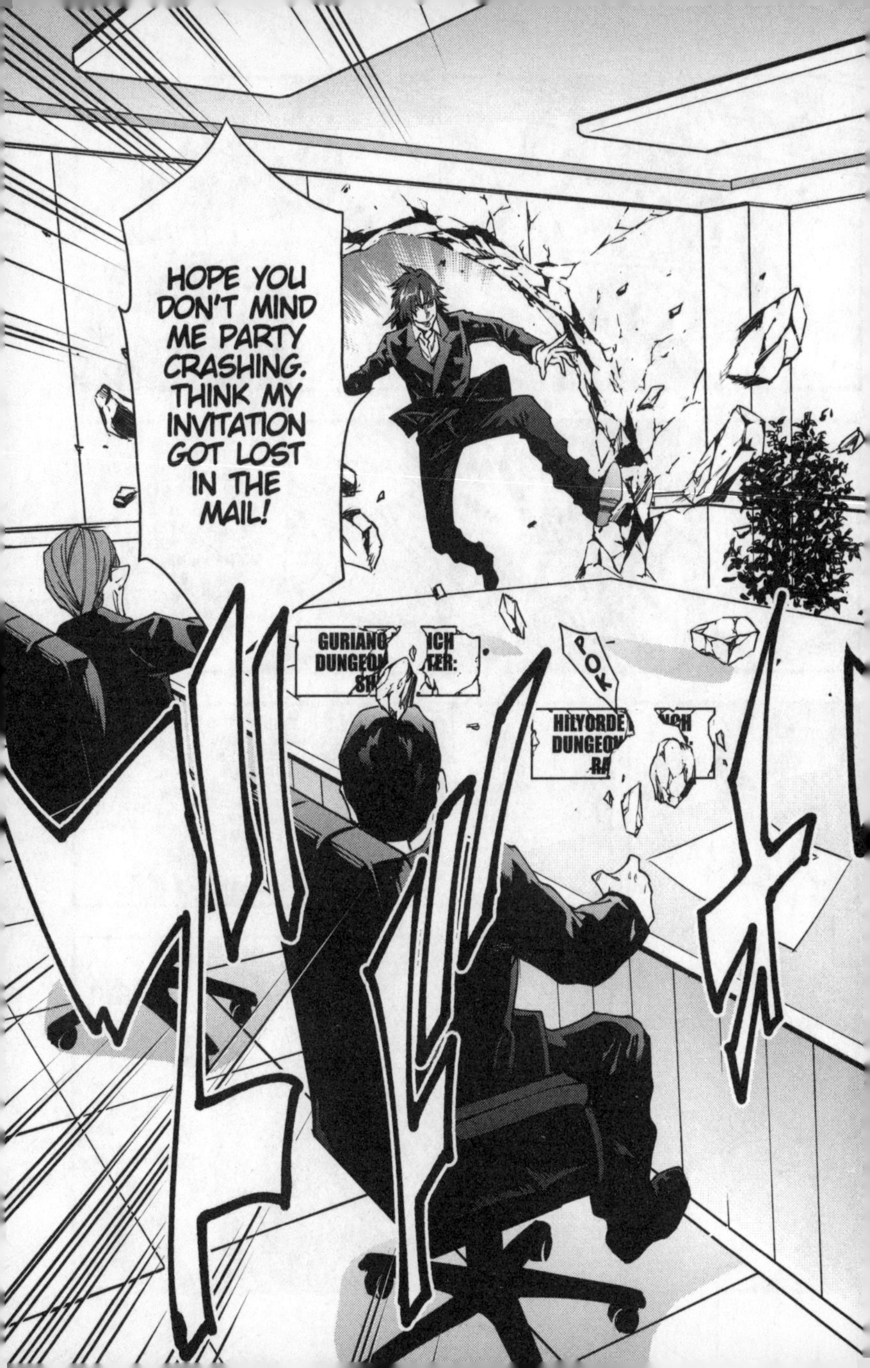
HOPE YOU DON'T MIND ME PARTY CRASHING. THINK MY INVITATION GOT LOST IN THE MAIL!
GURIANO ICH
DUNGEON TER:
SH
POK
HILYORDE ICH
DUNGEON
RA

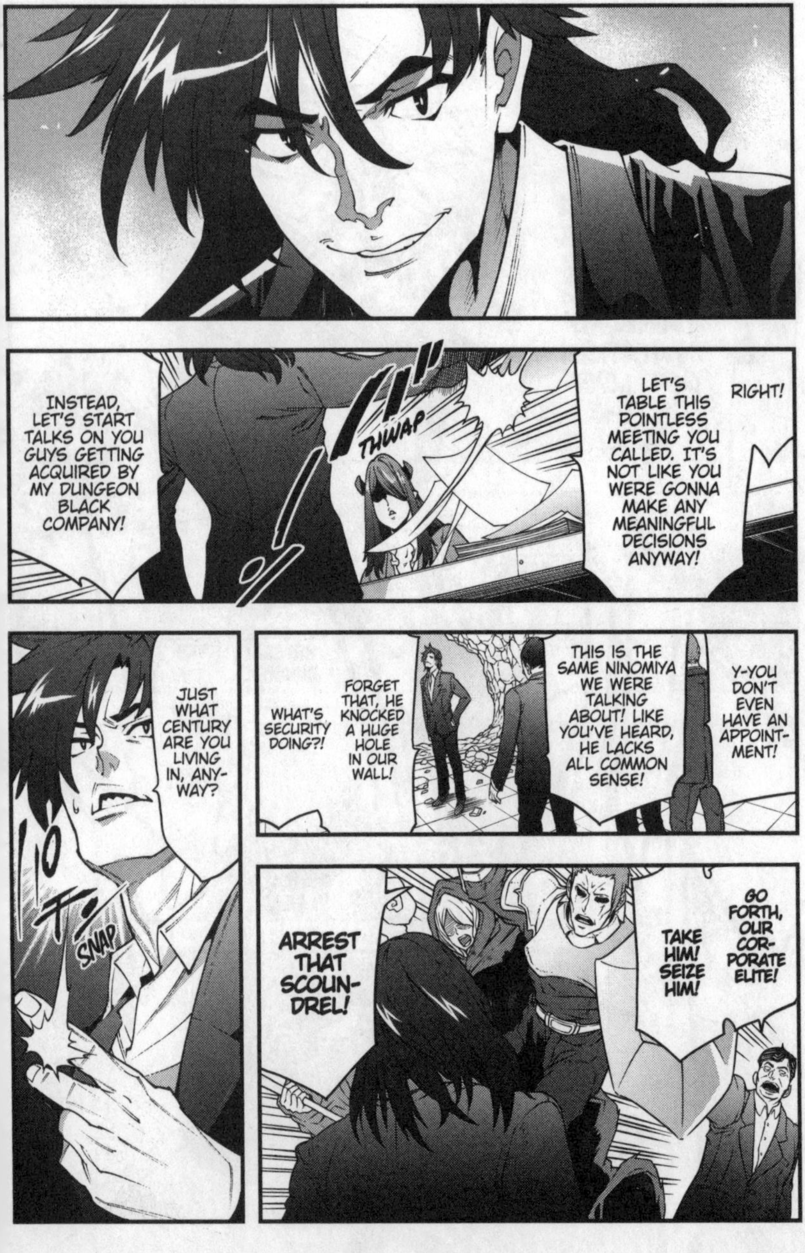
RIGHT!
LET'S TABLE THIS POINTLESS MEETING YOU CALLED. IT'S NOT LIKE YOU WERE GONNA MAKE ANY MEANINGFUL DECISIONS ANYWAY!
THWAP
INSTEAD, LET'S START TALKS ON YOU GUYS GETTING ACQUIRED BY MY DUNGEON BLACK COMPANY!
Y-YOU DON'T EVEN HAVE AN APPOINT-MENT!
THIS IS THE SAME NINOMIYA WE WERE TALKING ABOUT! LIKE YOU'VE HEARD, HE LACKS ALL COMMON SENSE!
FORGET THAT, HE KNOCKED A HUGE HOLE IN OUR WALL!
WHAT'S SECURITY DOING?!
GO FORTH, OUR COR-PORATE ELITE!
TAKE HIM! SEIZE HIM!
ARREST THAT SCOUN-DREL!
JUST WHAT CENTURY ARE YOU LIVING IN, ANY-WAY?
SNAP

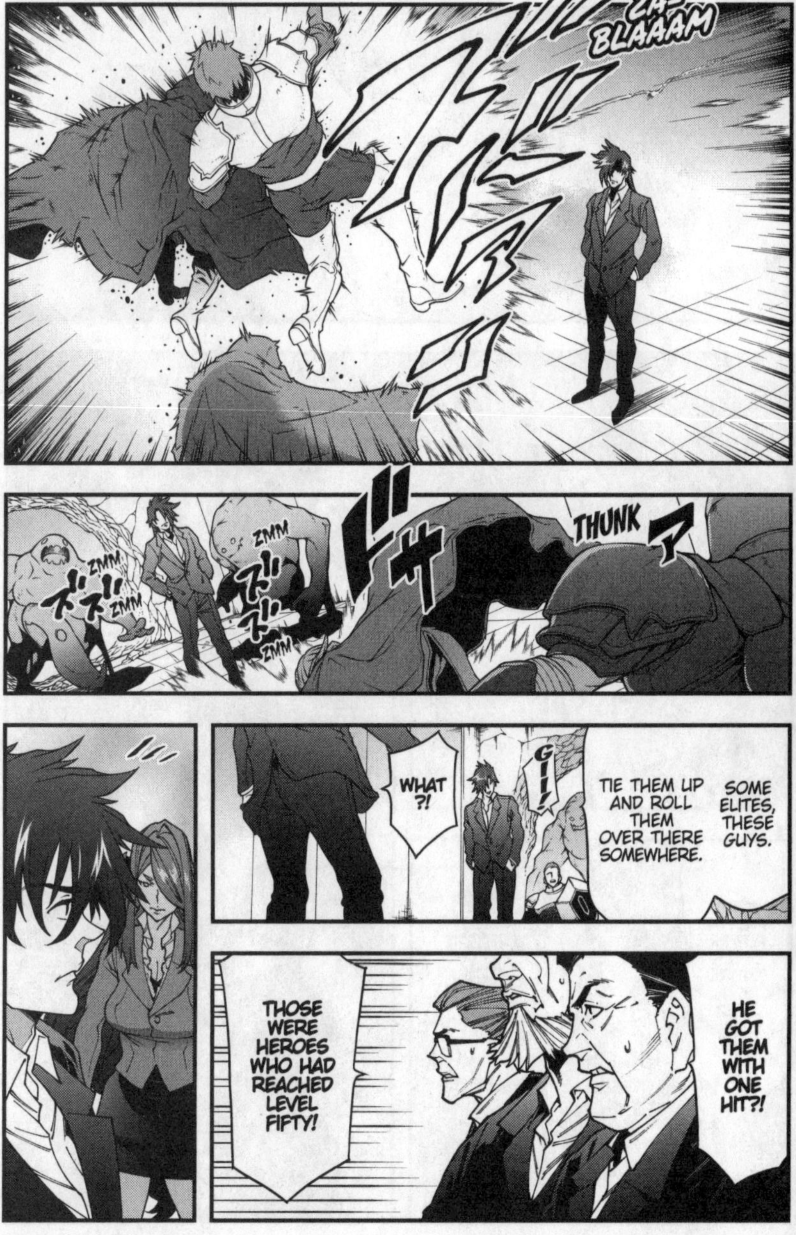

ZA-BLAAAM
THUNK
ドサァ
ZMM
ZMM
ZMM
ZMM
SOME ELITES, THESE GUYS.
TIE THEM UP AND ROLL THEM OVER THERE SOMEWHERE.
GI!!
WHAT?!
HE GOT THEM WITH ONE HIT?!
THOSE WERE HEROES WHO HAD REACHED LEVEL FIFTY!

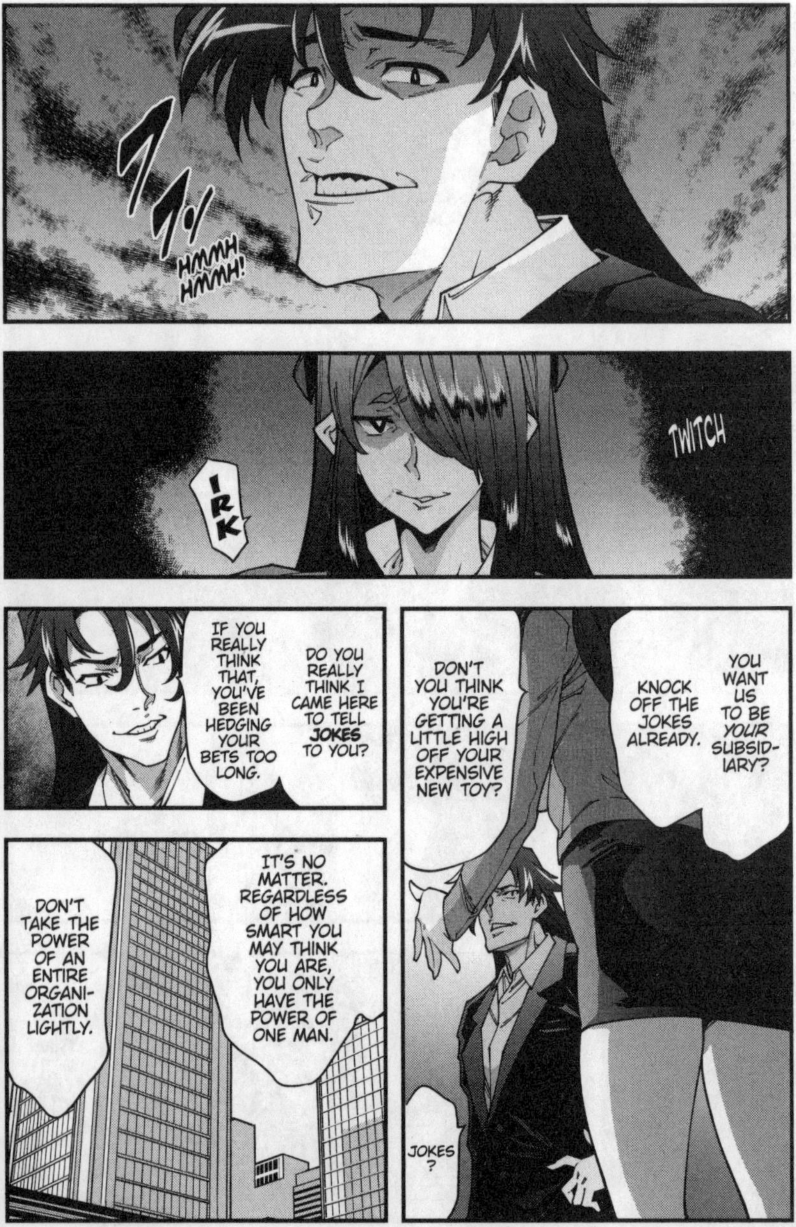
HMMH HMMH!
TWITCH
IRK
YOU WANT US TO BE *YOUR* SUBSIDIARY?
KNOCK OFF THE JOKES ALREADY.
DON'T YOU THINK YOU'RE GETTING A LITTLE HIGH OFF YOUR EXPENSIVE NEW TOY?
JOKES?
DO YOU REALLY THINK I CAME HERE TO TELL **JOKES** TO YOU?
IF YOU REALLY THINK THAT, YOU'VE BEEN HEDGING YOUR BETS TOO LONG.
IT'S NO MATTER. REGARDLESS OF HOW SMART YOU MAY THINK YOU ARE, YOU ONLY HAVE THE POWER OF ONE MAN.
DON'T TAKE THE POWER OF AN ENTIRE ORGANIZATION LIGHTLY.

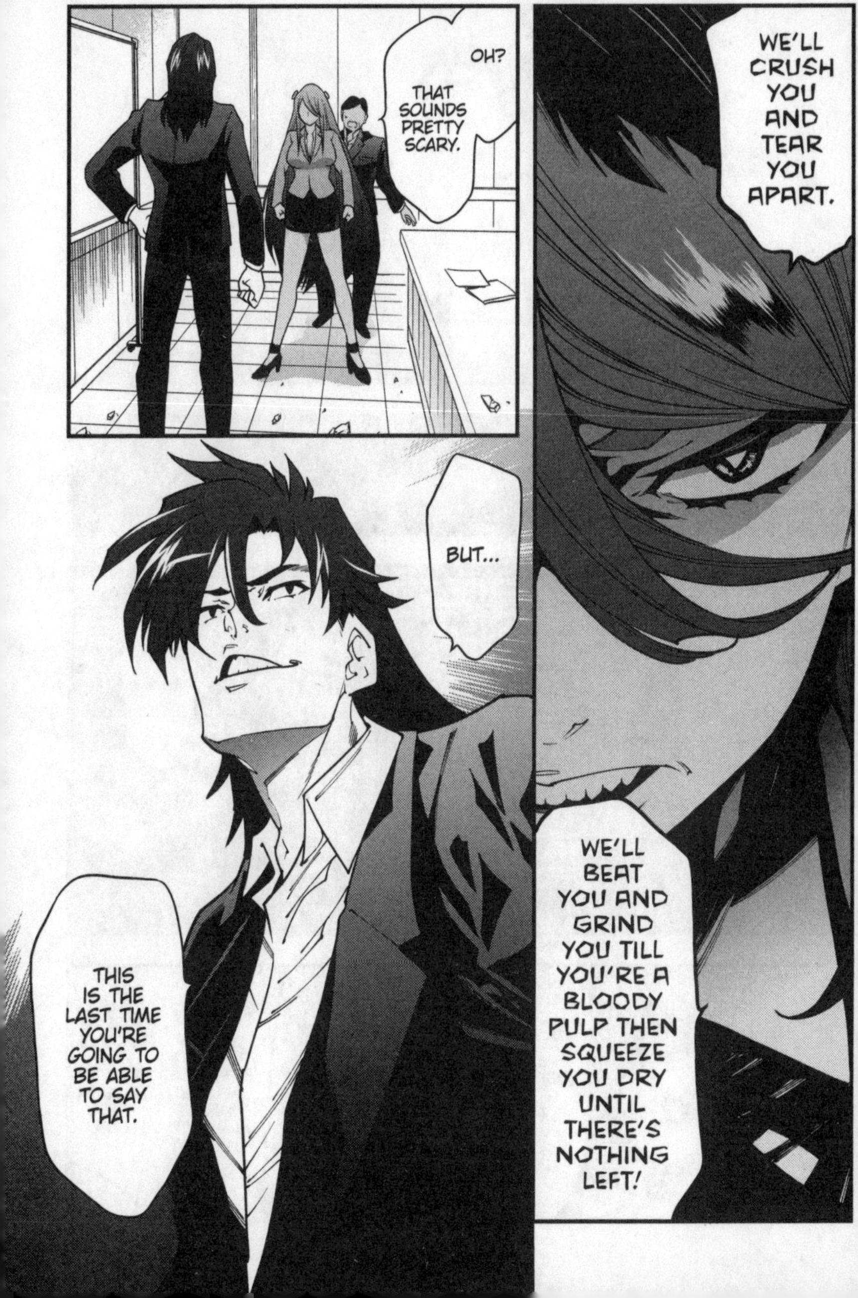
WE'LL CRUSH YOU AND TEAR YOU APART.
WE'LL BEAT YOU AND GRIND YOU TILL YOU'RE A BLOODY PULP THEN SQUEEZE YOU DRY UNTIL THERE'S NOTHING LEFT!
OH?
THAT SOUNDS PRETTY SCARY.
BUT...
THIS IS THE LAST TIME YOU'RE GOING TO BE ABLE TO SAY THAT.

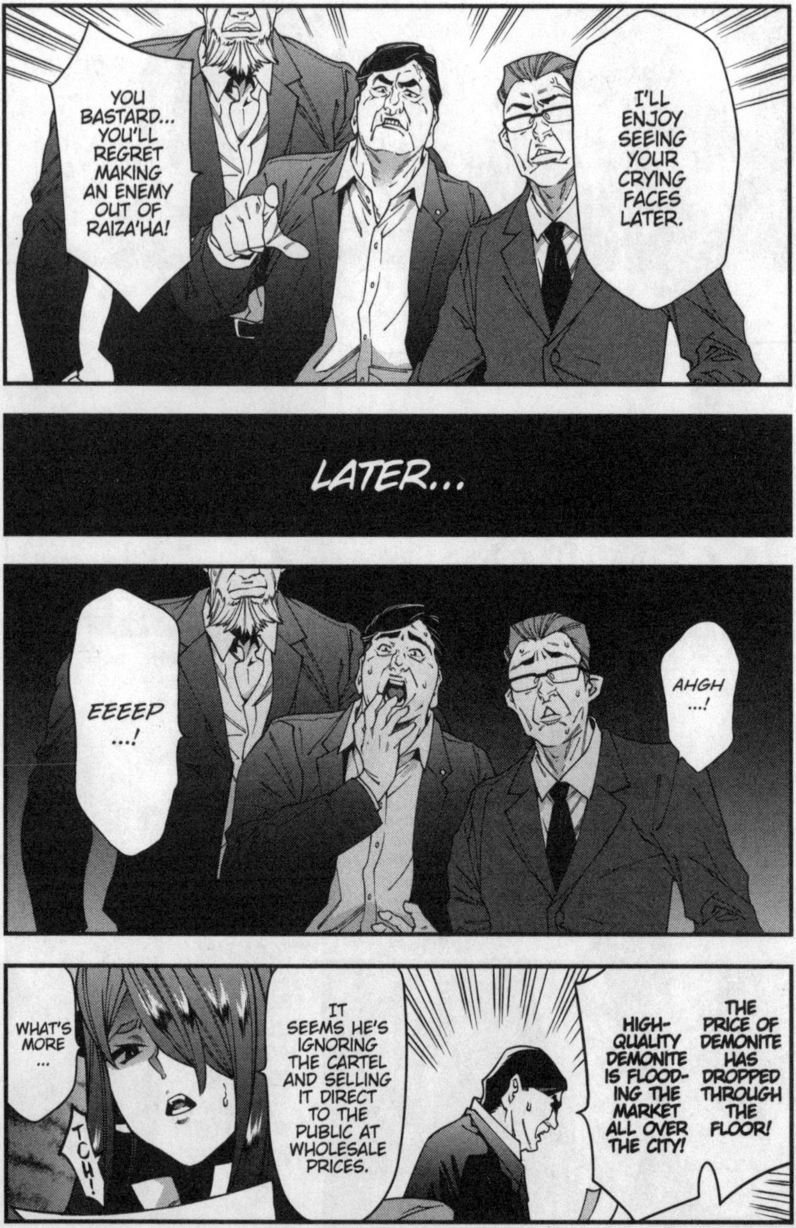
I'LL ENJOY SEEING YOUR CRYING FACES LATER.
YOU BASTARD... YOU'LL REGRET MAKING AN ENEMY OUT OF RAIZA'HA!
LATER...
AHGH ...!
EEEEP ...!
THE PRICE OF DEMONITE HAS DROPPED THROUGH THE FLOOR!
HIGH-QUALITY DEMONITE IS FLOODING THE MARKET ALL OVER THE CITY!
IT SEEMS HE'S IGNORING THE CARTEL AND SELLING IT DIRECT TO THE PUBLIC AT WHOLESALE PRICES.
TCH!
WHAT'S MORE ...

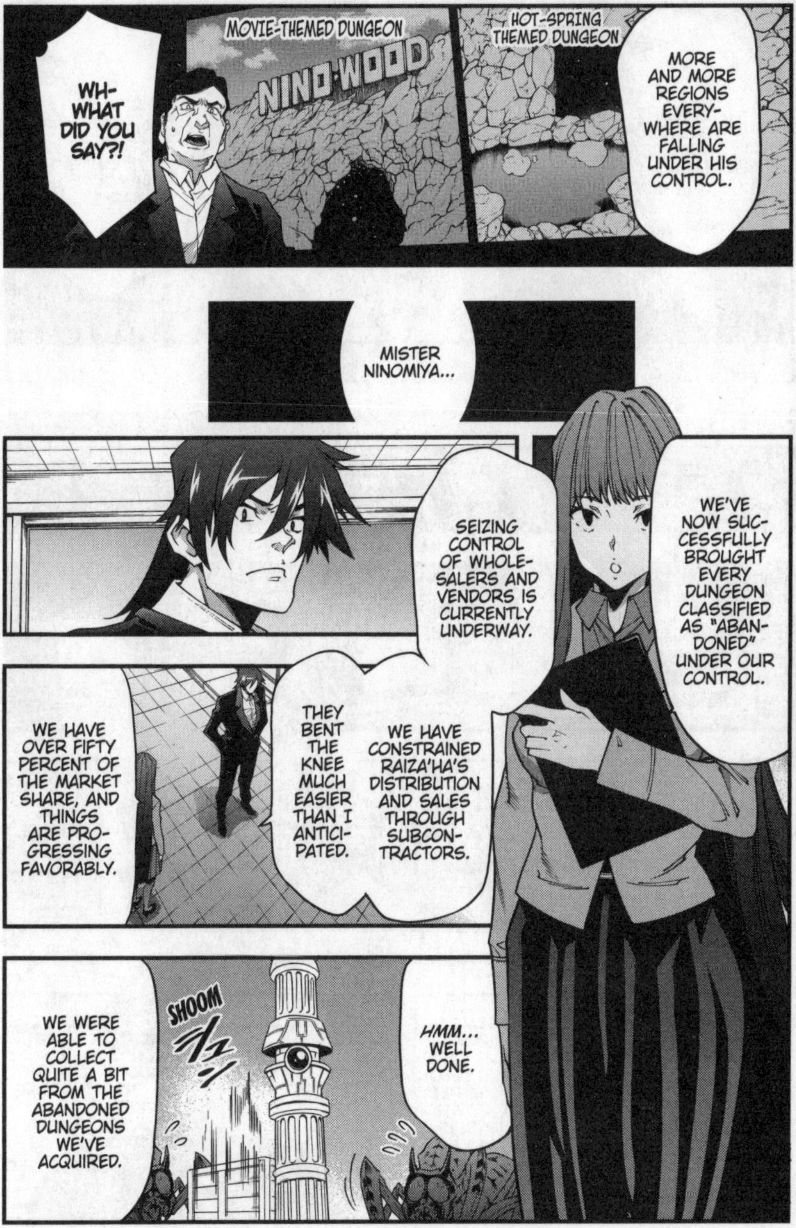
HOT-SPRING THEMED DUNGEON
MORE AND MORE REGIONS EVERY-WHERE ARE FALLING UNDER HIS CONTROL.
MOVIE-THEMED DUNGEON
NINO-WOOD
WH-WHAT DID YOU SAY?!
MISTER NINOMIYA...
WE'VE NOW SUC-CESSFULLY BROUGHT EVERY DUNGEON CLASSIFIED AS "ABAN-DONED" UNDER OUR CONTROL.
SEIZING CONTROL OF WHOLE-SALERS AND VENDORS IS CURRENTLY UNDERWAY.
WE HAVE CONSTRAINED RAIZA'HA'S DISTRIBUTION AND SALES THROUGH SUBCON-TRACTORS.
THEY BENT THE KNEE MUCH EASIER THAN I ANTICI-PATED.
WE HAVE OVER FIFTY PERCENT OF THE MARKET SHARE, AND THINGS ARE PRO-GRESSING FAVORABLY.
HMM... WELL DONE.
SHOOM
WE WERE ABLE TO COLLECT QUITE A BIT FROM THE ABANDONED DUNGEONS WE'VE ACQUIRED.

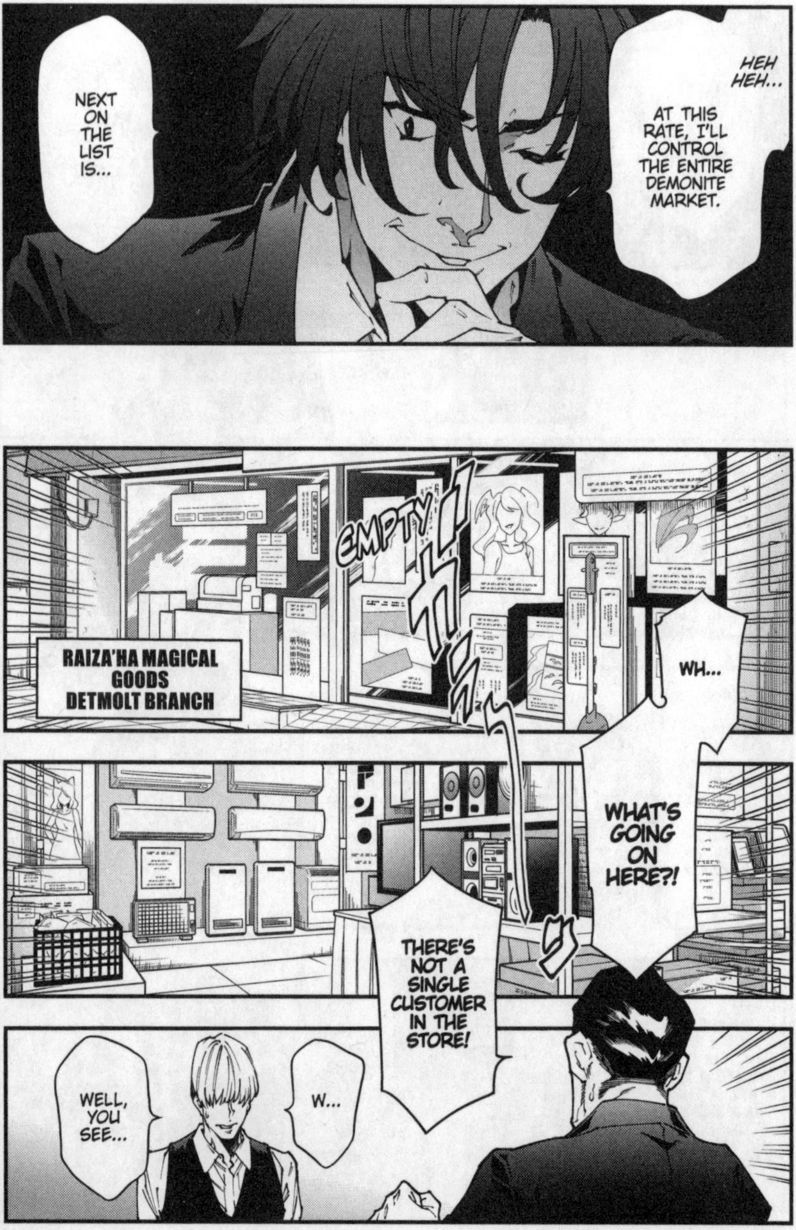
HEH HEH...
AT THIS RATE, I'LL CONTROL THE ENTIRE DEMONITE MARKET.
NEXT ON THE LIST IS...
EMPTY
WH...
RAIZA'HA MAGICAL GOODS DETMOLT BRANCH
WHAT'S GOING ON HERE?!
THERE'S NOT A SINGLE CUSTOMER IN THE STORE!
W...
WELL, YOU SEE...

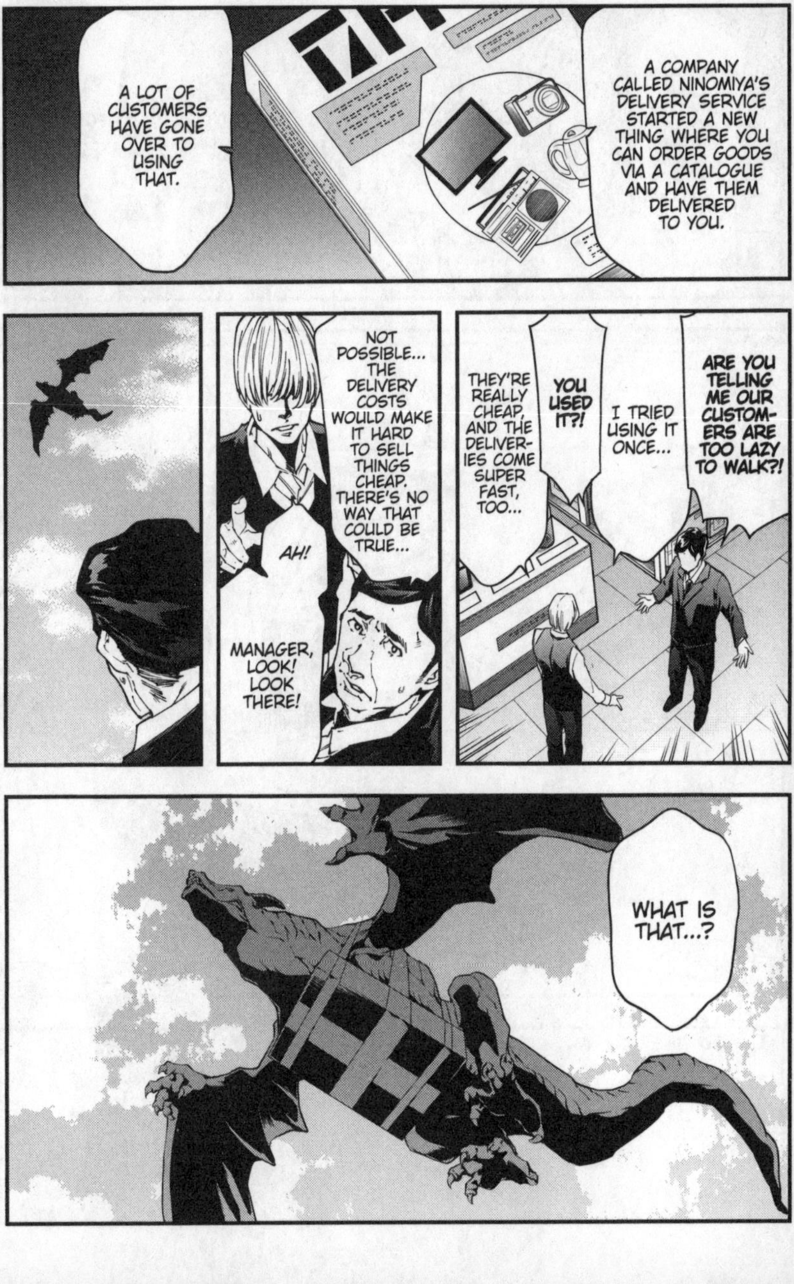
A COMPANY CALLED NINOMIYA'S DELIVERY SERVICE STARTED A NEW THING WHERE YOU CAN ORDER GOODS VIA A CATALOGUE AND HAVE THEM DELIVERED TO YOU.
A LOT OF CUSTOMERS HAVE GONE OVER TO USING THAT.
ARE YOU TELLING ME OUR CUSTOM-ERS ARE TOO LAZY TO WALK?!
I TRIED USING IT ONCE...
YOU USED IT?!
THEY'RE REALLY CHEAP, AND THE DELIVER-IES COME SUPER FAST, TOO...
NOT POSSIBLE... THE DELIVERY COSTS WOULD MAKE IT HARD TO SELL THINGS CHEAP. THERE'S NO WAY THAT COULD BE TRUE...
AH!
MANAGER, LOOK! LOOK THERE!
WHAT IS THAT...?

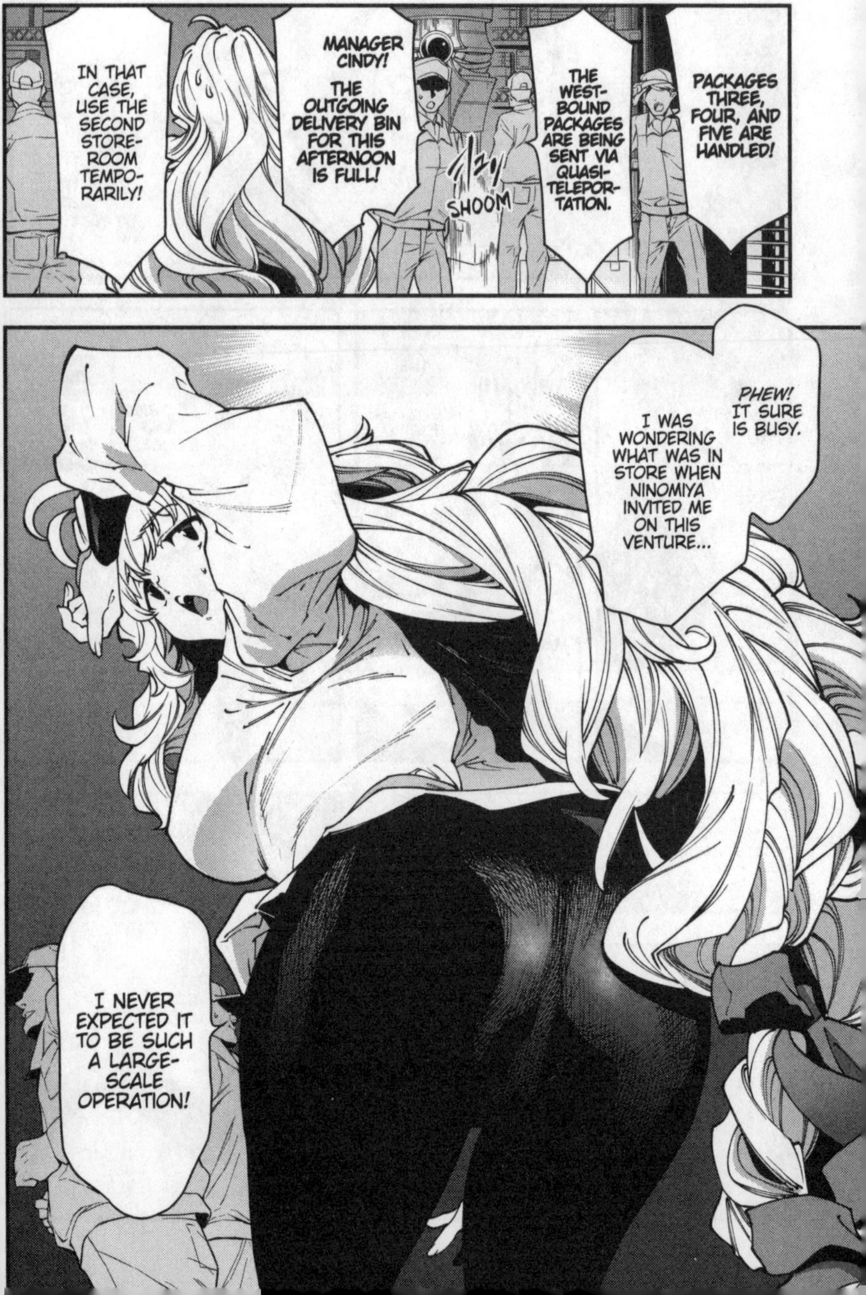
PACKAGES THREE, FOUR, AND FIVE ARE HANDLED!
THE WEST-BOUND PACKAGES ARE BEING SENT VIA QUASI-TELEPORTATION.
SHOOM
MANAGER CINDY!
THE OUTGOING DELIVERY BIN FOR THIS AFTERNOON IS FULL!
IN THAT CASE, USE THE SECOND STOREROOM TEMPORARILY!
PHEW! IT SURE IS BUSY.
I WAS WONDERING WHAT WAS IN STORE WHEN NINOMIYA INVITED ME ON THIS VENTURE...
I NEVER EXPECTED IT TO BE SUCH A LARGE-SCALE OPERATION!

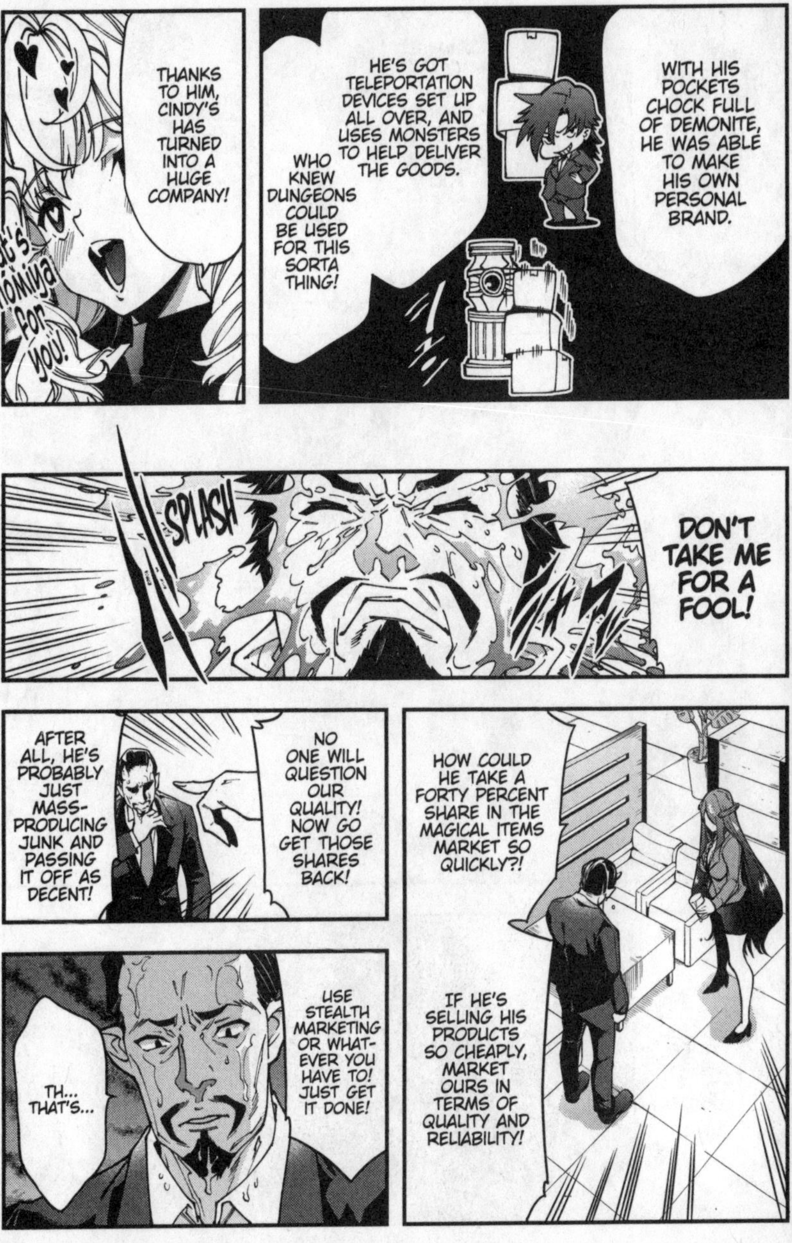
WITH HIS POCKETS CHOCK FULL OF DEMONITE, HE WAS ABLE TO MAKE HIS OWN PERSONAL BRAND.
HE'S GOT TELEPORTATION DEVICES SET UP ALL OVER, AND USES MONSTERS TO HELP DELIVER THE GOODS.
WHO KNEW DUNGEONS COULD BE USED FOR THIS SORTA THING!
THANKS TO HIM, CINDY'S HAS TURNED INTO A HUGE COMPANY!
That's Ninomiya for you!
DON'T TAKE ME FOR A FOOL!
SPLASH
HOW COULD HE TAKE A FORTY PERCENT SHARE IN THE MAGICAL ITEMS MARKET SO QUICKLY?!
IF HE'S SELLING HIS PRODUCTS SO CHEAPLY, MARKET OURS IN TERMS OF QUALITY AND RELIABILITY!
NO ONE WILL QUESTION OUR QUALITY! NOW GO GET THOSE SHARES BACK!
AFTER ALL, HE'S PROBABLY JUST MASS-PRODUCING JUNK AND PASSING IT OFF AS DECENT!
USE STEALTH MARKETING OR WHATEVER YOU HAVE TO! JUST GET IT DONE!
TH... THAT'S...

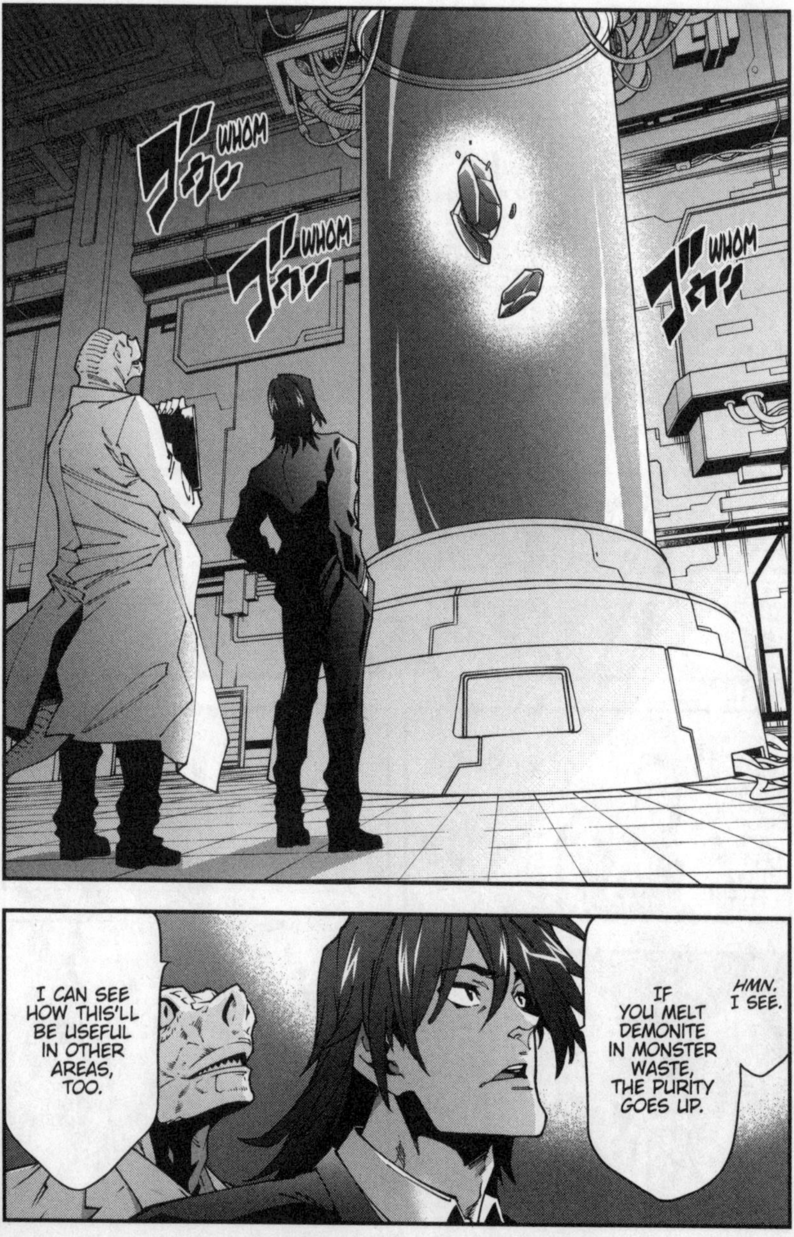
ゴウン WHOM
ゴウン WHOM
ゴウン WHOM
HMN. I SEE.
IF YOU MELT DEMONITE IN MONSTER WASTE, THE PURITY GOES UP.
I CAN SEE HOW THIS'LL BE USEFUL IN OTHER AREAS, TOO.

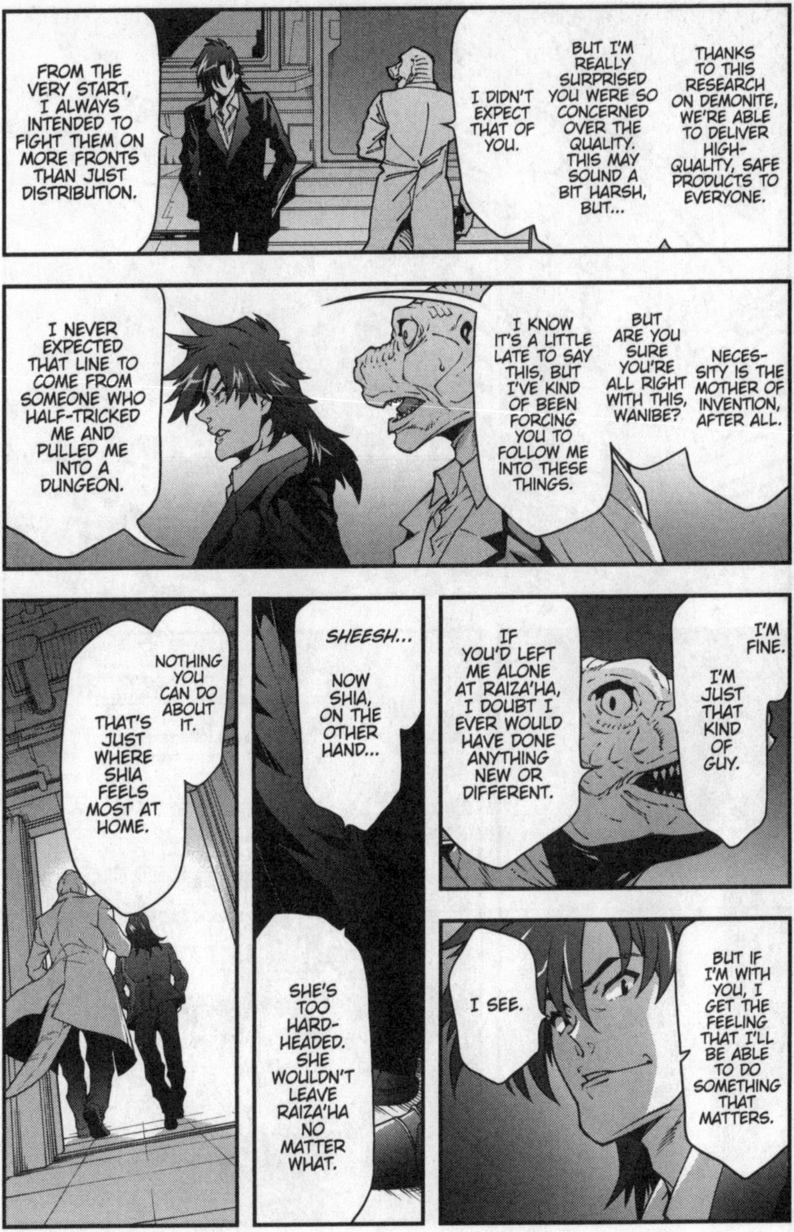
THANKS TO THIS RESEARCH ON DEMONITE, WE'RE ABLE TO DELIVER HIGH-QUALITY, SAFE PRODUCTS TO EVERYONE.
BUT I'M REALLY SURPRISED YOU WERE SO CONCERNED OVER THE QUALITY. THIS MAY SOUND A BIT HARSH, BUT...
I DIDN'T EXPECT THAT OF YOU.
FROM THE VERY START, I ALWAYS INTENDED TO FIGHT THEM ON MORE FRONTS THAN JUST DISTRIBUTION.
NECESSITY IS THE MOTHER OF INVENTION, AFTER ALL.
BUT ARE YOU SURE YOU'RE ALL RIGHT WITH THIS, WANIBE?
I KNOW IT'S A LITTLE LATE TO SAY THIS, BUT I'VE KIND OF BEEN FORCING YOU TO FOLLOW ME INTO THESE THINGS.
I NEVER EXPECTED THAT LINE TO COME FROM SOMEONE WHO HALF-TRICKED ME AND PULLED ME INTO A DUNGEON.
I'M FINE.
I'M JUST THAT KIND OF GUY.
IF YOU'D LEFT ME ALONE AT RAIZA'HA, I DOUBT I EVER WOULD HAVE DONE ANYTHING NEW OR DIFFERENT.
BUT IF I'M WITH YOU, I GET THE FEELING THAT I'LL BE ABLE TO DO SOMETHING THAT MATTERS.
I SEE.
SHEESH...
NOW SHIA, ON THE OTHER HAND...
SHE'S TOO HARD-HEADED. SHE WOULDN'T LEAVE RAIZA'HA NO MATTER WHAT.
NOTHING YOU CAN DO ABOUT IT.
THAT'S JUST WHERE SHIA FEELS MOST AT HOME.

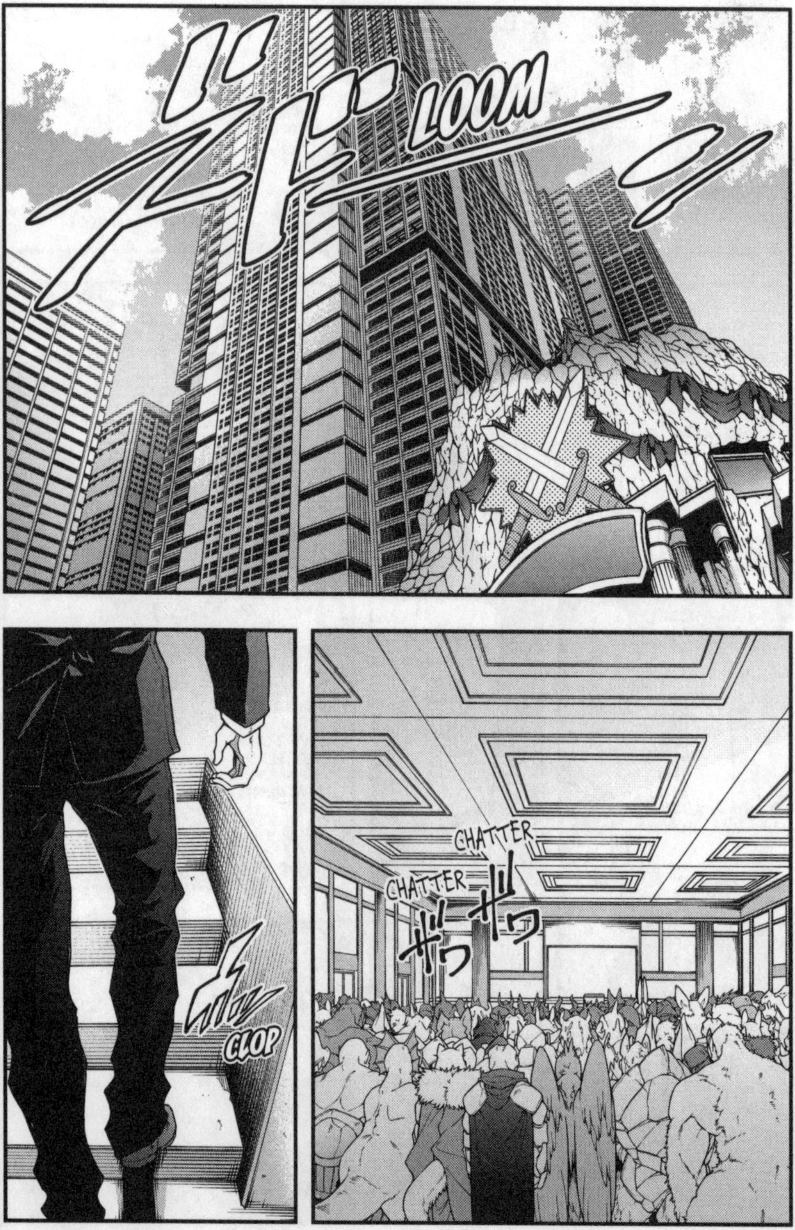
LOOM
CHATTER
CHATTER
CLOP

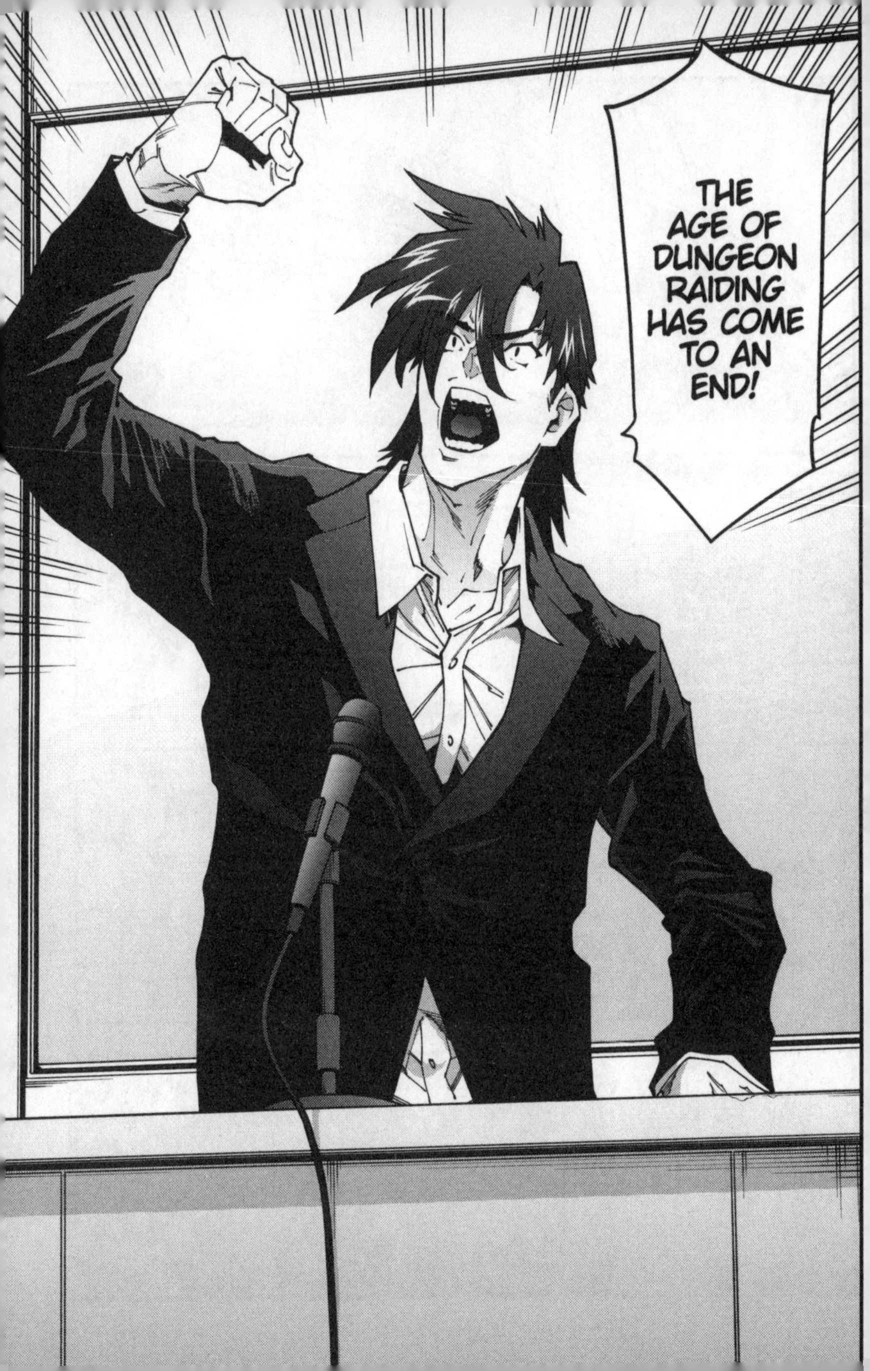
THE AGE OF DUNGEON RAIDING HAS COME TO AN END!

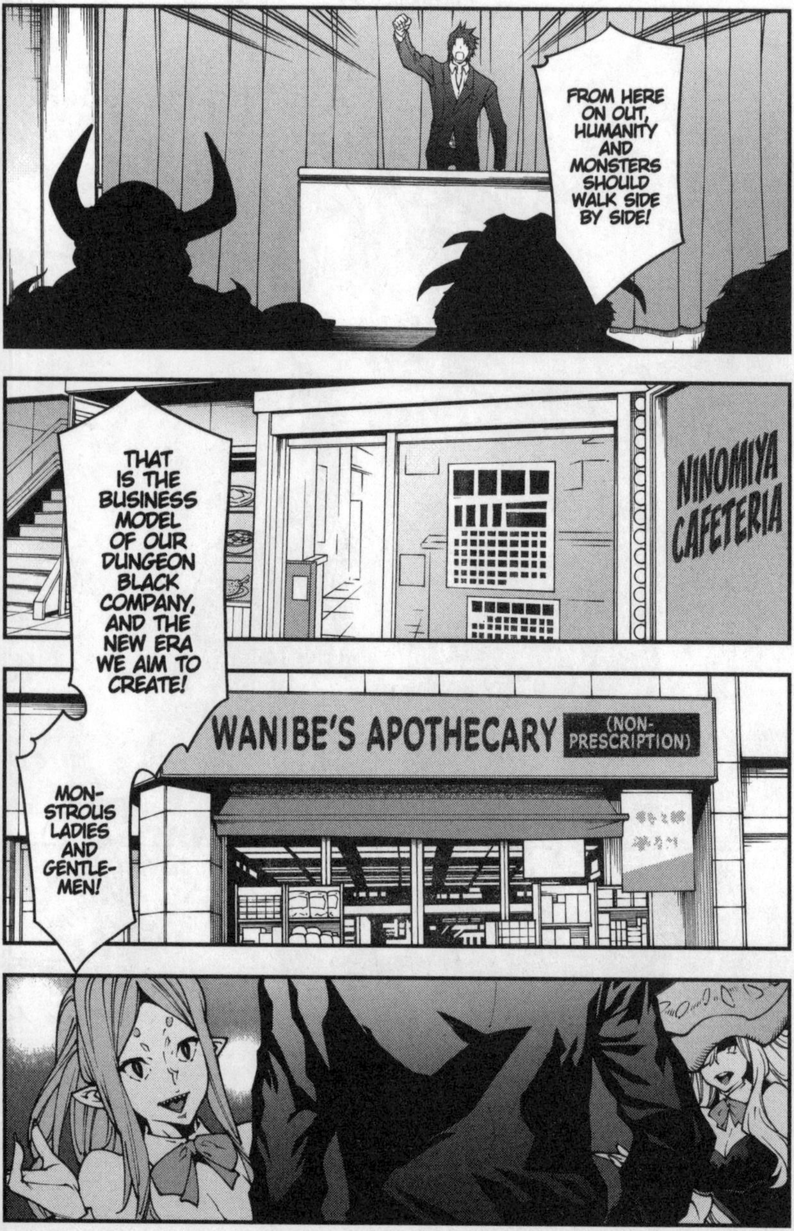
FROM HERE ON OUT, HUMANITY AND MONSTERS SHOULD WALK SIDE BY SIDE!
NINOMIYA CAFETERIA
THAT IS THE BUSINESS MODEL OF OUR DUNGEON BLACK COMPANY, AND THE NEW ERA WE AIM TO CREATE!
WANIBE'S APOTHECARY
(NON-PRESCRIPTION)
MON-STROUS LADIES AND GENTLE-MEN!

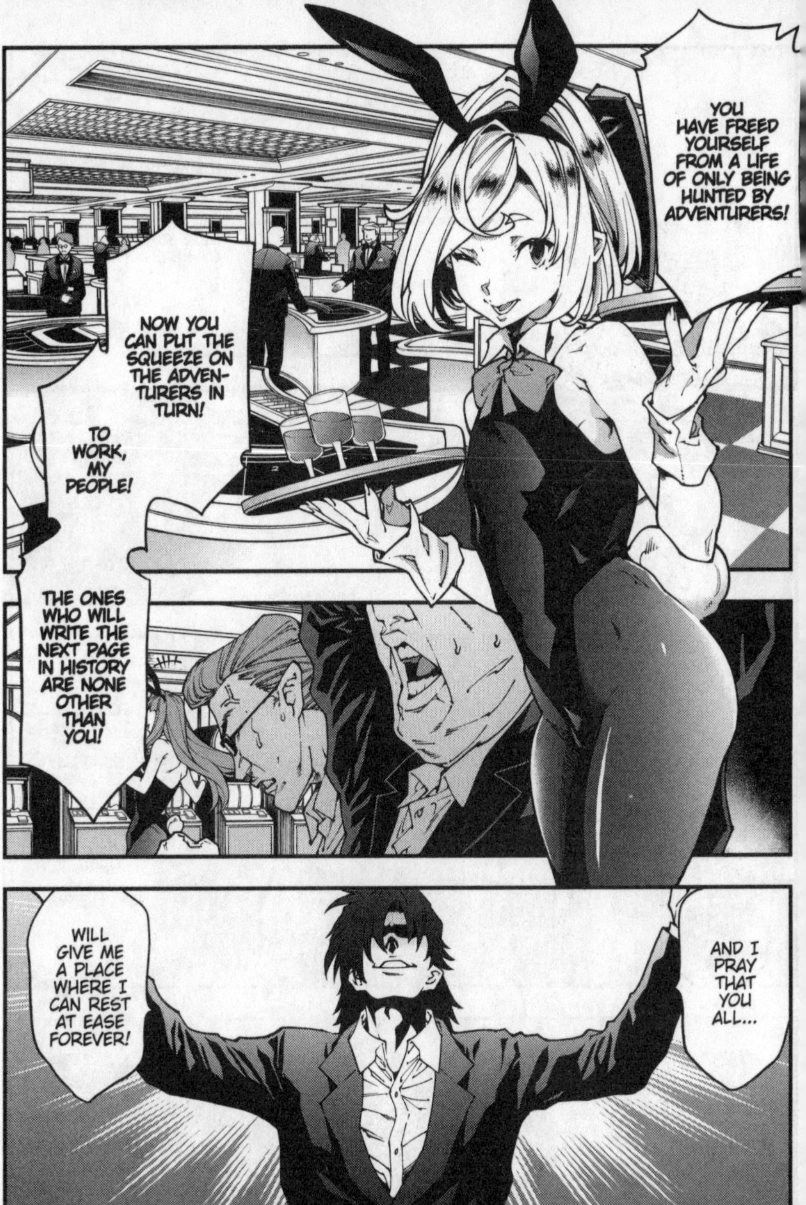
YOU HAVE FREED YOURSELF FROM A LIFE OF ONLY BEING HUNTED BY ADVENTURERS!
NOW YOU CAN PUT THE SQUEEZE ON THE ADVEN-TURERS IN TURN!
TO WORK, MY PEOPLE!
THE ONES WHO WILL WRITE THE NEXT PAGE IN HISTORY ARE NONE OTHER THAN YOU!
AND I PRAY THAT YOU ALL...
WILL GIVE ME A PLACE WHERE I CAN REST AT EASE FOREVER!

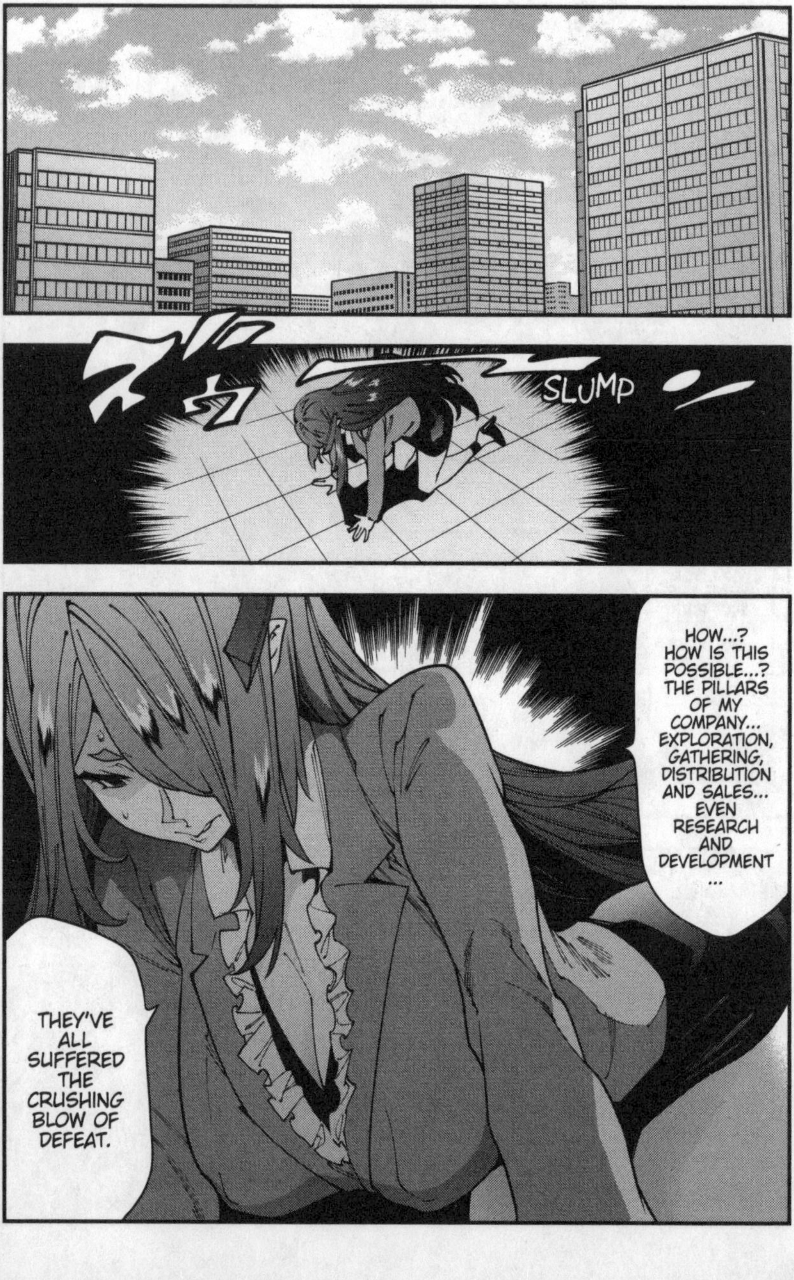
SLUMP
HOW...? HOW IS THIS POSSIBLE...? THE PILLARS OF MY COMPANY... EXPLORATION, GATHERING, DISTRIBUTION AND SALES... EVEN RESEARCH AND DEVELOPMENT ...
THEY'VE ALL SUFFERED THE CRUSHING BLOW OF DEFEAT.

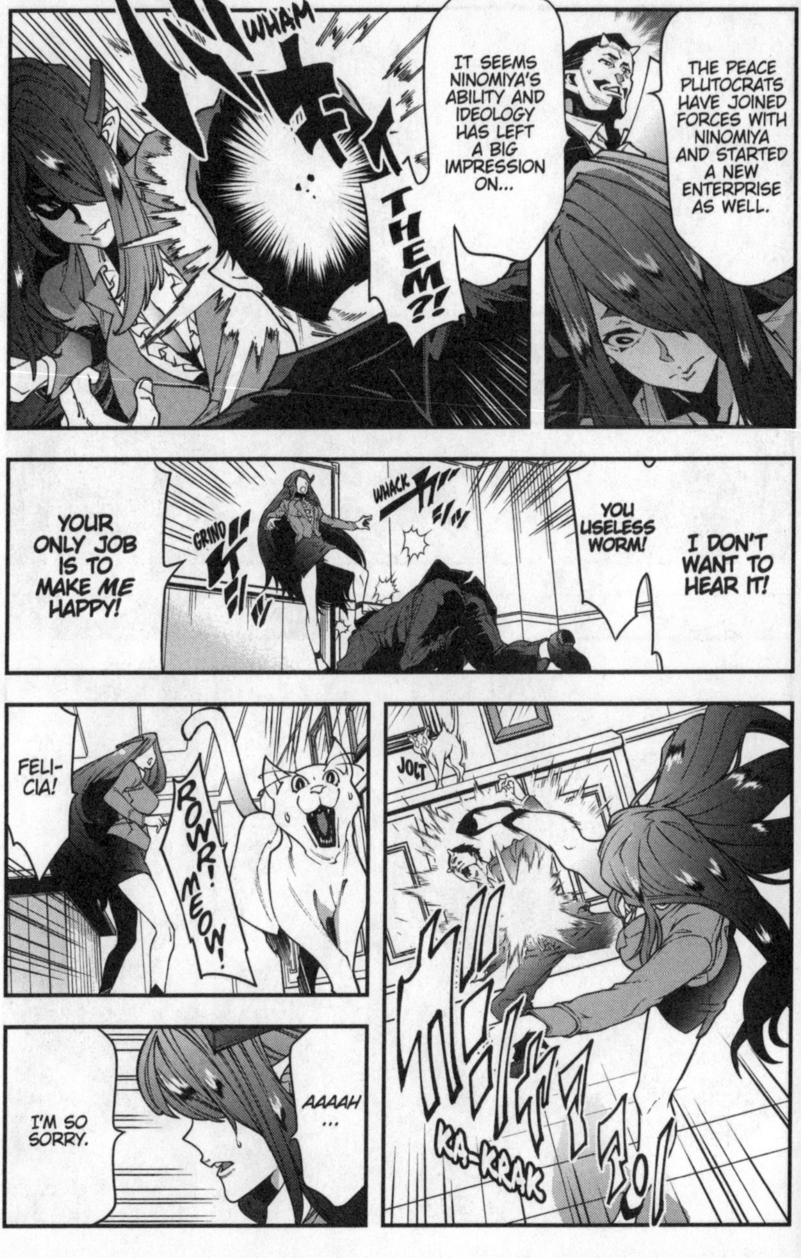
THE PEACE PLUTOCRATS HAVE JOINED FORCES WITH NINOMIYA AND STARTED A NEW ENTERPRISE AS WELL.
IT SEEMS NINOMIYA'S ABILITY AND IDEOLOGY HAS LEFT A BIG IMPRESSION ON...
WHAM
THEM?!
I DON'T WANT TO HEAR IT!
YOU USELESS WORM!
WHACK
GRIND
YOUR ONLY JOB IS TO MAKE ME HAPPY!
JOLT
KA-KRAK
FELI-CIA!
ROWR! MEOW!
AAAAH ...
I'M SO SORRY.

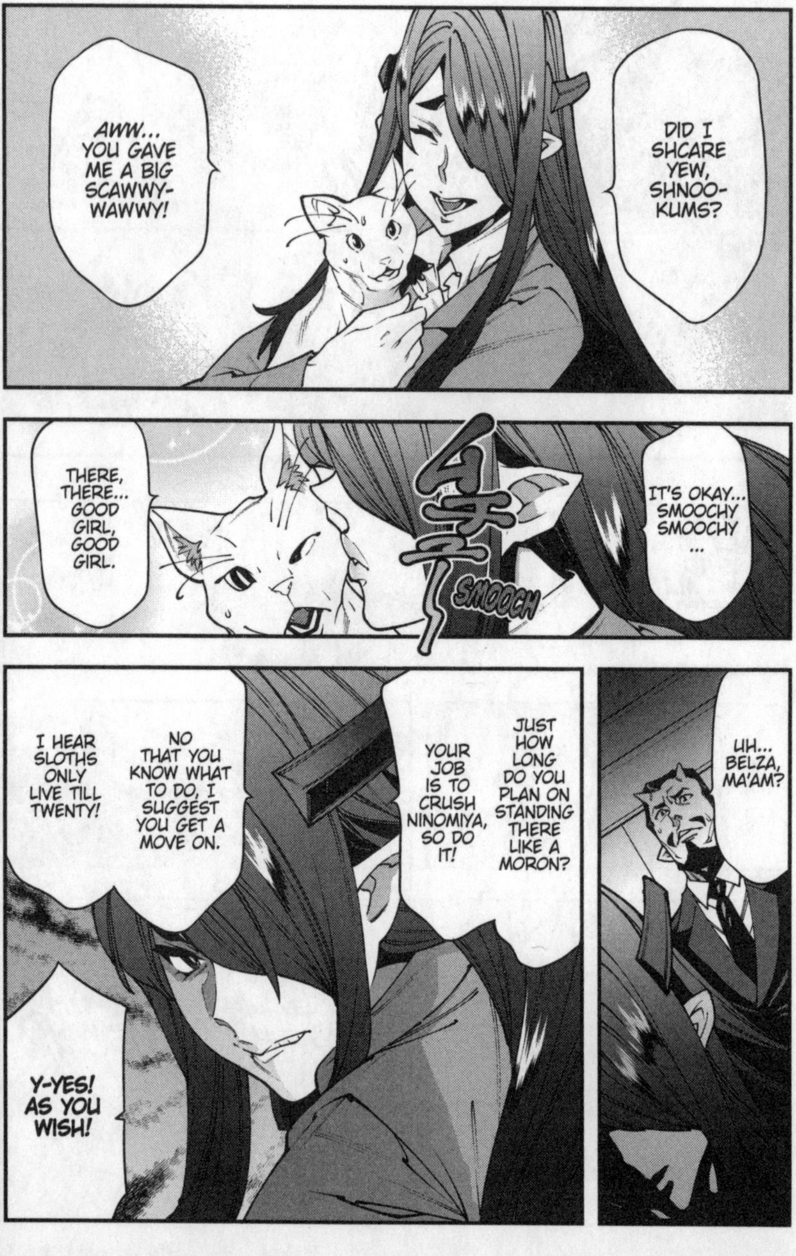
DID I SHCARE YEW, SHNOO-KUMS?
AWW... YOU GAVE ME A BIG SCAWWY-WAWWY!
IT'S OKAY... SMOOCHY SMOOCHY ...
SMOOCH
THERE, THERE... GOOD GIRL, GOOD GIRL.
UH... BELZA, MA'AM?
JUST HOW LONG DO YOU PLAN ON STANDING THERE LIKE A MORON?
YOUR JOB IS TO CRUSH NINOMIYA, SO DO IT!
NO THAT YOU KNOW WHAT TO DO, I SUGGEST YOU GET A MOVE ON.
I HEAR SLOTHS ONLY LIVE TILL TWENTY!
Y-YES! AS YOU WISH!

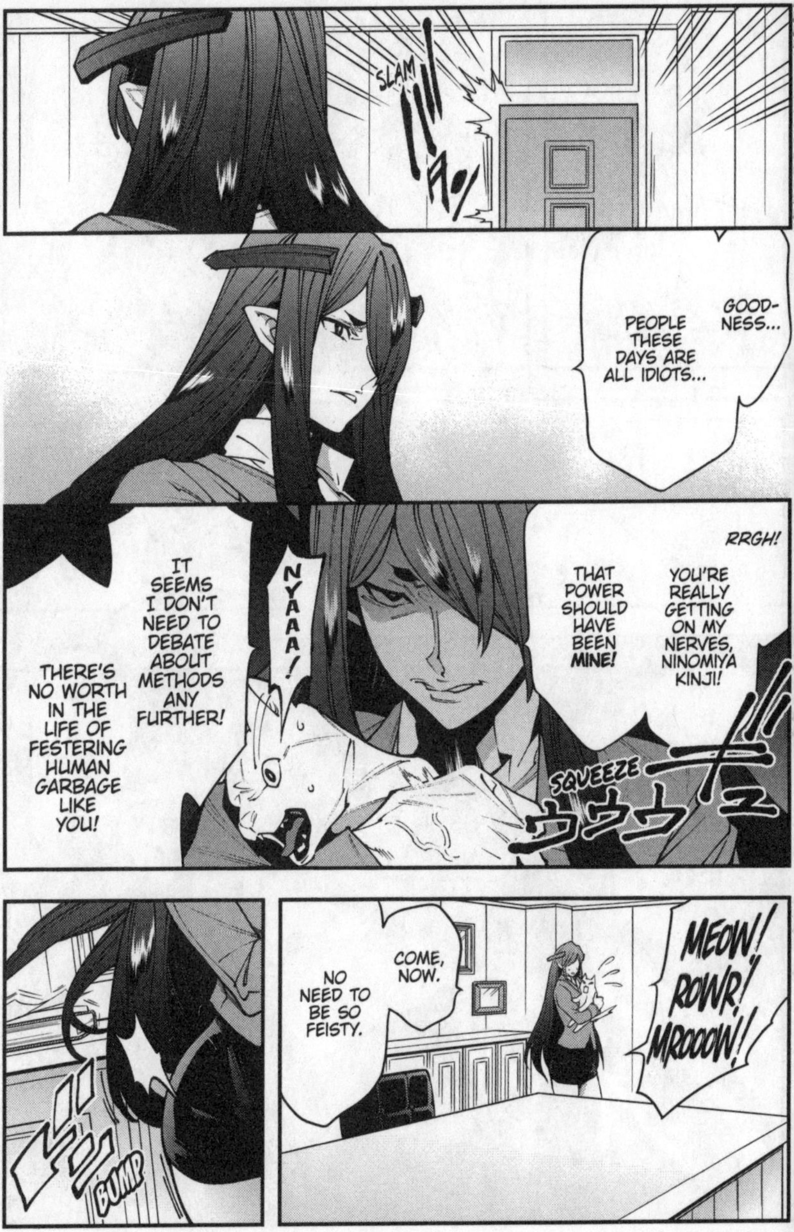
SLAM
GOODNESS...
PEOPLE THESE DAYS ARE ALL IDIOTS...
RRGH!
YOU'RE REALLY GETTING ON MY NERVES, NINOMIYA KINJI!
THAT POWER SHOULD HAVE BEEN MINE!
SQUEEZE
NYAAA!
IT SEEMS I DON'T NEED TO DEBATE ABOUT METHODS ANY FURTHER!
THERE'S NO WORTH IN THE LIFE OF FESTERING HUMAN GARBAGE LIKE YOU!
MEOW! ROWR! MROOOW!
COME, NOW.
NO NEED TO BE SO FEISTY.
BUMP

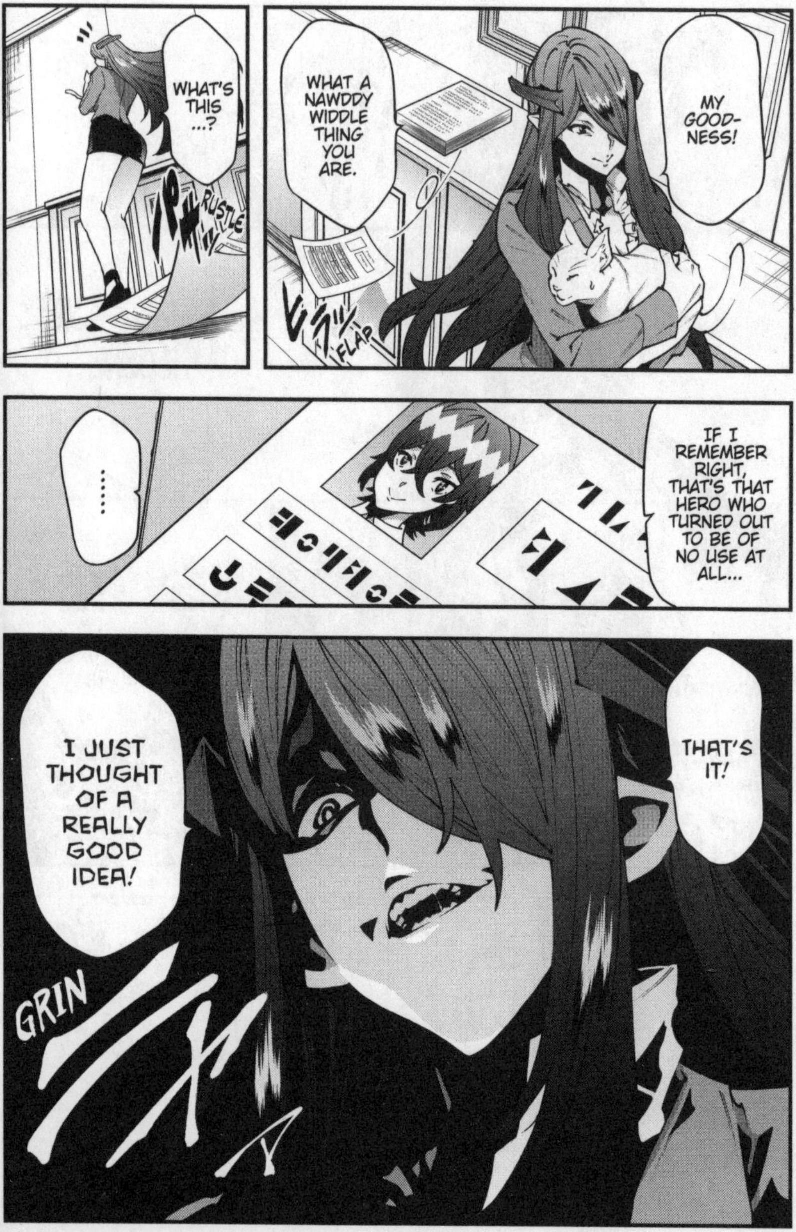
MY GOODNESS!
WHAT A NAWDDY WIDDLE THING YOU ARE.
FLAP
WHAT'S THIS ...?
RUSTLE
IF I REMEMBER RIGHT, THAT'S THAT HERO WHO TURNED OUT TO BE OF NO USE AT ALL...
......
THAT'S IT!
I JUST THOUGHT OF A REALLY GOOD IDEA!
GRIN

RANGA
BELZA
COSTUME
VERSION

THE DUNGEON OF
BLACK COMPANY

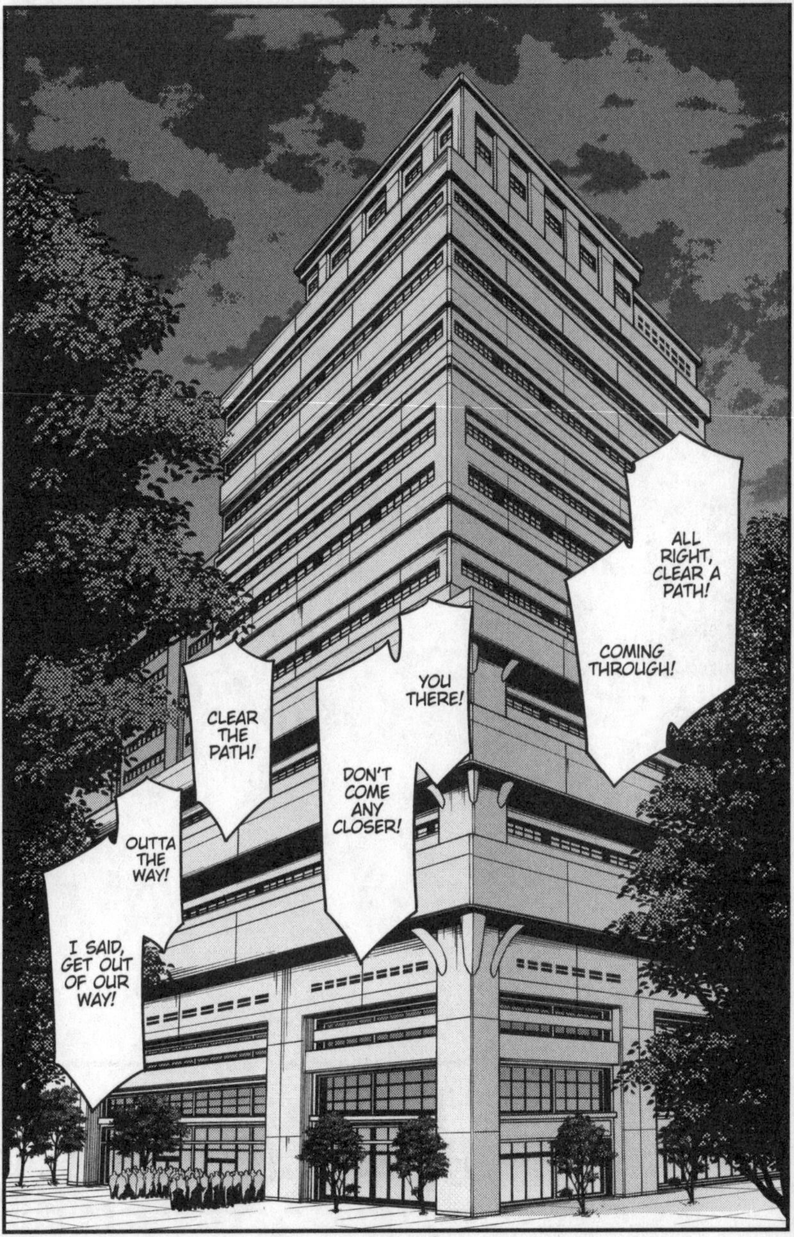
ALL RIGHT, CLEAR A PATH!
COMING THROUGH!
YOU THERE!
DON'T COME ANY CLOSER!
CLEAR THE PATH!
OUTTA THE WAY!
I SAID, GET OUT OF OUR WAY!

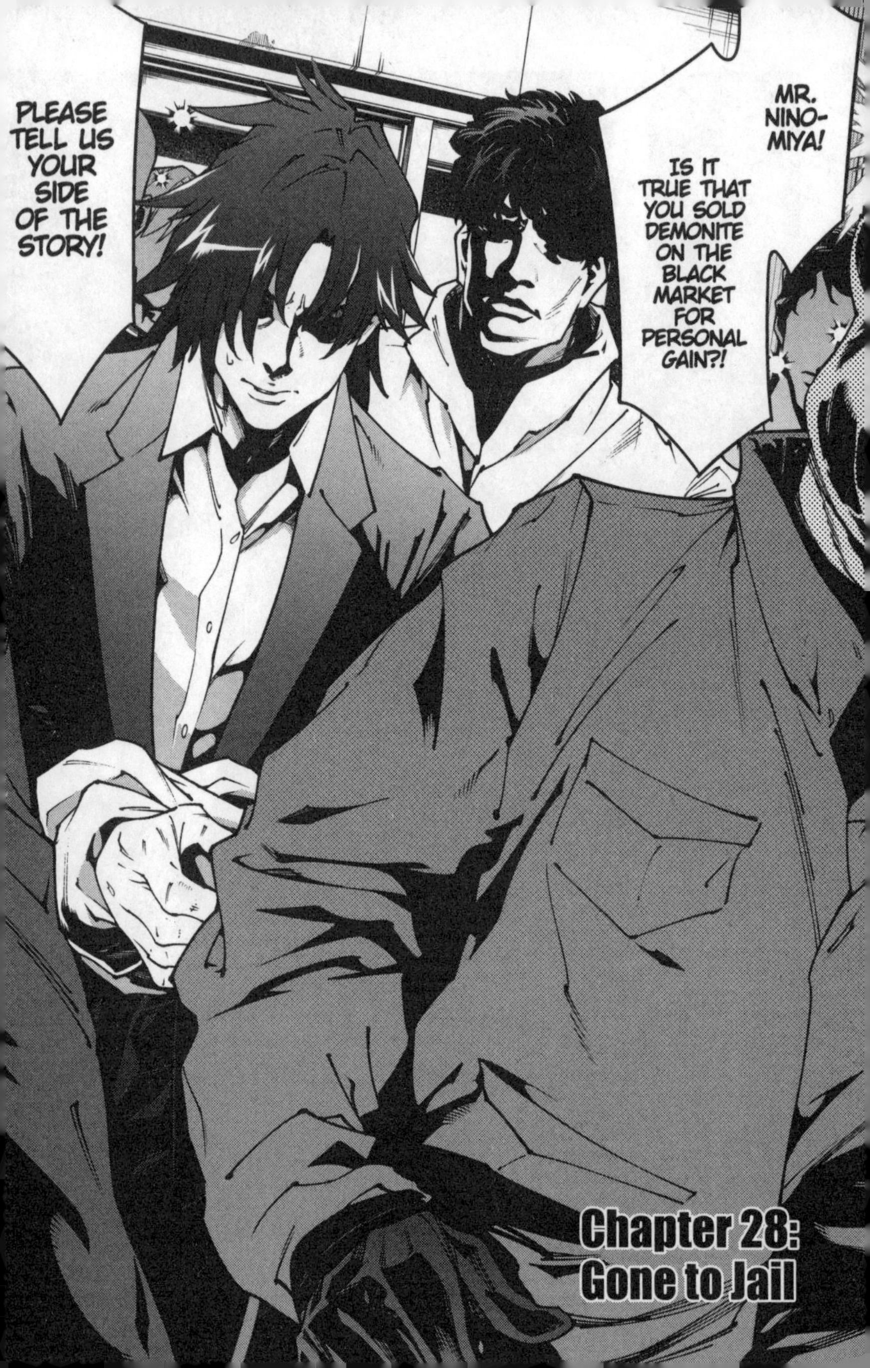
MR. NINO-MIYA!
IS IT TRUE THAT YOU SOLD DEMONITE ON THE BLACK MARKET FOR PERSONAL GAIN?!
PLEASE TELL US YOUR SIDE OF THE STORY!

Chapter 28: Gone to Jail

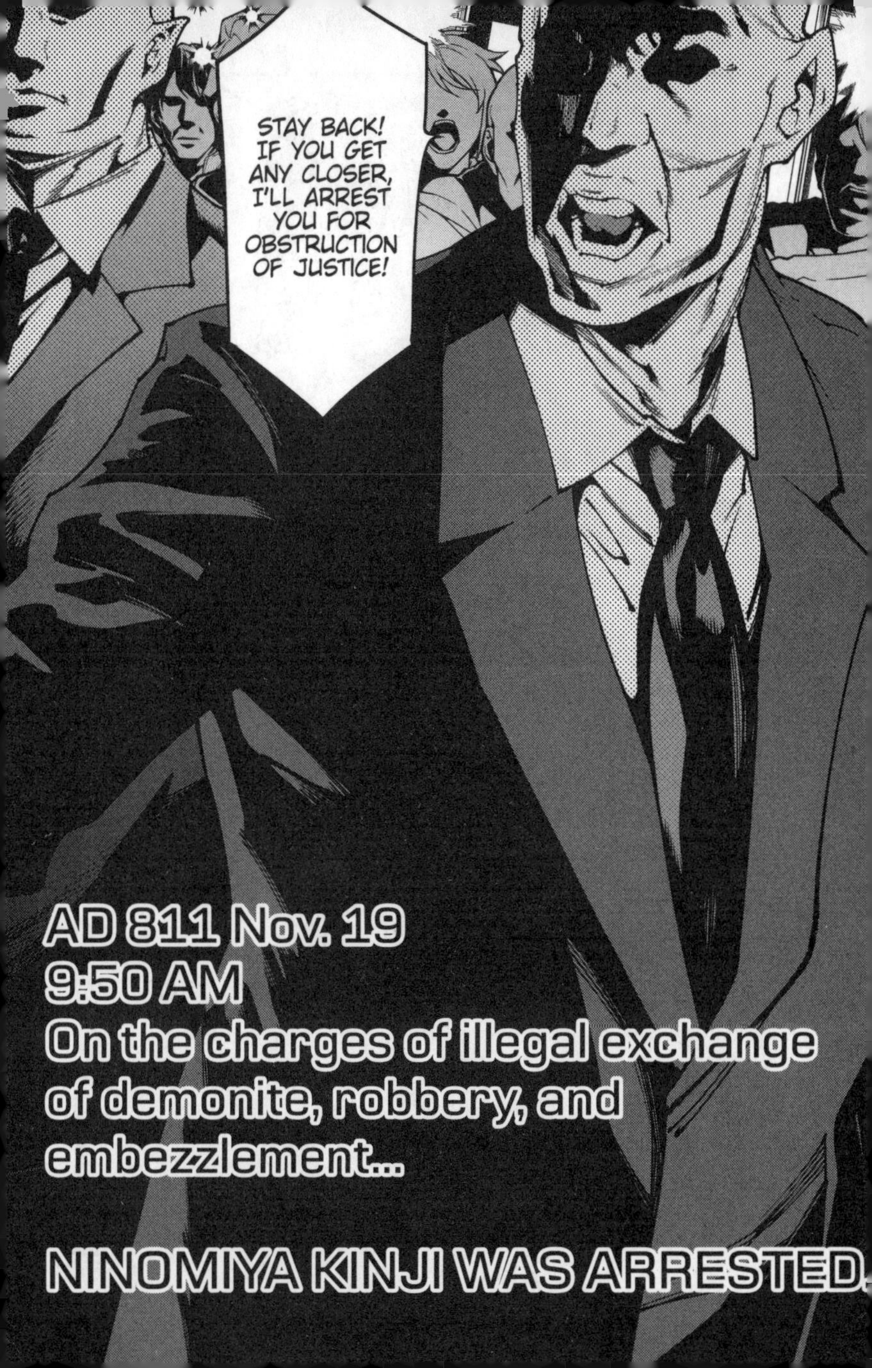
STAY BACK! IF YOU GET ANY CLOSER, I'LL ARREST YOU FOR OBSTRUCTION OF JUSTICE!
AD 811 Nov. 19
9:50 AM
On the charges of illegal exchange of demonite, robbery, and embezzlement...
NINOMIYA KINJI WAS ARRESTED.

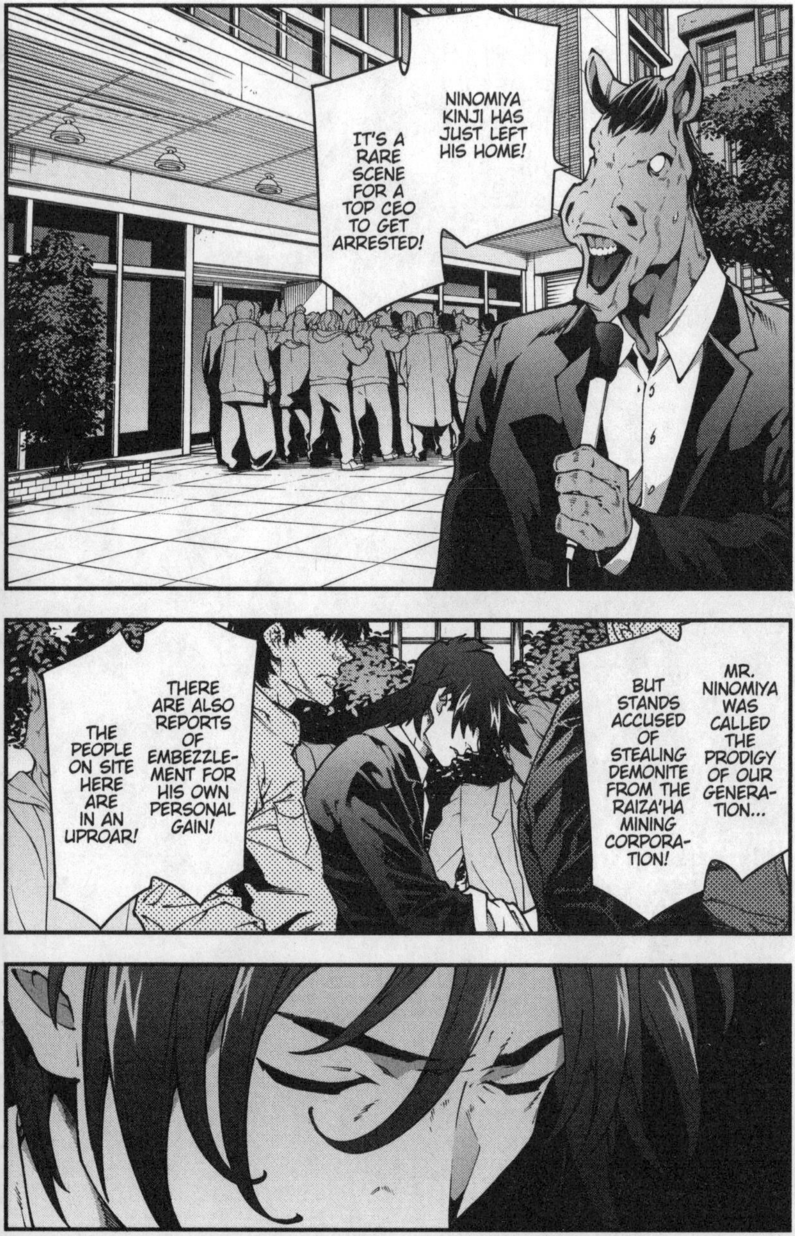
NINOMIYA KINJI HAS JUST LEFT HIS HOME!
IT'S A RARE SCENE FOR A TOP CEO TO GET ARRESTED!
MR. NINOMIYA WAS CALLED THE PRODIGY OF OUR GENERATION...
BUT STANDS ACCUSED OF STEALING DEMONITE FROM THE RAIZA'HA MINING CORPORATION!
THERE ARE ALSO REPORTS OF EMBEZZLEMENT FOR HIS OWN PERSONAL GAIN!
THE PEOPLE ON SITE HERE ARE IN AN UPROAR!

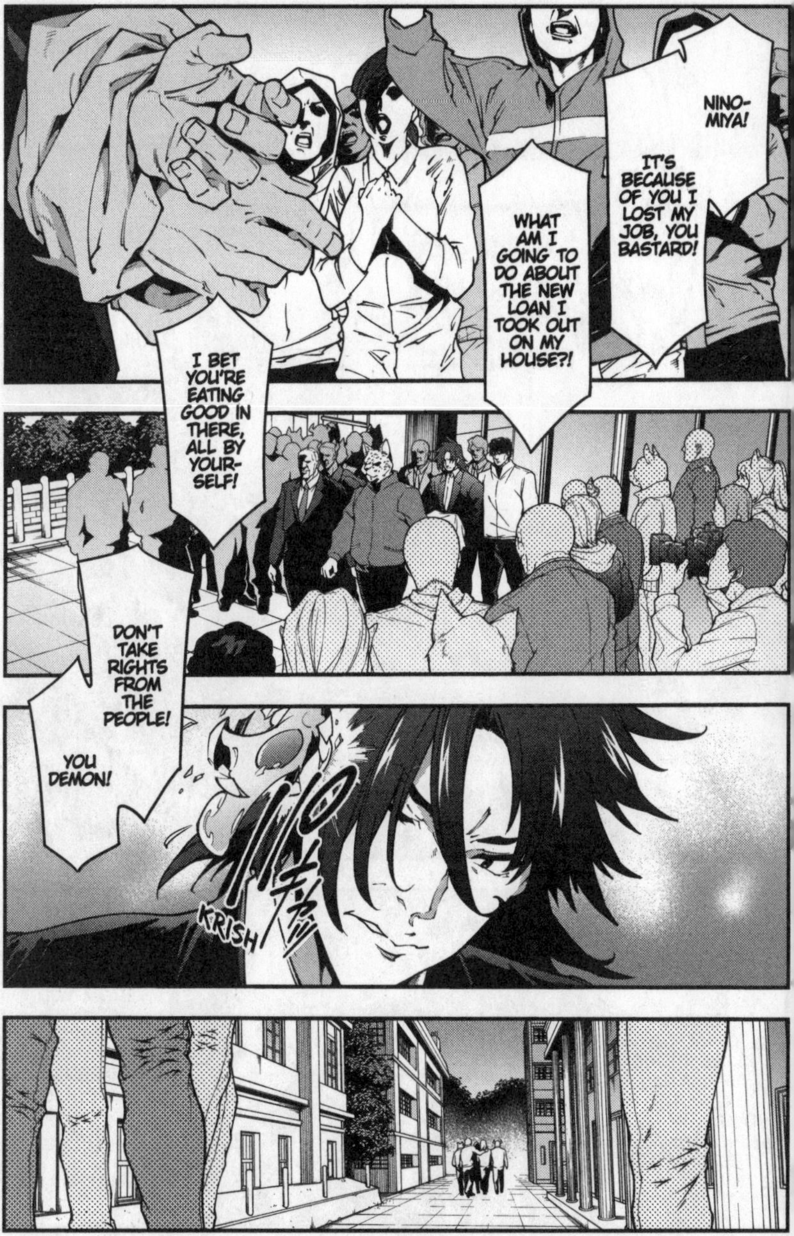
NINO-MIYA!
IT'S BECAUSE OF YOU I LOST MY JOB, YOU BASTARD!
WHAT AM I GOING TO DO ABOUT THE NEW LOAN I TOOK OUT ON MY HOUSE?!
I BET YOU'RE EATING GOOD IN THERE, ALL BY YOUR-SELF!
DON'T TAKE RIGHTS FROM THE PEOPLE!
YOU DEMON!
KRISH

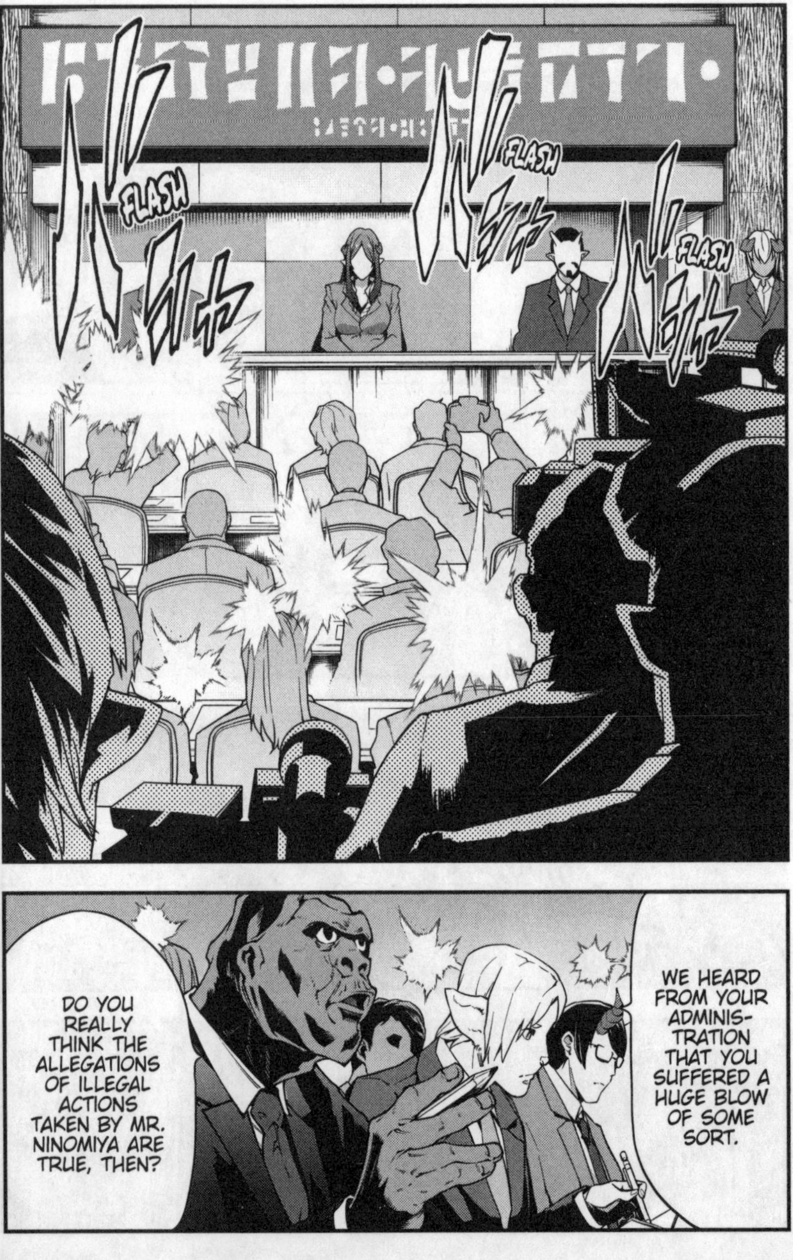
FLASH
FLASH
FLASH
WE HEARD FROM YOUR ADMINIS-TRATION THAT YOU SUFFERED A HUGE BLOW OF SOME SORT.
DO YOU REALLY THINK THE ALLEGATIONS OF ILLEGAL ACTIONS TAKEN BY MR. NINOMIYA ARE TRUE, THEN?

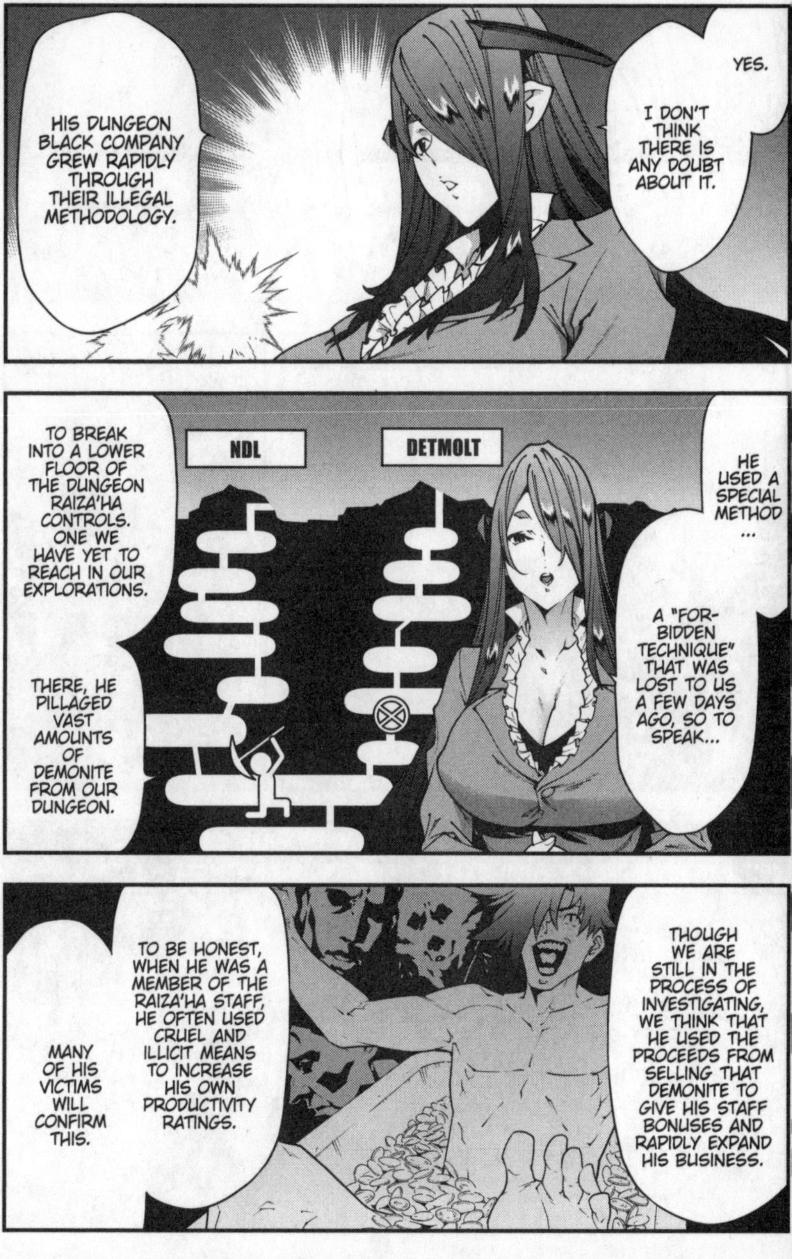
YES.
I DON'T THINK THERE IS ANY DOUBT ABOUT IT.
HIS DUNGEON BLACK COMPANY GREW RAPIDLY THROUGH THEIR ILLEGAL METHODOLOGY.
HE USED A SPECIAL METHOD ...
A "FOR-BIDDEN TECHNIQUE" THAT WAS LOST TO US A FEW DAYS AGO, SO TO SPEAK...
DETMOLT
NDL
TO BREAK INTO A LOWER FLOOR OF THE DUNGEON RAIZA'HA CONTROLS. ONE WE HAVE YET TO REACH IN OUR EXPLORATIONS.
THERE, HE PILLAGED VAST AMOUNTS OF DEMONITE FROM OUR DUNGEON.
THOUGH WE ARE STILL IN THE PROCESS OF INVESTIGATING, WE THINK THAT HE USED THE PROCEEDS FROM SELLING THAT DEMONITE TO GIVE HIS STAFF BONUSES AND RAPIDLY EXPAND HIS BUSINESS.
TO BE HONEST, WHEN HE WAS A MEMBER OF THE RAIZA'HA STAFF, HE OFTEN USED CRUEL AND ILLICIT MEANS TO INCREASE HIS OWN PRODUCTIVITY RATINGS.
MANY OF HIS VICTIMS WILL CONFIRM THIS.

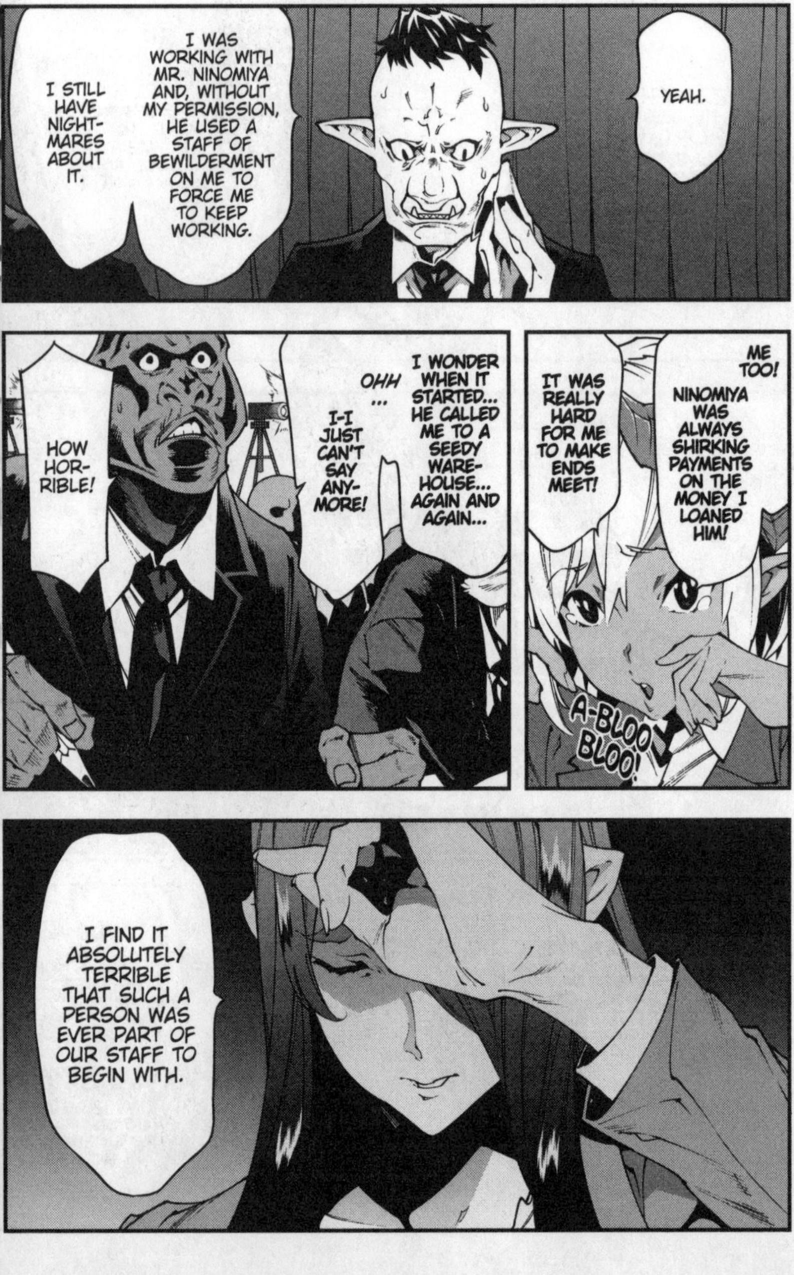
YEAH.
I WAS WORKING WITH MR. NINOMIYA AND, WITHOUT MY PERMISSION, HE USED A STAFF OF BEWILDERMENT ON ME TO FORCE ME TO KEEP WORKING.
I STILL HAVE NIGHTMARES ABOUT IT.
ME TOO! NINOMIYA WAS ALWAYS SHIRKING PAYMENTS ON THE MONEY I LOANED HIM!
IT WAS REALLY HARD FOR ME TO MAKE ENDS MEET!
A-BLOO BLOO!
I WONDER WHEN IT STARTED... HE CALLED ME TO A SEEDY WAREHOUSE... AGAIN AND AGAIN...
OHH ... I-I JUST CAN'T SAY ANYMORE!
HOW HORRIBLE!
I FIND IT ABSOLUTELY TERRIBLE THAT SUCH A PERSON WAS EVER PART OF OUR STAFF TO BEGIN WITH.

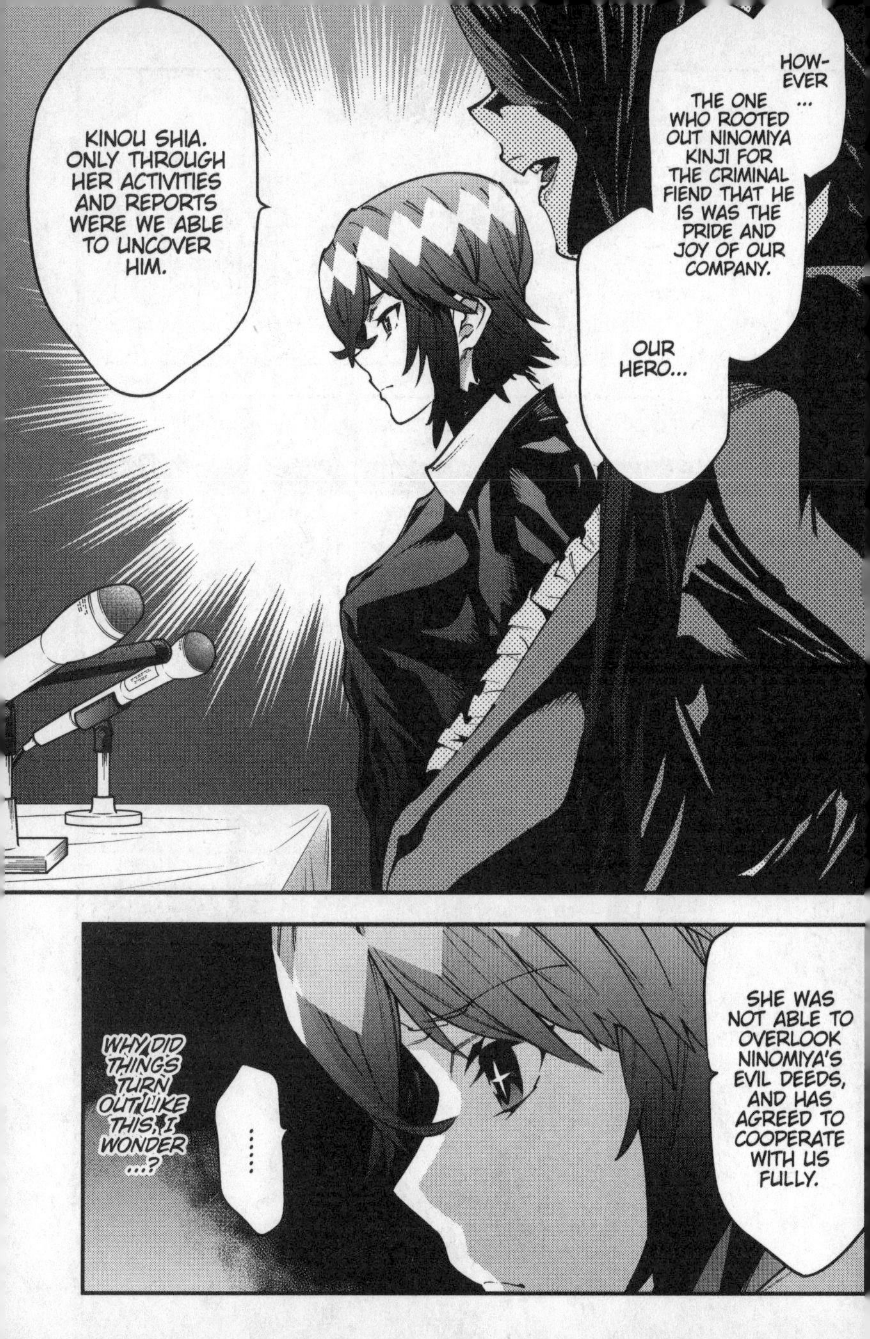
HOW-EVER... THE ONE WHO ROOTED OUT NINOMIYA KINJI FOR THE CRIMINAL FIEND THAT HE IS WAS THE PRIDE AND JOY OF OUR COMPANY.
OUR HERO...
KINOU SHIA. ONLY THROUGH HER ACTIVITIES AND REPORTS WERE WE ABLE TO UNCOVER HIM.
SHE WAS NOT ABLE TO OVERLOOK NINOMIYA'S EVIL DEEDS, AND HAS AGREED TO COOPERATE WITH US FULLY.
......
WHY DID THINGS TURN OUT LIKE THIS, I WONDER...?

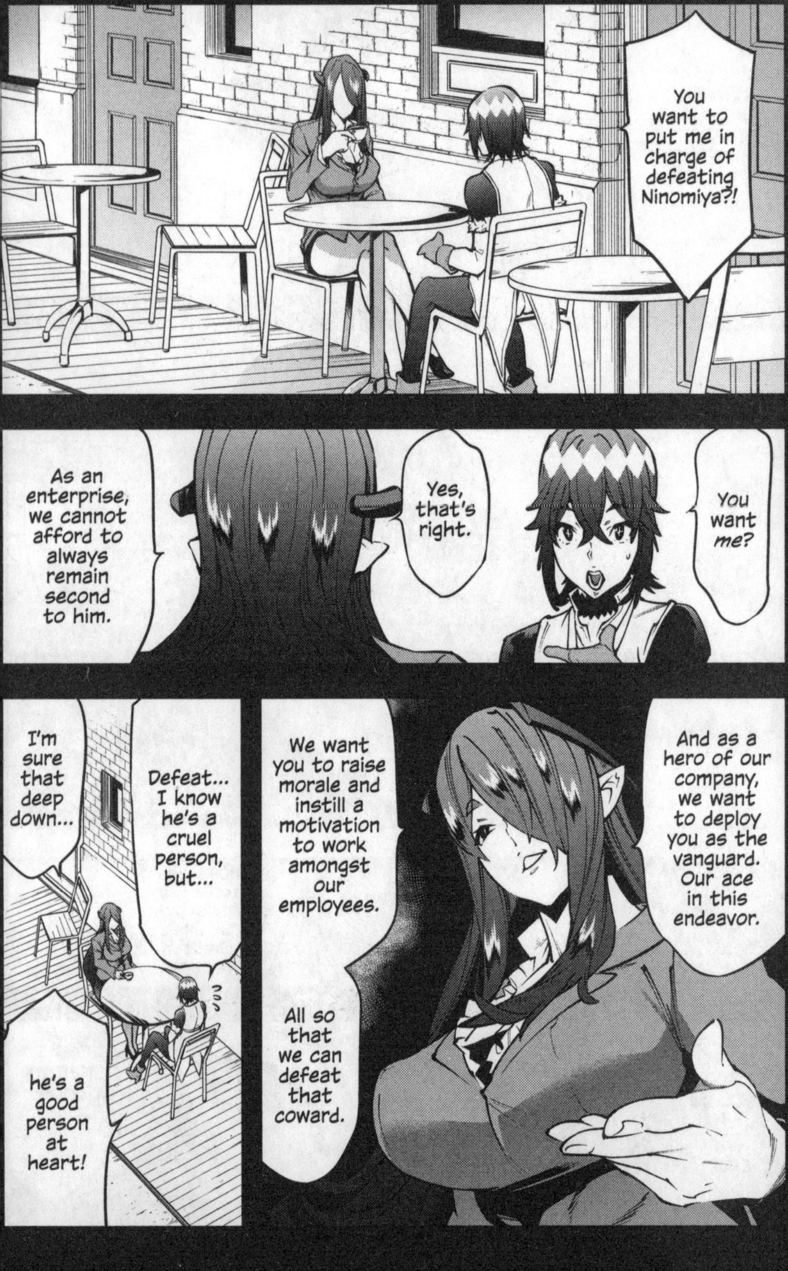
You want to put me in charge of defeating Ninomiya?!
You want *me*?
Yes, that's right.
As an enterprise, we cannot afford to always remain second to him.
And as a hero of our company, we want to deploy you as the vanguard. Our ace in this endeavor.
We want you to raise morale and instill a motivation to work amongst our employees.
All so that we can defeat that coward.
Defeat... I know he's a cruel person, but...
I'm sure that deep down...
he's a good person at heart!

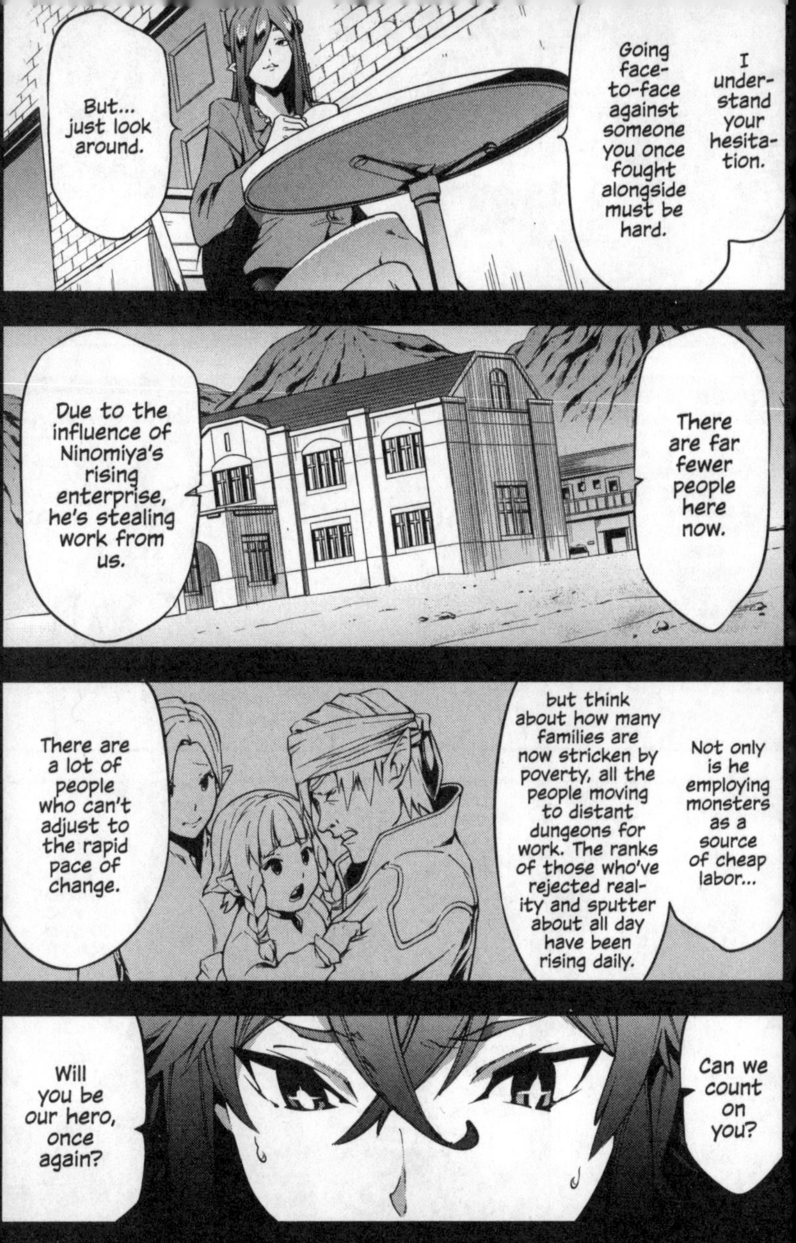
I understand your hesitation.
Going face-to-face against someone you once fought alongside must be hard.
But... just look around.
There are far fewer people here now.
Due to the influence of Ninomiya's rising enterprise, he's stealing work from us.
Not only is he employing monsters as a source of cheap labor...
but think about how many families are now stricken by poverty, all the people moving to distant dungeons for work. The ranks of those who've rejected reality and sputter about all day have been rising daily.
There are a lot of people who can't adjust to the rapid pace of change.
Can we count on you?
Will you be our hero, once again?

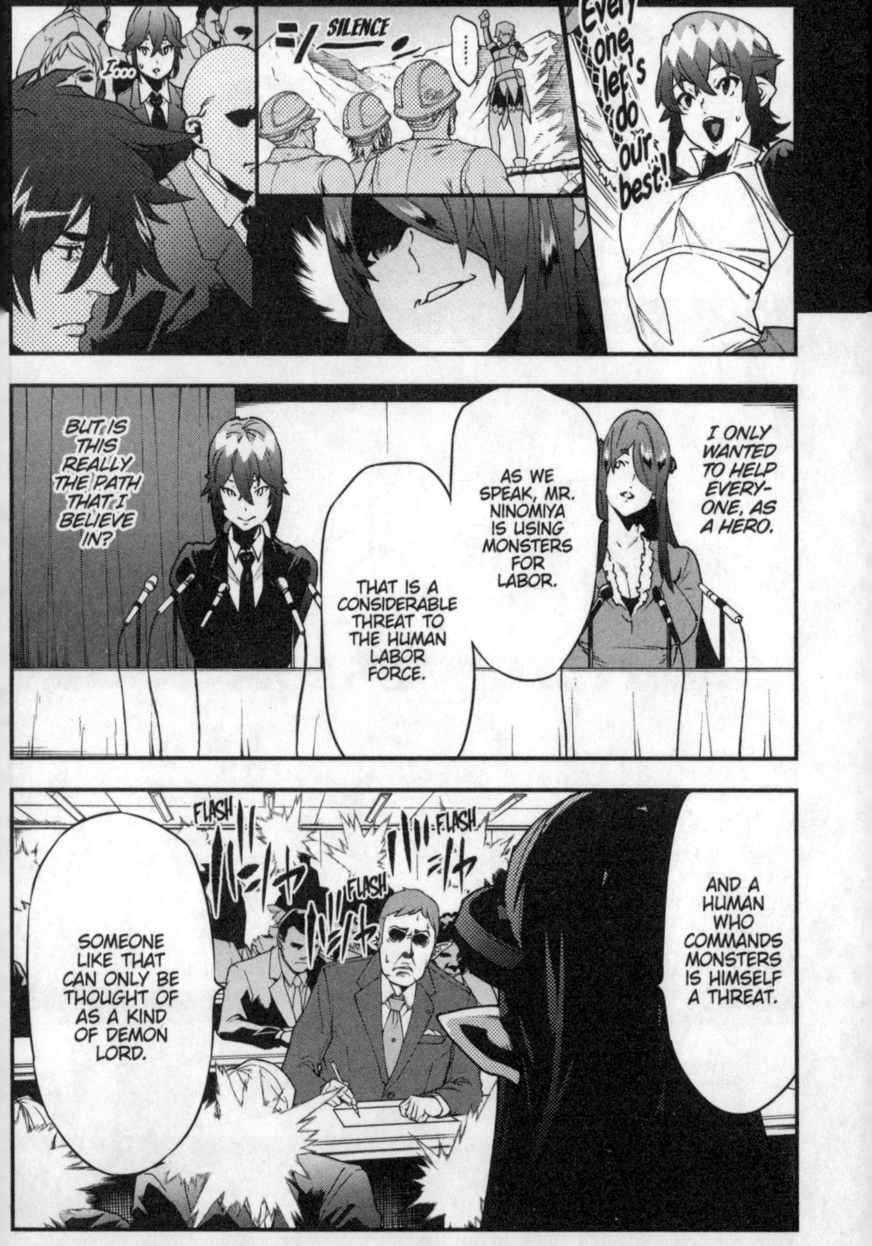
Every-one let's do our best!
SILENCE
......
I...
I ONLY WANTED TO HELP EVERY-ONE, AS A HERO.
AS WE SPEAK, MR. NINOMIYA IS USING MONSTERS FOR LABOR.
THAT IS A CONSIDERABLE THREAT TO THE HUMAN LABOR FORCE.
BUT IS THIS REALLY THE PATH THAT I BELIEVE IN?
AND A HUMAN WHO COMMANDS MONSTERS IS HIMSELF A THREAT.
FLASH
FLASH
FLASH
SOMEONE LIKE THAT CAN ONLY BE THOUGHT OF AS A KIND OF DEMON LORD.

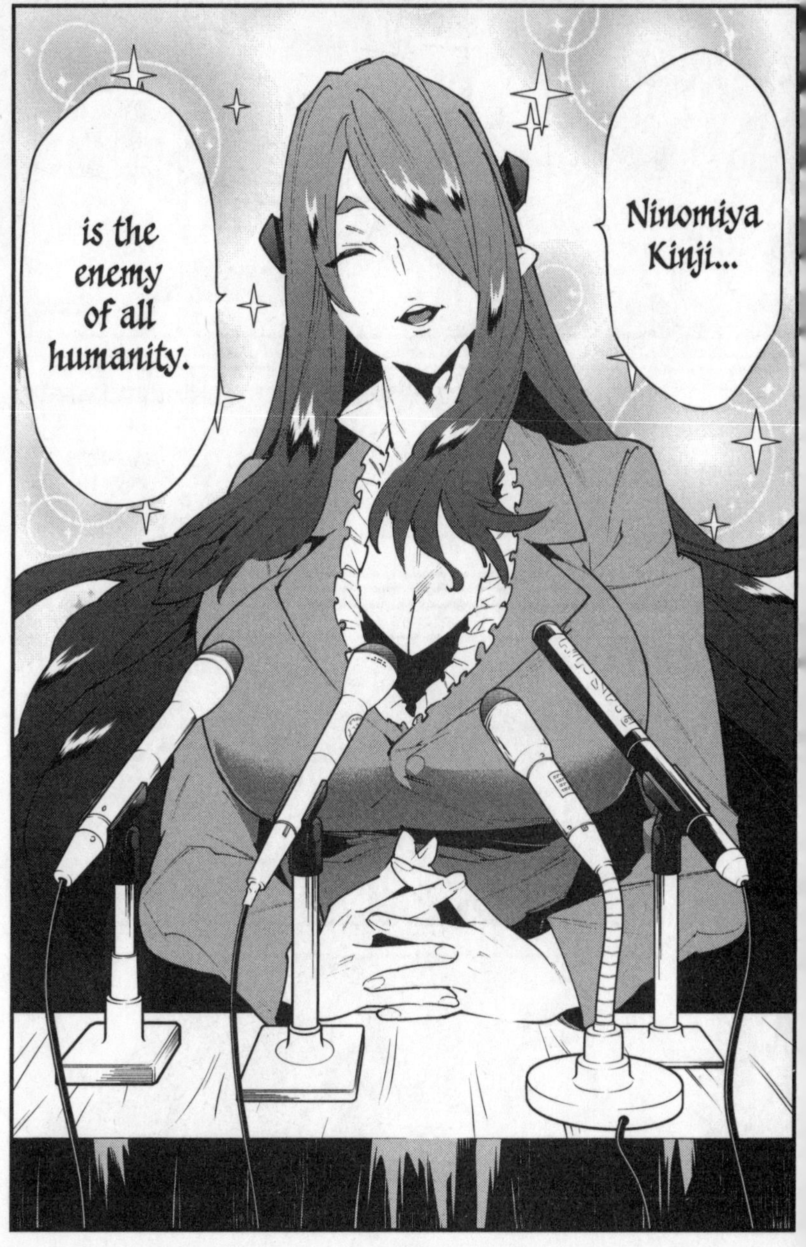
Ninomiya Kinji...
is the enemy of all humanity.

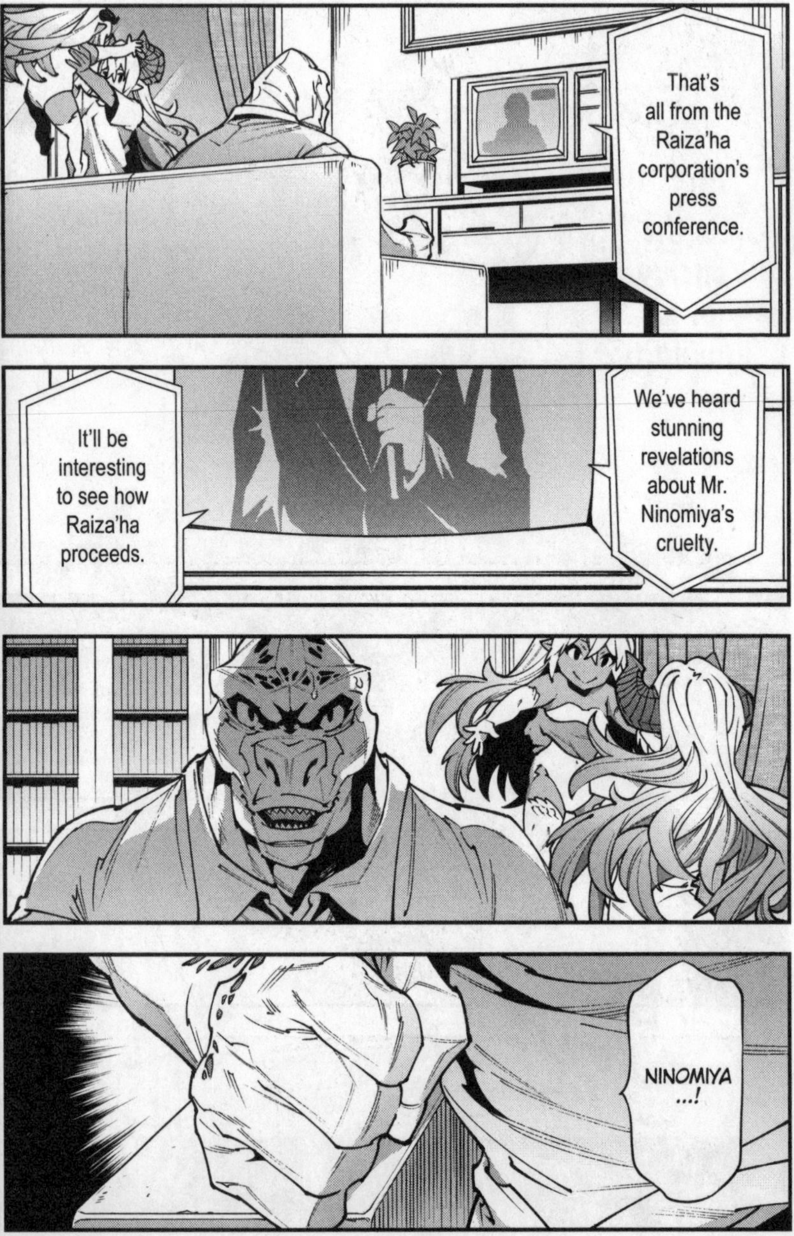
That's all from the Raiza'ha corporation's press conference.
We've heard stunning revelations about Mr. Ninomiya's cruelty.
It'll be interesting to see how Raiza'ha proceeds.
NINOMIYA ...!

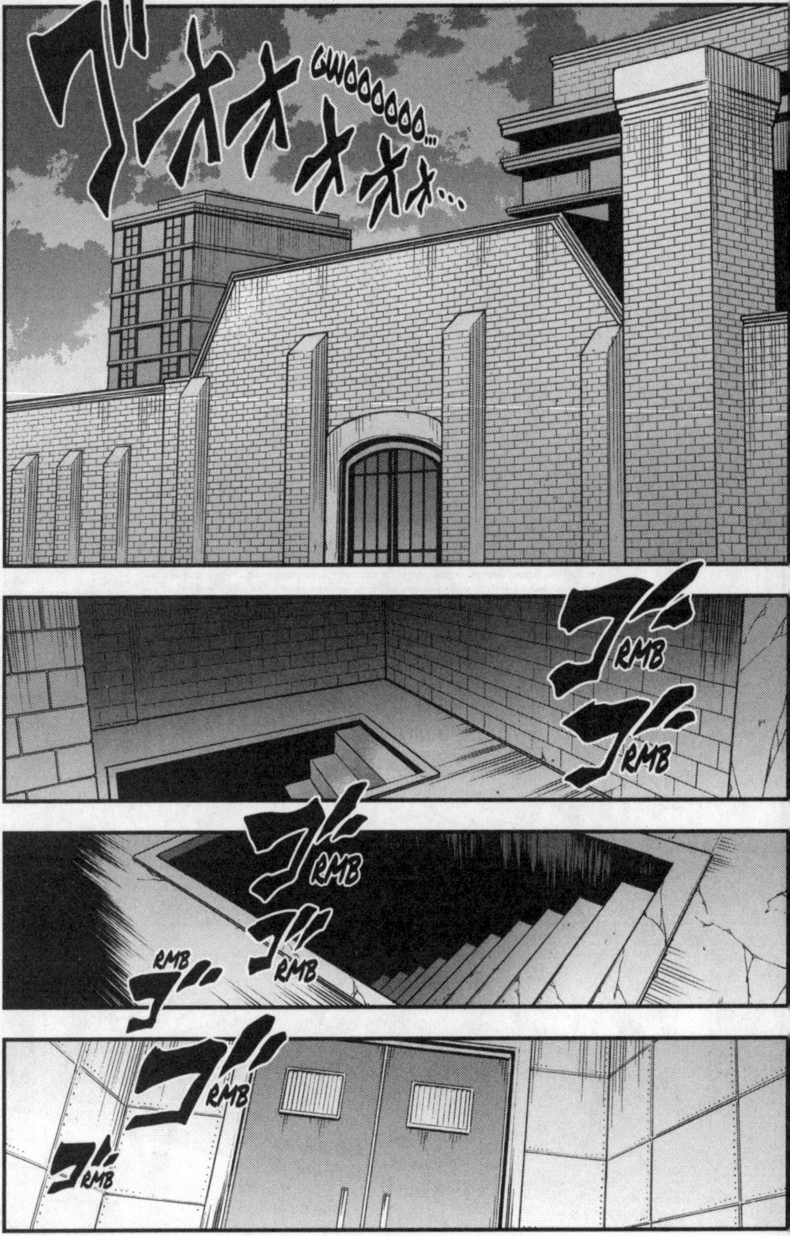
ヴォオオ
GWOOOOOOO...
オォォ…
RMB
RMB
RMB
RMB
RMB
RMB
RMB

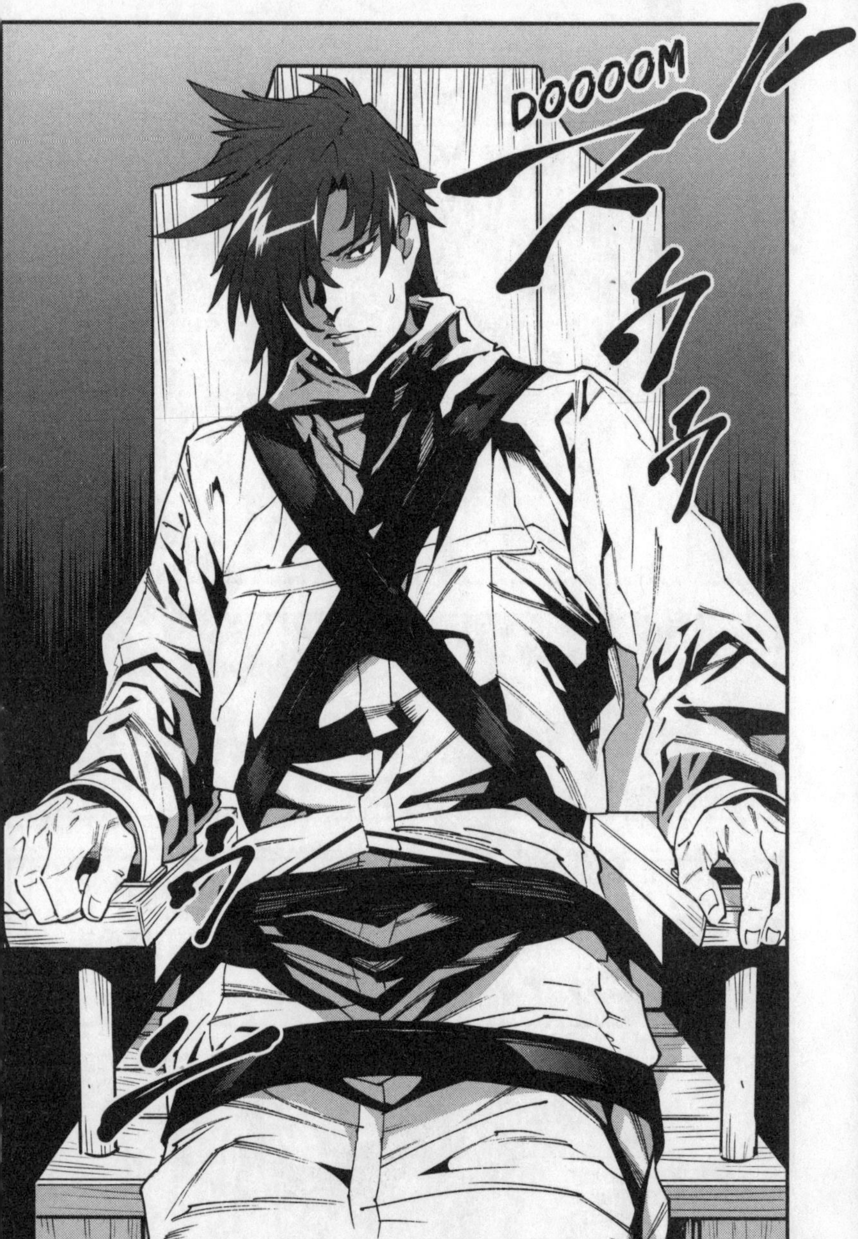
DOOOOM

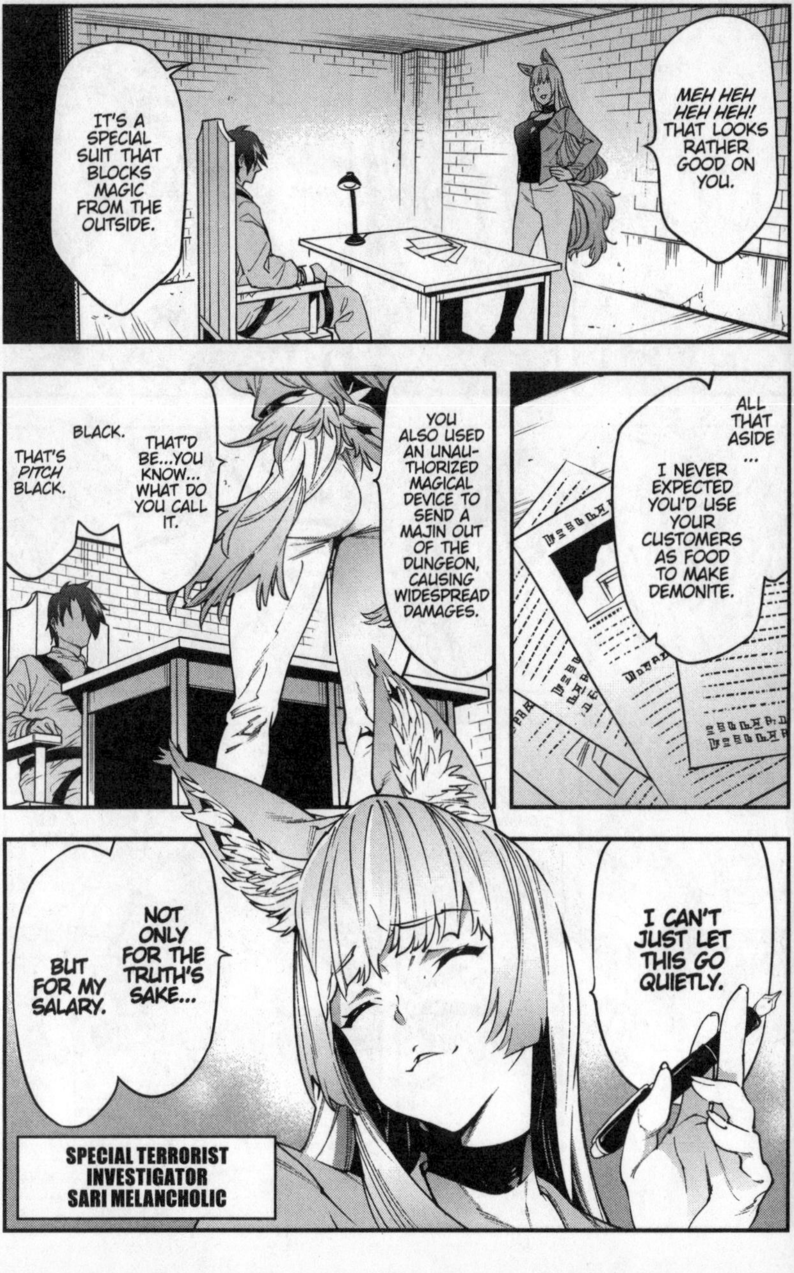
MEH HEH HEH HEH! THAT LOOKS RATHER GOOD ON YOU.
IT'S A SPECIAL SUIT THAT BLOCKS MAGIC FROM THE OUTSIDE.
ALL THAT ASIDE...
I NEVER EXPECTED YOU'D USE YOUR CUSTOMERS AS FOOD TO MAKE DEMONITE.
YOU ALSO USED AN UNAUTHORIZED MAGICAL DEVICE TO SEND A MAJIN OUT OF THE DUNGEON, CAUSING WIDESPREAD DAMAGES.
THAT'D BE...YOU KNOW... WHAT DO YOU CALL IT.
BLACK.
THAT'S *PITCH* BLACK.
I CAN'T JUST LET THIS GO QUIETLY.
NOT ONLY FOR THE TRUTH'S SAKE...
BUT FOR MY SALARY.
SPECIAL TERRORIST INVESTIGATOR SARI MELANCHOLIC

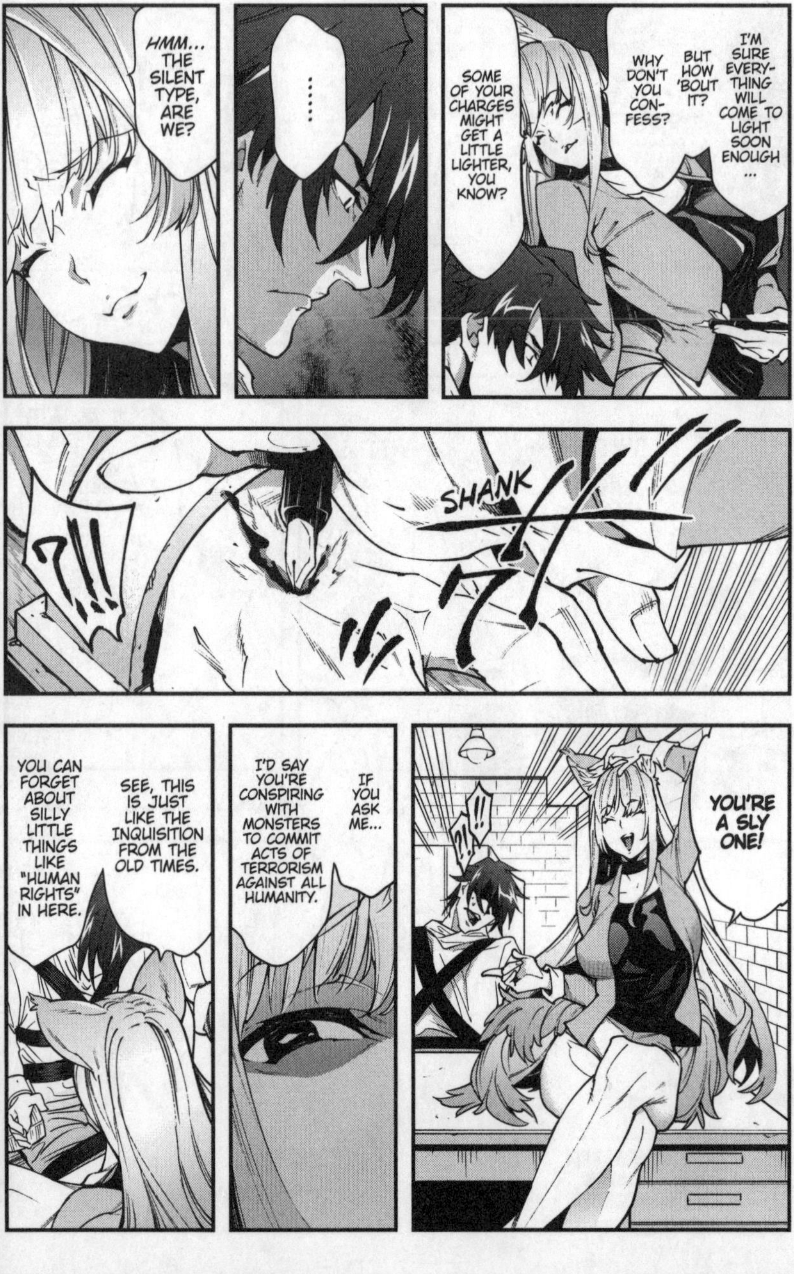

I'M SURE EVERY-THING WILL COME TO LIGHT SOON ENOUGH...
BUT HOW 'BOUT IT?
WHY DON'T YOU CON-FESS?
SOME OF YOUR CHARGES MIGHT GET A LITTLE LIGHTER, YOU KNOW?
......
HMM... THE SILENT TYPE, ARE WE?
SHANK
?!!
YOU'RE A SLY ONE!
?!!
IF YOU ASK ME...
I'D SAY YOU'RE CONSPIRING WITH MONSTERS TO COMMIT ACTS OF TERRORISM AGAINST ALL HUMANITY.
SEE, THIS IS JUST LIKE THE INQUISITION FROM THE OLD TIMES.
YOU CAN FORGET ABOUT SILLY LITTLE THINGS LIKE "HUMAN RIGHTS" IN HERE.

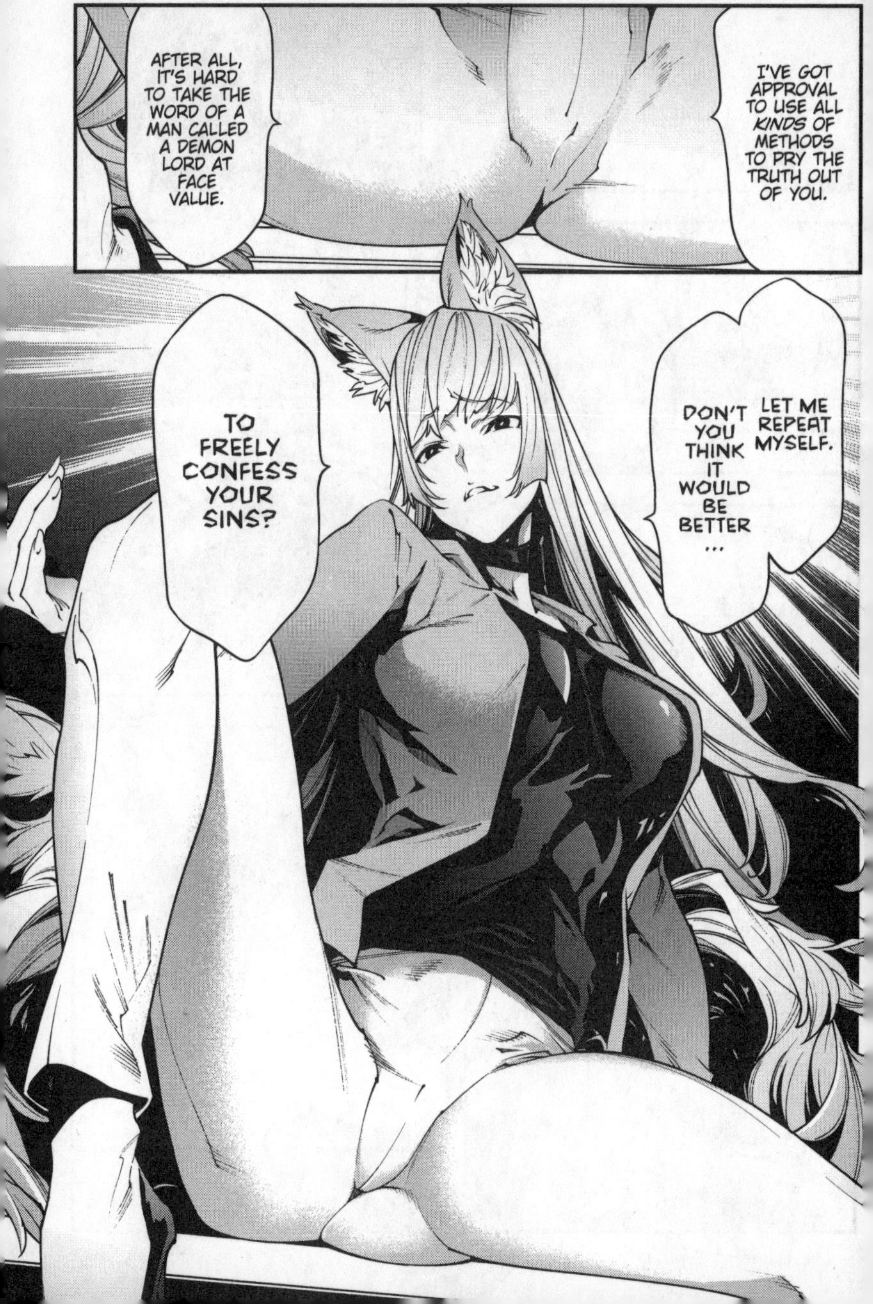
I'VE GOT APPROVAL TO USE ALL KINDS OF METHODS TO PRY THE TRUTH OUT OF YOU.
AFTER ALL, IT'S HARD TO TAKE THE WORD OF A MAN CALLED A DEMON LORD AT FACE VALUE.
LET ME REPEAT MYSELF.
DON'T YOU THINK IT WOULD BE BETTER...
TO FREELY CONFESS YOUR SINS?

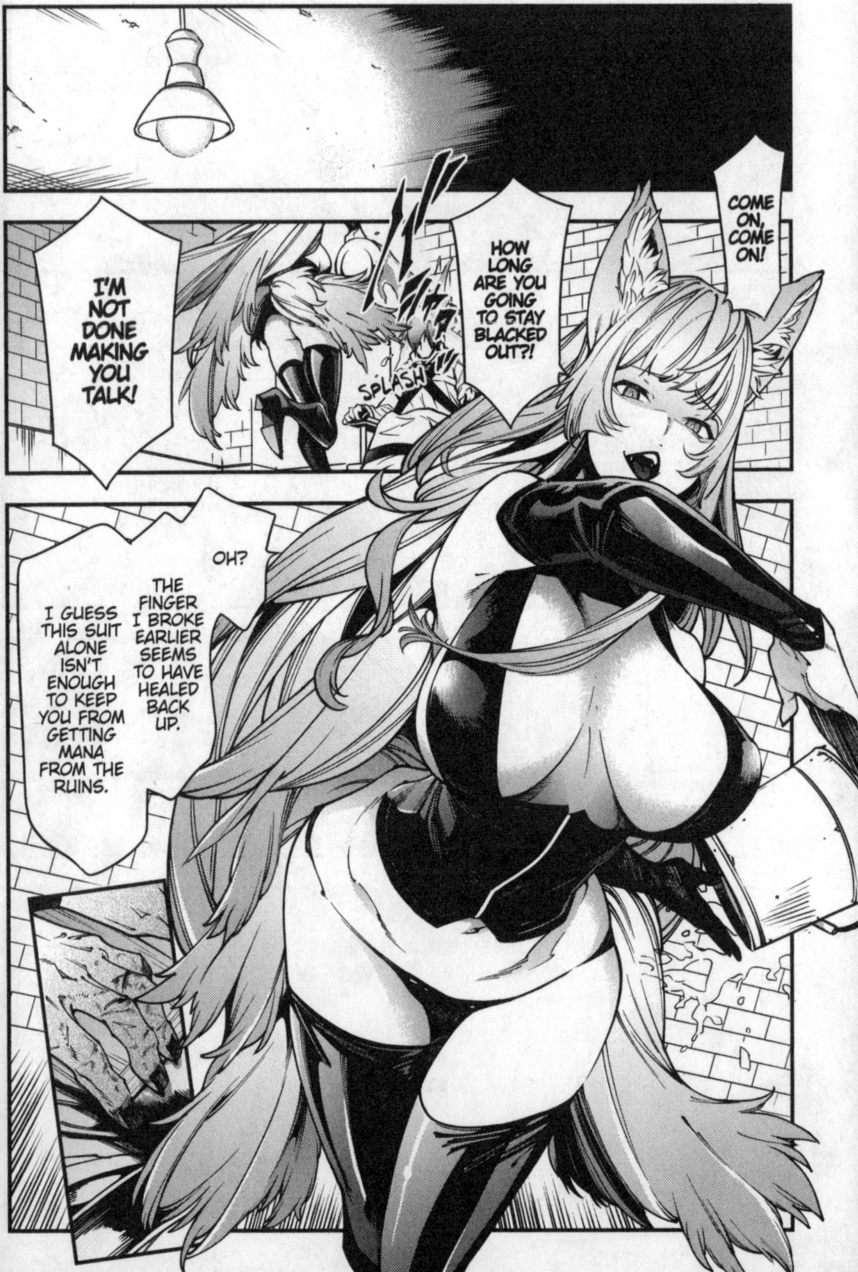
COME ON, COME ON!
HOW LONG ARE YOU GOING TO STAY BLACKED OUT?!
SPLASH
I'M NOT DONE MAKING YOU TALK!
OH?
THE FINGER I BROKE EARLIER SEEMS TO HAVE HEALED BACK UP.
I GUESS THIS SUIT ALONE ISN'T ENOUGH TO KEEP YOU FROM GETTING MANA FROM THE RUINS.

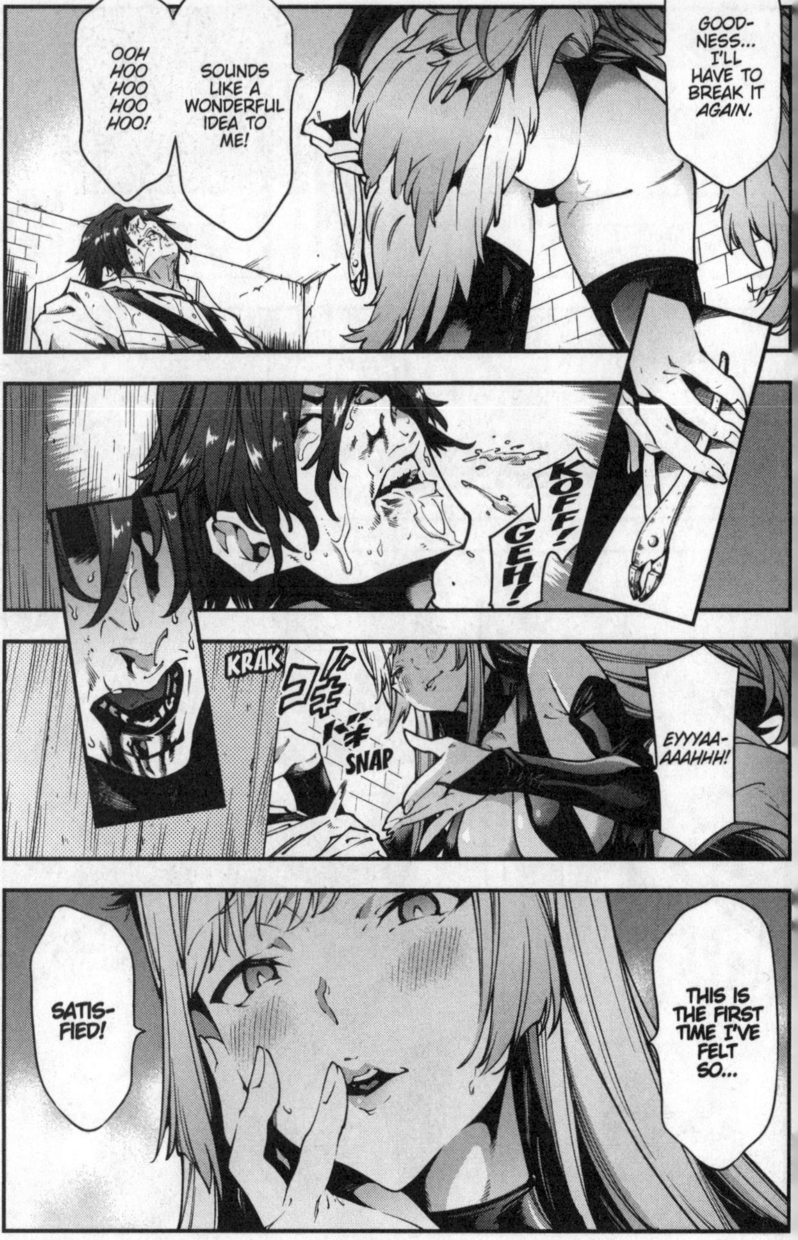

GOOD-NESS... I'LL HAVE TO BREAK IT AGAIN.
SOUNDS LIKE A WONDERFUL IDEA TO ME!
OOH HOO HOO HOO HOO!
KOFF!
GEH!
EYYYAA-AAAHHH!
KRAK
SNAP
THIS IS THE FIRST TIME I'VE FELT SO...
SATIS-FIED!

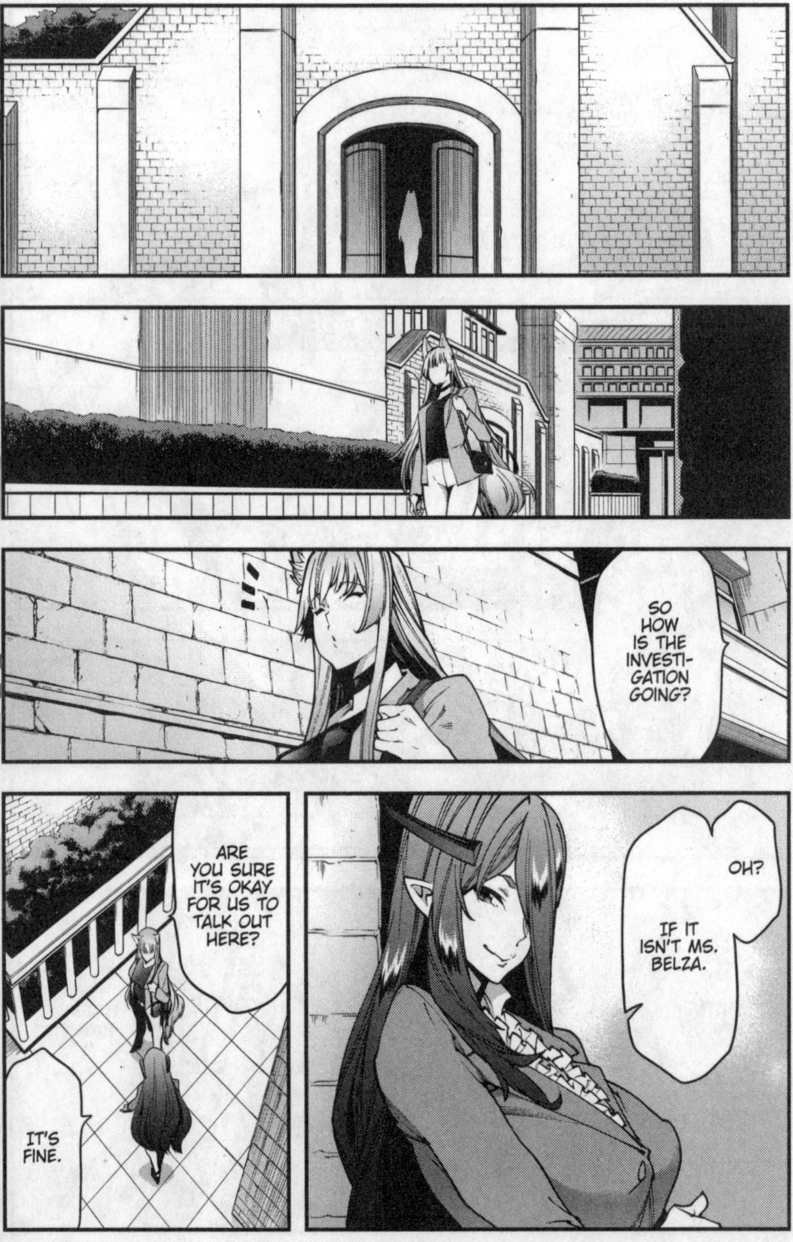
SO HOW IS THE INVESTIGATION GOING?
OH?
IF IT ISN'T MS. BELZA.
ARE YOU SURE IT'S OKAY FOR US TO TALK OUT HERE?
IT'S FINE.

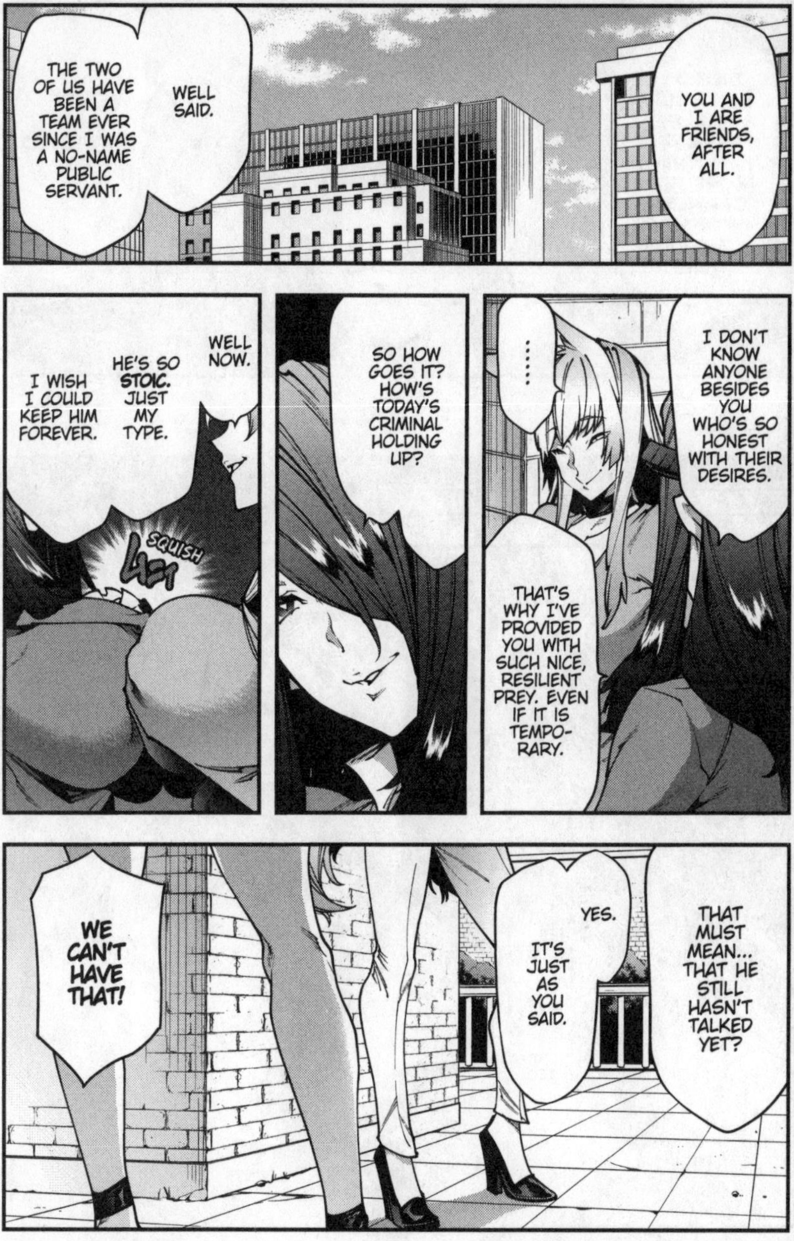
YOU AND I ARE FRIENDS, AFTER ALL.
WELL SAID.
THE TWO OF US HAVE BEEN A TEAM EVER SINCE I WAS A NO-NAME PUBLIC SERVANT.
I DON'T KNOW ANYONE BESIDES YOU WHO'S SO HONEST WITH THEIR DESIRES.
......
THAT'S WHY I'VE PROVIDED YOU WITH SUCH NICE, RESILIENT PREY. EVEN IF IT IS TEMPO-RARY.
SO HOW GOES IT? HOW'S TODAY'S CRIMINAL HOLDING UP?
WELL NOW.
HE'S SO STOIC. JUST MY TYPE.
I WISH I COULD KEEP HIM FOREVER.
SQUISH
THAT MUST MEAN... THAT HE STILL HASN'T TALKED YET?
YES.
IT'S JUST AS YOU SAID.
WE CAN'T HAVE THAT!

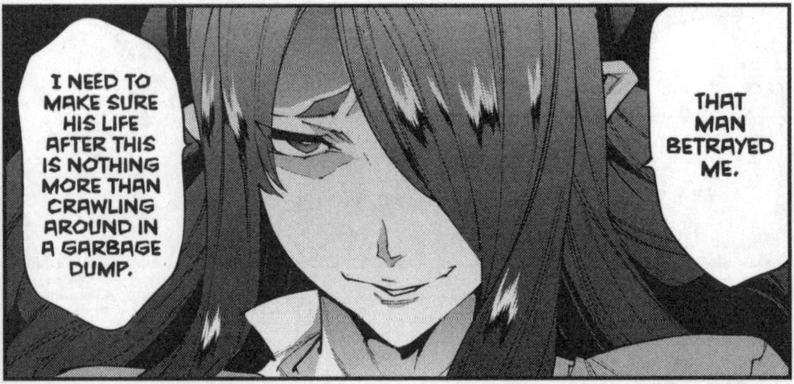
THAT MAN BETRAYED ME.
I NEED TO MAKE SURE HIS LIFE AFTER THIS IS NOTHING MORE THAN CRAWLING AROUND IN A GARBAGE DUMP.

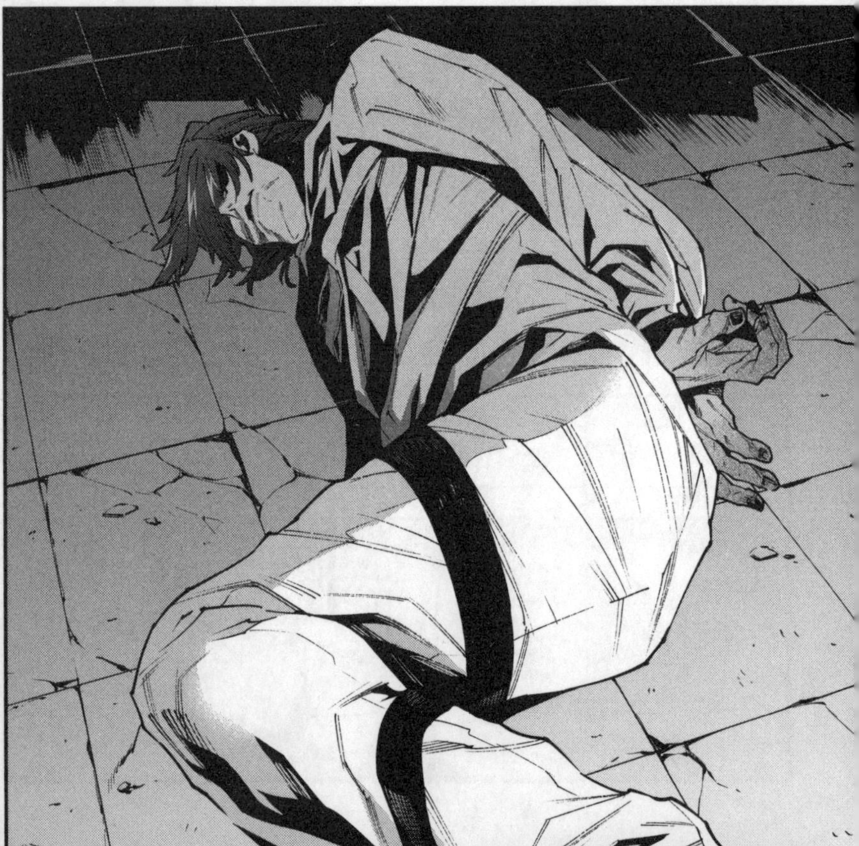

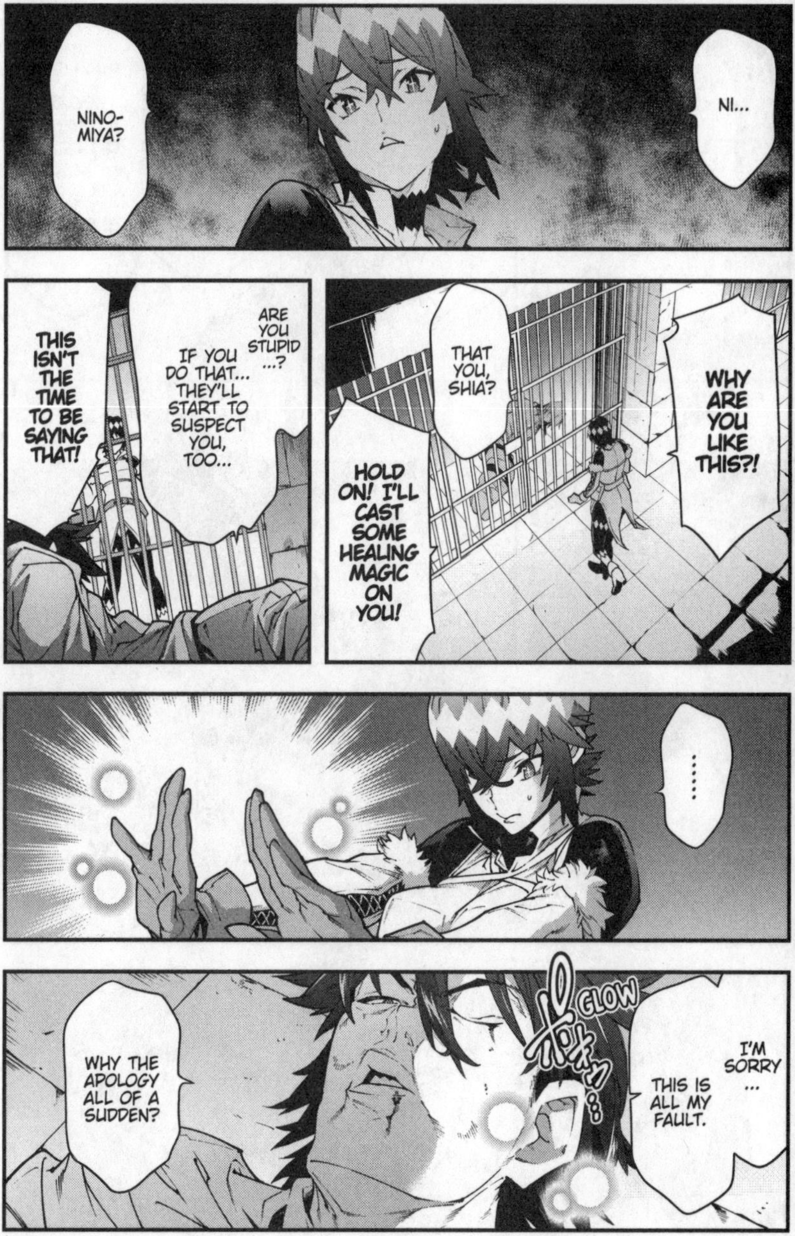
NI...
NINO-MIYA?
THAT YOU, SHIA?
WHY ARE YOU LIKE THIS?!
HOLD ON! I'LL CAST SOME HEALING MAGIC ON YOU!
ARE YOU STUPID ...?
IF YOU DO THAT... THEY'LL START TO SUSPECT YOU, TOO...
THIS ISN'T THE TIME TO BE SAYING THAT!
......
I'M SORRY ...
THIS IS ALL MY FAULT.
GLOW
WHY THE APOLOGY ALL OF A SUDDEN?

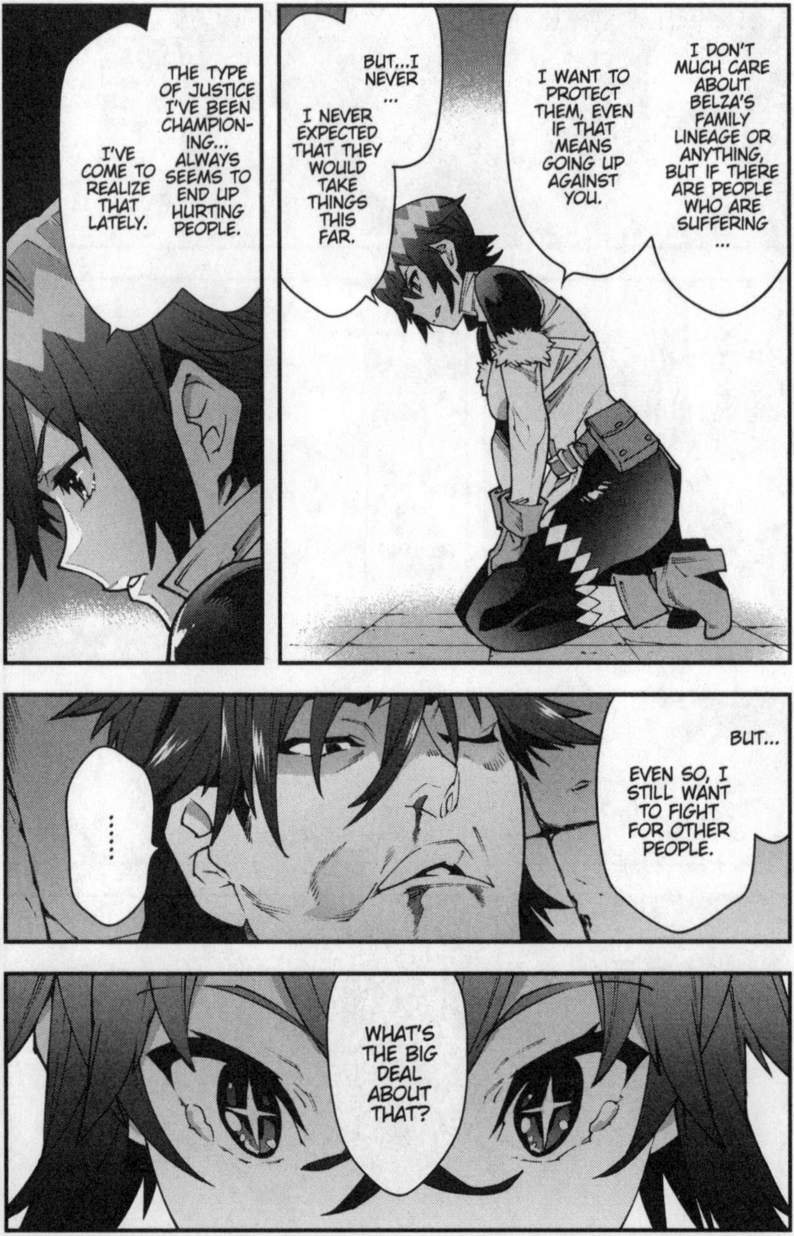
I DON'T MUCH CARE ABOUT BELZA'S FAMILY LINEAGE OR ANYTHING, BUT IF THERE ARE PEOPLE WHO ARE SUFFERING...
I WANT TO PROTECT THEM, EVEN IF THAT MEANS GOING UP AGAINST YOU.
BUT...I NEVER...
I NEVER EXPECTED THAT THEY WOULD TAKE THINGS THIS FAR.
THE TYPE OF JUSTICE I'VE BEEN CHAMPIONING... ALWAYS SEEMS TO END UP HURTING PEOPLE.
I'VE COME TO REALIZE THAT LATELY.
BUT...
EVEN SO, I STILL WANT TO FIGHT FOR OTHER PEOPLE.
......
WHAT'S THE BIG DEAL ABOUT THAT?

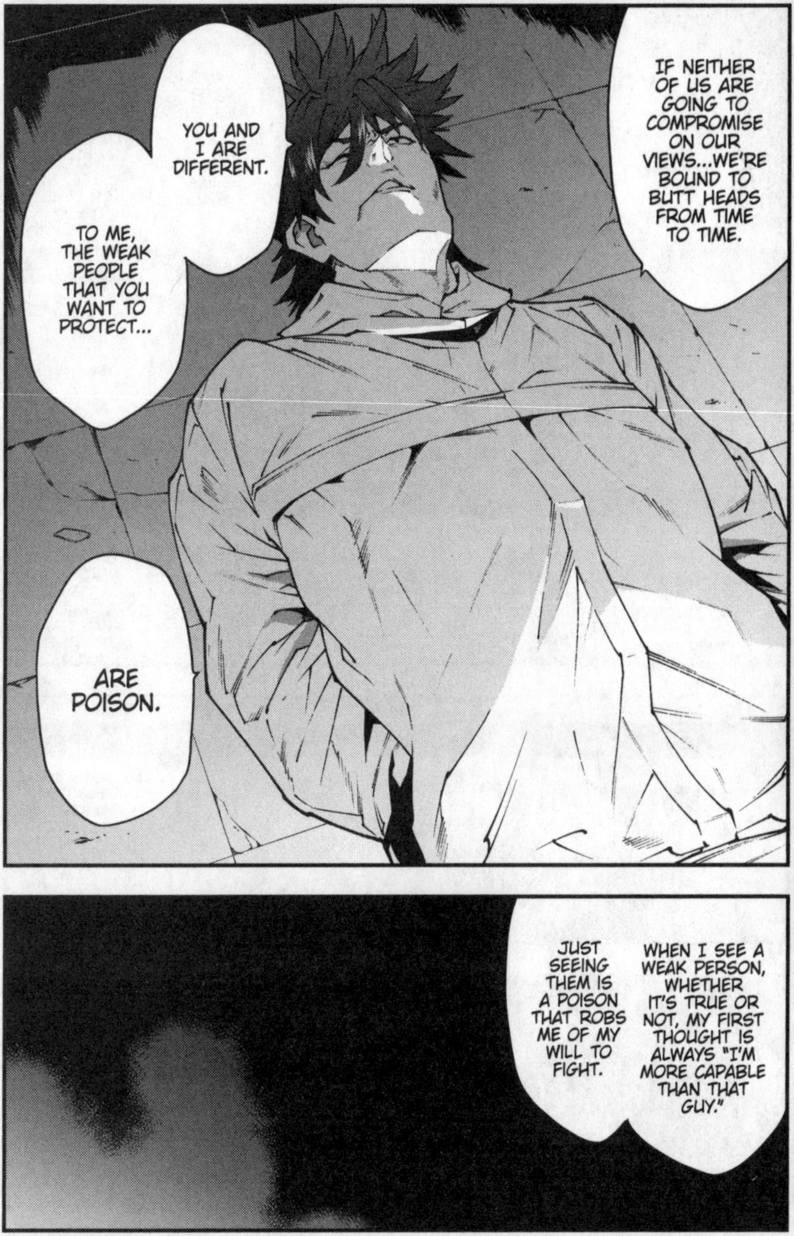
IF NEITHER OF US ARE GOING TO COMPROMISE ON OUR VIEWS...WE'RE BOUND TO BUTT HEADS FROM TIME TO TIME.
YOU AND I ARE DIFFERENT.
TO ME, THE WEAK PEOPLE THAT YOU WANT TO PROTECT...
ARE POISON.
WHEN I SEE A WEAK PERSON, WHETHER IT'S TRUE OR NOT, MY FIRST THOUGHT IS ALWAYS "I'M MORE CAPABLE THAN THAT GUY."
JUST SEEING THEM IS A POISON THAT ROBS ME OF MY WILL TO FIGHT.

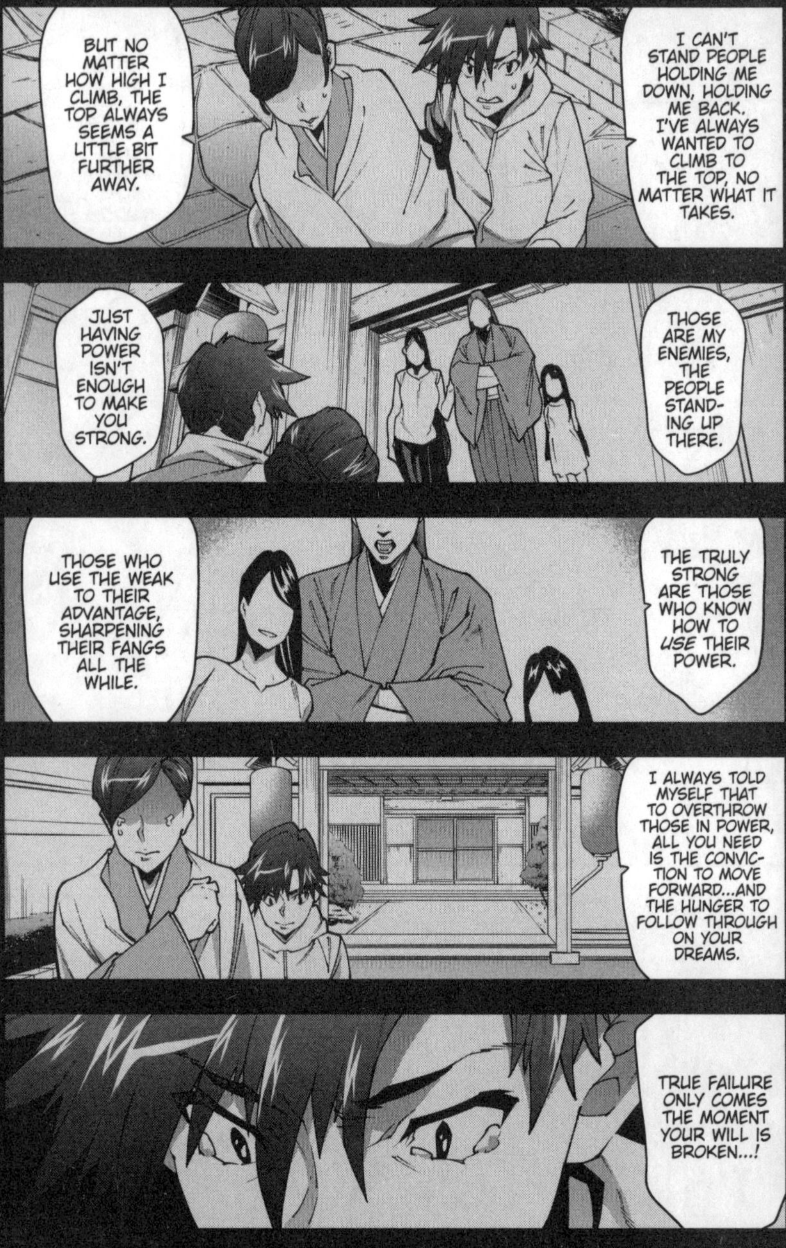
I CAN'T STAND PEOPLE HOLDING ME DOWN, HOLDING ME BACK. I'VE ALWAYS WANTED TO CLIMB TO THE TOP, NO MATTER WHAT IT TAKES.
BUT NO MATTER HOW HIGH I CLIMB, THE TOP ALWAYS SEEMS A LITTLE BIT FURTHER AWAY.
THOSE ARE MY ENEMIES, THE PEOPLE STANDING UP THERE.
JUST HAVING POWER ISN'T ENOUGH TO MAKE YOU STRONG.
THE TRULY STRONG ARE THOSE WHO KNOW HOW TO *USE* THEIR POWER.
THOSE WHO USE THE WEAK TO THEIR ADVANTAGE, SHARPENING THEIR FANGS ALL THE WHILE.
I ALWAYS TOLD MYSELF THAT TO OVERTHROW THOSE IN POWER, ALL YOU NEED IS THE CONVICTION TO MOVE FORWARD...AND THE HUNGER TO FOLLOW THROUGH ON YOUR DREAMS.
TRUE FAILURE ONLY COMES THE MOMENT YOUR WILL IS BROKEN...!

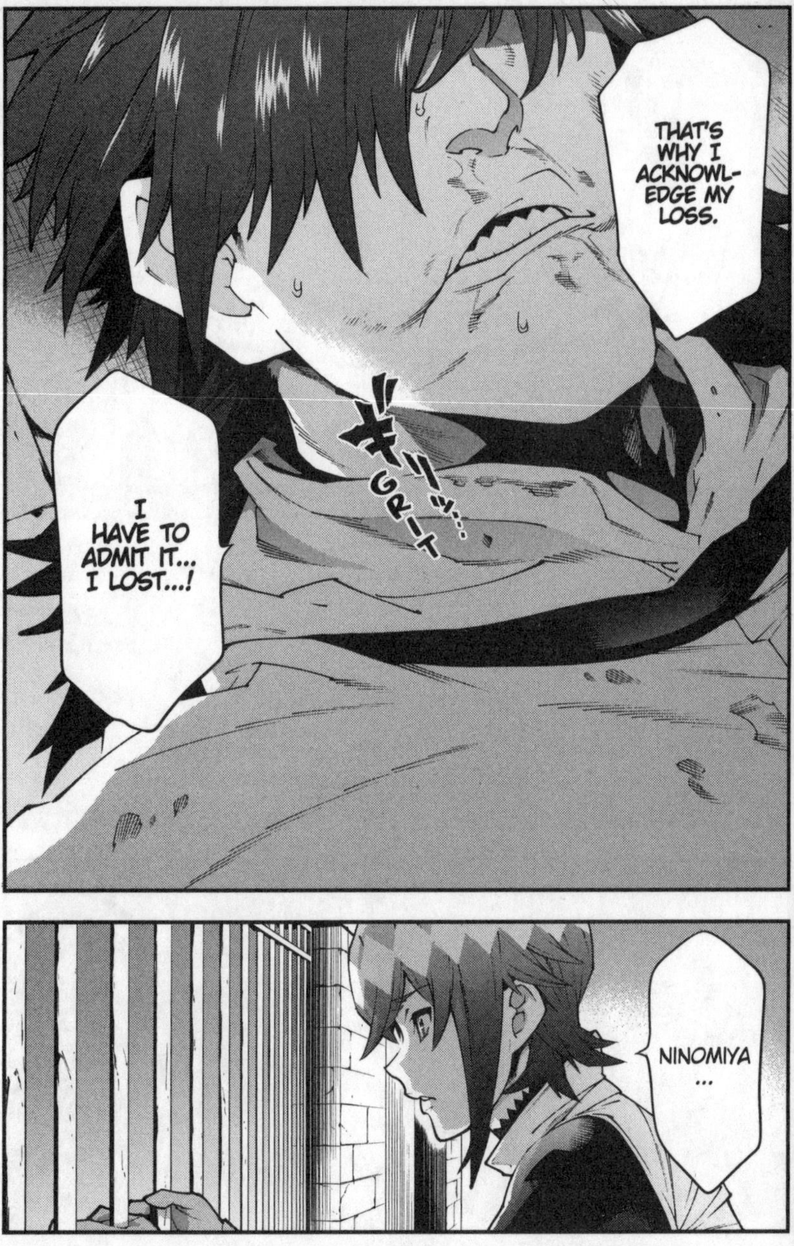
THAT'S WHY I ACKNOWL-EDGE MY LOSS.
ギリッ...
GRIT
I HAVE TO ADMIT IT... I LOST...!
NINOMIYA ...

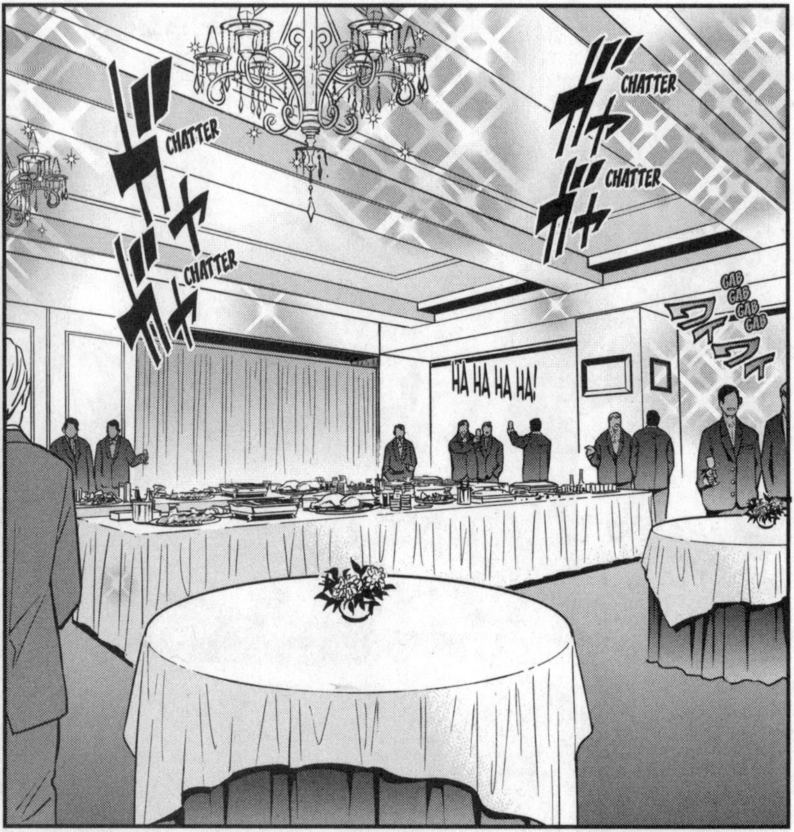
ガヤガヤ
CHATTER
CHATTER
GAB GAB GAB GAB
ワイワイ
HA HA HA HA!
ガヤガヤ
CHATTER
CHATTER

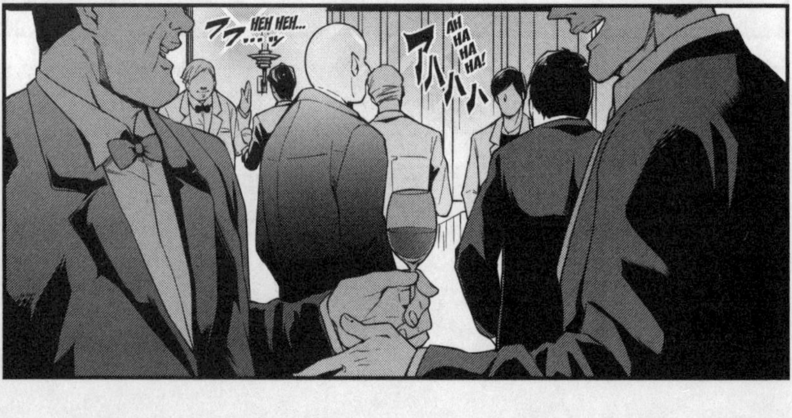
AH HA HA HA!
アハハハ
HEH HEH...
フフ...ッ

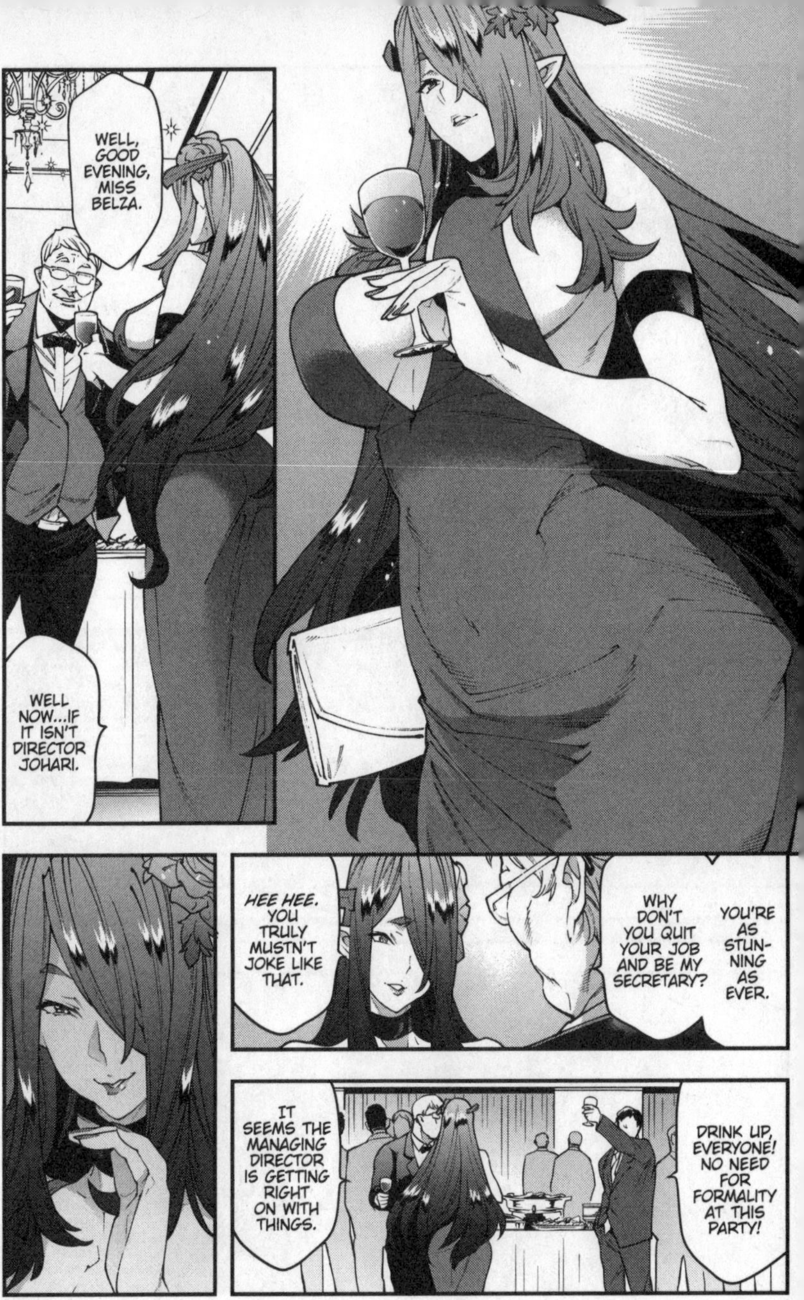
WELL, GOOD EVENING, MISS BELZA.
WELL NOW...IF IT ISN'T DIRECTOR JOHARI.
YOU'RE AS STUN-NING AS EVER.
WHY DON'T YOU QUIT YOUR JOB AND BE MY SECRETARY?
HEE HEE. YOU TRULY MUSTN'T JOKE LIKE THAT.
DRINK UP, EVERYONE! NO NEED FOR FORMALITY AT THIS PARTY!
IT SEEMS THE MANAGING DIRECTOR IS GETTING RIGHT ON WITH THINGS.

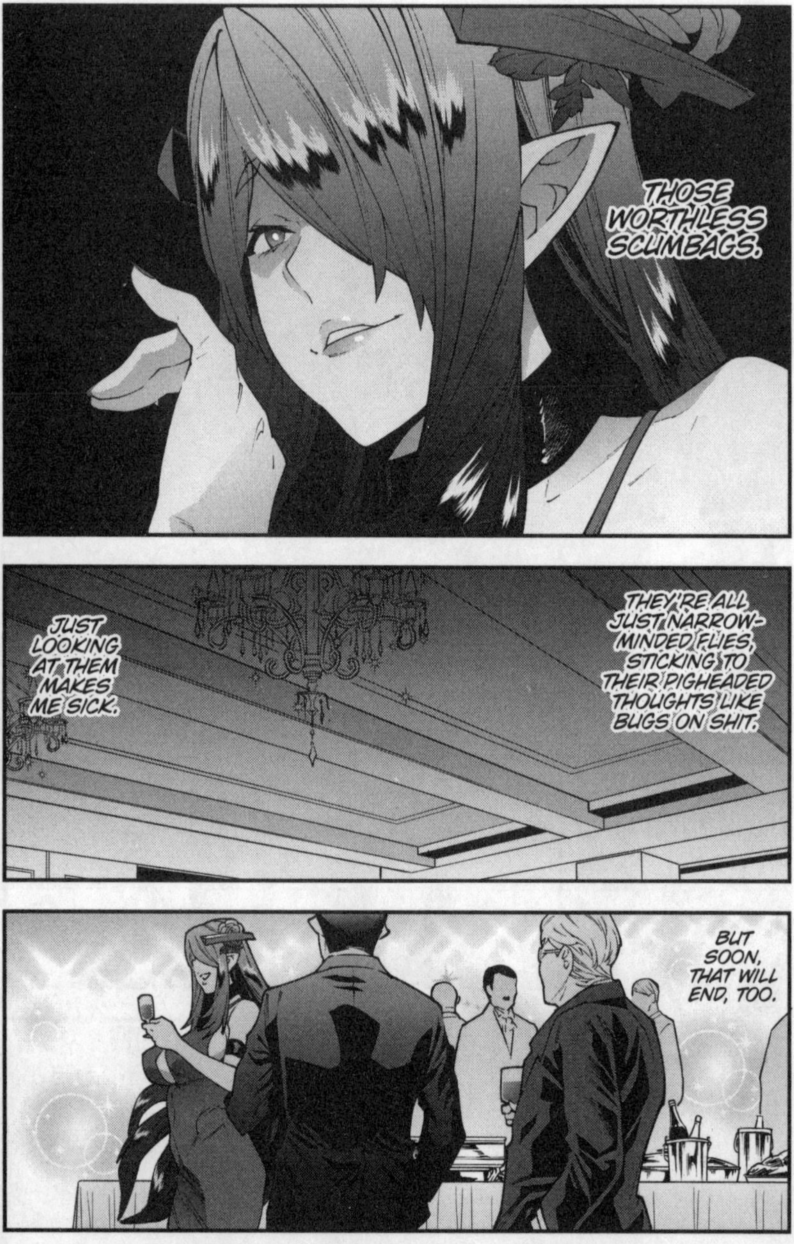
THOSE WORTHLESS SCUMBAGS.
THEY'RE ALL JUST NARROW-MINDED FLIES, STICKING TO THEIR PIGHEADED THOUGHTS LIKE BUGS ON SHIT.
JUST LOOKING AT THEM MAKES ME SICK.
BUT SOON, THAT WILL END, TOO.

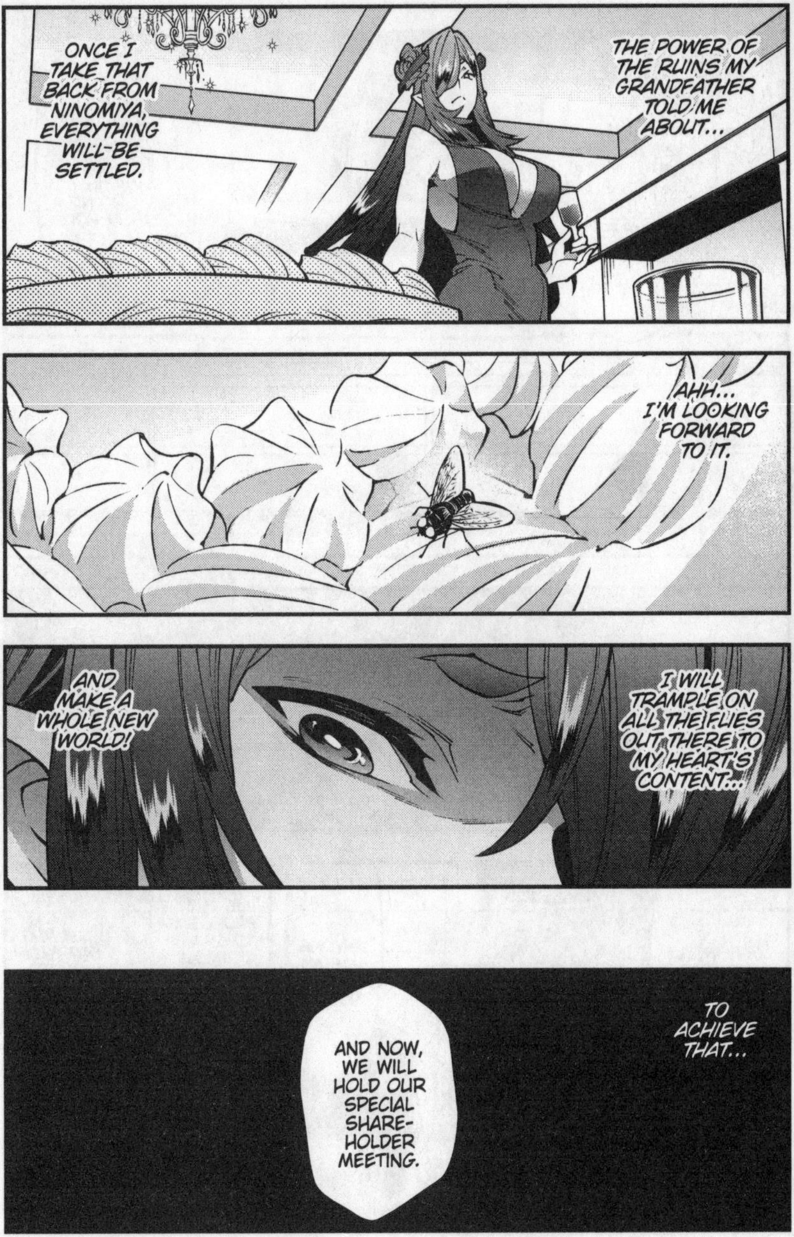
THE POWER OF THE RUINS MY GRANDFATHER TOLD ME ABOUT...
ONCE I TAKE THAT BACK FROM NINOMIYA, EVERYTHING WILL BE SETTLED.
AHH... I'M LOOKING FORWARD TO IT.
I WILL TRAMPLE ON ALL THE FLIES OUT THERE TO MY HEART'S CONTENT...
AND MAKE A WHOLE NEW WORLD!
TO ACHIEVE THAT...
AND NOW, WE WILL HOLD OUR SPECIAL SHARE-HOLDER MEETING.

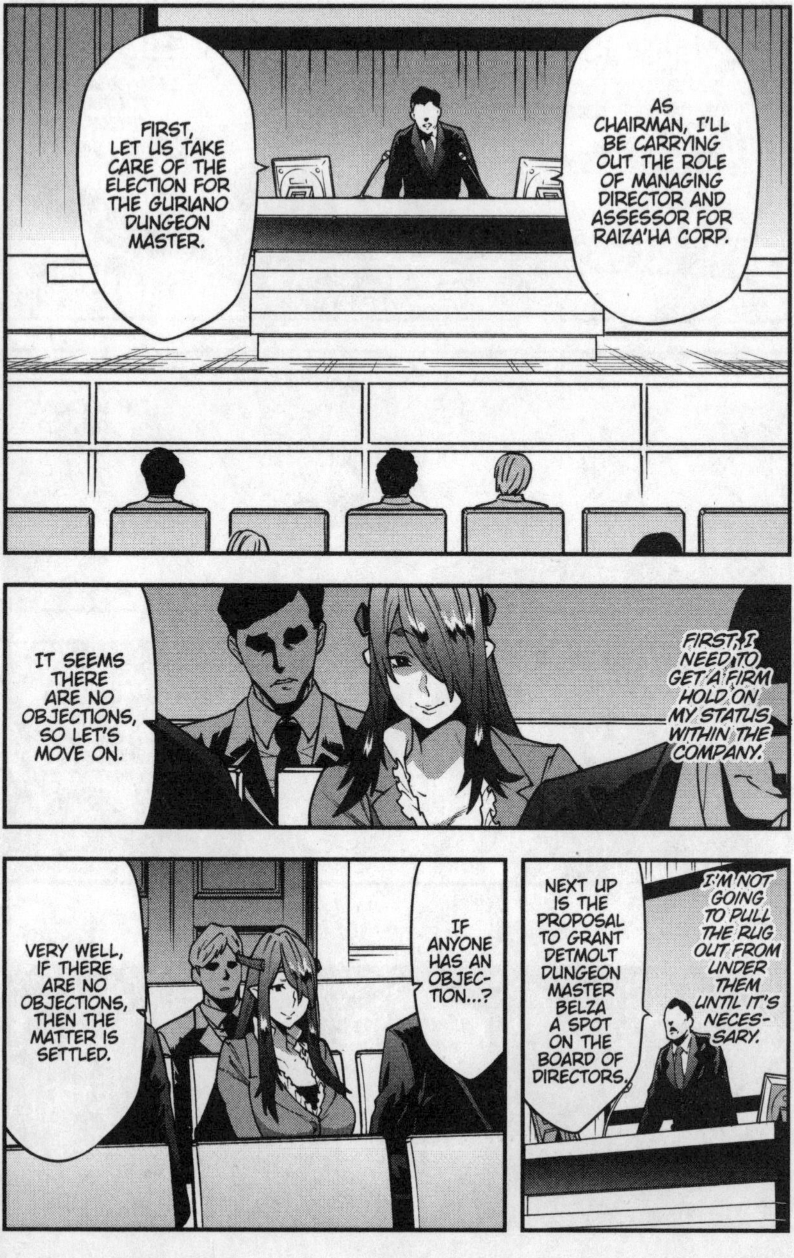
AS CHAIRMAN, I'LL BE CARRYING OUT THE ROLE OF MANAGING DIRECTOR AND ASSESSOR FOR RAIZA'HA CORP.
FIRST, LET US TAKE CARE OF THE ELECTION FOR THE GURIANO DUNGEON MASTER.
FIRST, I NEED TO GET A FIRM HOLD ON MY STATUS WITHIN THE COMPANY.
IT SEEMS THERE ARE NO OBJECTIONS, SO LET'S MOVE ON.
I'M NOT GOING TO PULL THE RUG OUT FROM UNDER THEM UNTIL IT'S NECES-SARY.
NEXT UP IS THE PROPOSAL TO GRANT DETMOLT DUNGEON MASTER BELZA A SPOT ON THE BOARD OF DIRECTORS.
IF ANYONE HAS AN OBJEC-TION...?
VERY WELL, IF THERE ARE NO OBJECTIONS, THEN THE MATTER IS SETTLED.

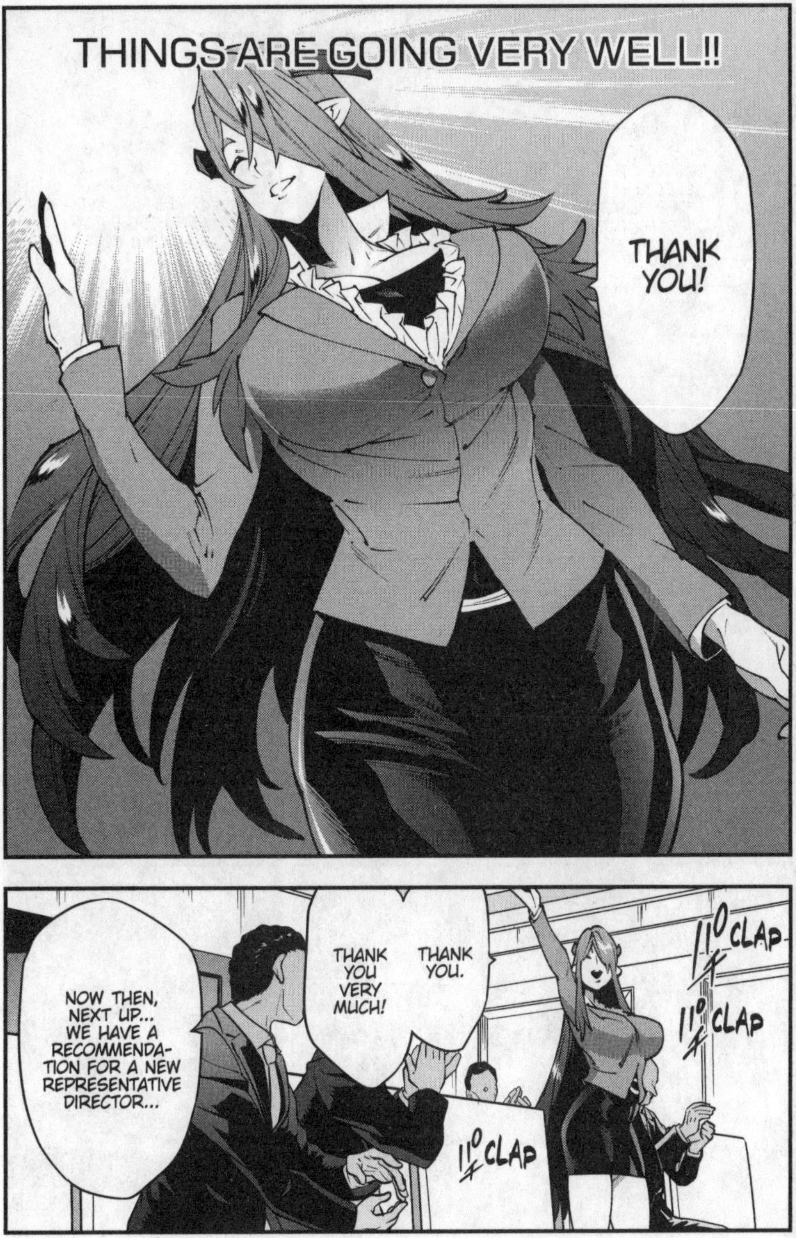
THINGS ARE GOING VERY WELL!!
THANK YOU!
CLAP
CLAP
THANK YOU.
THANK YOU VERY MUCH!
NOW THEN, NEXT UP... WE HAVE A RECOMMENDATION FOR A NEW REPRESENTATIVE DIRECTOR...
CLAP

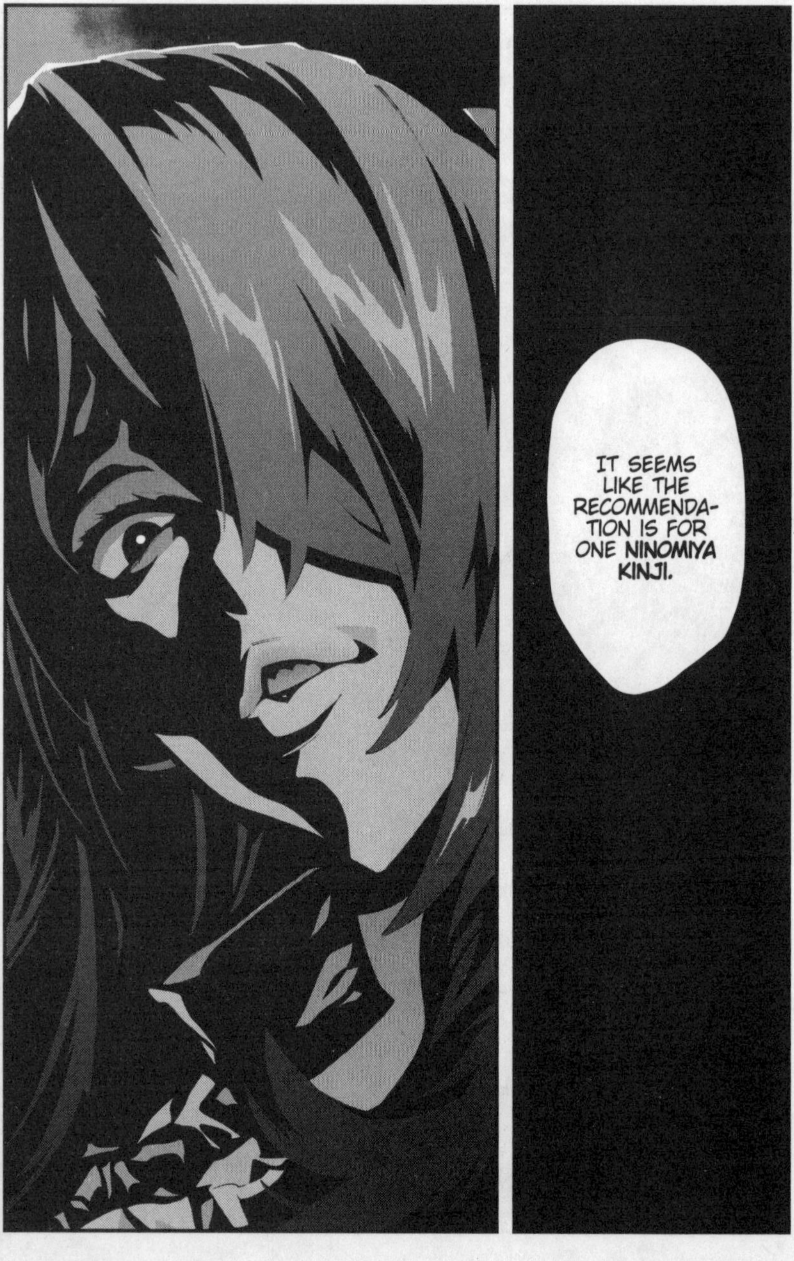
IT SEEMS LIKE THE RECOMMENDA-TION IS FOR ONE NINOMIYA KINJI.

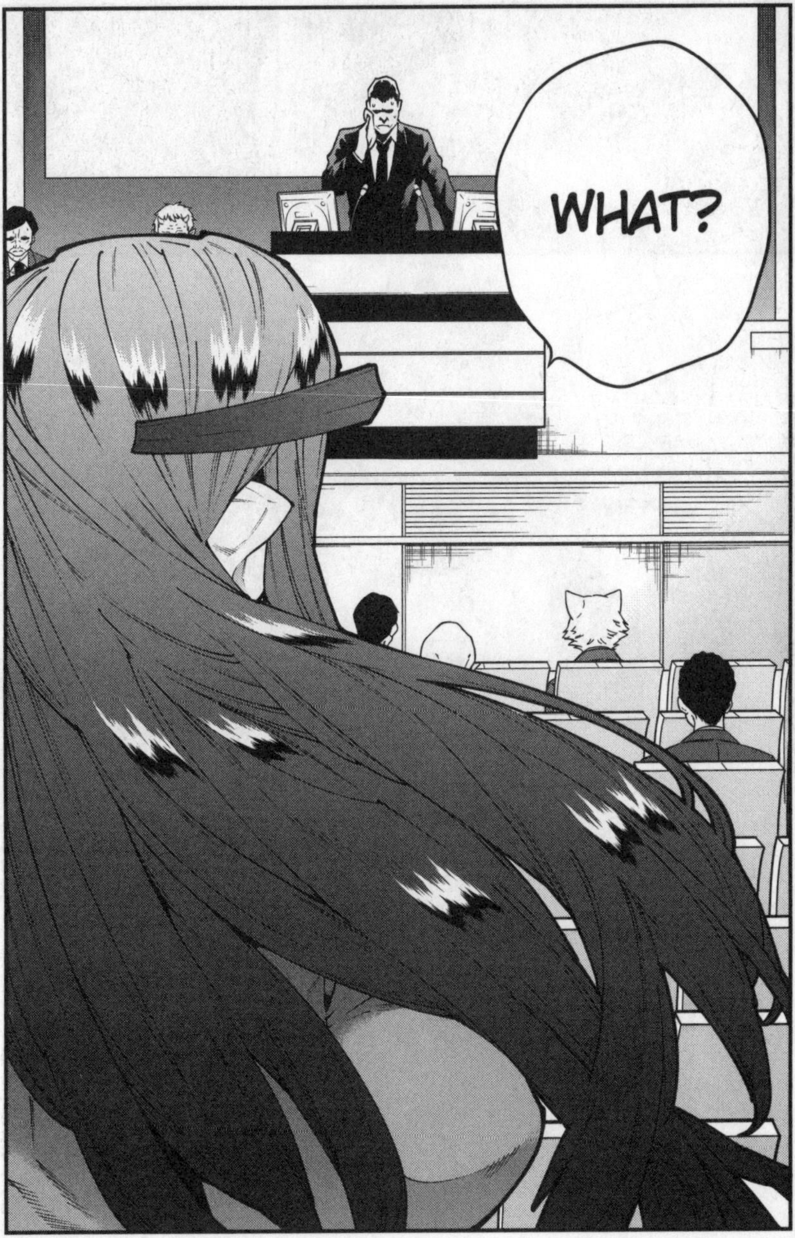
WHAT?

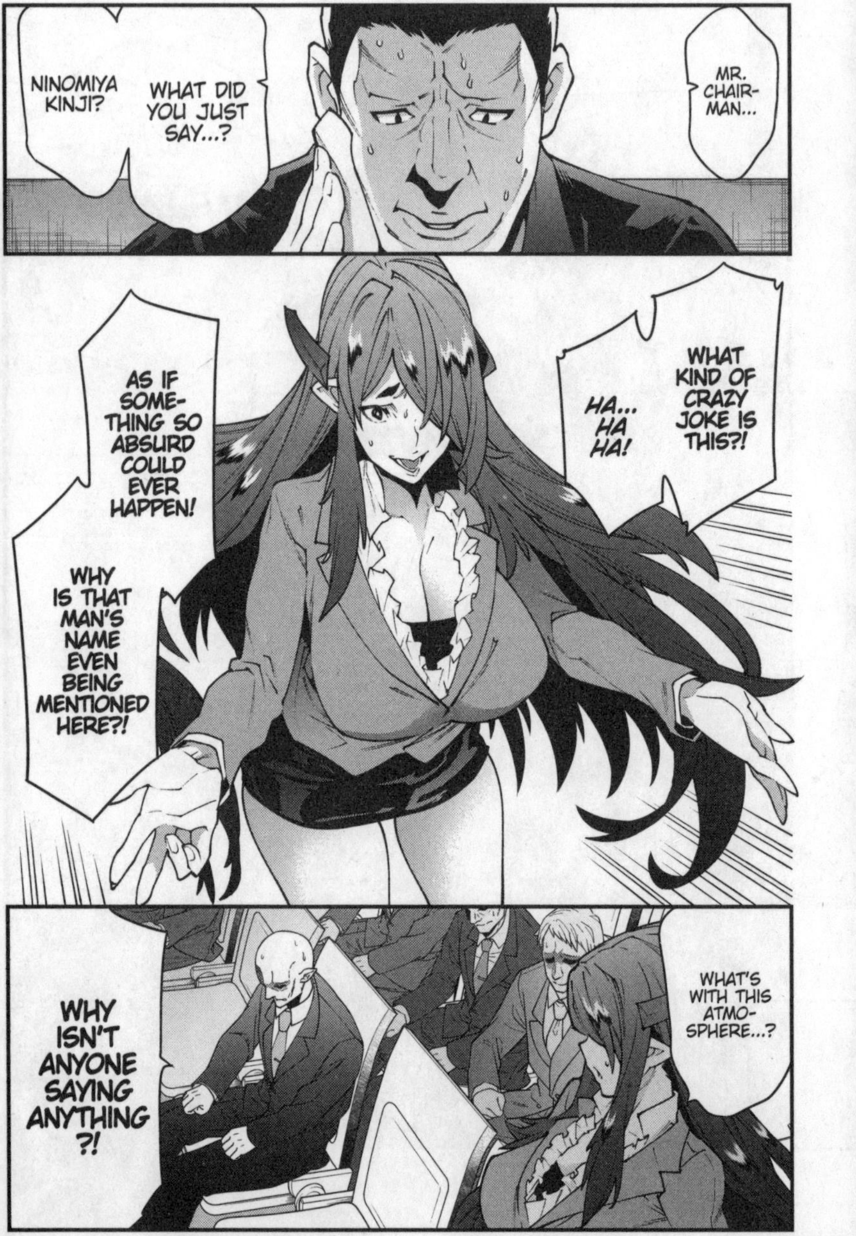
MR. CHAIR-MAN...
NINOMIYA KINJI? WHAT DID YOU JUST SAY...?
HA... HA HA! WHAT KIND OF CRAZY JOKE IS THIS?!
AS IF SOME-THING SO ABSURD COULD EVER HAPPEN!
WHY IS THAT MAN'S NAME EVEN BEING MENTIONED HERE?!
WHAT'S WITH THIS ATMO-SPHERE...?
WHY ISN'T ANYONE SAYING ANYTHING?!

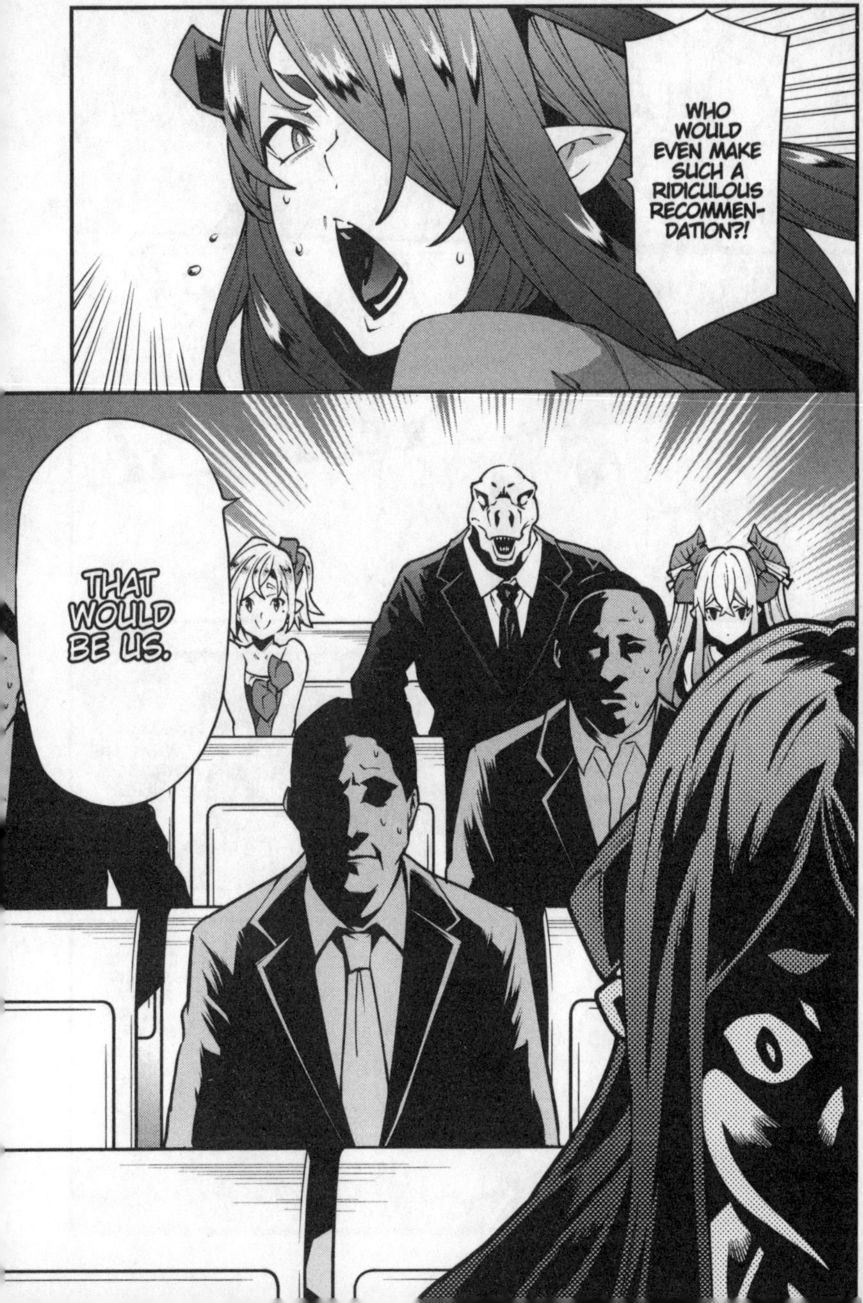
WHO WOULD EVEN MAKE SUCH A RIDICULOUS RECOMMEN-DATION?!
THAT WOULD BE US.

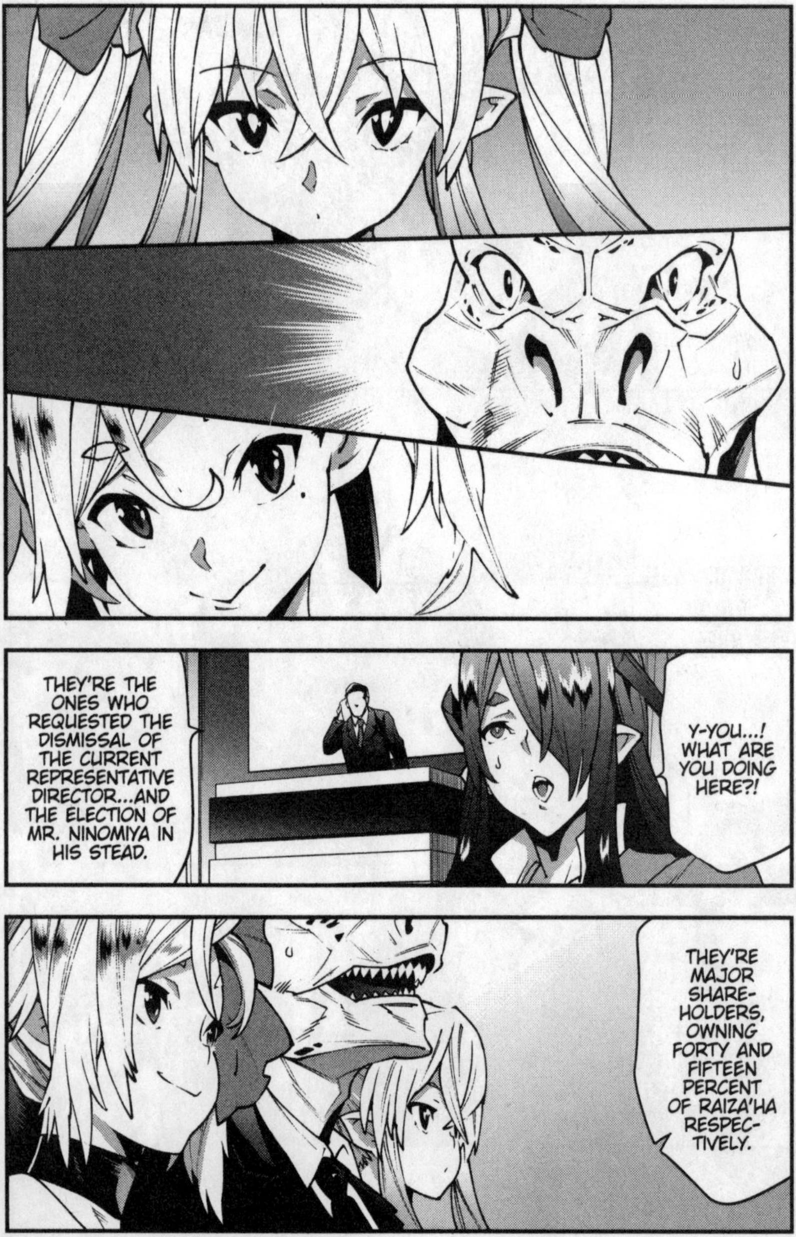
Y-YOU...! WHAT ARE YOU DOING HERE?!
THEY'RE THE ONES WHO REQUESTED THE DISMISSAL OF THE CURRENT REPRESENTATIVE DIRECTOR...AND THE ELECTION OF MR. NINOMIYA IN HIS STEAD.
THEY'RE MAJOR SHARE-HOLDERS, OWNING FORTY AND FIFTEEN PERCENT OF RAIZA'HA RESPEC-TIVELY.

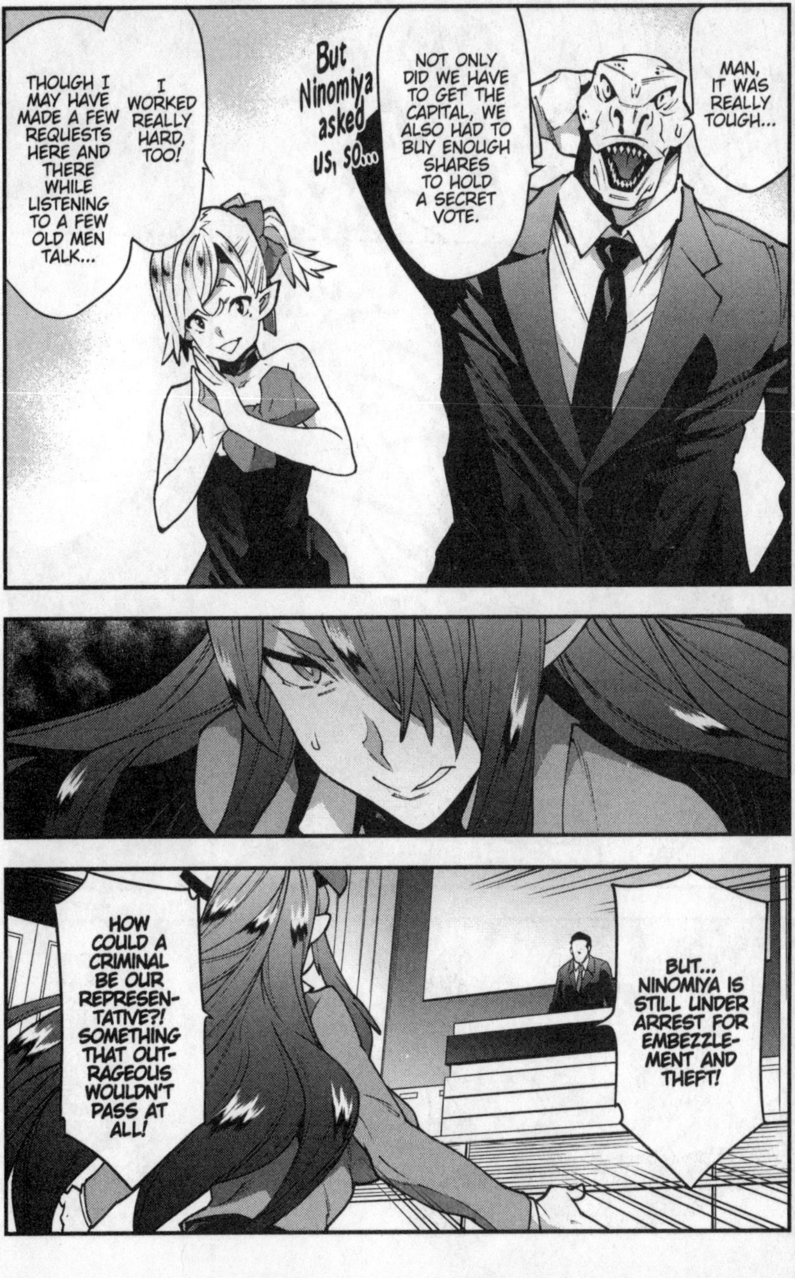
MAN, IT WAS REALLY TOUGH...
NOT ONLY DID WE HAVE TO GET THE CAPITAL, WE ALSO HAD TO BUY ENOUGH SHARES TO HOLD A SECRET VOTE.
But Ninomiya asked us, so...
I WORKED REALLY HARD, TOO!
THOUGH I MAY HAVE MADE A FEW REQUESTS HERE AND THERE WHILE LISTENING TO A FEW OLD MEN TALK...
BUT... NINOMIYA IS STILL UNDER ARREST FOR EMBEZZLE-MENT AND THEFT!
HOW COULD A CRIMINAL BE OUR REPRESEN-TATIVE?! SOMETHING THAT OUT-RAGEOUS WOULDN'T PASS AT ALL!

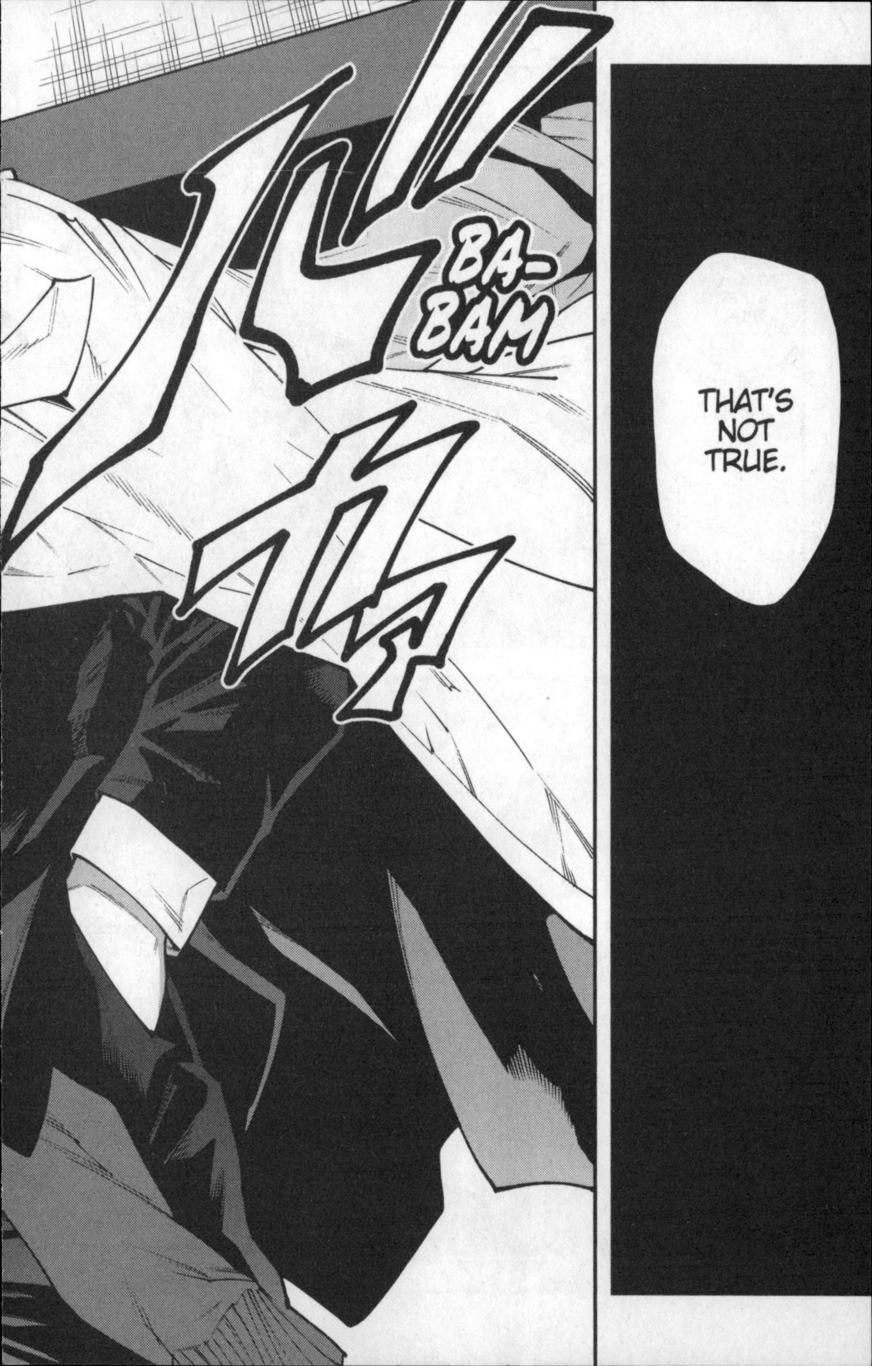
THAT'S NOT TRUE.
BA-BAM

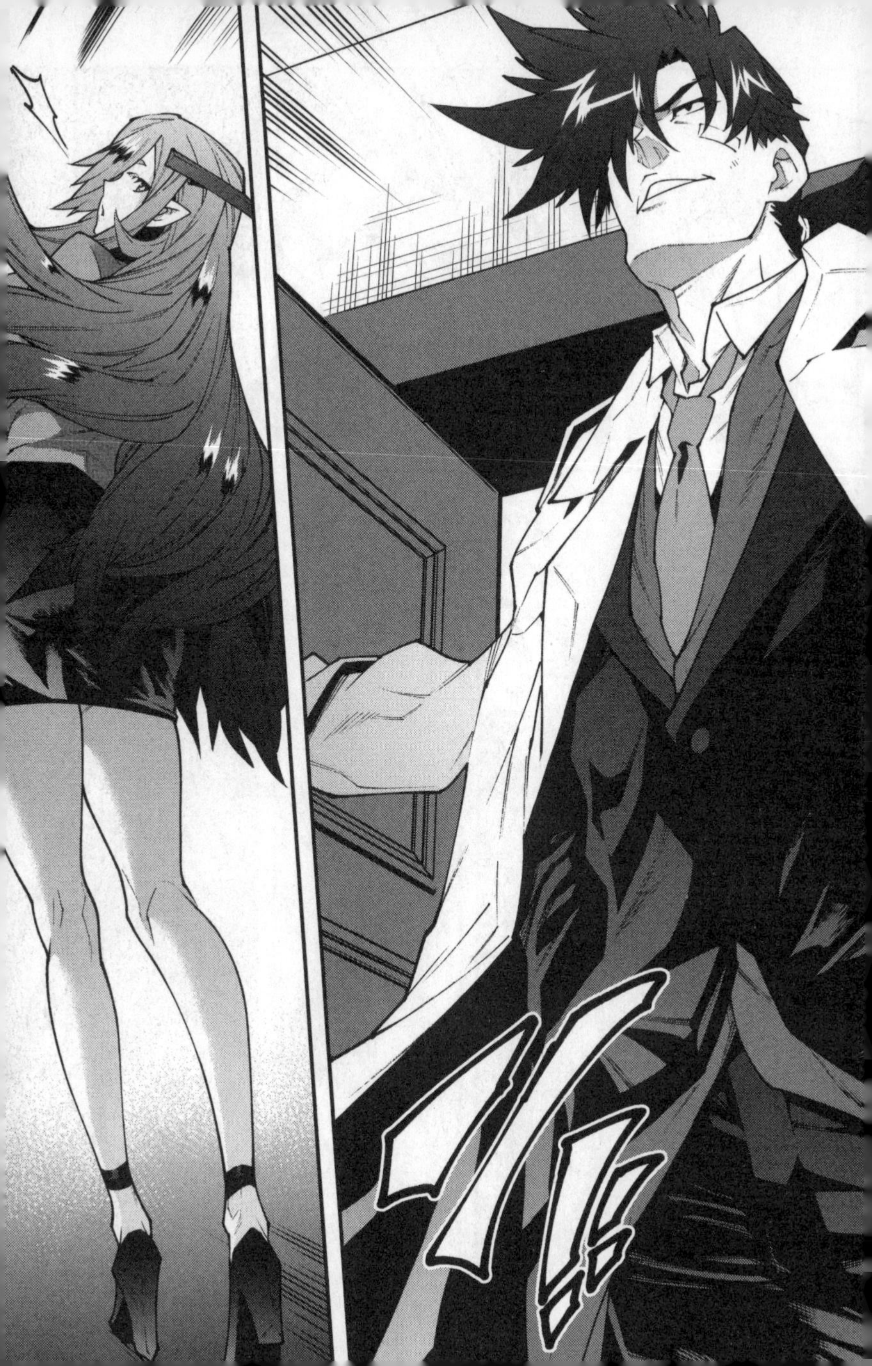

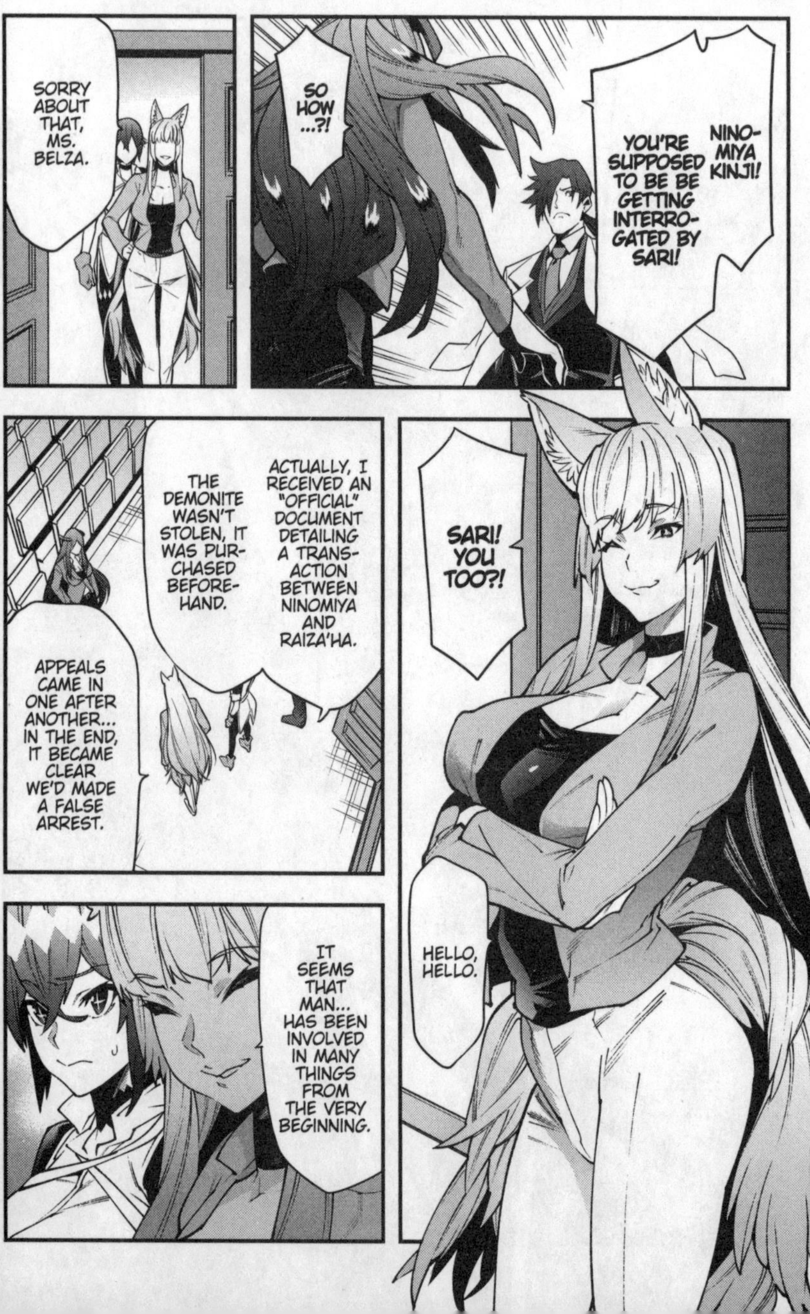
NINOMIYA KINJI! YOU'RE SUPPOSED TO BE BE GETTING INTERROGATED BY SARI!
SO HOW ...?!
SORRY ABOUT THAT, MS. BELZA.
SARI! YOU TOO?!
HELLO, HELLO.
ACTUALLY, I RECEIVED AN "OFFICIAL" DOCUMENT DETAILING A TRANSACTION BETWEEN NINOMIYA AND RAIZA'HA.
THE DEMONITE WASN'T STOLEN, IT WAS PURCHASED BEFOREHAND.
APPEALS CAME IN ONE AFTER ANOTHER... IN THE END, IT BECAME CLEAR WE'D MADE A FALSE ARREST.
IT SEEMS THAT MAN... HAS BEEN INVOLVED IN MANY THINGS FROM THE VERY BEGINNING.

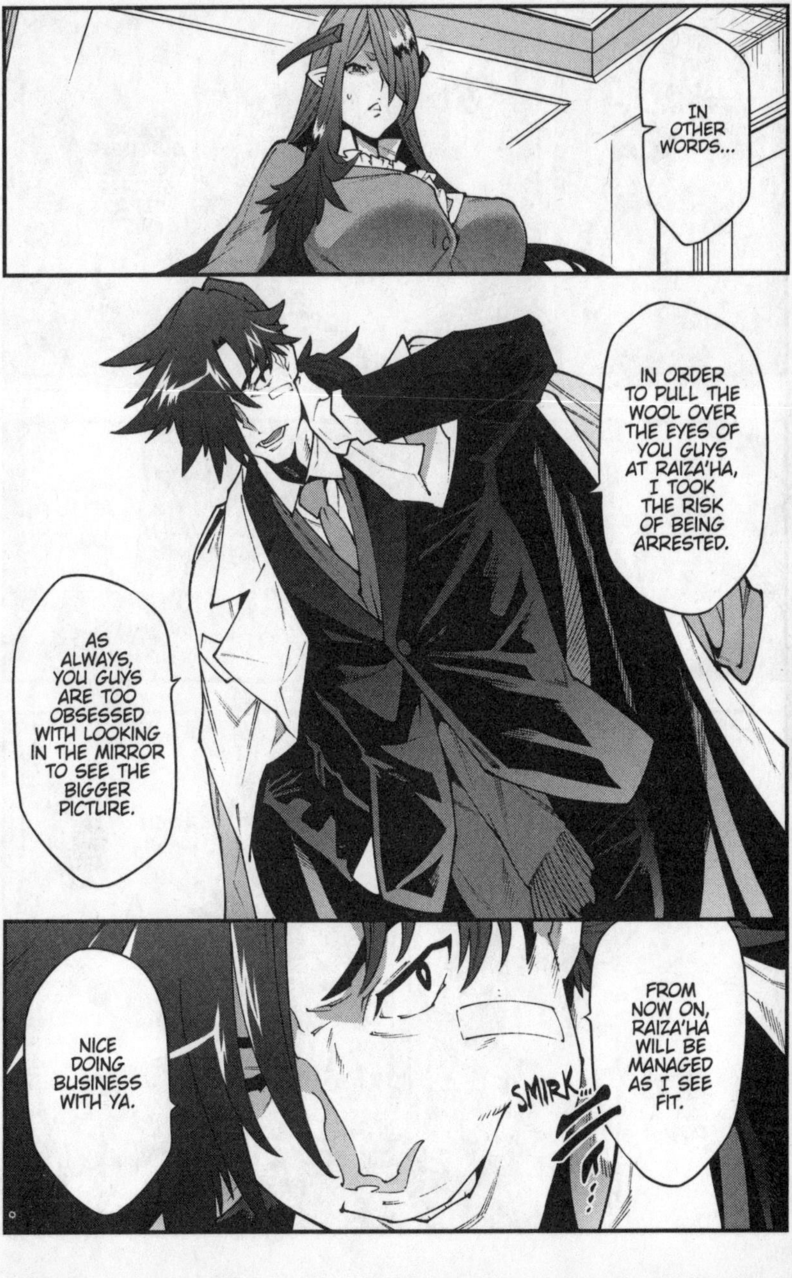
IN OTHER WORDS...
IN ORDER TO PULL THE WOOL OVER THE EYES OF YOU GUYS AT RAIZA'HA, I TOOK THE RISK OF BEING ARRESTED.
AS ALWAYS, YOU GUYS ARE TOO OBSESSED WITH LOOKING IN THE MIRROR TO SEE THE BIGGER PICTURE.
FROM NOW ON, RAIZA'HA WILL BE MANAGED AS I SEE FIT.
SMIRK...
NICE DOING BUSINESS WITH YA.

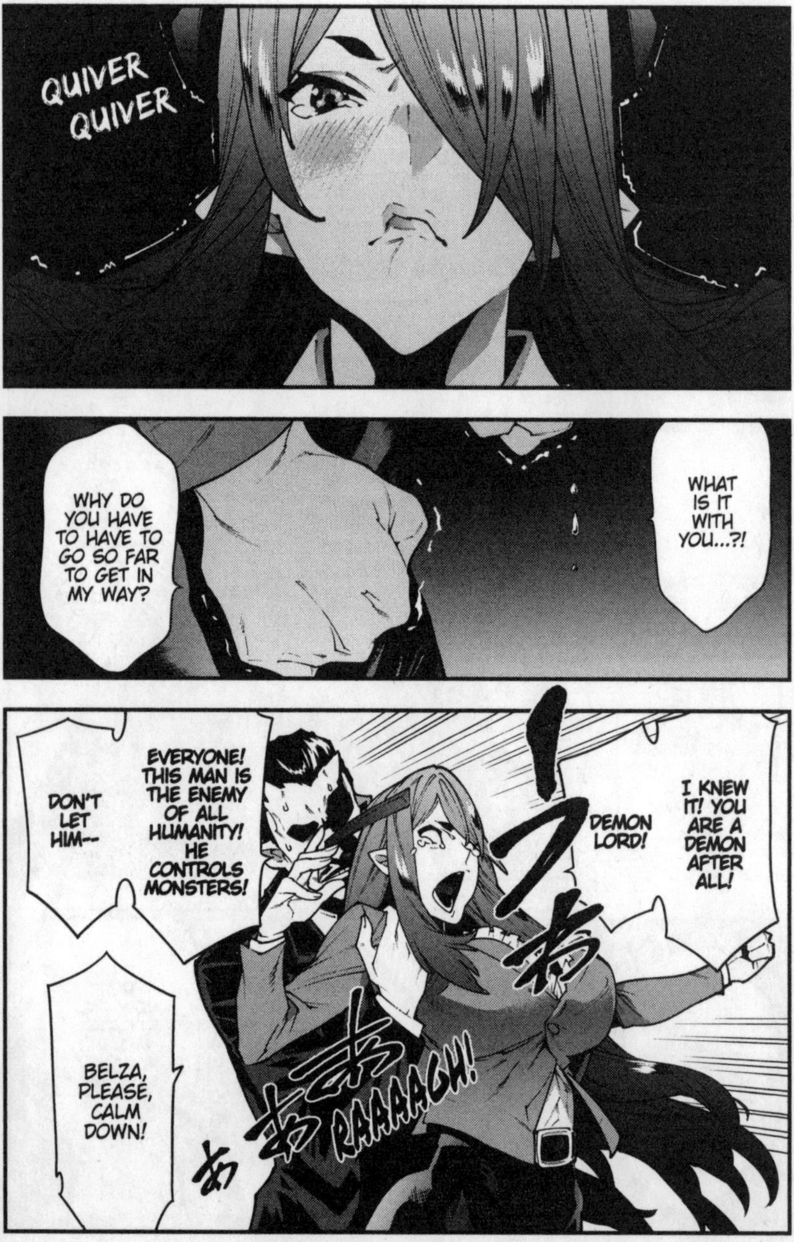
QUIVER QUIVER
WHAT IS IT WITH YOU...?!
WHY DO YOU HAVE TO HAVE TO GO SO FAR TO GET IN MY WAY?
I KNEW IT! YOU ARE A DEMON AFTER ALL!
DEMON LORD!
EVERYONE! THIS MAN IS THE ENEMY OF ALL HUMANITY! HE CONTROLS MONSTERS!
DON'T LET HIM--
RAAAAGH!
BELZA, PLEASE, CALM DOWN!

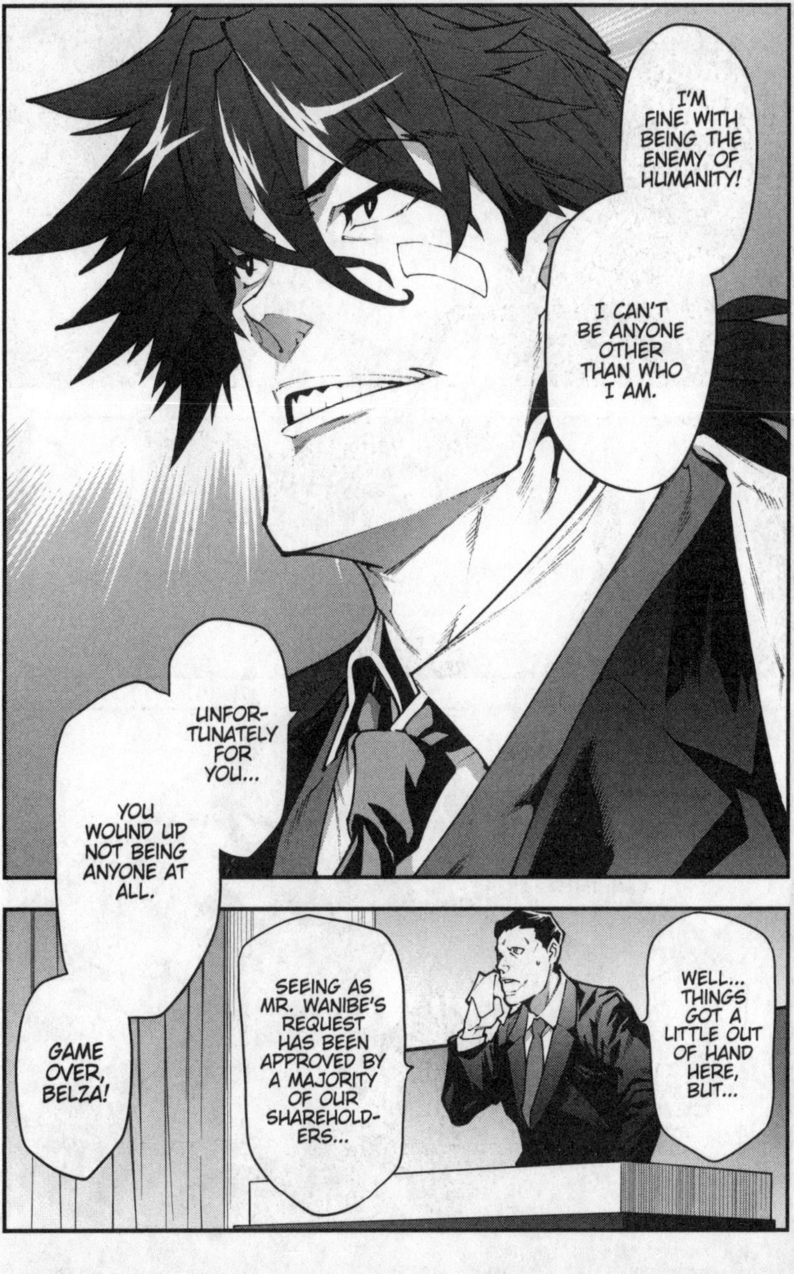

I'M FINE WITH BEING THE ENEMY OF HUMANITY!
I CAN'T BE ANYONE OTHER THAN WHO I AM.
UNFOR-TUNATELY FOR YOU...
YOU WOUND UP NOT BEING ANYONE AT ALL.
WELL... THINGS GOT A LITTLE OUT OF HAND HERE, BUT...
SEEING AS MR. WANIBE'S REQUEST HAS BEEN APPROVED BY A MAJORITY OF OUR SHAREHOLD-ERS...
GAME OVER, BELZA!

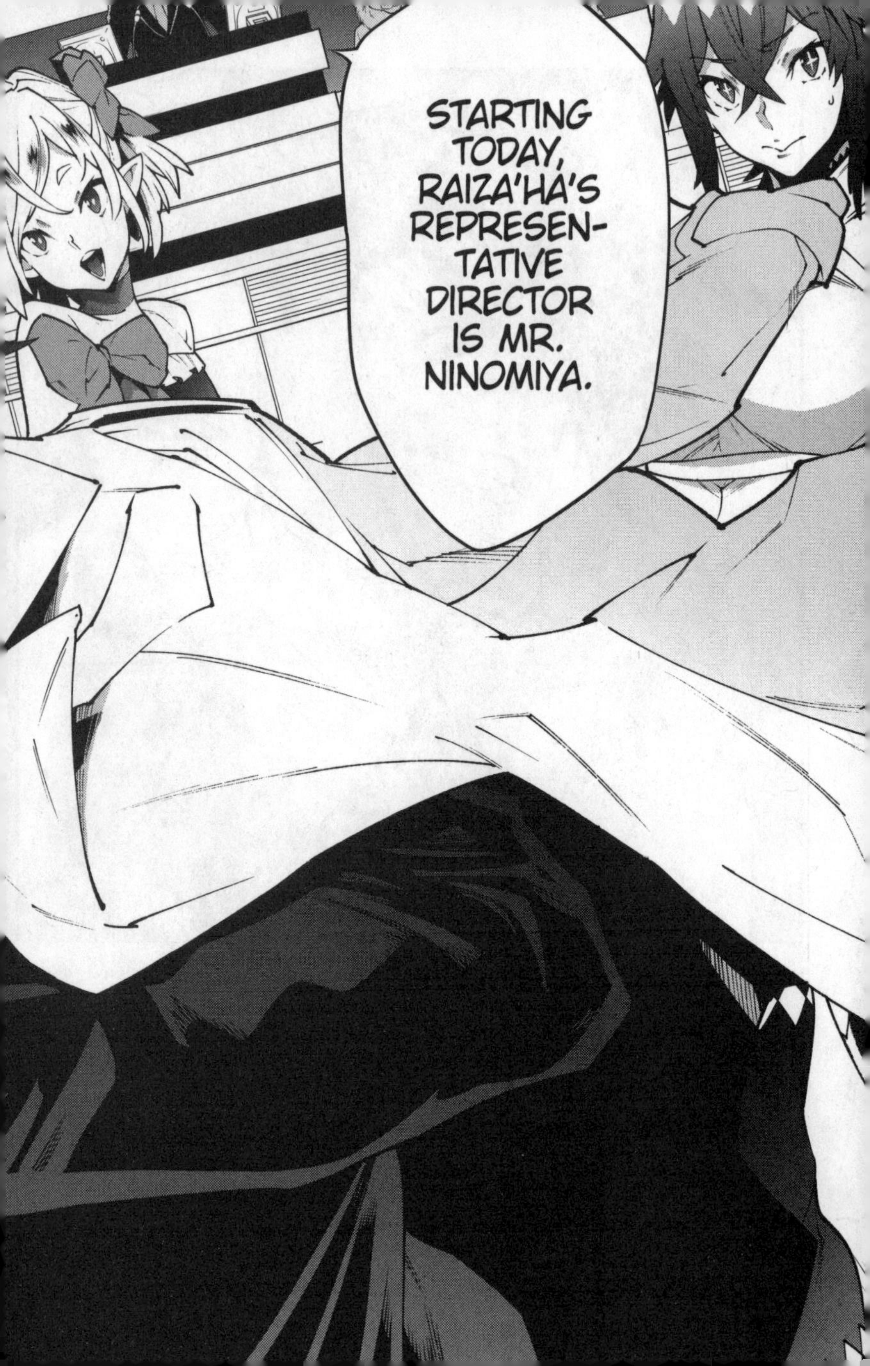
STARTING TODAY, RAIZA'HA'S REPRESEN-TATIVE DIRECTOR IS MR. NINOMIYA.

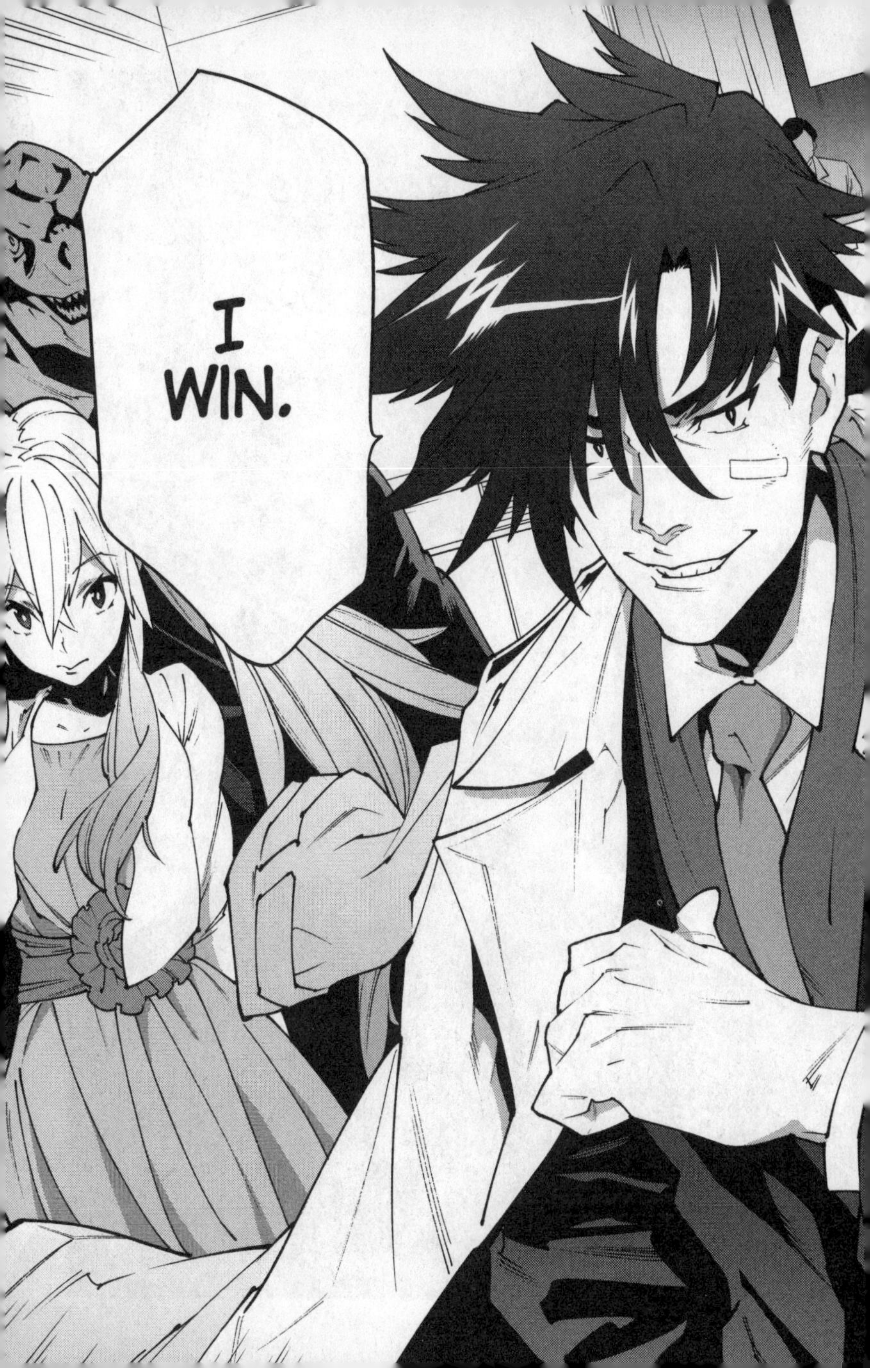
I WIN.

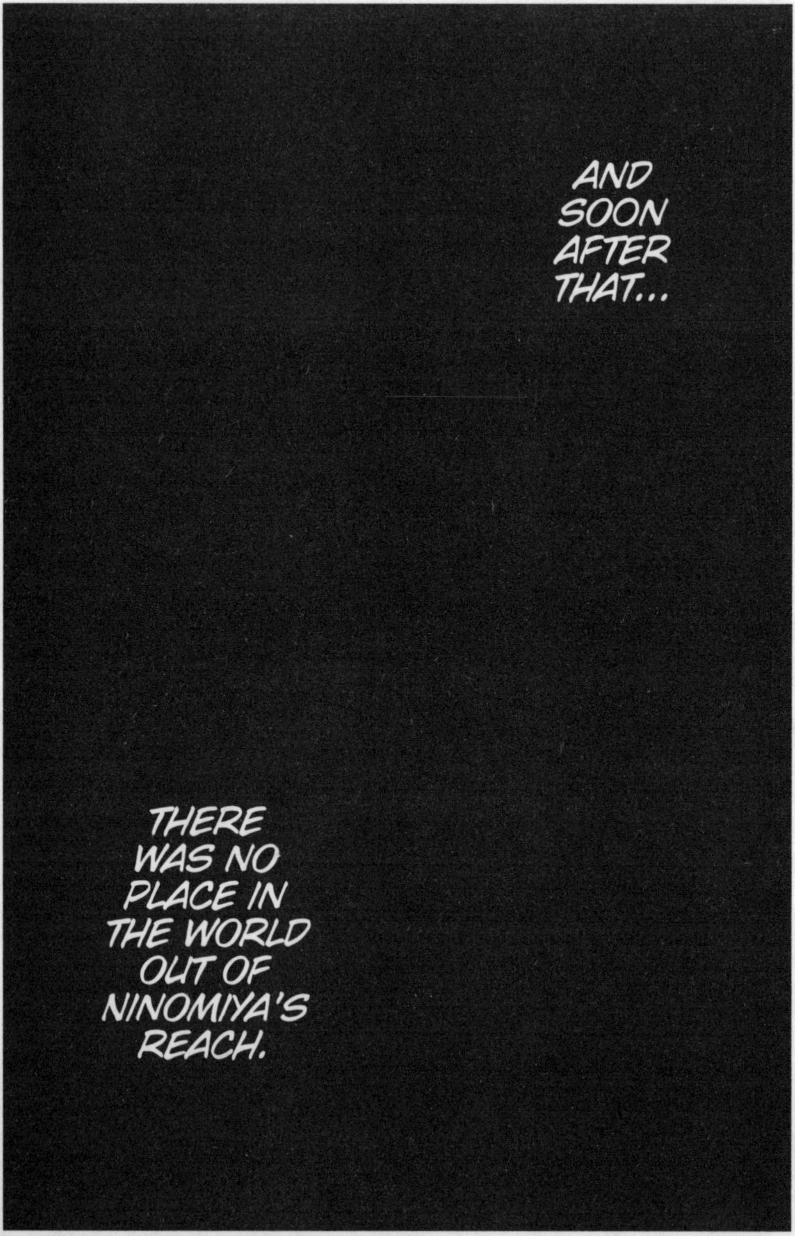
AND SOON AFTER THAT...
THERE WAS NO PLACE IN THE WORLD OUT OF NINOMIYA'S REACH.

RIM
SHIA COSTUME
VERSION

THE DUNGEON OF
BLACK COMPANY

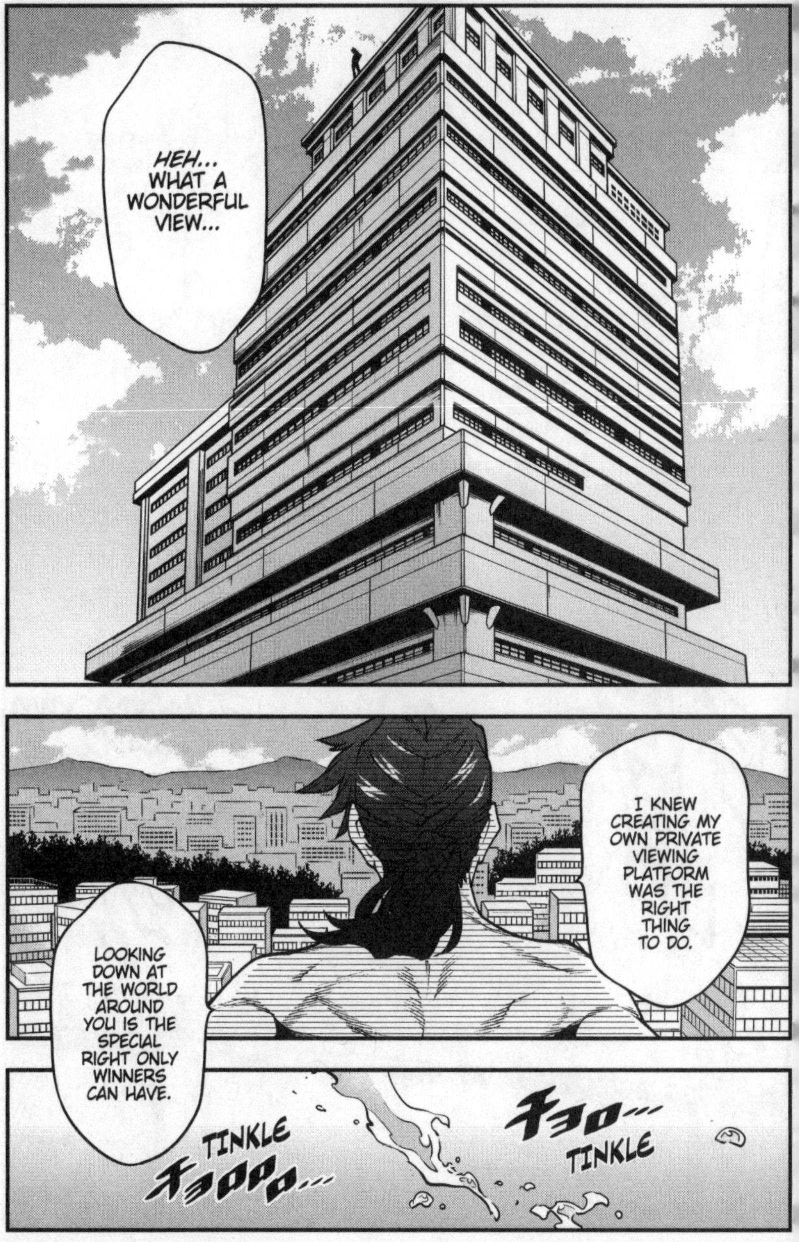
HEH... WHAT A WONDERFUL VIEW...
I KNEW CREATING MY OWN PRIVATE VIEWING PLATFORM WAS THE RIGHT THING TO DO.
LOOKING DOWN AT THE WORLD AROUND YOU IS THE SPECIAL RIGHT ONLY WINNERS CAN HAVE.
チョロ...
TINKLE
TINKLE
チョロロロ...

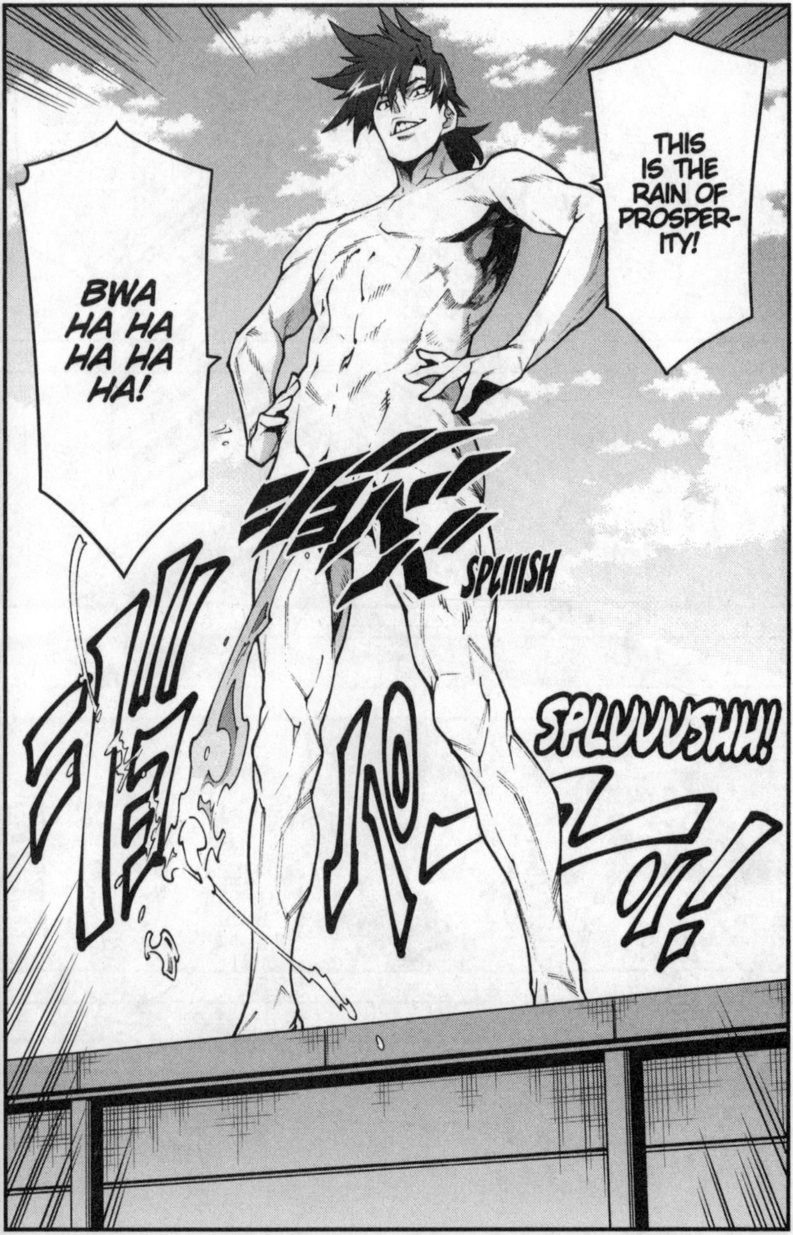
THIS IS THE RAIN OF PROSPER-ITY!
BWA HA HA HA HA HA!
SPLIIISH
SPLUUUSHH!

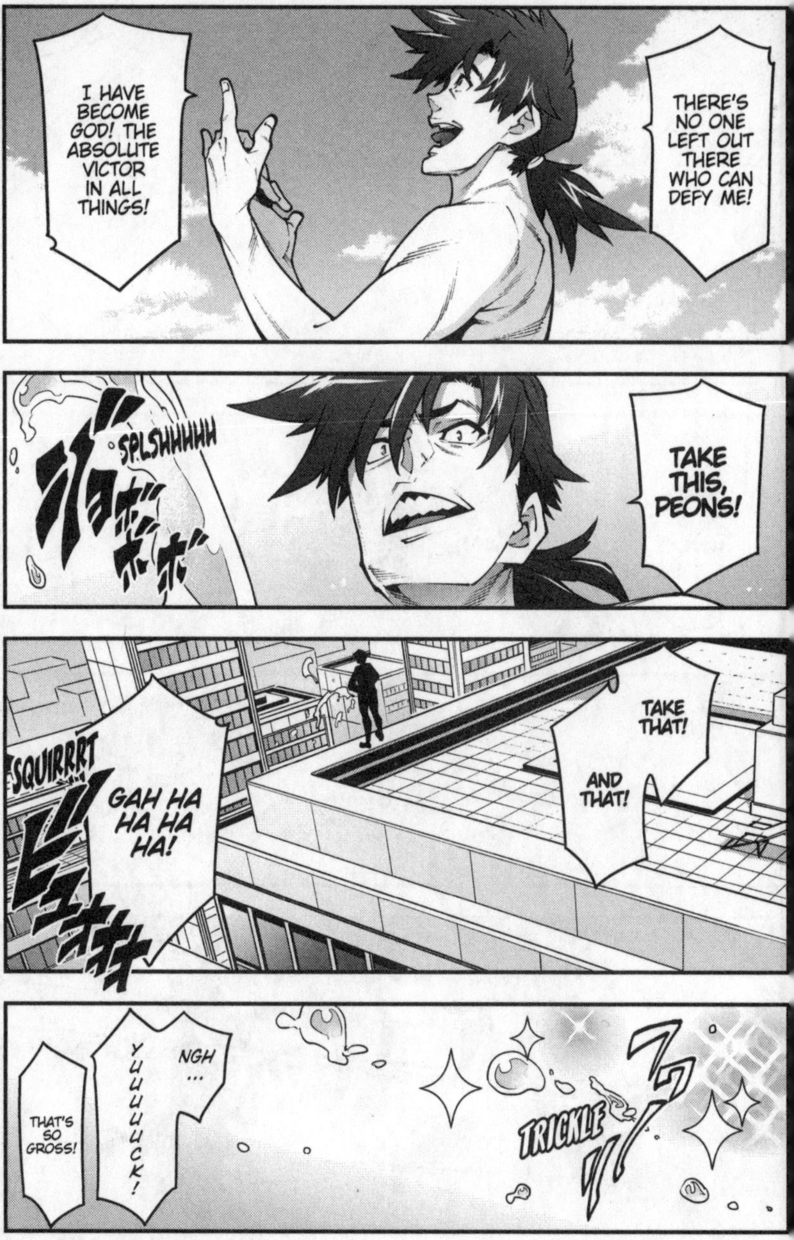
THERE'S NO ONE LEFT OUT THERE WHO CAN DEFY ME!
I HAVE BECOME GOD! THE ABSOLUTE VICTOR IN ALL THINGS!
TAKE THIS, PEONS!
SPLSHHHHH
TAKE THAT!
AND THAT!
GAH HA HA HA HA!
SQUIRRRT
TRICKLE
NGH...
YUUUUUCK!
THAT'S SO GROSS!

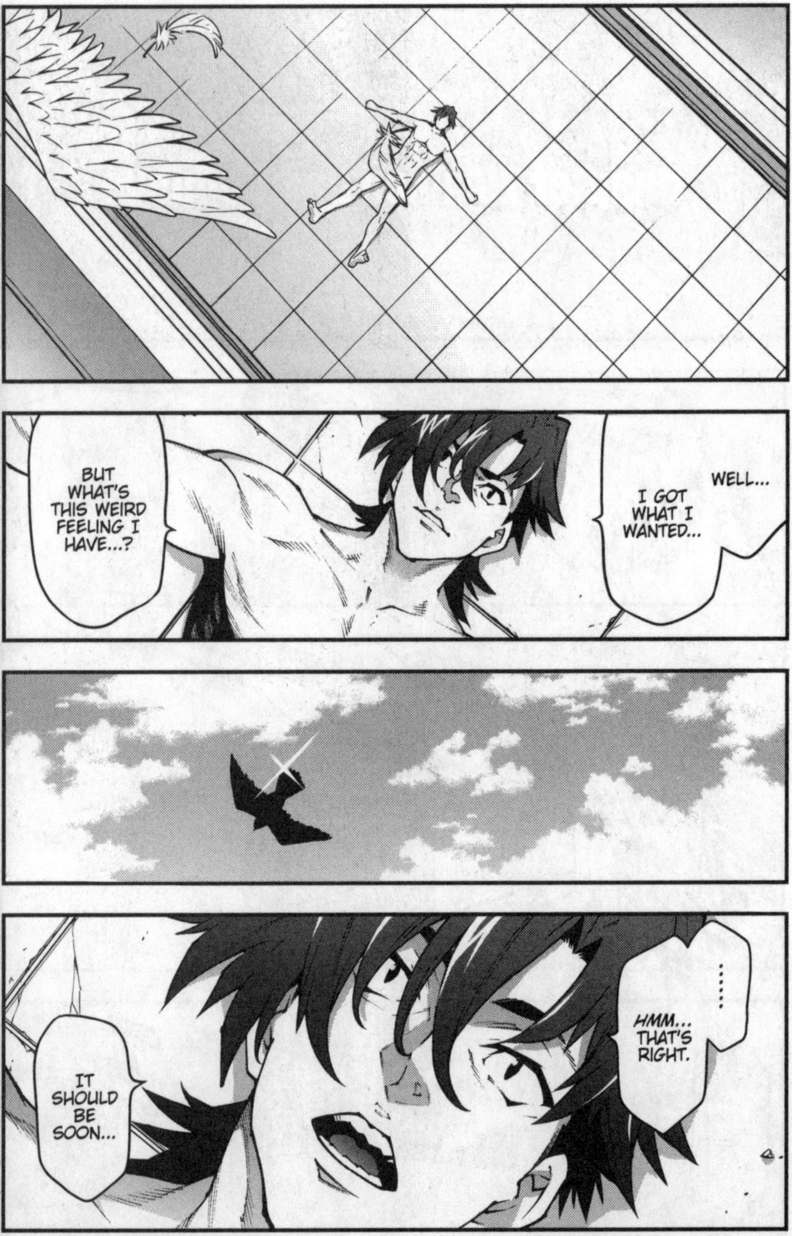
WELL...
I GOT WHAT I WANTED...
BUT WHAT'S THIS WEIRD FEELING I HAVE...?
......
HMM... THAT'S RIGHT.
IT SHOULD BE SOON...

Chapter 29: Good Day, Goodbye

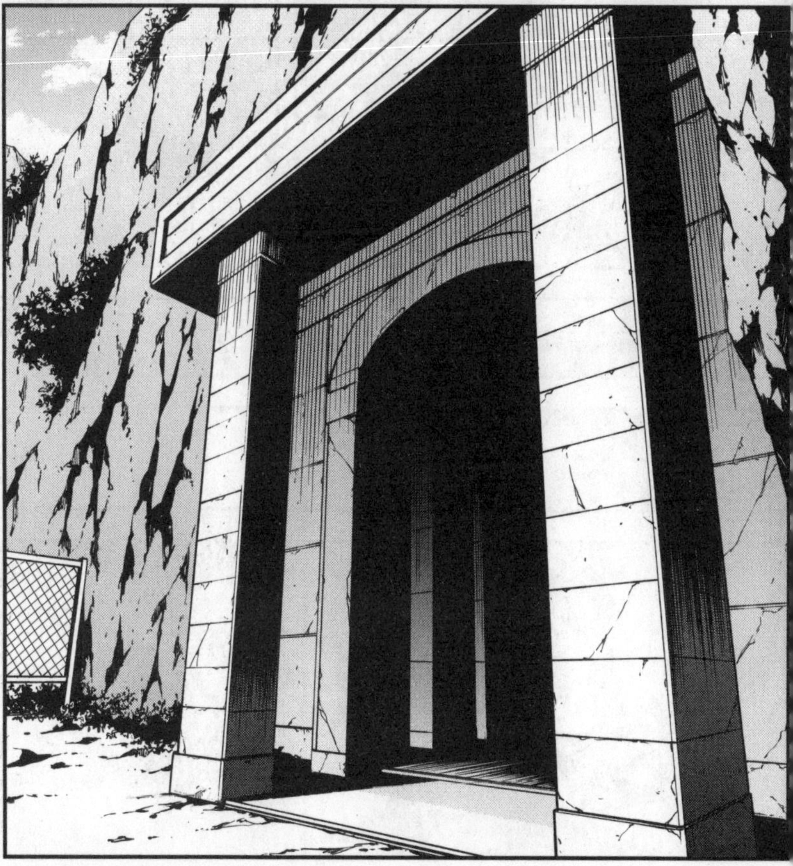

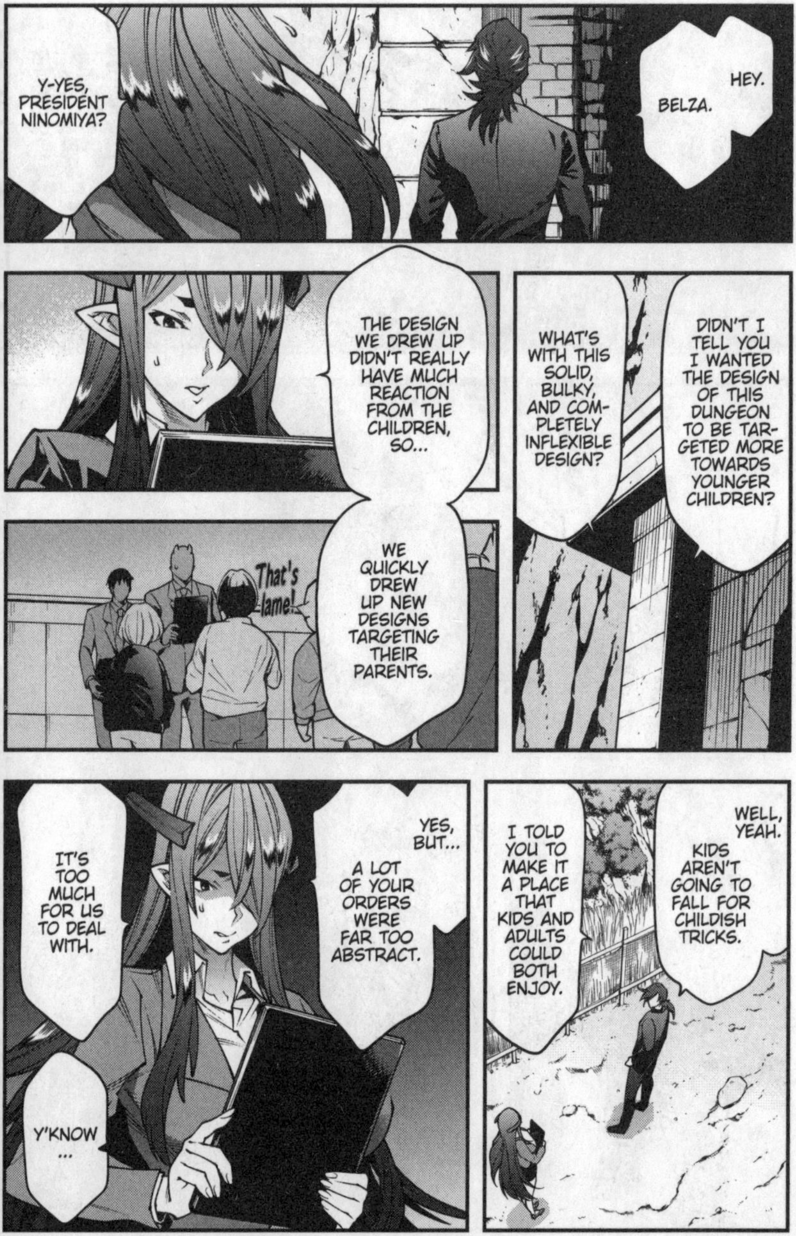
HEY. BELZA.
Y-YES, PRESIDENT NINOMIYA?
DIDN'T I TELL YOU I WANTED THE DESIGN OF THIS DUNGEON TO BE TARGETED MORE TOWARDS YOUNGER CHILDREN?
WHAT'S WITH THIS SOLID, BULKY, AND COMPLETELY INFLEXIBLE DESIGN?
THE DESIGN WE DREW UP DIDN'T REALLY HAVE MUCH REACTION FROM THE CHILDREN, SO...
WE QUICKLY DREW UP NEW DESIGNS TARGETING THEIR PARENTS.
That's lame!
WELL, YEAH. KIDS AREN'T GOING TO FALL FOR CHILDISH TRICKS.
I TOLD YOU TO MAKE IT A PLACE THAT KIDS AND ADULTS COULD BOTH ENJOY.
YES, BUT...
A LOT OF YOUR ORDERS WERE FAR TOO ABSTRACT.
IT'S TOO MUCH FOR US TO DEAL WITH.
Y'KNOW ...

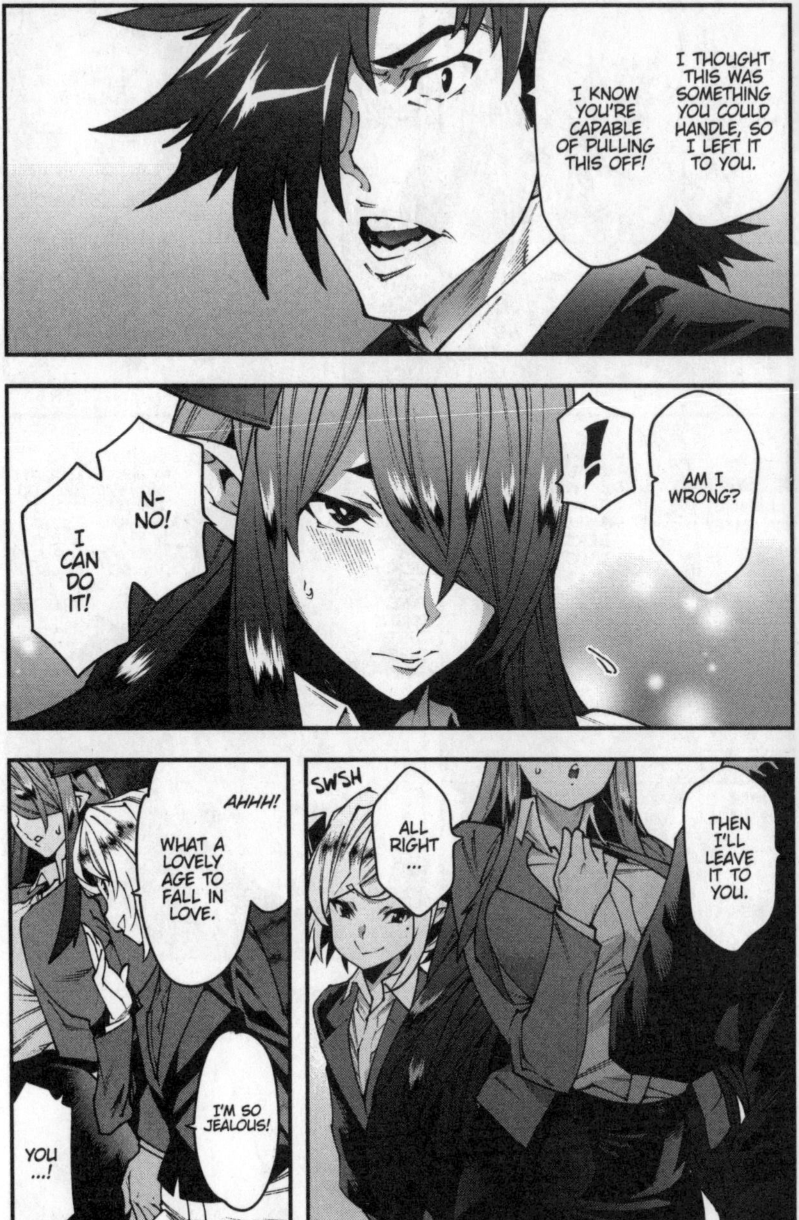
I THOUGHT THIS WAS SOMETHING YOU COULD HANDLE, SO I LEFT IT TO YOU.
I KNOW YOU'RE CAPABLE OF PULLING THIS OFF!
AM I WRONG?
!
N-NO!
I CAN DO IT!
THEN I'LL LEAVE IT TO YOU.
SWSH
ALL RIGHT ...
AHHH!
WHAT A LOVELY AGE TO FALL IN LOVE.
I'M SO JEALOUS!
YOU ...!

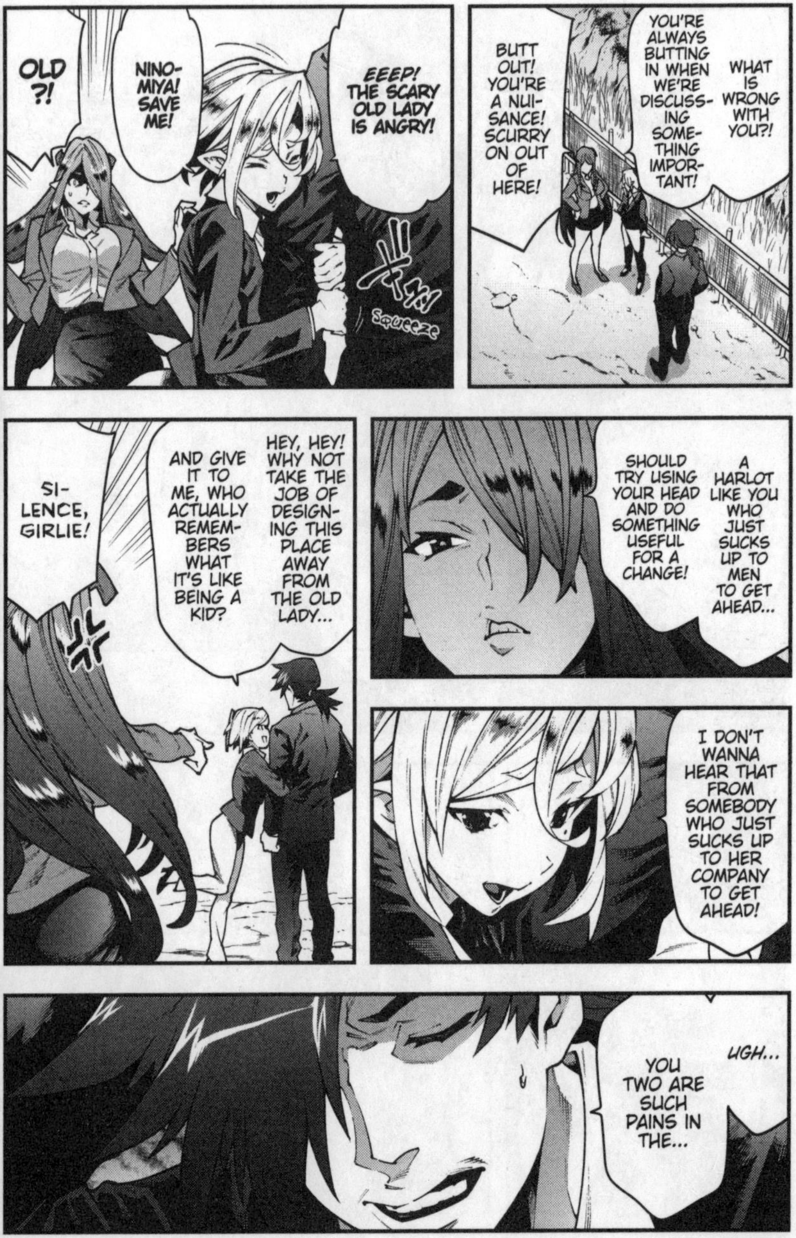
WHAT IS WRONG WITH YOU?!
YOU'RE ALWAYS BUTTING IN WHEN WE'RE DISCUSS-ING SOME-THING IMPORT-TANT!
BUTT OUT! YOU'RE A NUI-SANCE! SCURRY ON OUT OF HERE!
EEEP! THE SCARY OLD LADY IS ANGRY!
Squeeze
NINO-MIYA! SAVE ME!
OLD ?!
A HARLOT LIKE YOU WHO JUST SUCKS UP TO MEN TO GET AHEAD...
SHOULD TRY USING YOUR HEAD AND DO SOMETHING USEFUL FOR A CHANGE!
I DON'T WANNA HEAR THAT FROM SOMEBODY WHO JUST SUCKS UP TO HER COMPANY TO GET AHEAD!
HEY, HEY! WHY NOT TAKE THE JOB OF DESIGN-ING THIS PLACE AWAY FROM THE OLD LADY...
AND GIVE IT TO ME, WHO ACTUALLY REMEM-BERS WHAT IT'S LIKE BEING A KID?
SI-LENCE, GIRLIE!
UGH...
YOU TWO ARE SUCH PAINS IN THE...

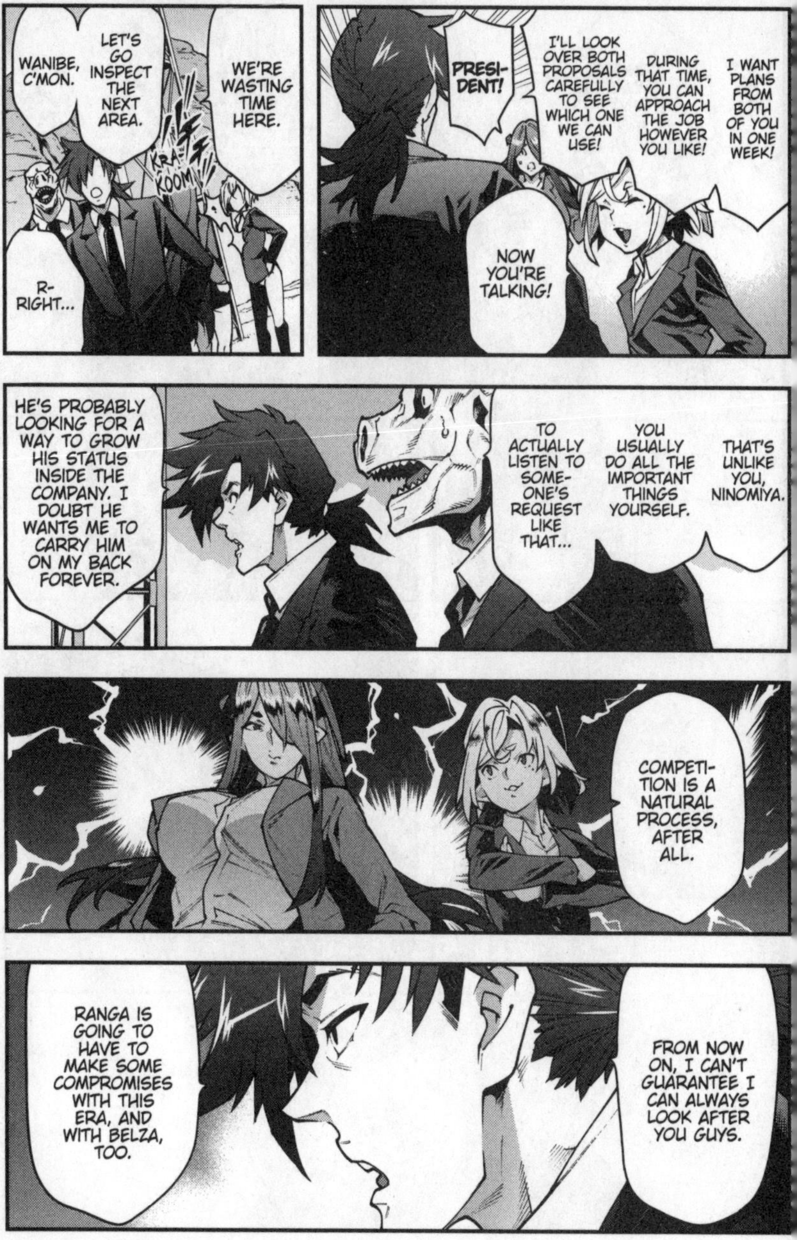
I WANT PLANS FROM BOTH OF YOU IN ONE WEEK!
DURING THAT TIME, YOU CAN APPROACH THE JOB HOWEVER YOU LIKE!
I'LL LOOK OVER BOTH PROPOSALS CAREFULLY TO SEE WHICH ONE WE CAN USE!
PRESIDENT!
NOW YOU'RE TALKING!
WE'RE WASTING TIME HERE.
LET'S GO INSPECT THE NEXT AREA.
WANIBE, C'MON.
KRA-KOOM
R-RIGHT...
THAT'S UNLIKE YOU, NINOMIYA.
YOU USUALLY DO ALL THE IMPORTANT THINGS YOURSELF.
TO ACTUALLY LISTEN TO SOMEONE'S REQUEST LIKE THAT...
HE'S PROBABLY LOOKING FOR A WAY TO GROW HIS STATUS INSIDE THE COMPANY. I DOUBT HE WANTS ME TO CARRY HIM ON MY BACK FOREVER.
COMPETITION IS A NATURAL PROCESS, AFTER ALL.
FROM NOW ON, I CAN'T GUARANTEE I CAN ALWAYS LOOK AFTER YOU GUYS.
RANGA IS GOING TO HAVE TO MAKE SOME COMPROMISES WITH THIS ERA, AND WITH BELZA, TOO.

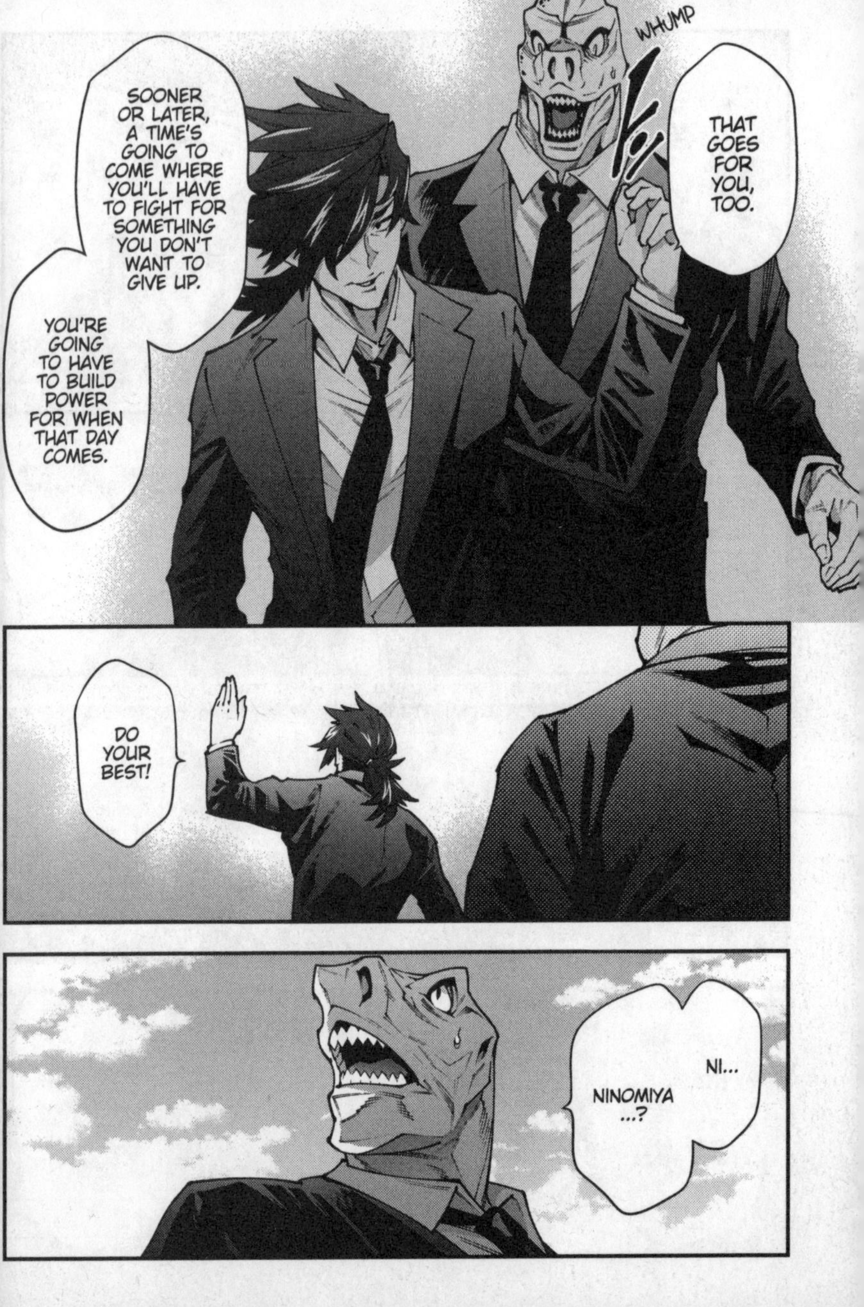
WHUMP
THAT GOES FOR YOU, TOO.
SOONER OR LATER, A TIME'S GOING TO COME WHERE YOU'LL HAVE TO FIGHT FOR SOMETHING YOU DON'T WANT TO GIVE UP.
YOU'RE GOING TO HAVE TO BUILD POWER FOR WHEN THAT DAY COMES.
DO YOUR BEST!
NI... NINOMIYA ...?

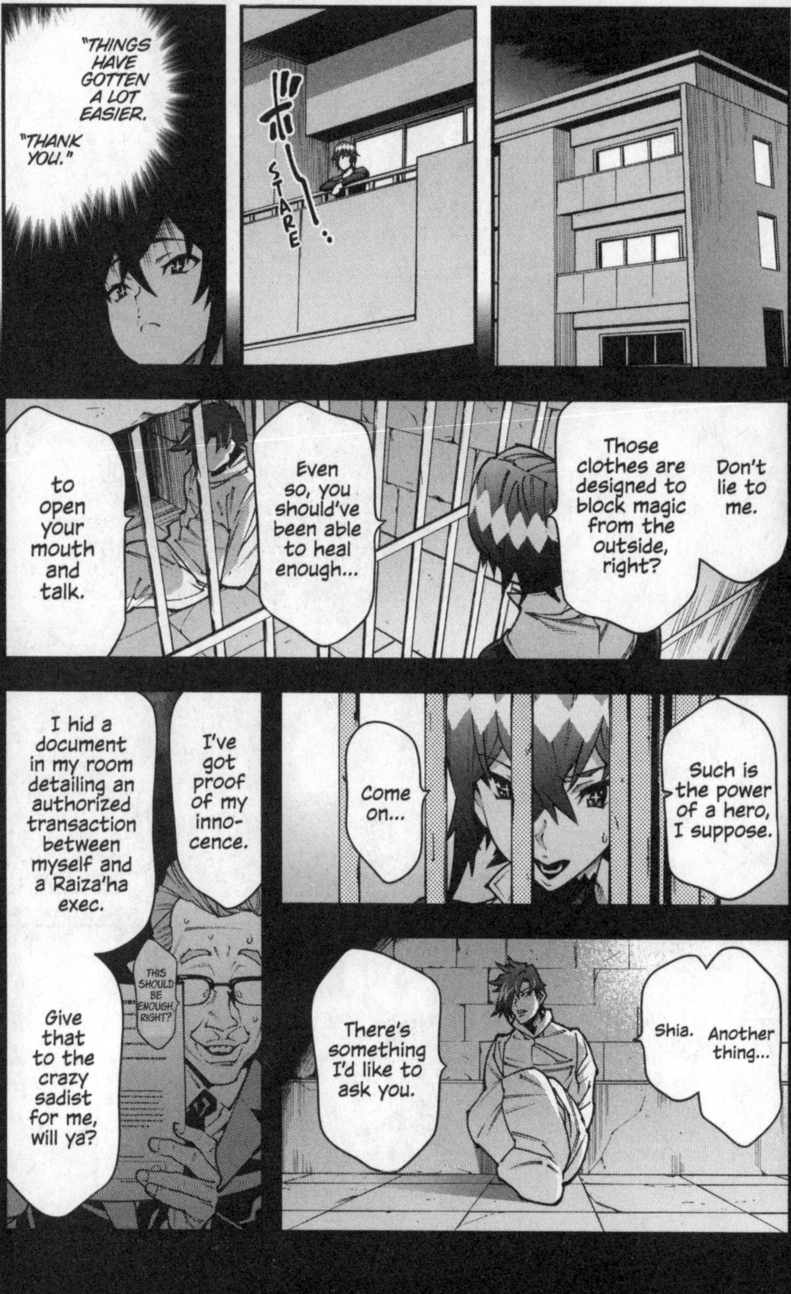
STARE
"THINGS HAVE GOTTEN A LOT EASIER.
"THANK YOU."
Don't lie to me.
Those clothes are designed to block magic from the outside, right?
Even so, you should've been able to heal enough...
to open your mouth and talk.
Such is the power of a hero, I suppose.
Come on...
Another thing...
Shia.
There's something I'd like to ask you.
I've got proof of my innocence.
I hid a document in my room detailing an authorized transaction between myself and a Raiza'ha exec.
Give that to the crazy sadist for me, will ya?
THIS SHOULD BE ENOUGH, RIGHT?

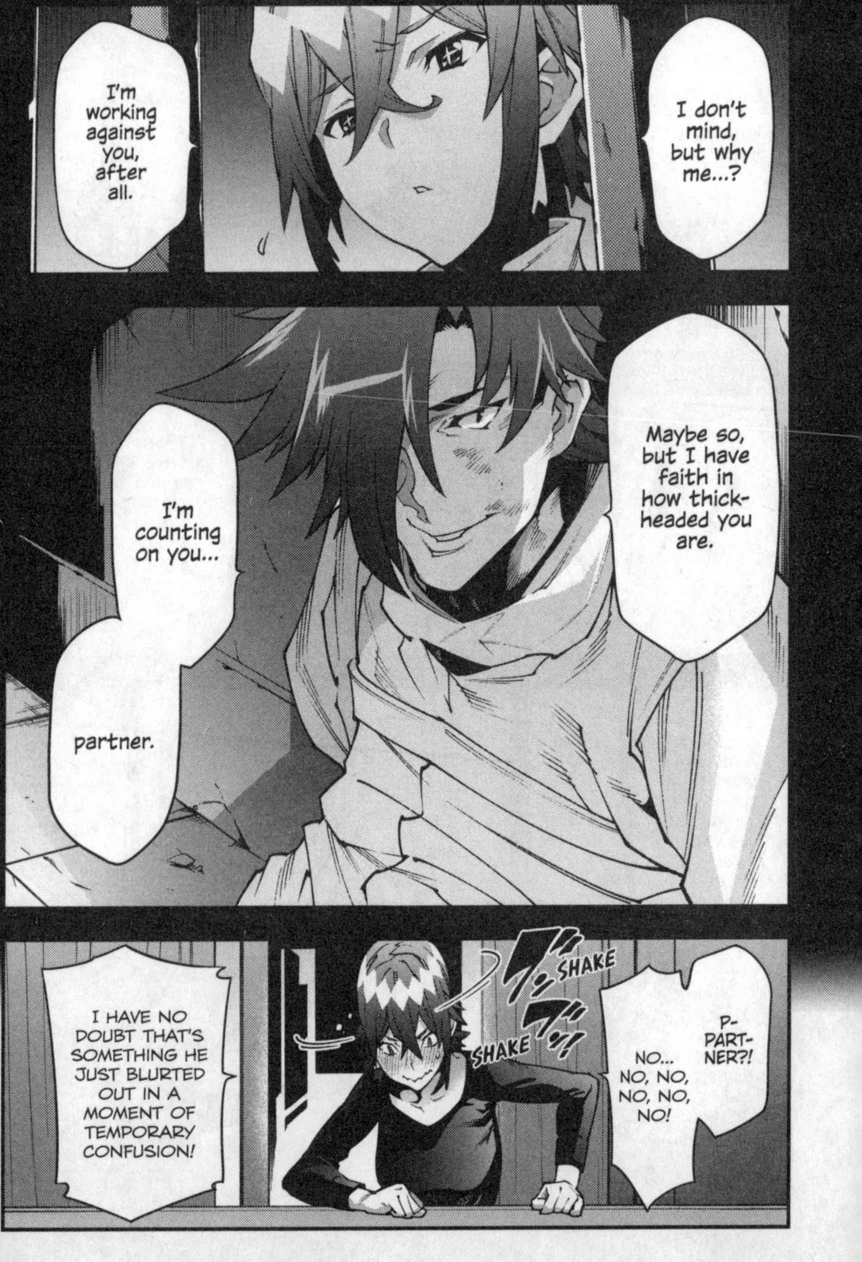
I don't mind, but why me...?
I'm working against you, after all.
Maybe so, but I have faith in how thick-headed you are.
I'm counting on you...
partner.
P-PARTNER?!
SHAKE
SHAKE
NO... NO, NO, NO, NO, NO!
I HAVE NO DOUBT THAT'S SOMETHING HE JUST BLURTED OUT IN A MOMENT OF TEMPORARY CONFUSION!

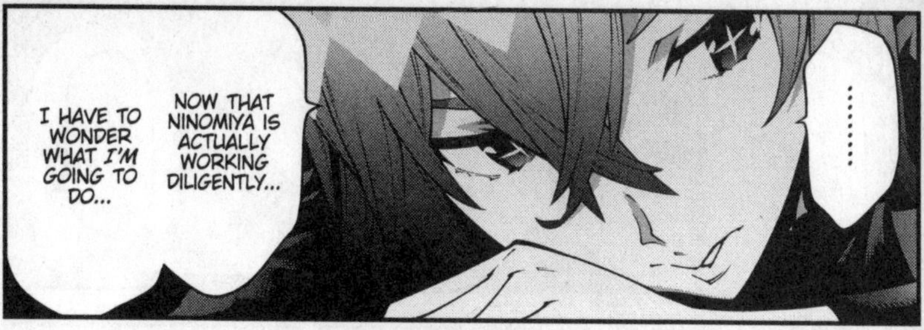
......
NOW THAT NINOMIYA IS ACTUALLY WORKING DILIGENTLY...
I HAVE TO WONDER WHAT *I'M* GOING TO DO...

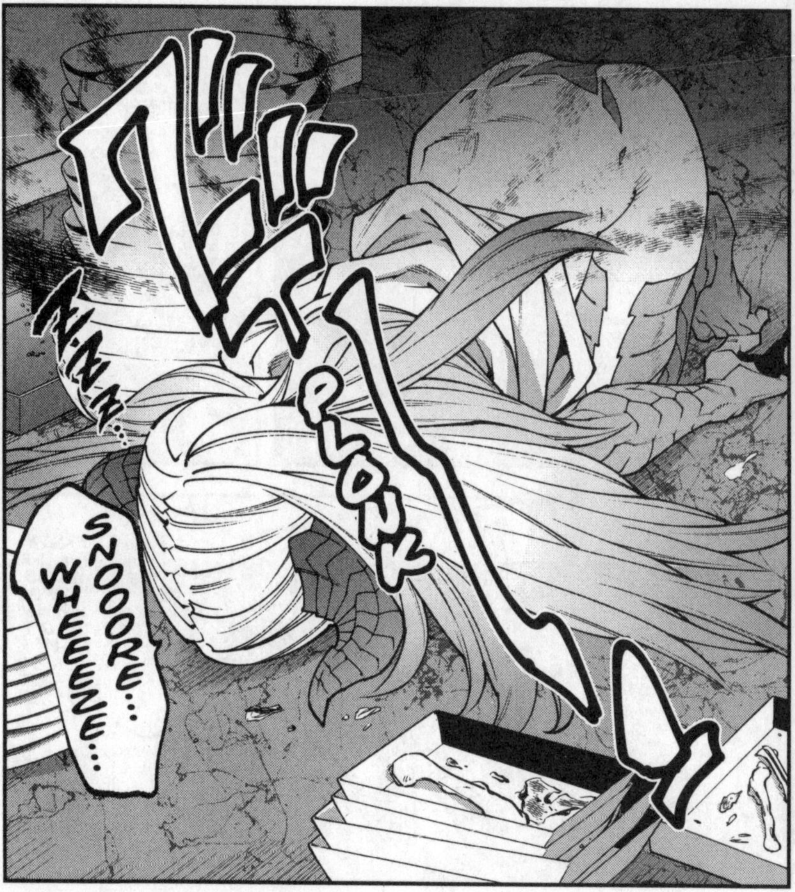
PLONK
NNN...
SNOOORE... WHEEEZE...

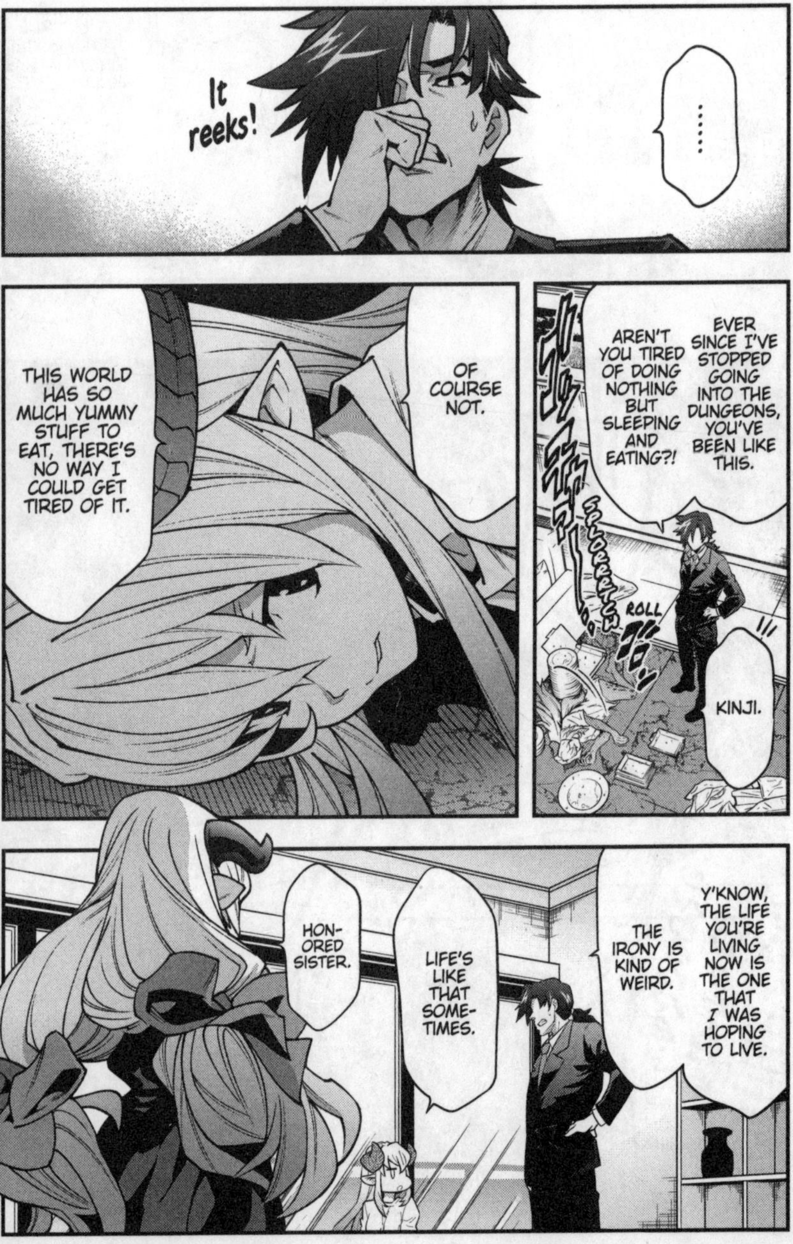
......
It reeks!
EVER SINCE I'VE STOPPED GOING INTO THE DUNGEONS, YOU'VE BEEN LIKE THIS.
AREN'T YOU TIRED OF DOING NOTHING BUT SLEEPING AND EATING?!
SPLORRRTCH
ROLL
!!!
KINJI.
OF COURSE NOT.
THIS WORLD HAS SO MUCH YUMMY STUFF TO EAT, THERE'S NO WAY I COULD GET TIRED OF IT.
Y'KNOW, THE LIFE YOU'RE LIVING NOW IS THE ONE THAT I WAS HOPING TO LIVE.
THE IRONY IS KIND OF WEIRD.
LIFE'S LIKE THAT SOMETIMES.
HON-ORED SISTER.

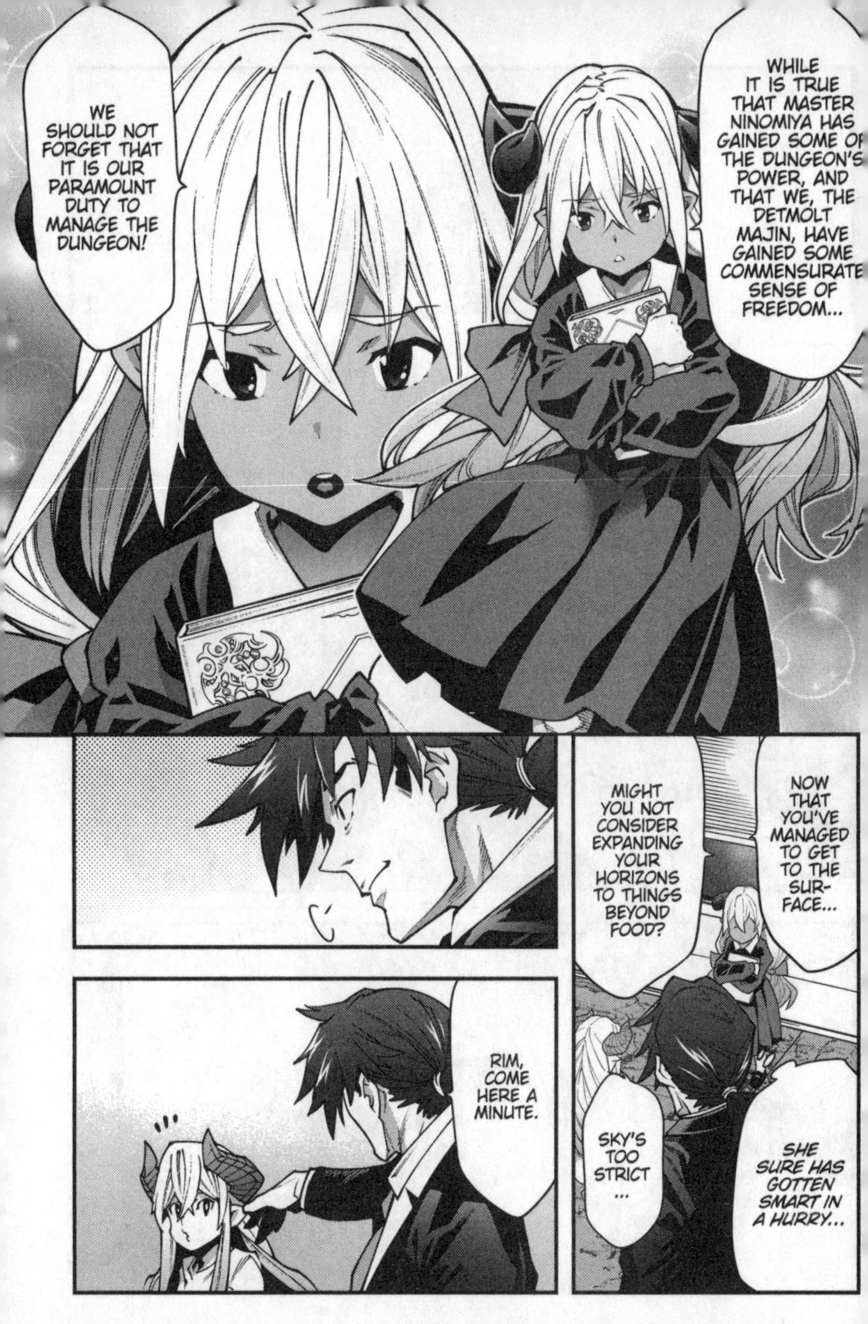
WHILE IT IS TRUE THAT MASTER NINOMIYA HAS GAINED SOME OF THE DUNGEON'S POWER, AND THAT WE, THE DETMOLT MAJIN, HAVE GAINED SOME COMMENSURATE SENSE OF FREEDOM...
WE SHOULD NOT FORGET THAT IT IS OUR PARAMOUNT DUTY TO MANAGE THE DUNGEON!
NOW THAT YOU'VE MANAGED TO GET TO THE SUR-FACE...
MIGHT YOU NOT CONSIDER EXPANDING YOUR HORIZONS TO THINGS BEYOND FOOD?
SHE SURE HAS GOTTEN SMART IN A HURRY...
SKY'S TOO STRICT ...
RIM, COME HERE A MINUTE.

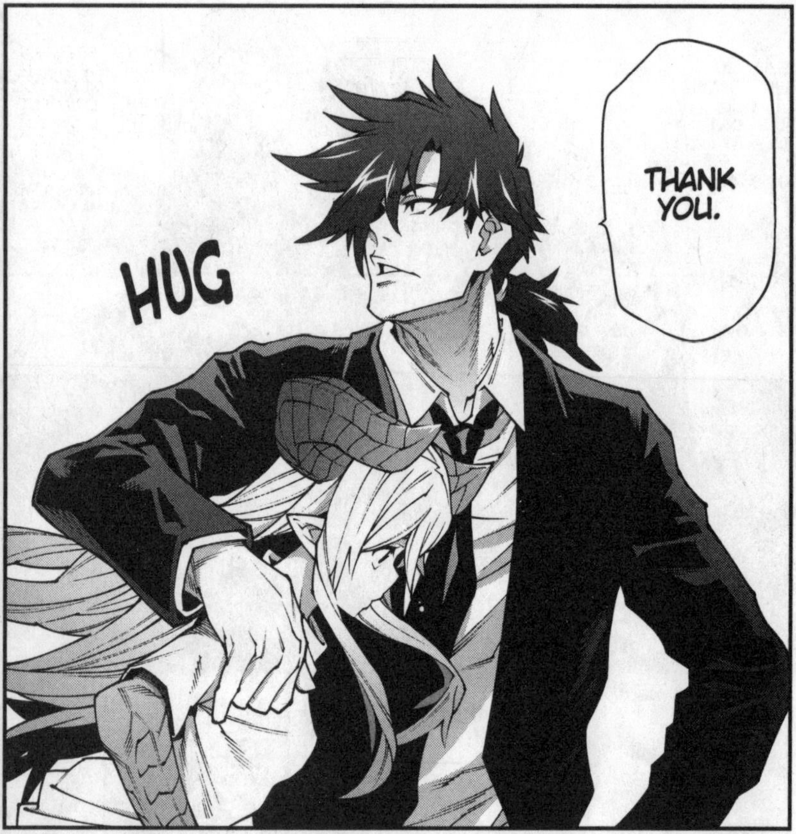
THANK YOU.
HUG
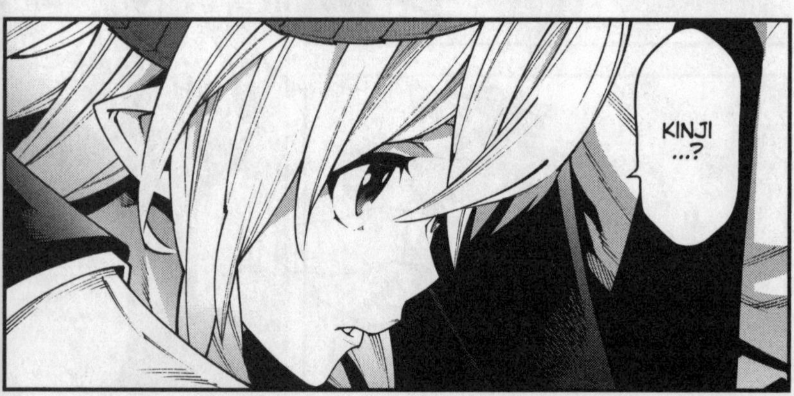
KINJI ...?

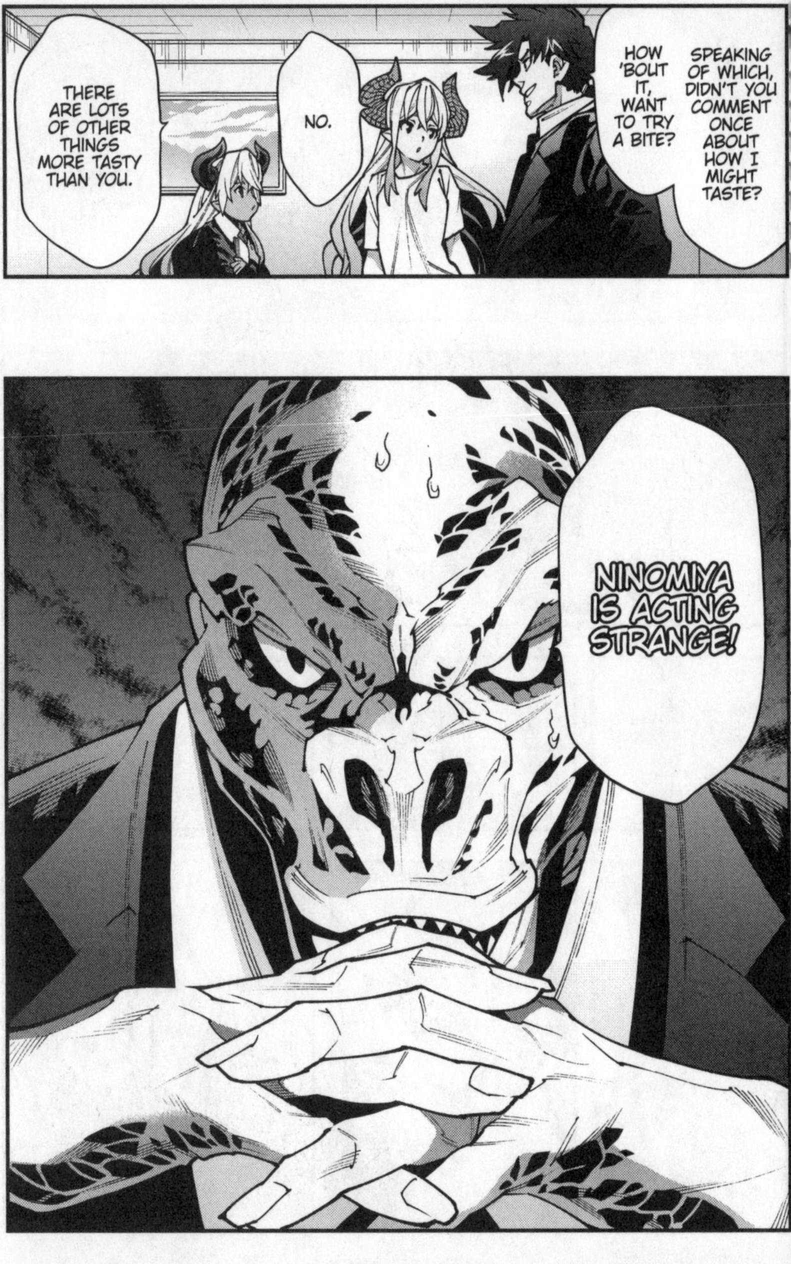
SPEAKING OF WHICH, DIDN'T YOU COMMENT ONCE ABOUT HOW I MIGHT TASTE?
HOW 'BOUT IT, WANT TO TRY A BITE?
NO.
THERE ARE LOTS OF OTHER THINGS MORE TASTY THAN YOU.
NINOMIYA IS ACTING STRANGE!

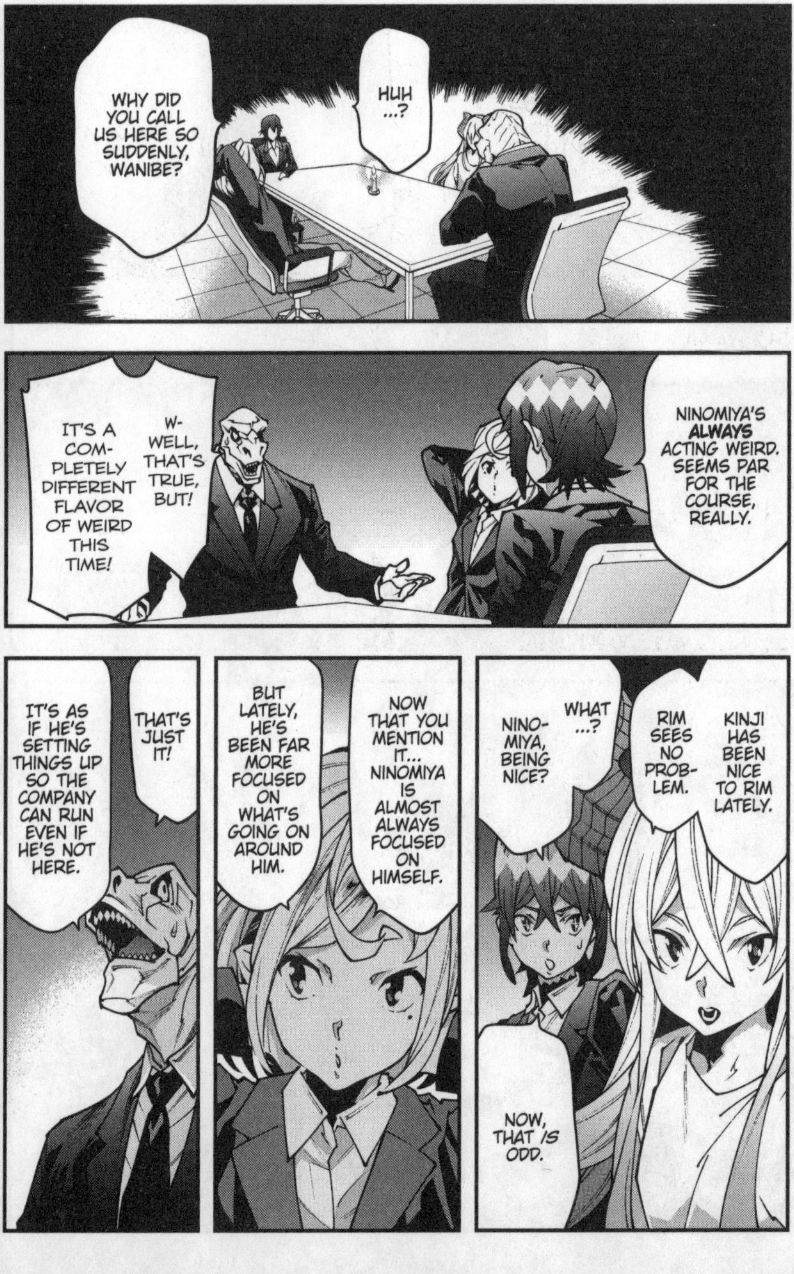
HUH ...?
WHY DID YOU CALL US HERE SO SUDDENLY, WANIBE?
NINOMIYA'S **ALWAYS** ACTING WEIRD. SEEMS PAR FOR THE COURSE, REALLY.
W-WELL, THAT'S TRUE, BUT!
IT'S A COMPLETELY DIFFERENT FLAVOR OF WEIRD THIS TIME!
KINJI HAS BEEN NICE TO RIM LATELY.
RIM SEES NO PROBLEM.
WHAT ...?
NINOMIYA, BEING NICE?
NOW, THAT *IS* ODD.
NOW THAT YOU MENTION IT... NINOMIYA IS ALMOST ALWAYS FOCUSED ON HIMSELF.
BUT LATELY, HE'S BEEN FAR MORE FOCUSED ON WHAT'S GOING ON AROUND HIM.
THAT'S JUST IT!
IT'S AS IF HE'S SETTING THINGS UP SO THE COMPANY CAN RUN EVEN IF HE'S NOT HERE.

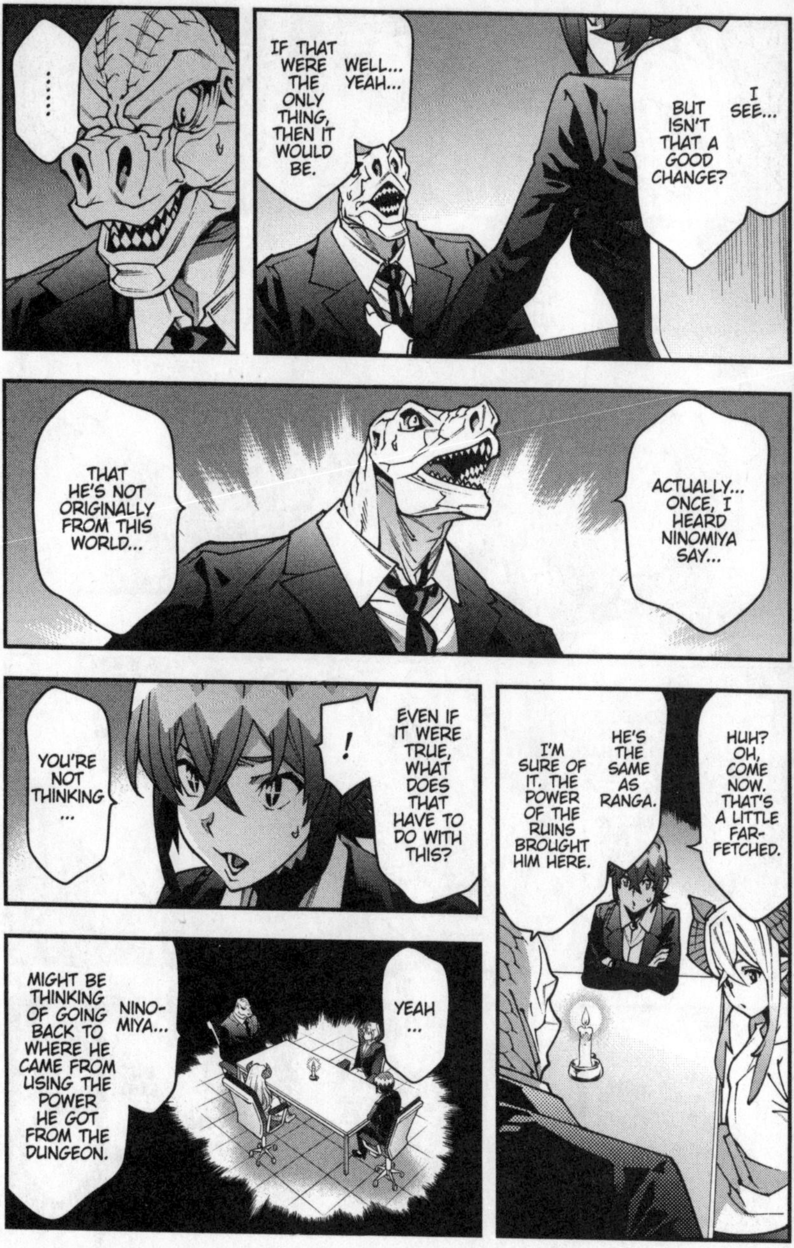
I SEE... BUT ISN'T THAT A GOOD CHANGE?
WELL... YEAH... IF THAT WERE THE ONLY THING, THEN IT WOULD BE.
......
ACTUALLY... ONCE, I HEARD NINOMIYA SAY...
THAT HE'S NOT ORIGINALLY FROM THIS WORLD...
HUH? OH, COME NOW. THAT'S A LITTLE FAR-FETCHED.
HE'S THE SAME AS RANGA.
I'M SURE OF IT. THE POWER OF THE RUINS BROUGHT HIM HERE.
!
EVEN IF IT WERE TRUE, WHAT DOES THAT HAVE TO DO WITH THIS?
YOU'RE NOT THINKING...
YEAH...
NINO-MIYA...
MIGHT BE THINKING OF GOING BACK TO WHERE HE CAME FROM USING THE POWER HE GOT FROM THE DUNGEON.

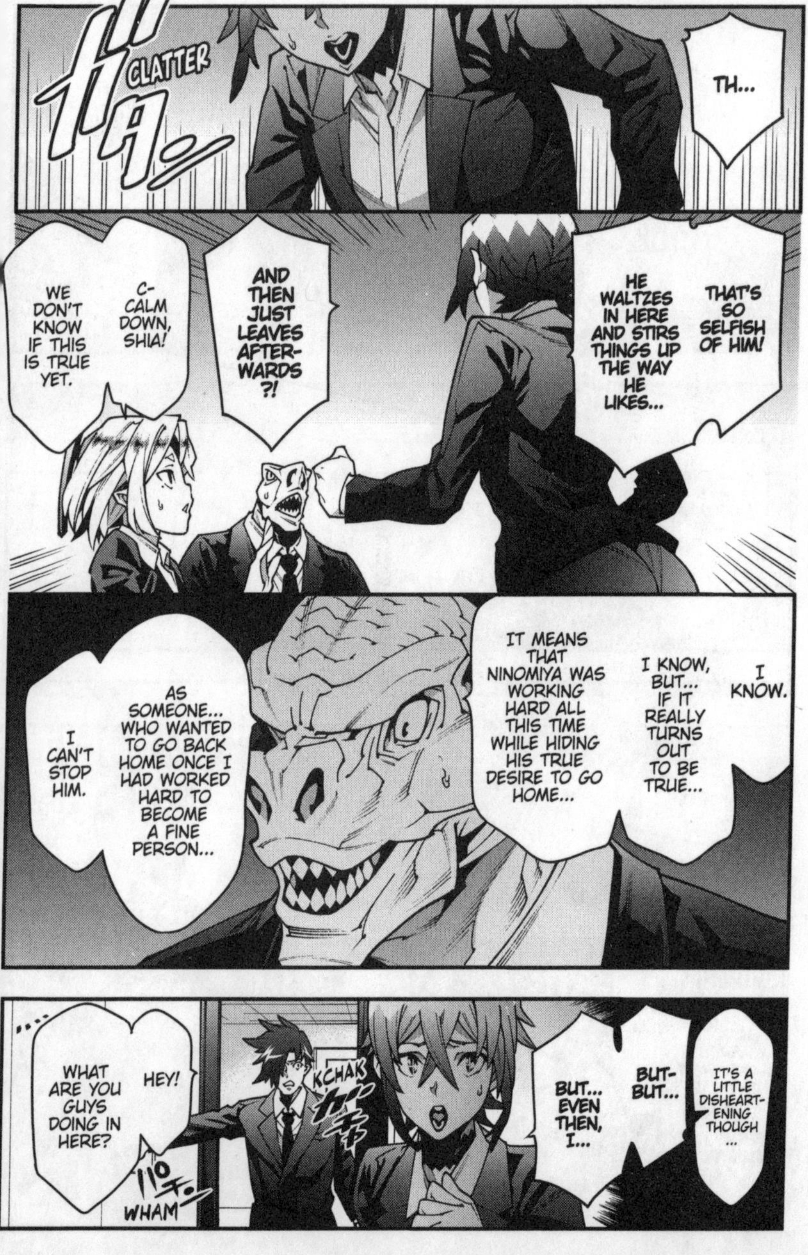
TH...
CLATTER
THAT'S SO SELFISH OF HIM!
HE WALTZES IN HERE AND STIRS THINGS UP THE WAY HE LIKES...
AND THEN JUST LEAVES AFTER-WARDS?!
C-CALM DOWN, SHIA!
WE DON'T KNOW IF THIS IS TRUE YET.
I KNOW.
I KNOW, BUT... IF IT REALLY TURNS OUT TO BE TRUE...
IT MEANS THAT NINOMIYA WAS WORKING HARD ALL THIS TIME WHILE HIDING HIS TRUE DESIRE TO GO HOME...
AS SOMEONE... WHO WANTED TO GO BACK HOME ONCE I HAD WORKED HARD TO BECOME A FINE PERSON...
I CAN'T STOP HIM.
IT'S A LITTLE DISHEART-ENING THOUGH...
BUT-BUT...
BUT... EVEN THEN, I...
KCHAK
HEY!
WHAT ARE YOU GUYS DOING IN HERE?
WHAM
....

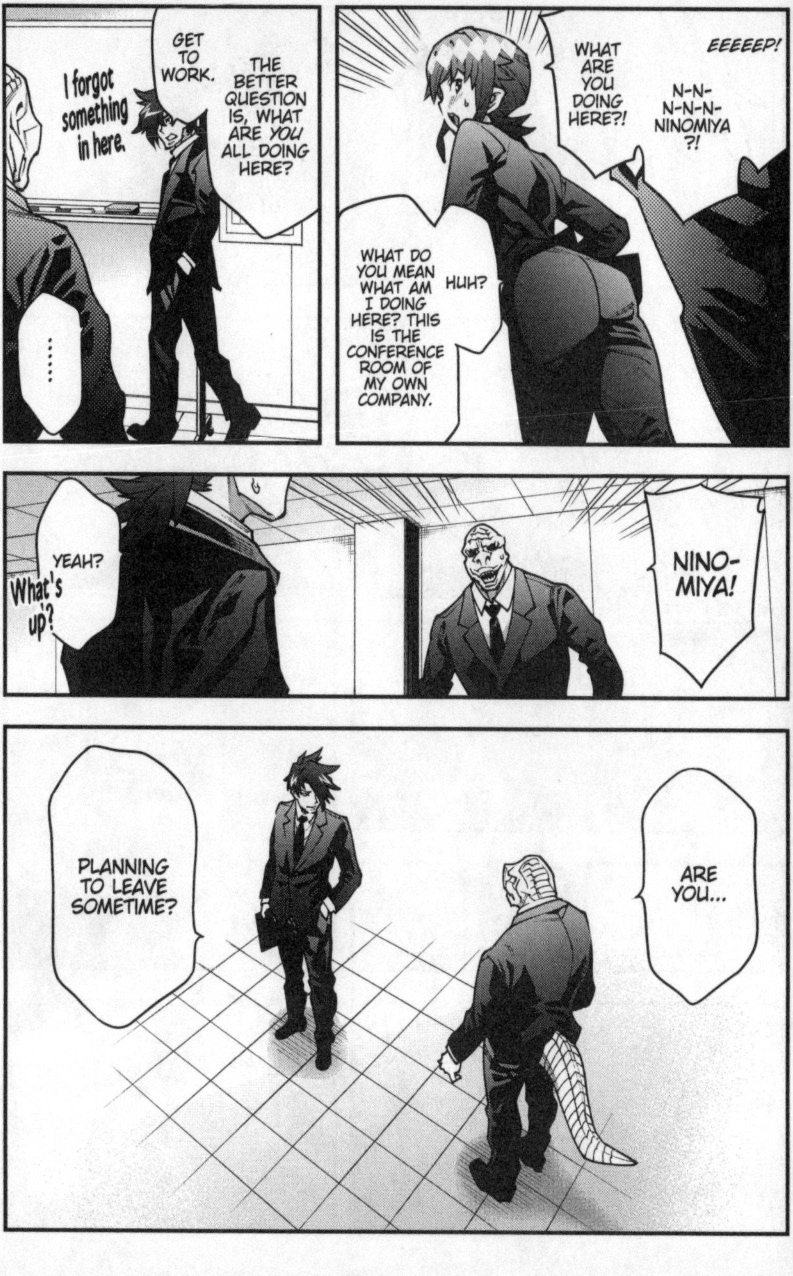
EEEEEP!
N-N-N-N-N-NINOMIYA?!
WHAT ARE YOU DOING HERE?!
HUH?
WHAT DO YOU MEAN WHAT AM I DOING HERE? THIS IS THE CONFERENCE ROOM OF MY OWN COMPANY.
THE BETTER QUESTION IS, WHAT ARE YOU ALL DOING HERE?
GET TO WORK.
I forgot something in here.
......
NINO-MIYA!
YEAH?
What's up?
ARE YOU...
PLANNING TO LEAVE SOMETIME?

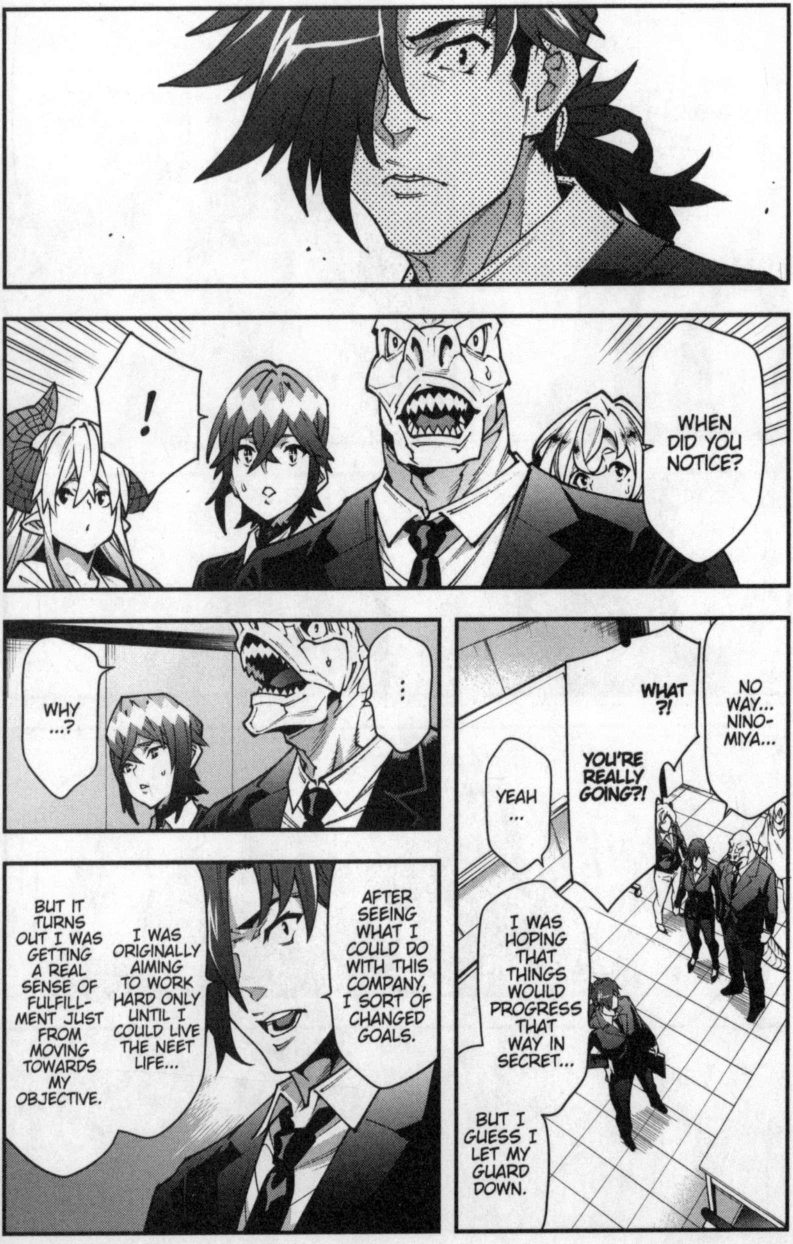
WHEN DID YOU NOTICE?
!
NO WAY... NINO-MIYA...
WHAT ?!
YOU'RE REALLY GOING?!
YEAH ...
I WAS HOPING THAT THINGS WOULD PROGRESS THAT WAY IN SECRET...
BUT I GUESS I LET MY GUARD DOWN.
...
WHY ...?
AFTER SEEING WHAT I COULD DO WITH THIS COMPANY, I SORT OF CHANGED GOALS.
I WAS ORIGINALLY AIMING TO WORK HARD ONLY UNTIL I COULD LIVE THE NEET LIFE...
BUT IT TURNS OUT I WAS GETTING A REAL SENSE OF FULFILL-MENT JUST FROM MOVING TOWARDS MY OBJECTIVE.

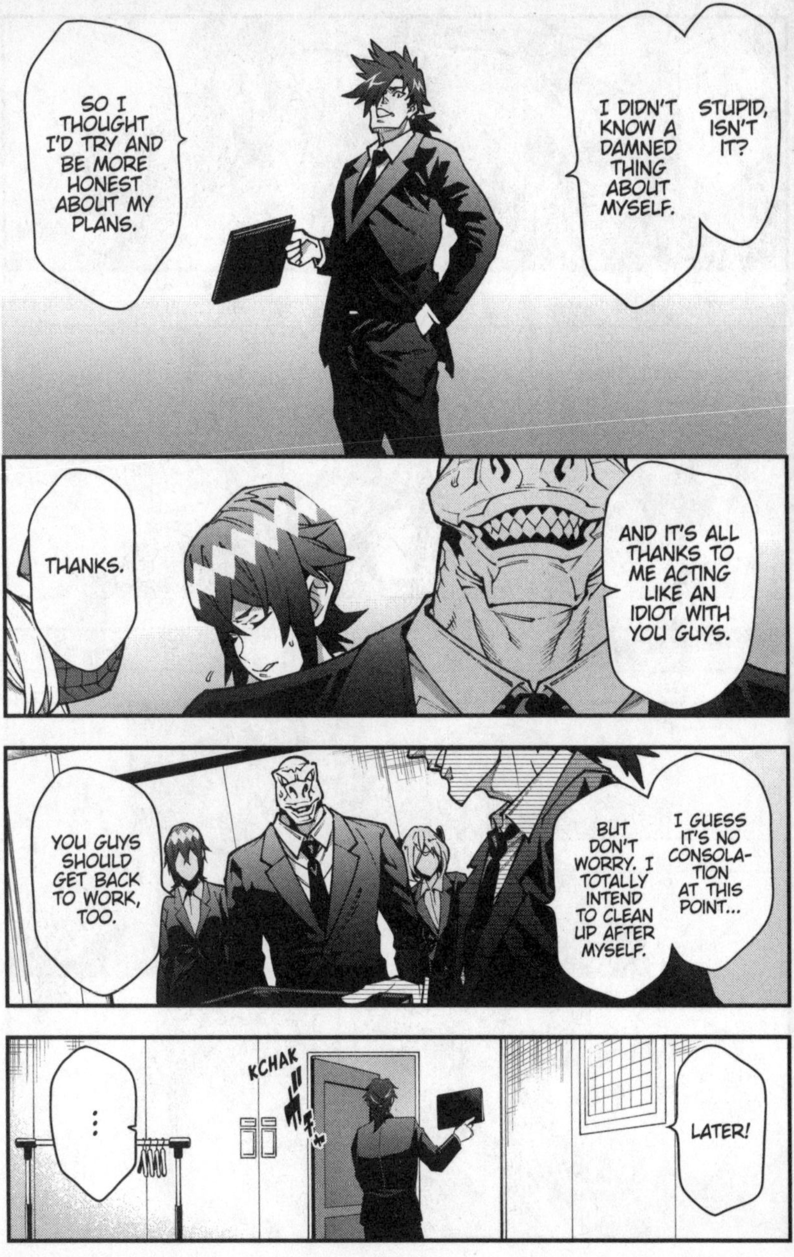
STUPID, ISN'T IT?
I DIDN'T KNOW A DAMNED THING ABOUT MYSELF.
SO I THOUGHT I'D TRY AND BE MORE HONEST ABOUT MY PLANS.
AND IT'S ALL THANKS TO ME ACTING LIKE AN IDIOT WITH YOU GUYS.
THANKS.
I GUESS IT'S NO CONSOLA-TION AT THIS POINT...
BUT DON'T WORRY. I TOTALLY INTEND TO CLEAN UP AFTER MYSELF.
YOU GUYS SHOULD GET BACK TO WORK, TOO.
LATER!
KCHAK
...

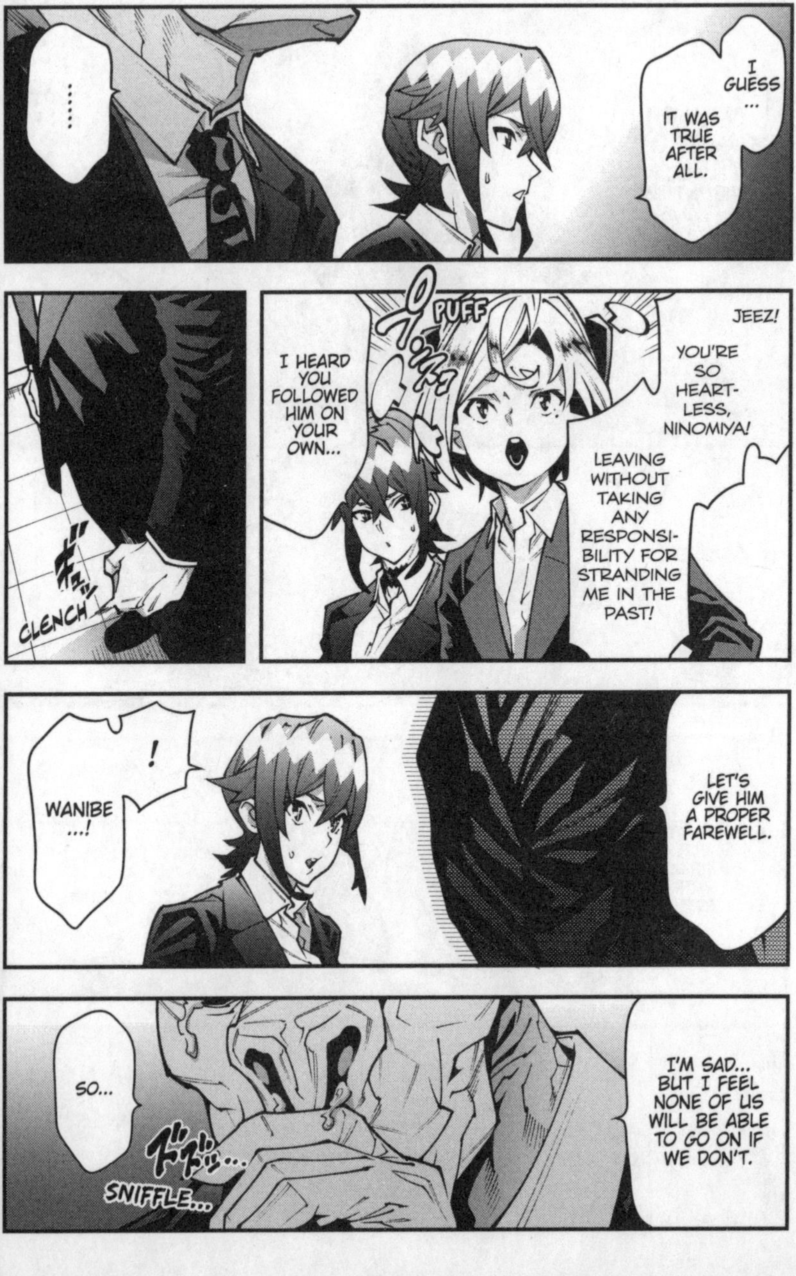
I GUESS...
IT WAS TRUE AFTER ALL.
......
JEEZ!
YOU'RE SO HEART-LESS, NINOMIYA!
LEAVING WITHOUT TAKING ANY RESPONSI-BILITY FOR STRANDING ME IN THE PAST!
PUFF
I HEARD YOU FOLLOWED HIM ON YOUR OWN...
CLENCH
LET'S GIVE HIM A PROPER FAREWELL.
!
WANIBE...!
I'M SAD... BUT I FEEL NONE OF US WILL BE ABLE TO GO ON IF WE DON'T.
SO...
SNIFFLE...

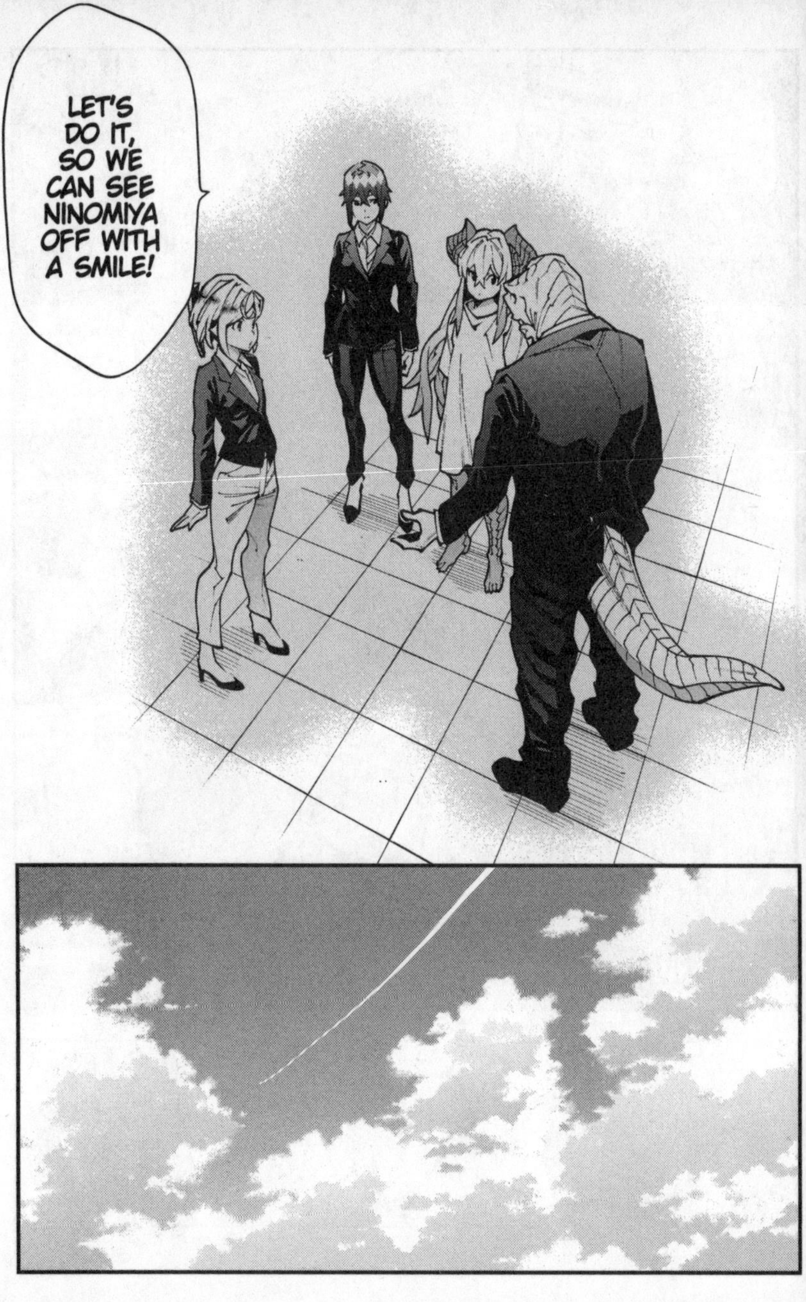
LET'S DO IT, SO WE CAN SEE NINOMIYA OFF WITH A SMILE!

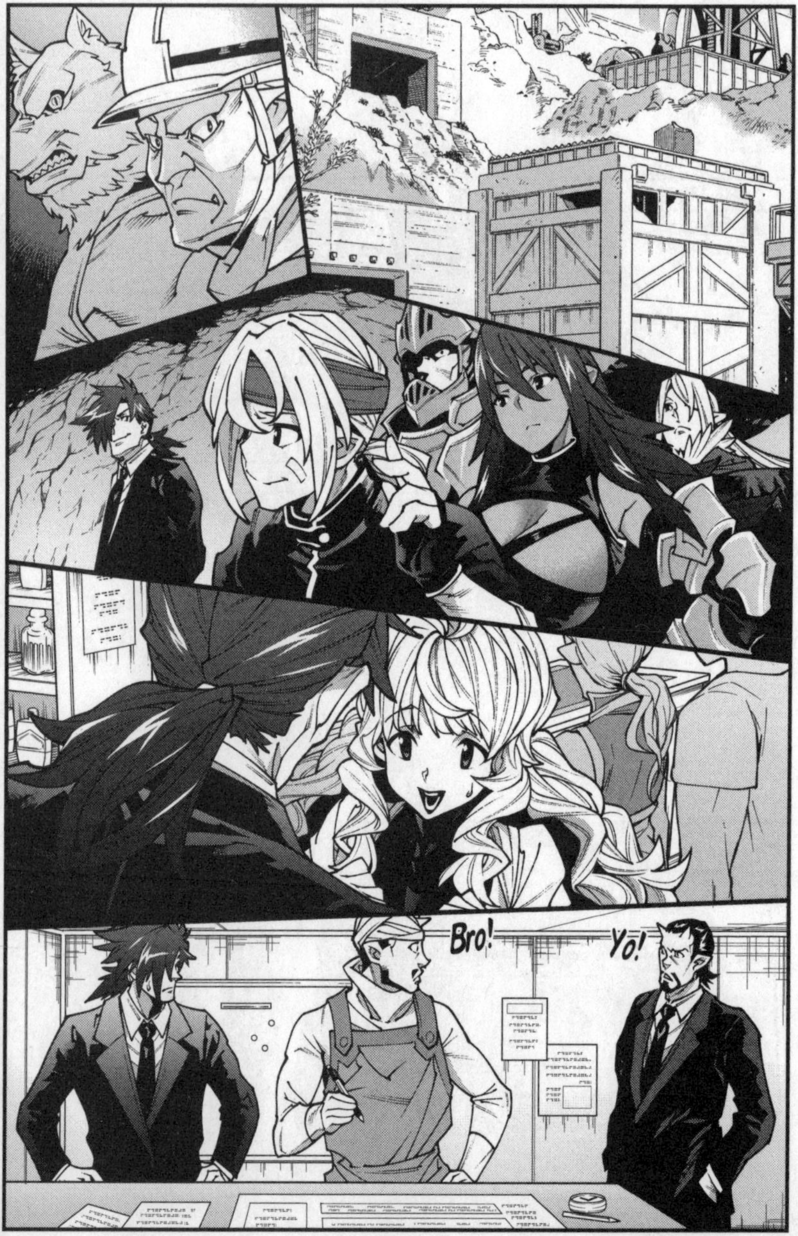
Yo!
Bro!

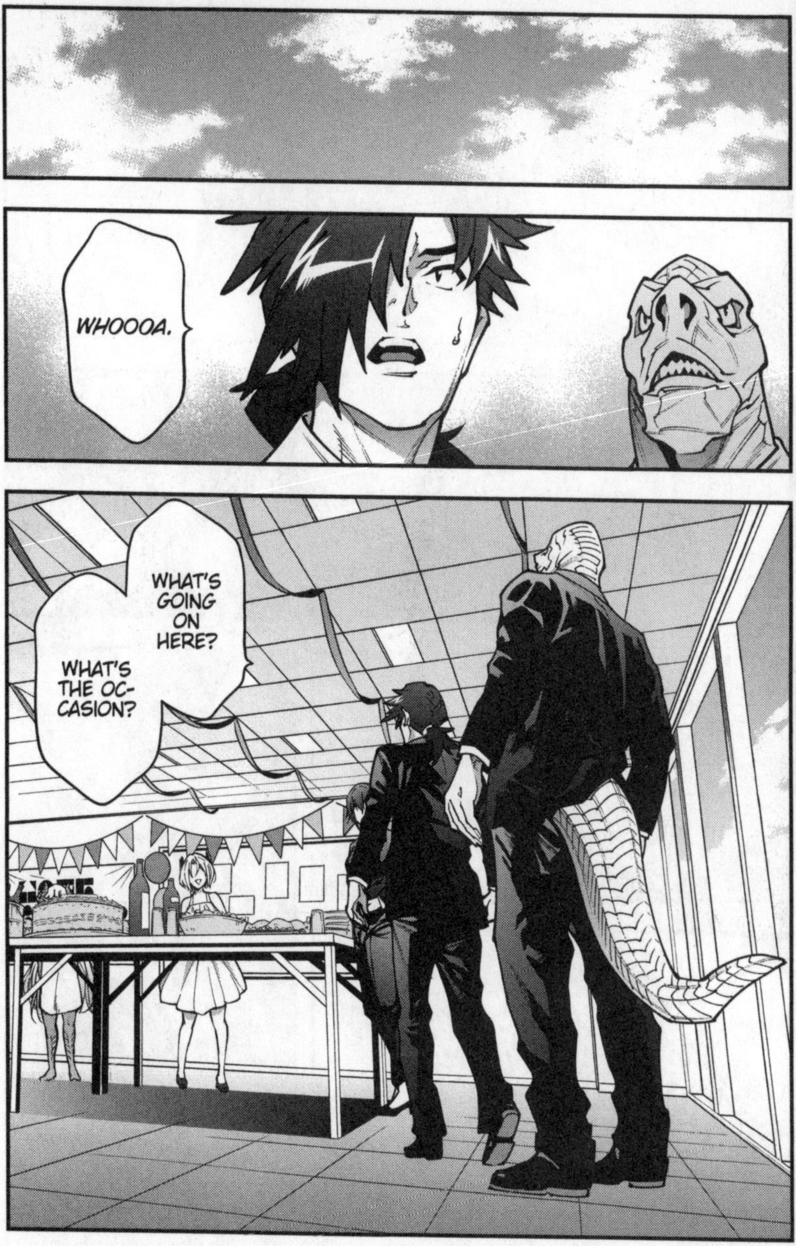
WHOOOA.
WHAT'S GOING ON HERE?
WHAT'S THE OC-CASION?

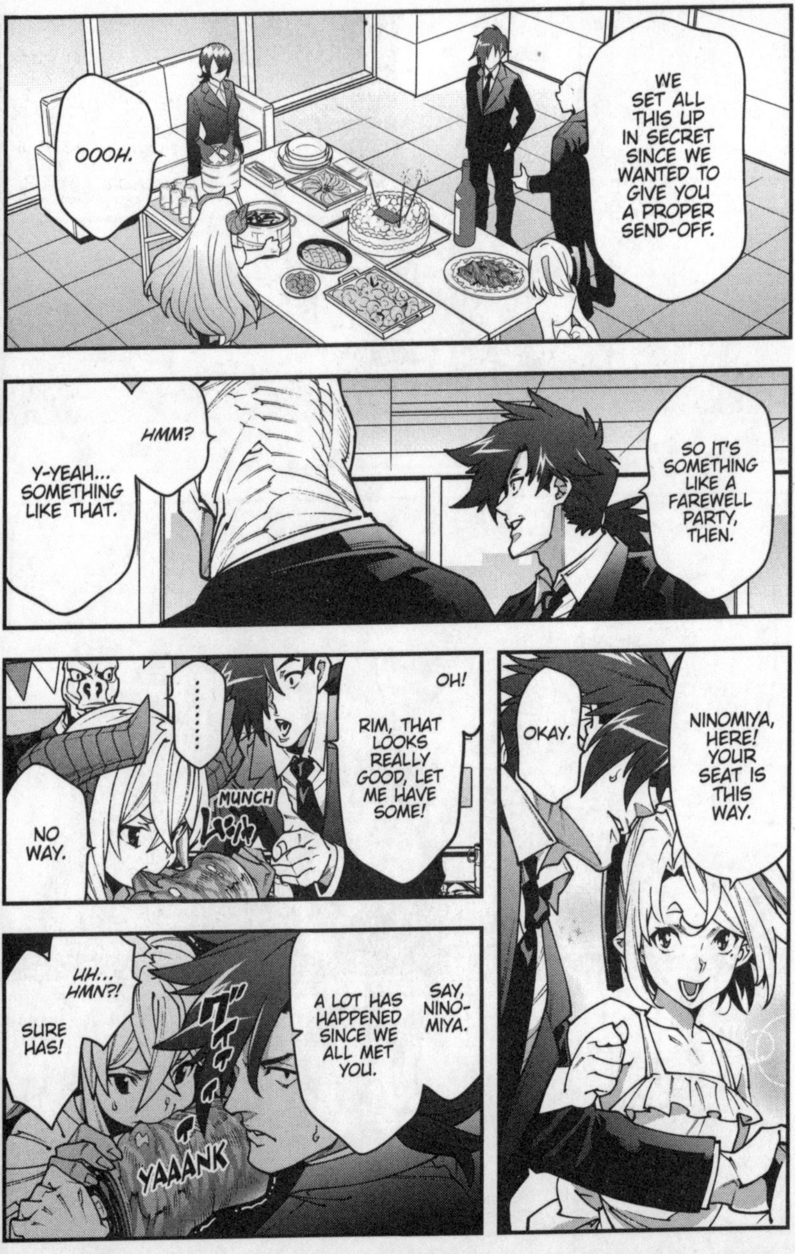
WE SET ALL THIS UP IN SECRET SINCE WE WANTED TO GIVE YOU A PROPER SEND-OFF.
OOOH.
SO IT'S SOMETHING LIKE A FAREWELL PARTY, THEN.
HMM?
Y-YEAH... SOMETHING LIKE THAT.
NINOMIYA, HERE! YOUR SEAT IS THIS WAY.
OKAY.
OH!
RIM, THAT LOOKS REALLY GOOD, LET ME HAVE SOME!
MUNCH
......
NO WAY.
SAY, NINO-MIYA.
A LOT HAS HAPPENED SINCE WE ALL MET YOU.
UH... HMN?!
SURE HAS!
YAAANK

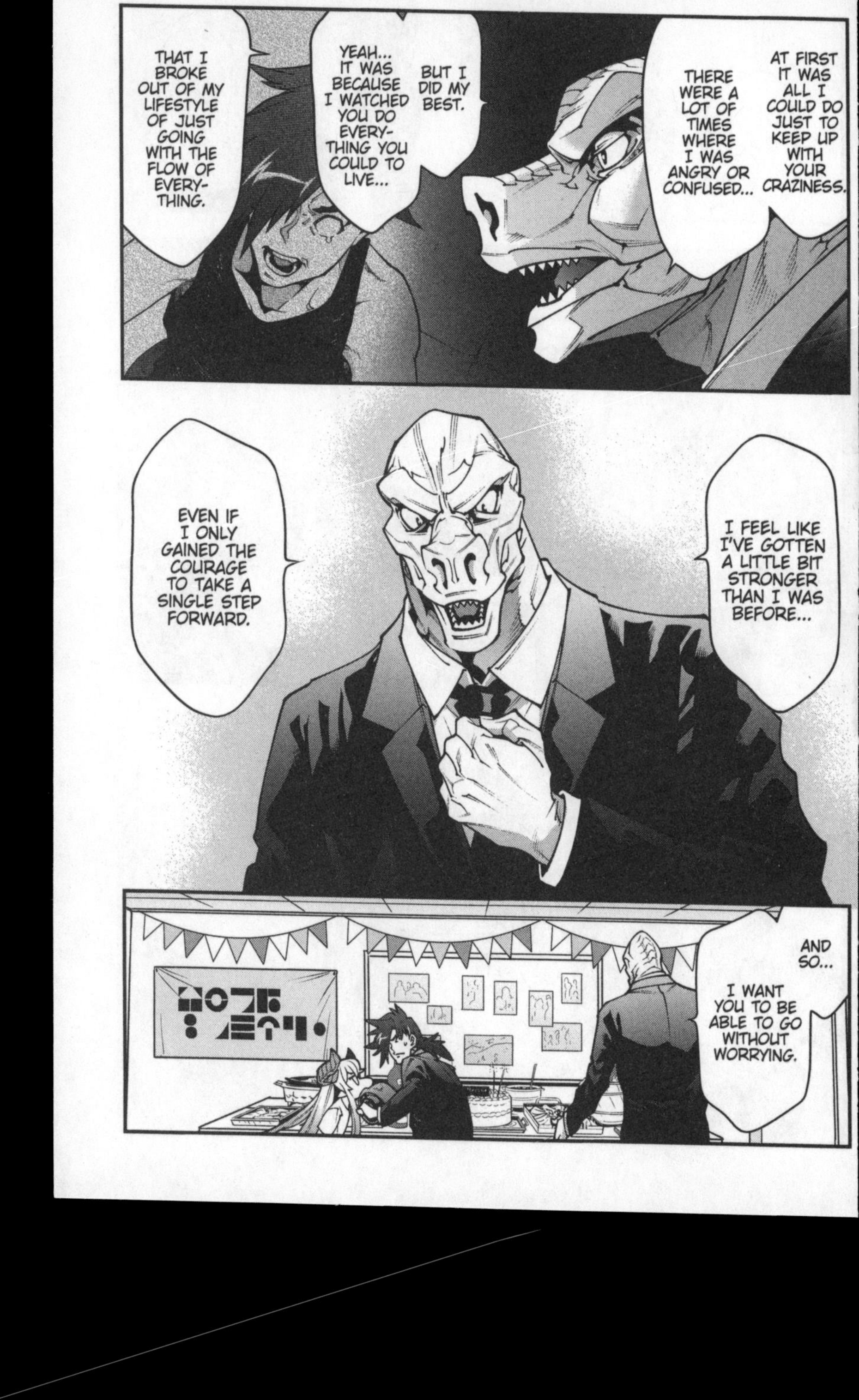
AT FIRST IT WAS ALL I COULD DO JUST TO KEEP UP WITH YOUR CRAZINESS.
THERE WERE A LOT OF TIMES WHERE I WAS ANGRY OR CONFUSED...
BUT I DID MY BEST.
YEAH... IT WAS BECAUSE I WATCHED YOU DO EVERY-THING YOU COULD TO LIVE...
THAT I BROKE OUT OF MY LIFESTYLE OF JUST GOING WITH THE FLOW OF EVERY-THING.
I FEEL LIKE I'VE GOTTEN A LITTLE BIT STRONGER THAN I WAS BEFORE...
EVEN IF I ONLY GAINED THE COURAGE TO TAKE A SINGLE STEP FORWARD.
AND SO...
I WANT YOU TO BE ABLE TO GO WITHOUT WORRYING.

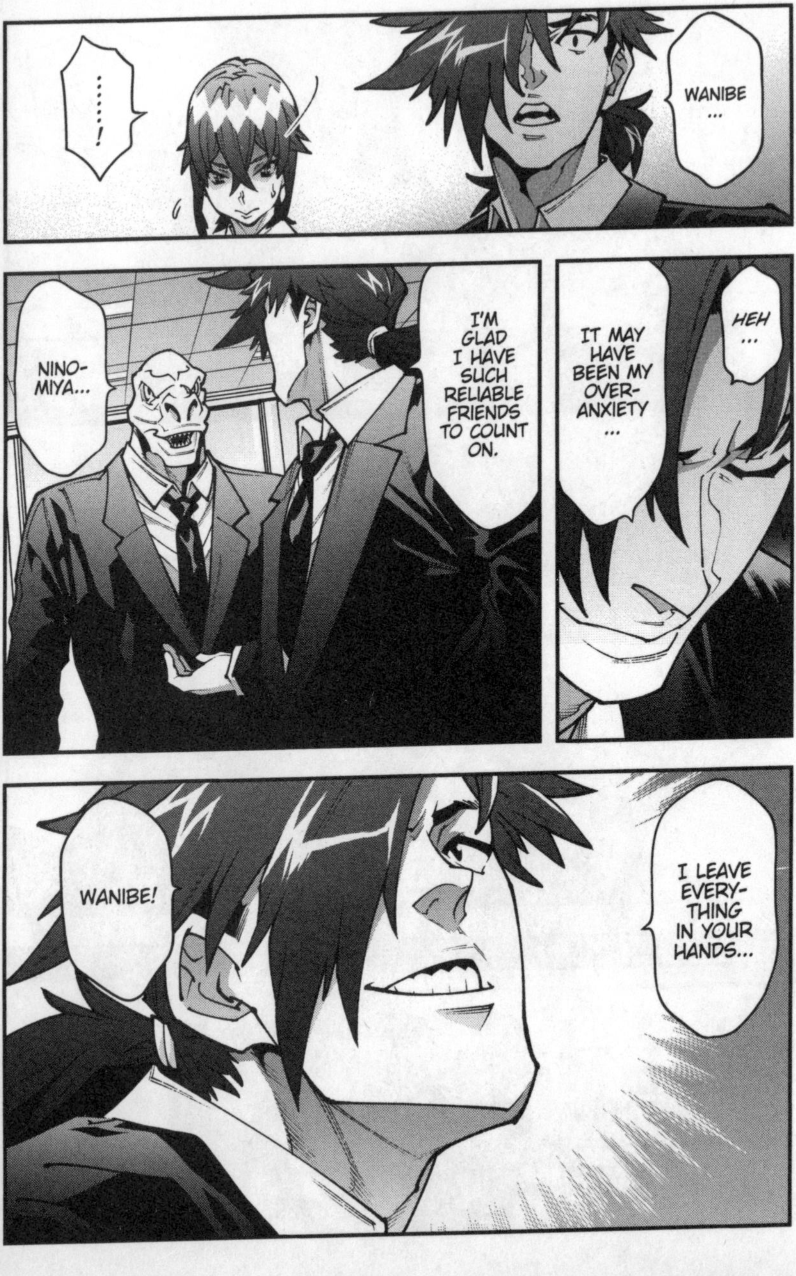
WANIBE ...
......!
HEH ...
IT MAY HAVE BEEN MY OVER-ANXIETY ...
I'M GLAD I HAVE SUCH RELIABLE FRIENDS TO COUNT ON.
NINO-MIYA...
I LEAVE EVERY-THING IN YOUR HANDS...
WANIBE!

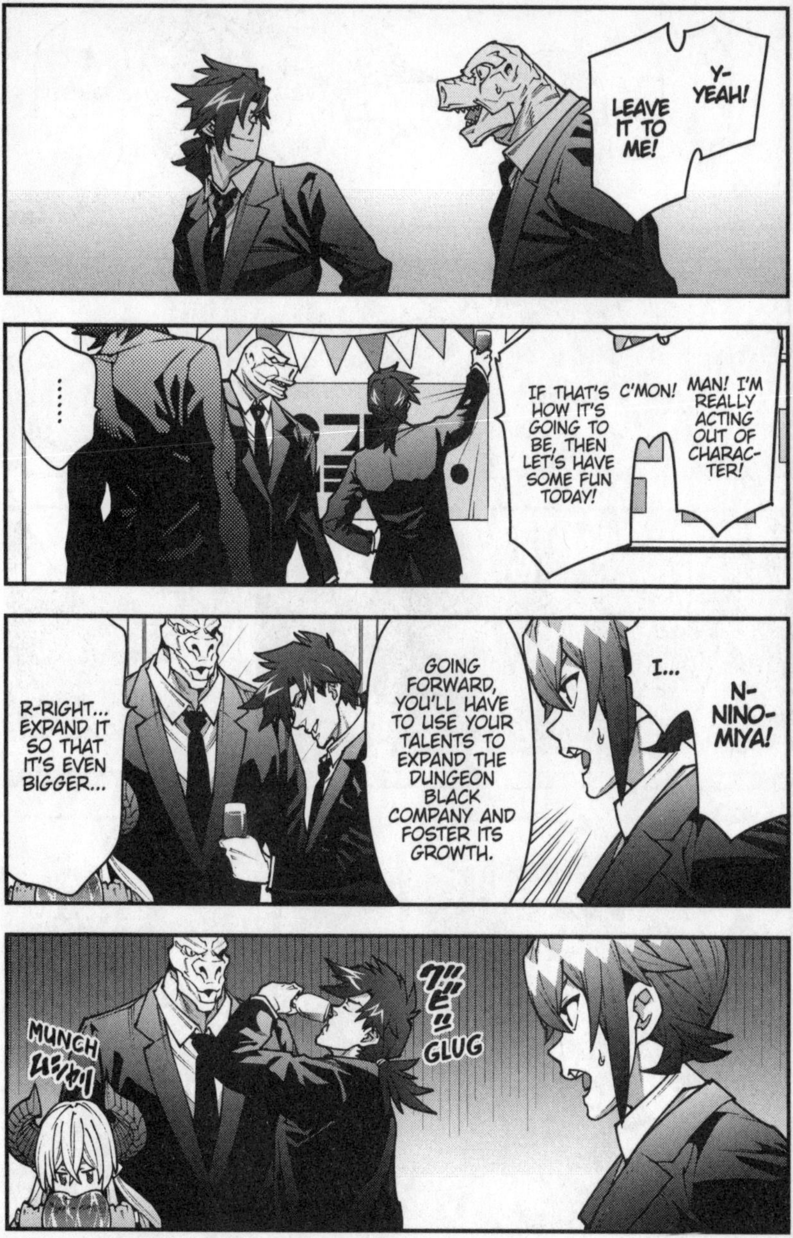
Y-YEAH! LEAVE IT TO ME!
MAN! I'M REALLY ACTING OUT OF CHARAC-TER!
C'MON! IF THAT'S HOW IT'S GOING TO BE, THEN LET'S HAVE SOME FUN TODAY!
......
N-NINO-MIYA!
I...
GOING FORWARD, YOU'LL HAVE TO USE YOUR TALENTS TO EXPAND THE DUNGEON BLACK COMPANY AND FOSTER ITS GROWTH.
R-RIGHT... EXPAND IT SO THAT IT'S EVEN BIGGER...
GLUG
MUNCH

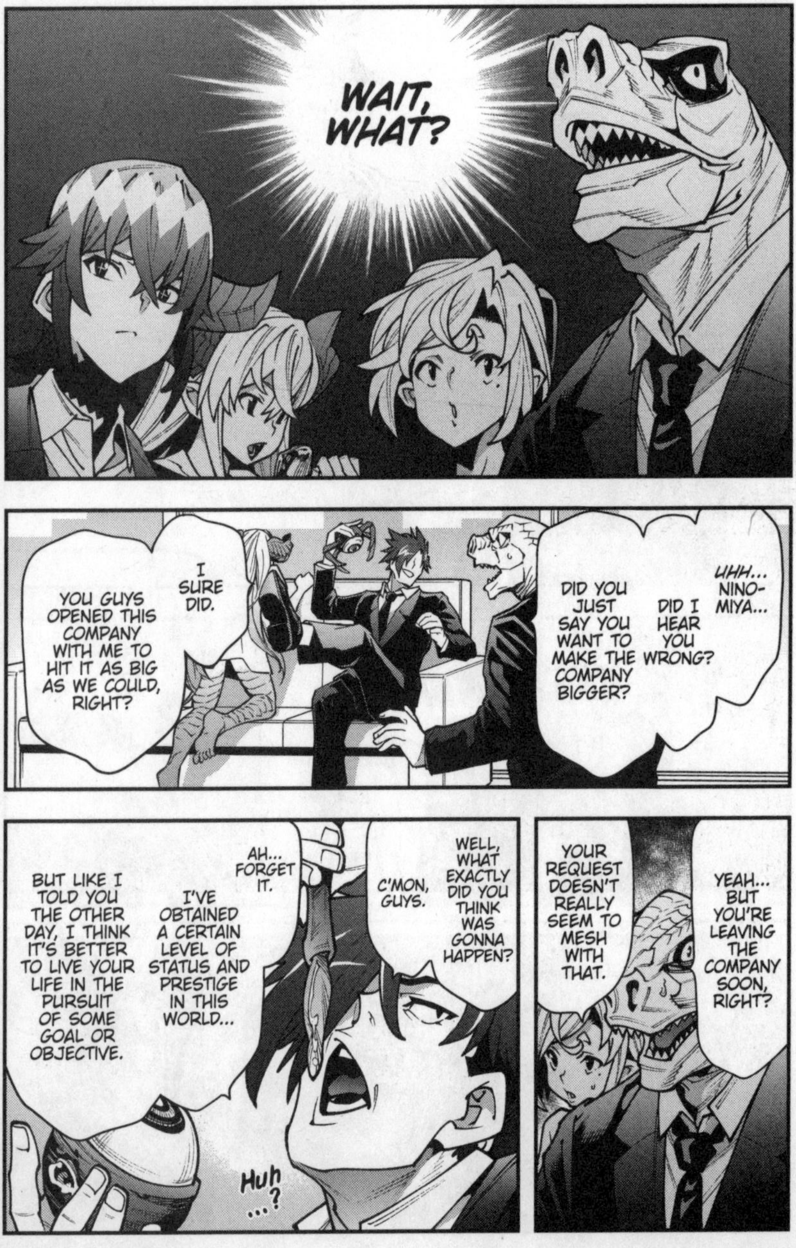
WAIT, WHAT?
UHH... NINO-MIYA...
DID I HEAR YOU WRONG?
DID YOU JUST SAY YOU WANT TO MAKE THE COMPANY BIGGER?
I SURE DID.
YOU GUYS OPENED THIS COMPANY WITH ME TO HIT IT AS BIG AS WE COULD, RIGHT?
YEAH... BUT YOU'RE LEAVING THE COMPANY SOON, RIGHT?
YOUR REQUEST DOESN'T REALLY SEEM TO MESH WITH THAT.
WELL, WHAT EXACTLY DID YOU THINK WAS GONNA HAPPEN?
C'MON, GUYS.
AH... FORGET IT.
I'VE OBTAINED A CERTAIN LEVEL OF STATUS AND PRESTIGE IN THIS WORLD...
BUT LIKE I TOLD YOU THE OTHER DAY, I THINK IT'S BETTER TO LIVE YOUR LIFE IN THE PURSUIT OF SOME GOAL OR OBJECTIVE.
Huh...?

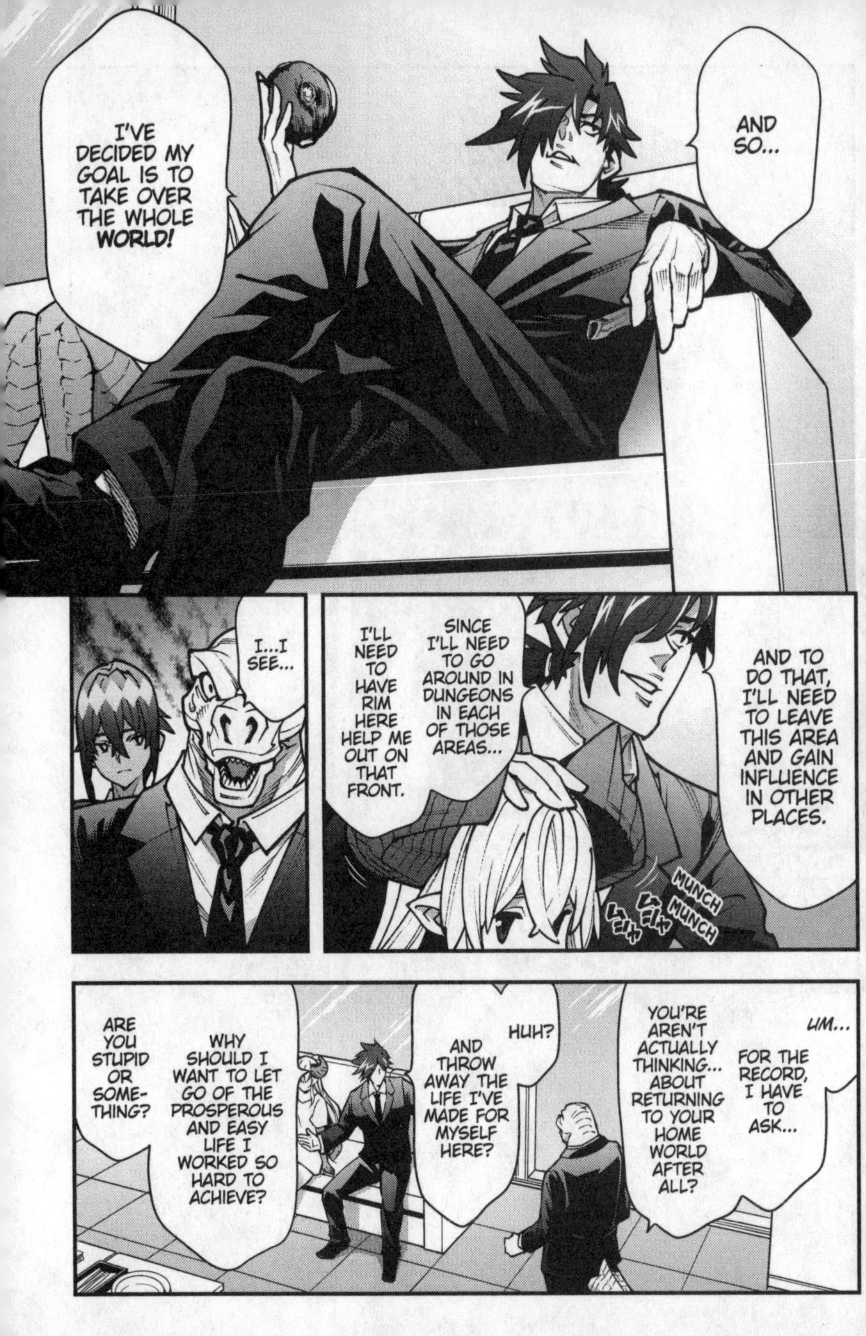
AND SO...
I'VE DECIDED MY GOAL IS TO TAKE OVER THE WHOLE WORLD!
AND TO DO THAT, I'LL NEED TO LEAVE THIS AREA AND GAIN INFLUENCE IN OTHER PLACES.
SINCE I'LL NEED TO GO AROUND IN DUNGEONS IN EACH OF THOSE AREAS...
I'LL NEED TO HAVE RIM HERE HELP ME OUT ON THAT FRONT.
MUNCH MUNCH
I...I SEE...
UM...
FOR THE RECORD, I HAVE TO ASK...
YOU'RE AREN'T ACTUALLY THINKING... ABOUT RETURNING TO YOUR HOME WORLD AFTER ALL?
HUH?
AND THROW AWAY THE LIFE I'VE MADE FOR MYSELF HERE?
WHY SHOULD I WANT TO LET GO OF THE PROSPEROUS AND EASY LIFE I WORKED SO HARD TO ACHIEVE?
ARE YOU STUPID OR SOME-THING?

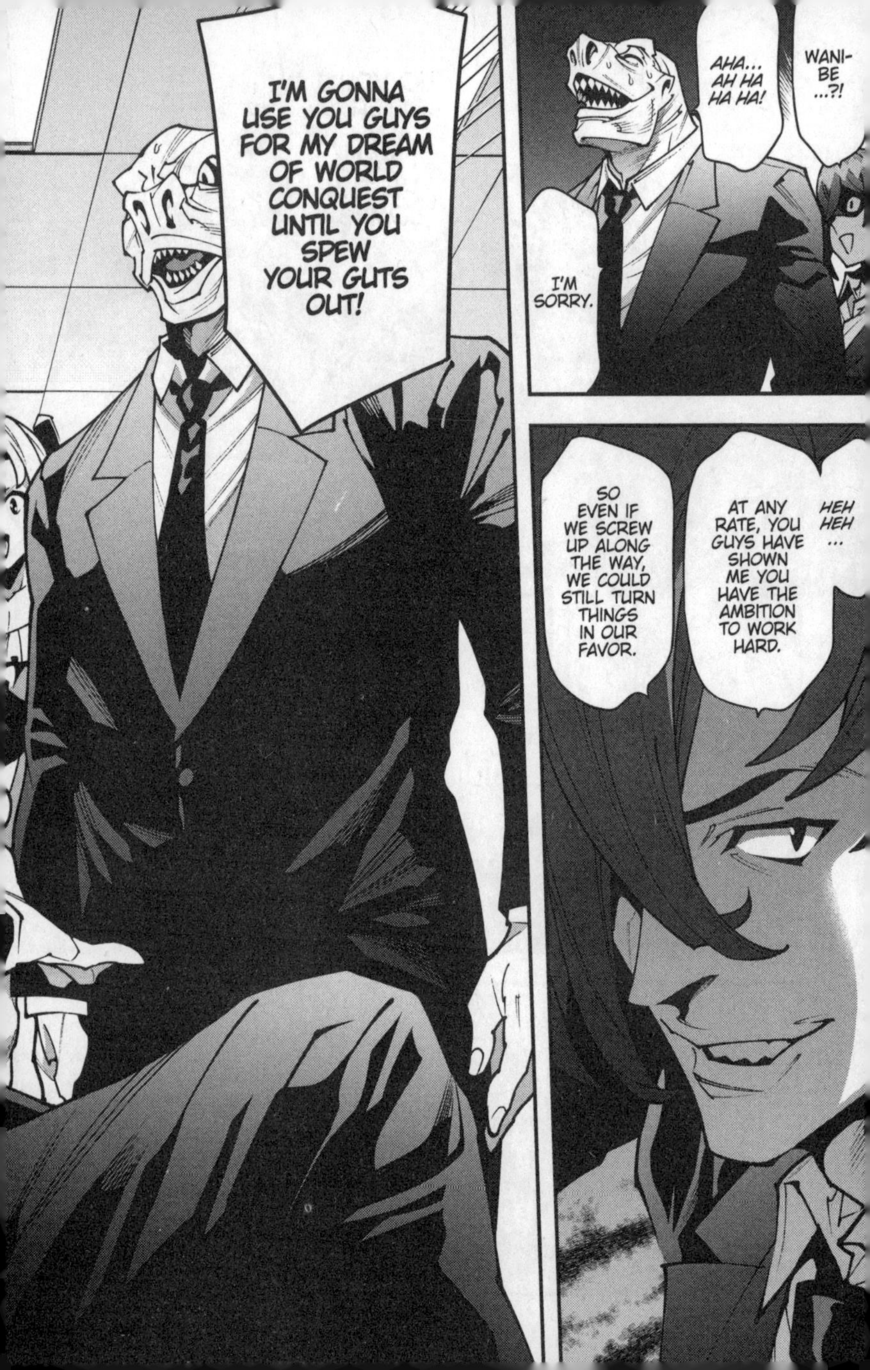
WANI-BE ...?!
AHA... AH HA HA HA!
I'M SORRY.
HEH HEH ...
AT ANY RATE, YOU GUYS HAVE SHOWN ME YOU HAVE THE AMBITION TO WORK HARD.
SO EVEN IF WE SCREW UP ALONG THE WAY, WE COULD STILL TURN THINGS IN OUR FAVOR.
I'M GONNA USE YOU GUYS FOR MY DREAM OF WORLD CONQUEST UNTIL YOU SPEW YOUR GUTS OUT!

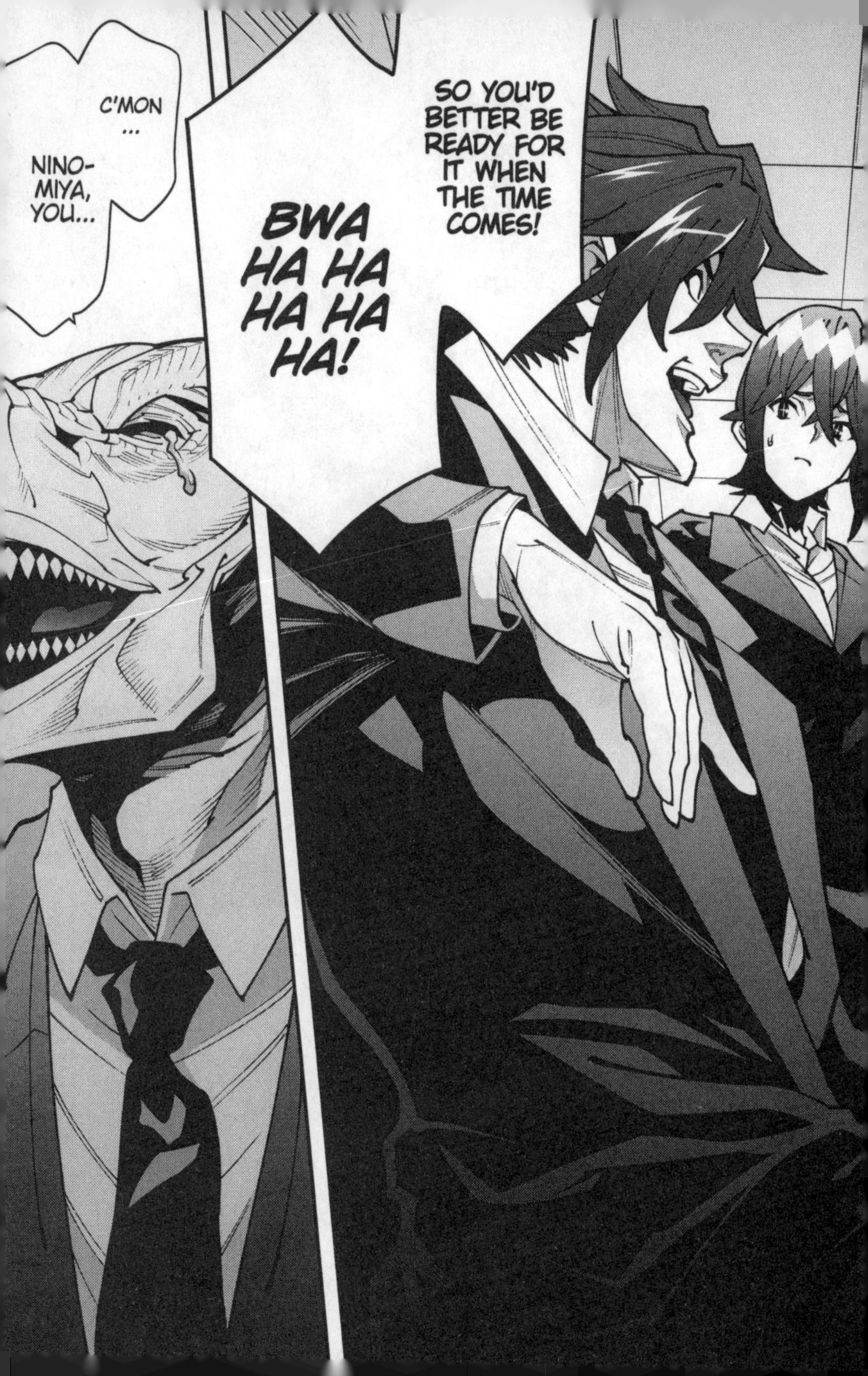
SO YOU'D BETTER BE READY FOR IT WHEN THE TIME COMES!
BWA HA HA HA HA HA!
C'MON ... NINO-MIYA, YOU...

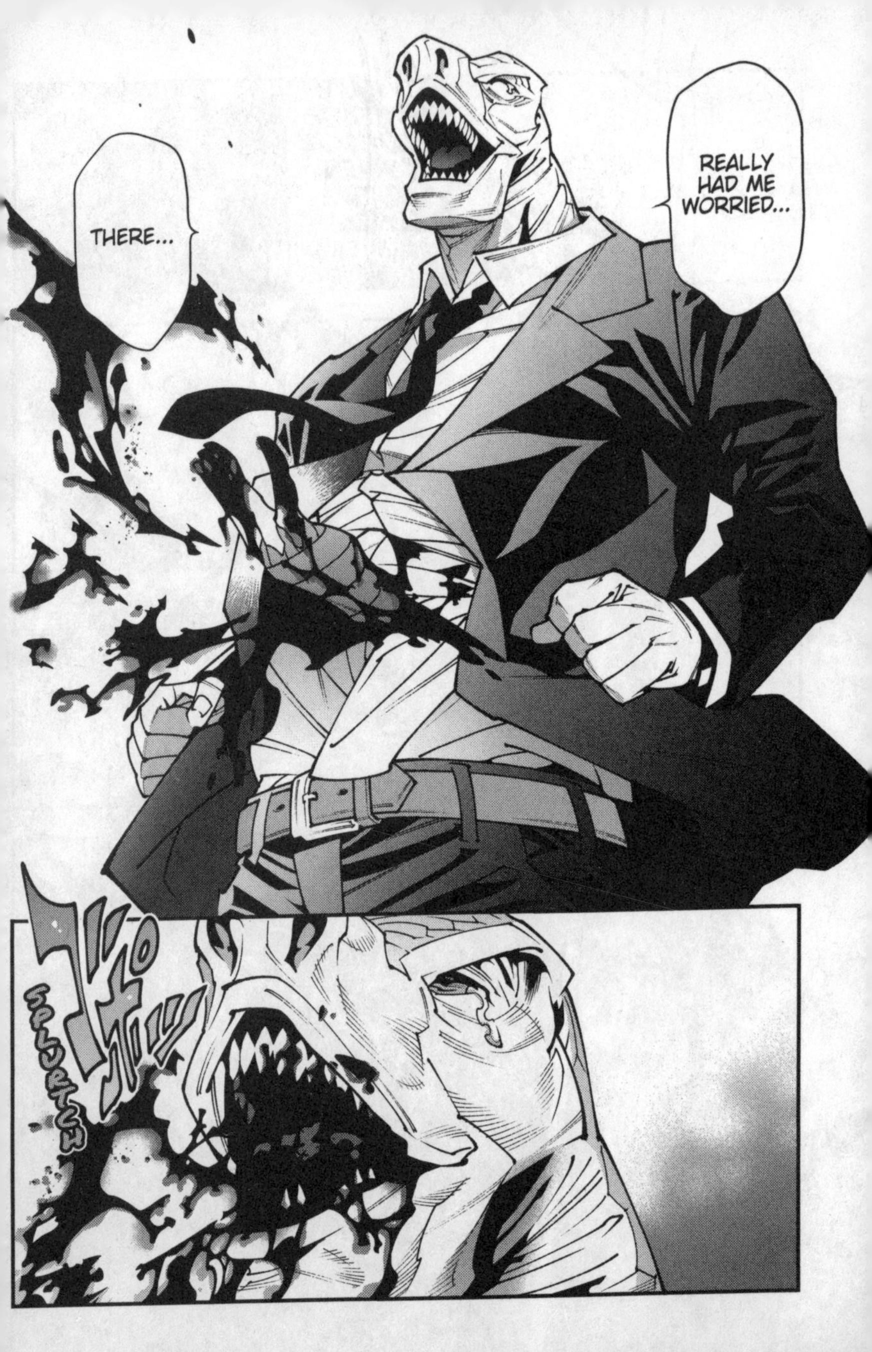
REALLY HAD ME WORRIED...
THERE...
SPLURCH

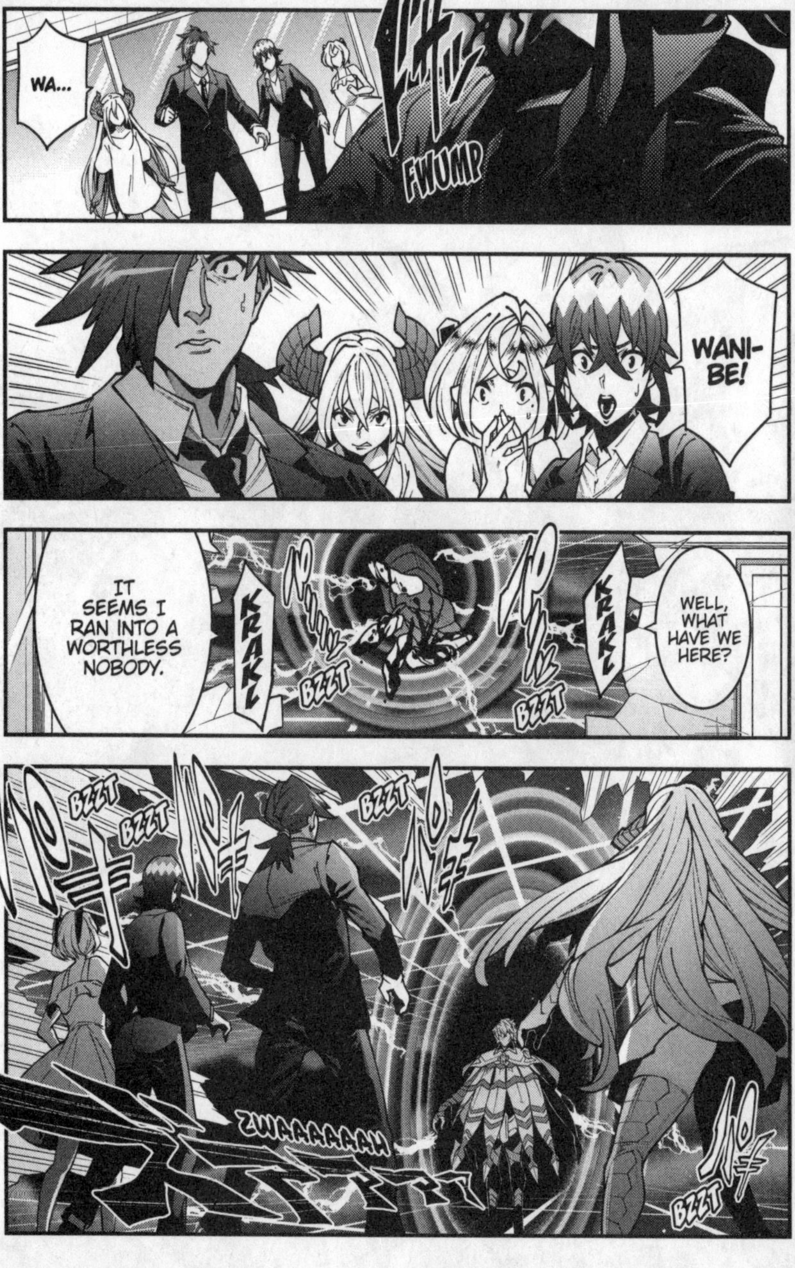
FWUMP
WA...
WANI-BE!
WELL, WHAT HAVE WE HERE?
KRAK!
BZZT
BZZT
IT SEEMS I RAN INTO A WORTHLESS NOBODY.
KRAK!
BZZT
BZZT
BZZT
BZZT
BZZT
ZWAAAAAAAH

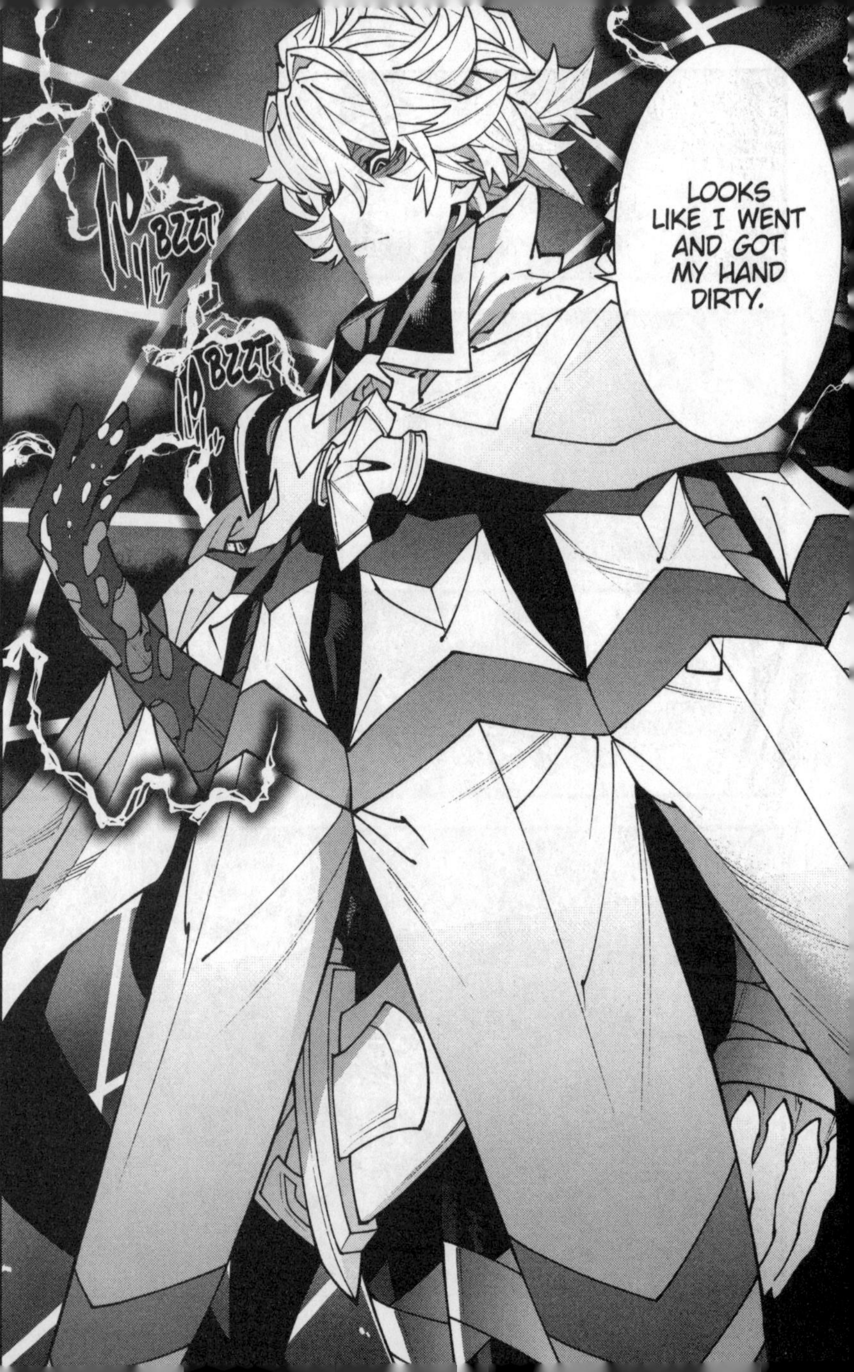
LOOKS LIKE I WENT AND GOT MY HAND DIRTY.
BZZT
BZZT

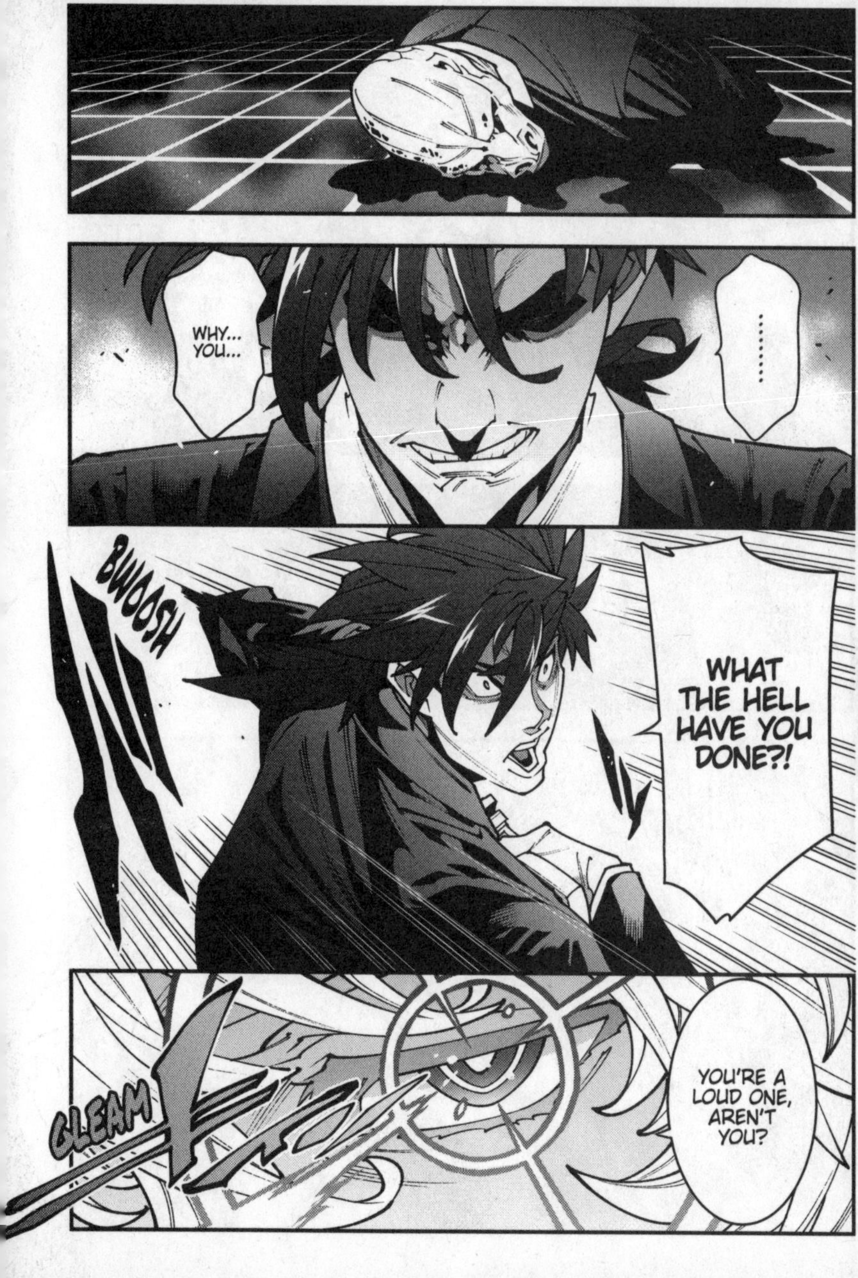
......
WHY... YOU...
BWOOSH
WHAT THE HELL HAVE YOU DONE?!
YOU'RE A LOUD ONE, AREN'T YOU?
GLEAM

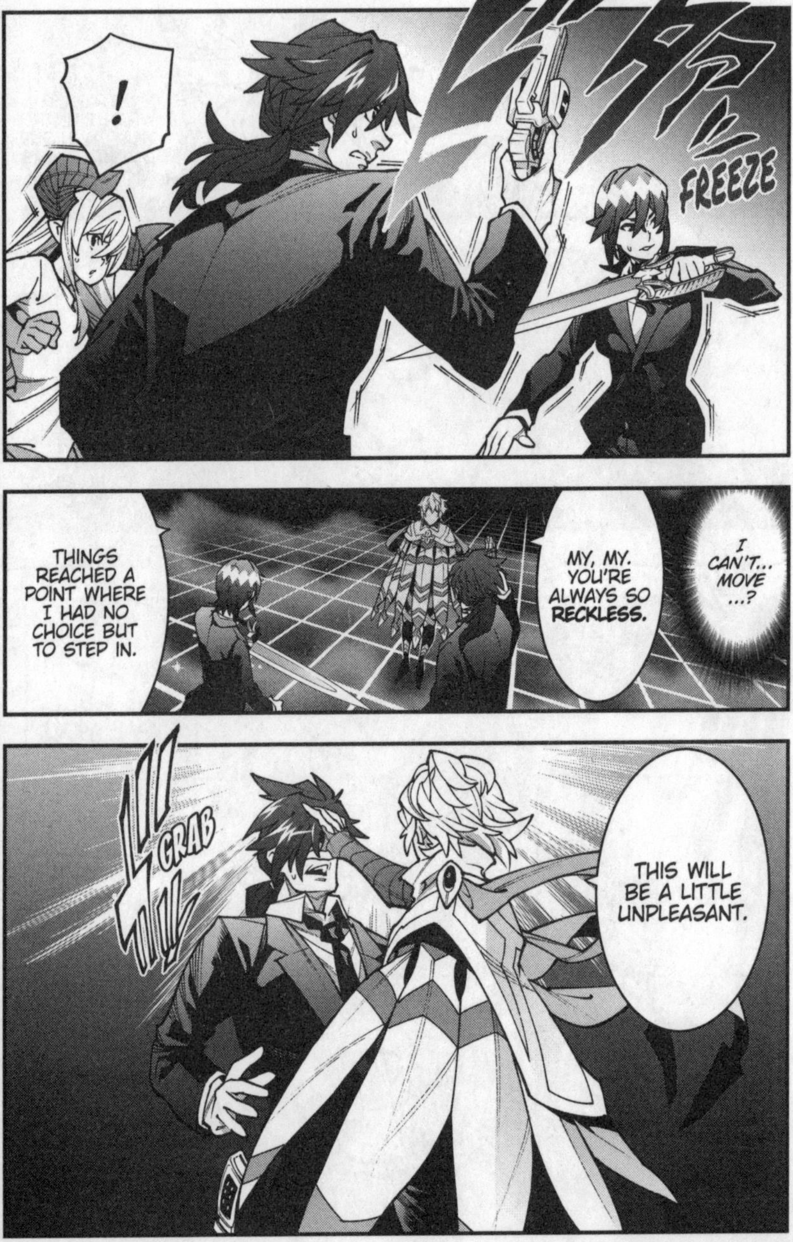
FREEZE
!
I CAN'T... MOVE ...?
MY, MY. YOU'RE ALWAYS SO RECKLESS.
THINGS REACHED A POINT WHERE I HAD NO CHOICE BUT TO STEP IN.
THIS WILL BE A LITTLE UNPLEASANT.
GRAB

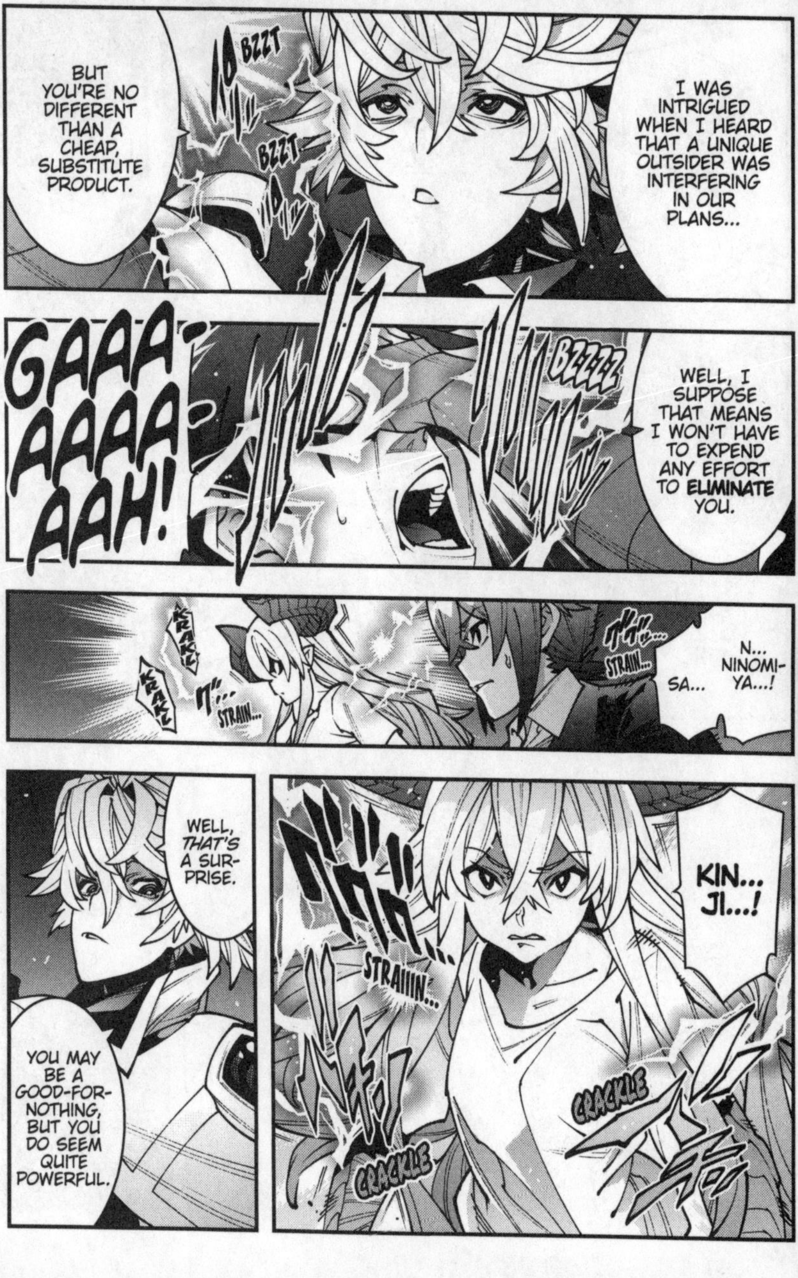
I WAS INTRIGUED WHEN I HEARD THAT A UNIQUE OUTSIDER WAS INTERFERING IN OUR PLANS...
BZZT
BZZT
BUT YOU'RE NO DIFFERENT THAN A CHEAP, SUBSTITUTE PRODUCT.
WELL, I SUPPOSE THAT MEANS I WON'T HAVE TO EXPEND ANY EFFORT TO **ELIMINATE** YOU.
BZZZZ
GAAAAAAAAAAH!
N... NINOMI-YA...!
SA...
STRAIN...
STRAIN...
KRAKL
KRAKL
KIN... JI...!
STRAIIIN...
CRACKLE
CRACKLE
WELL, *THAT'S* A SUR-PRISE.
YOU MAY BE A GOOD-FOR-NOTHING, BUT YOU DO SEEM QUITE POWERFUL.

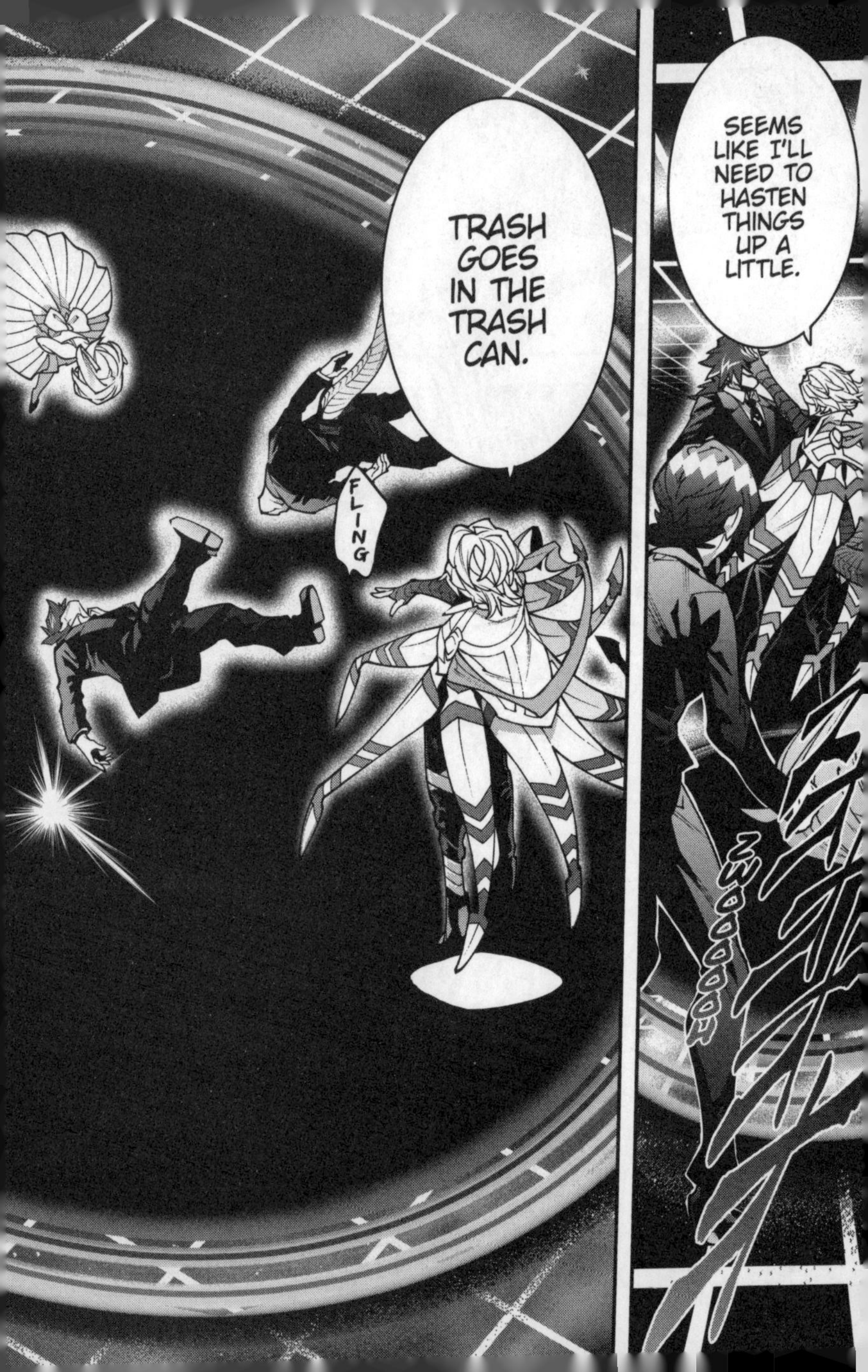
SEEMS LIKE I'LL NEED TO HASTEN THINGS UP A LITTLE.
ZWOOOOOOH
TRASH GOES IN THE TRASH CAN.
FLING

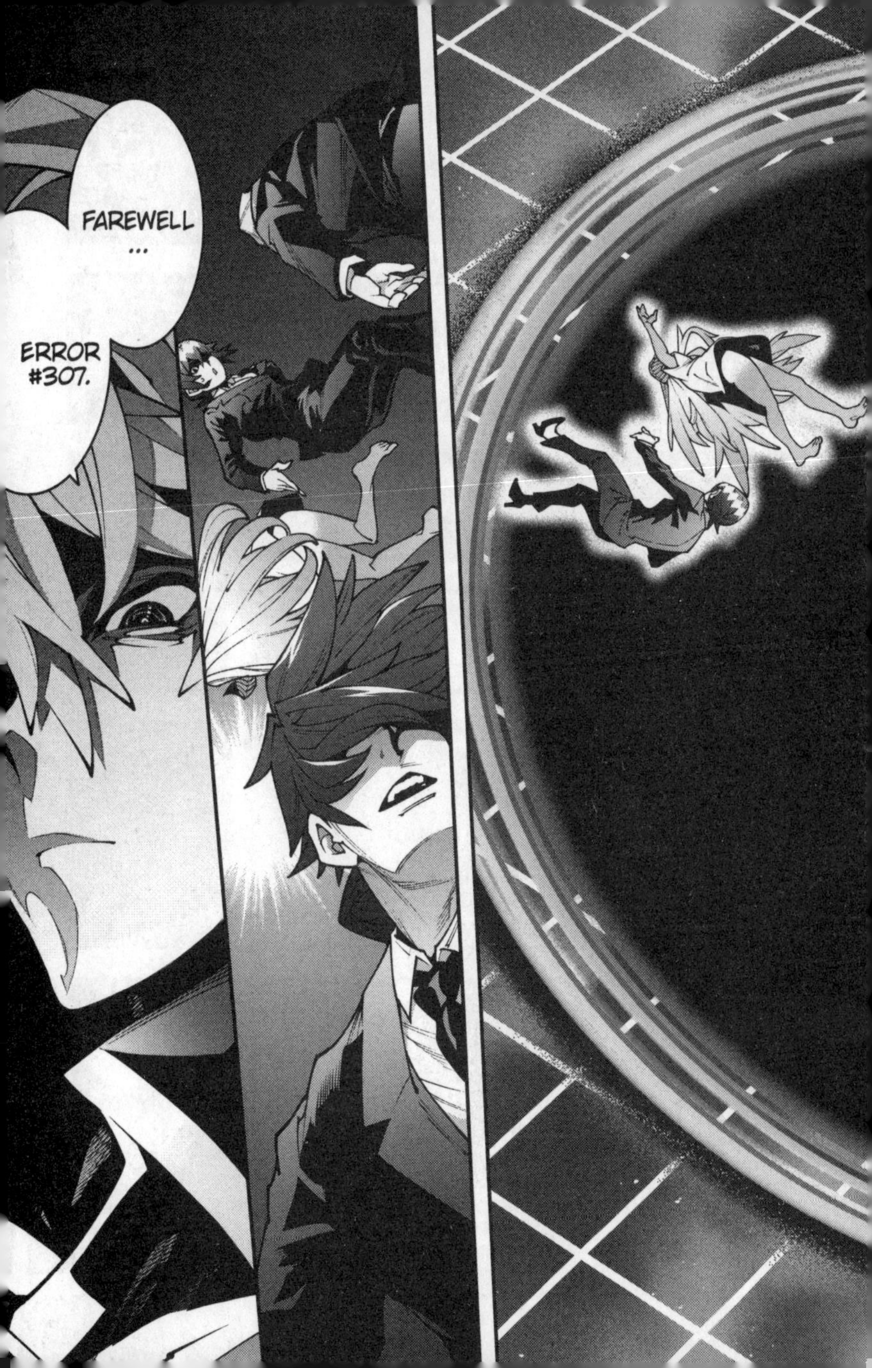
FAREWELL ...
ERROR #307.

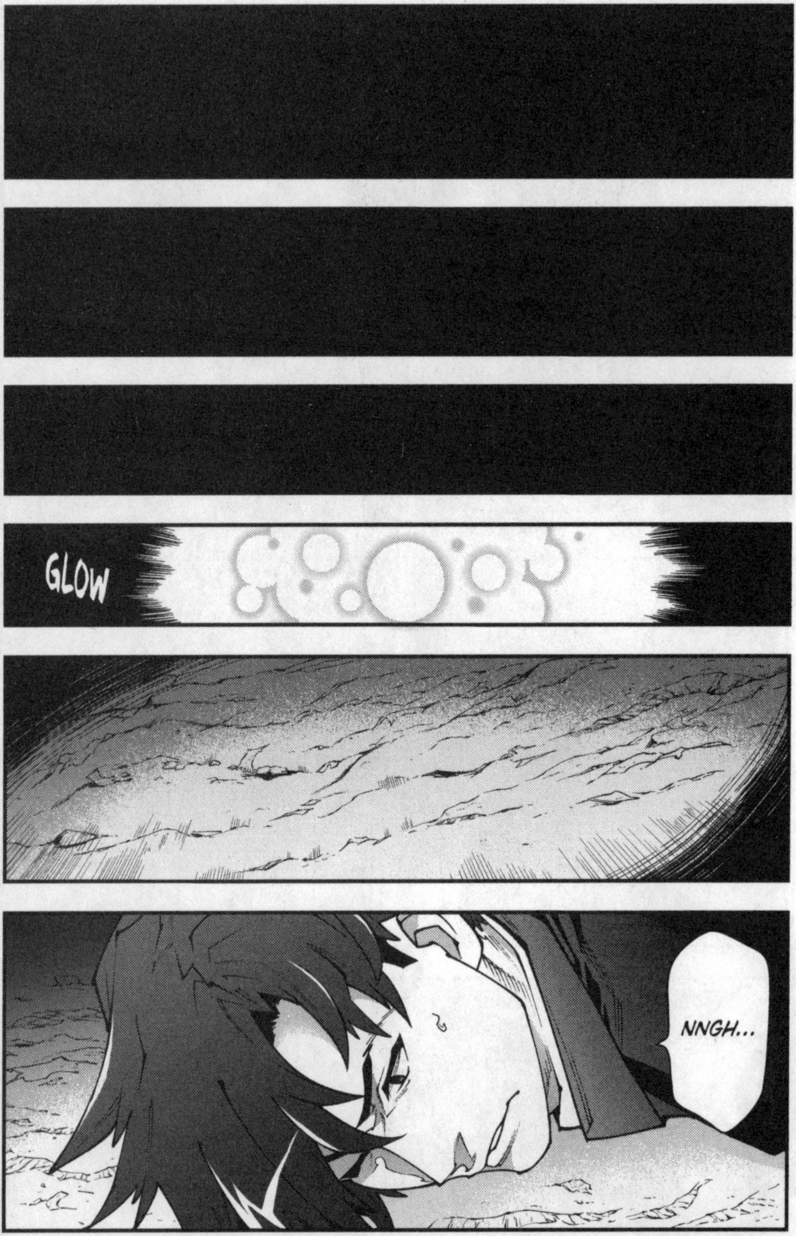
GLOW
NNGH...

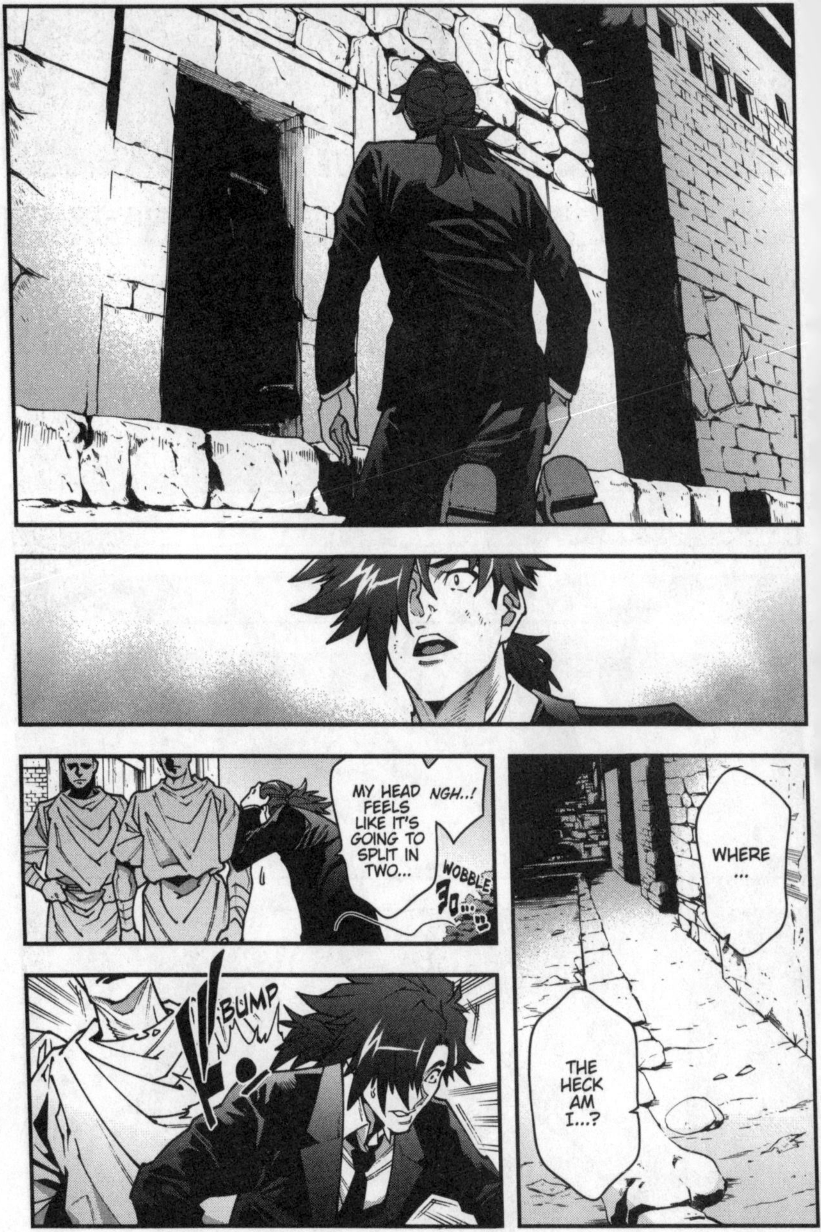
WHERE ...
THE HECK AM I...?
NGH..!
MY HEAD FEELS LIKE IT'S GOING TO SPLIT IN TWO...
WOBBLE
BUMP

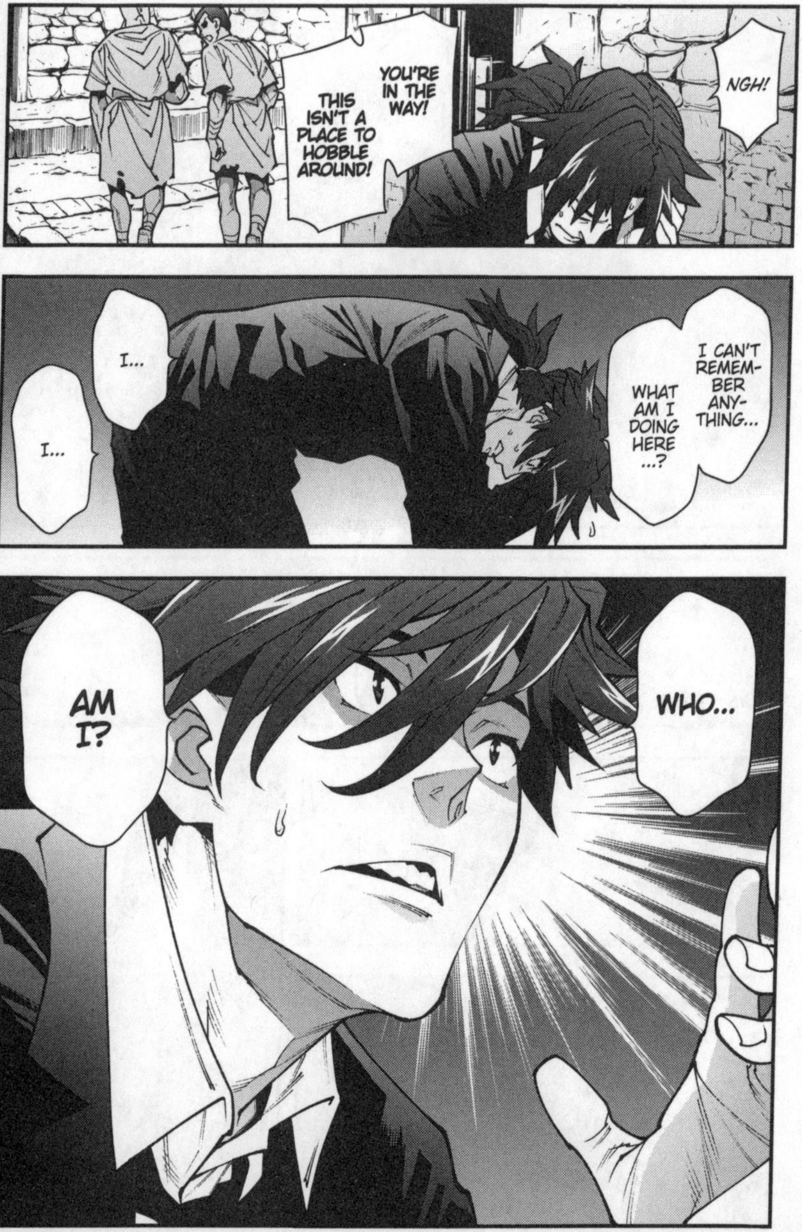
NGH!
YOU'RE IN THE WAY!
THIS ISN'T A PLACE TO HOBBLE AROUND!
I CAN'T REMEMBER ANYTHING...
WHAT AM I DOING HERE ...?
I...
I...
WHO...
AM I?

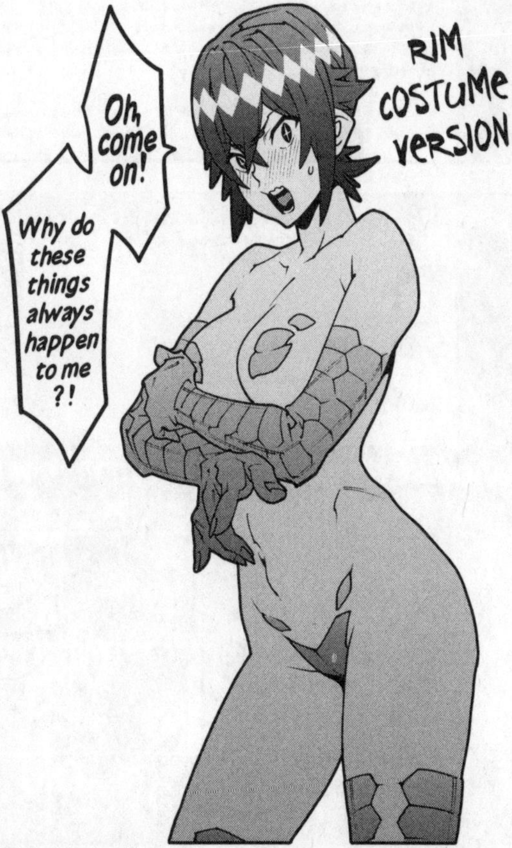
RIM COSTUME VERSION
Oh, come on!
Why do these things always happen to me ?!

SEVEN SEAS ENTERTAINMENT PRESENTS

THE DUNGEON OF BLACK COMPANY Vol. 6

story and art by YOUHEI YASUMURA

TRANSLATION
Wesley Bridges

LETTERING AND RETOUCH
Rina Mapa

COVER DESIGN
Kris Aubin

PROOFREADING
Danielle King

EDITOR
J.P. Sullivan

COPY EDITOR
Dawn Davis

PREPRESS TECHNICIAN
Rhiannon Rasmussen-Silverstein

PRODUCTION MANAGER
Lissa Pattillo

MANAGING EDITOR
Julie Davis

ASSOCIATE PUBLISHER
Adam Arnold

PUBLISHER
Jason DeAngelis

MEIKYUU BLACK COMPANY VOL. 6
© Youhei Yasumura 2020
Originally published in Japan in 2020 by MAG Garden Corporation, Tokyo.
English translation rights arranged through TOHAN CORPORATION, Tokyo.

Seven Seas press and purchase enquiries can be sent to Marketing Manager
Lianne Sentar at press@gomanga.com. Information regarding the distribution
and purchase of digital editions is available from Digital Manager CK Russell
at digital@gomanga.com.

Seven Seas and the Seven Seas logo are trademarks of
Seven Seas Entertainment. All rights reserved.

ISBN: 978-1-64505-773-4

Printed in Canada

First Printing: May 2021

10 9 8 7 6 5 4 3 2 1

FOLLOW US ONLINE: *www.sevenseasentertainment.com*

READING DIRECTIONS

This book reads from *right to left*, Japanese style.
If this is your first time reading manga, you start
reading from the top right panel on each page and
take it from there. If you get lost, just follow the
numbered diagram here. It may seem backwards at
first, but you'll get the hang of it! Have fun!!

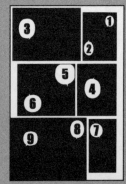